Mayor of the U

D0283596

ALSO BY LORNA LANDVIK
PUBLISHED BY THE UNIVERSITY OF MINNESOTA PRESS

Best to Laugh

Mayor of the Universe

A NOVEL

Lorna Landvik

UNIVERSITY OF MINNESOTA PRESS

MINNEAPOLIS • LONDON

Published by the University of Minnesota Press
111 Third Avenue South, Suite 290
Minneapolis, MN 55401–2520
http://www.upress.umn.edu

Library of Congress Cataloging-in-Publication Data
Landvik, Lorna.
Mayor of the universe : a novel / Lorna Landvik.
ISBN 978-0-8166-9455-6 (pb) I. Title.
PS3562.A4835M39 2014
813'.54—dc23

2014016890

Printed in the United States of America on acid-free paper

The University of Minnesota is an equal-opportunity educator and employer.

20 19 18 17 16 15 14   10 9 8 7 6 5 4 3 2 1

To Patty DeMarco
for friendship, counsel, and your big laugh

Prologue

In the desolation of a South Dakota field whose shorn wheat stubble poked through a lather of new snow, a boy in a maroon corduroy jacket danced. A bitter wind snatched at the music playing on the transistor radio held in his mittened hand, but still the boy shook his shoulders and swiveled his hips, a trillion stars his nightclub ceiling, the full moon his spotlight.

"Ladies, ladies, please, no fighting," he said, his boots raising tiny white clouds. "You'll all get your chance."

With studied cool, he flicked up his matted fake shearling collar and jumped into the air, bouncing to the ground in a half-split. He was James Brown, urging his hordes of fans to "Tighten up!" while his furious footwork generated heat that scorched the snow. He was Elvis Presley, whose teasing pelvic thrusts and wobbly knees caused multiple swooning. He was—his mitten rode up and he saw the face of his watch glint in the moonlight—he was Fletcher Weschel, and he was late.

"Ladies, please!" he exclaimed, batting away the keys and underpants and love notes thrown at him as he ran toward the Ford Galaxy he had just that day been licensed to drive. Before opening the door of the idling car, he tipped the brim of his plaid wool hat and pointed to a lovely redhead. "Now you, Ann-Margret—I'll see *you* in Vegas."

Even though the roads were empty in all directions, he turned on his blinker to indicate his merge into traffic and cautiously steered the car back toward town. Where there had once been music and dancing and adoration and sexual conquest, there was now only the wind blowing across a winter wheat field and, underneath its cold whistle, laughter.

Part I

1

For as long as his trial *Popular Mechanics* subscription lasted, Wendell Weschel, or WW as he insisted he be called, fancied himself an up-and-coming Alexander Graham Bell or Thomas Edison. He was certain that in him there was a creation as monumental as the telephone or the light bulb, but after a year of tinkering with transmitters, duct tape, and linseed oil, he gave up his dream of patent numbers and a fortune in royalties, complaining, "All the good stuff's been invented!"

WW was a man going places, the only trouble being he wasn't sure in what direction.

He provided for his family by working as an insurance agent—*For all your crop coverage, see WW!* read his card—and while he was considered one of the movers and shakers of the Pierre, South Dakota, business community, he knew it was only a matter of time before he shook the world at large.

"If they passed out a medal for confidence," he liked to tell his son, "WW would win solid gold."

"It's not what you can do, it's what they think you can do."

"Always walk like a warrior who knows he's going to win the war."

He believed the occasional pithy aphorism went a long way in fulfilling his duties as a father, although he did allow for quality time, too, which might mean calling Fletcher into supper with his sharp, mean whistle, or reading the paper on the front porch and shouting out baseball scores as his son passed by pushing the lawn mower, or letting the kid help him wash the Bel Air on Saturday mornings.

He didn't issue invitations to his *think tank* (a damp little corner in the basement where he spent much of his time), but apparently the boy didn't think he needed any and often visited WW at what inevitably were inopportune times.

Disappointed, but not undaunted by the fact he was not Bell or Edison, he was now focused on becoming the next Parker Bros. (if anyone could do it without the Brother, he could), inventing the board game that would usurp Monopoly and Clue. But other than a few doodles on his insurance stationery, WW had few ideas other than its name—*Cash-O!*—and that its tokens looked like coins. He tried to explain to his son that the game was still in the thinking stage and his concentration was bothered by questions like, "Daddy, why are you just sitting there?"

"Fletcher," he complained, "first and foremost, a man needs time and space to think. What you call 'just sitting there' is actually giving the mind the freedom to do what it does best: think."

"Oh," said Fletcher.

"Now why don't you run upstairs and do your homework?"

"I already did it."

"Then why don't you just run upstairs?"

As Fletcher climbed the worn green-painted stairs, he heard his father's shrill whistle and his admonition to straighten up and walk like a warrior. Discouraged, the son wondered what it was about him his father despised so much, while WW leaned back in his swivel chair, congratulating himself for putting in some father-son time. It's what Olive wanted, for Christ's sake, what Olive nagged him about night and day.

"Honestly, WW, just show him you don't think he's a complete washout!"

"Who says I don't?" joked WW, only Olive didn't laugh. But what the hell was he supposed to do with a chubby kid with a cowlick who dropped every ball ever thrown to him, who couldn't swim because of a propensity to ear infections (WW's backstroke had won his high school relay team a tri-county championship), who had the personality of a box turtle?

They just weren't a good match, WW had decided, and he had begun to wonder if this observation might include his wife, too.

And so when he volunteered to lead a Cub Scout den ("What their organization needs," he announced at the dinner table, "is WW's snappy ideas and innovative leadership"), both his wife and son had the same reaction. They nearly choked.

"Why, WW," said Olive red-faced, coughing into her napkin. "That's wonderful! You'll be absolutely wonderful!"

"Damn right." Then winking at Fletcher, he said, "Darn tootin'. Guess if I'm going to lead the Scouts, I'll have to do a little cleanup on the old language."

By chugging down a glass of water, Fletcher managed to dislodge the goulash that had taken a detour in his windpipe. He was equal parts stunned and elated.

"Gee, Dad, that's swell!" he ventured, and when WW reached over to tousle whatever part of his son's crew cut he could tousle, Fletcher had to sit on his hands to prevent himself from leaping up and embracing his father. WW had told him long ago that hugs were for sissies and that real men shook hands.

"Even good night?" the then four-year-old Fletcher had asked.

"Especially good night," said WW, offering instead a brisk clap on the shoulder before sending the boy off to bed.

Dressed in their matching navy shirts, their yellow kerchiefs smartly knotted, Fletcher felt, as soon as he and his father pushed open the doors of the community center, as close to invincible as an unpopular, chubby boy could feel. Building Popsicle stick birdhouses or three-dimensional maps of South America in a room that smelled of disinfectant and overperked coffee filled Fletcher with a happiness that made the rest of the week (full of teasing and threats) easier to bear.

Occasionally a fellow Scout would forget to be cowed by the fact that Fletcher's father was leading the meeting and would whisper orders to "Shut up, Lard-o!" or "Pass the paste, Four Eyes," but for the most part, the boys felt duty-bound to be nice to him.

As the season progressed, however, it was Mr. Rooney, the second Scout Master in command, who demonstrated knot tying on a piece of dirty rope ("Over, not under, Zimmerman!"), the one who explained the markings on the compass ("No, N does not stand for 'nowhere,' Gleisman, it's stands for 'north'"), the one who practiced bird calls with them ("Come on, Hilstead, enough with the screech owl!").

WW had lit a cigarette during the first meeting as the boys were introducing themselves, but Steve Rooney took him aside and said, "Say, WW, I don't think smoking in front of the kids is the Boy Scout thing to do," to which WW replied, "How 'bout if I teach them to blow smoke rings?"

In truth, taking a cigarette break was WW's favorite part of the meeting, especially when he discovered Shirley Quigley, the cute red-headed Brownie leader, doing the same thing. It didn't take them long to realize they shared more than a love of nicotine the night WW was out of matches and the Brownie leader lit his cigarette. Their eyes made contact across the trembling flame of light.

"Why, you're shaking," said WW.

"It's that community center coffee," said Shirley, stalling the inevitable with a nervous giggle. "The stuff's so strong, a half-cup makes me go all palsy."

"Hold me tight," said WW, flinging down his cigarette and wrapping the Brownie leader in his arms. "I'll show you some good vibrations."

From that night on, WW was present only at the beginning of the meetings to set out supplies and at the end to offer hearty praise for whatever gimcrack the boys had glued or woven or notched together. But it wasn't until Lincoln's Birthday, after the Scouts had made stovepipe hats out of construction paper and recited the Gettysburg Address, that the slow-to-burn Mr. Rooney finally got fed up. Deciding to punish the son for the sins of the father, he sent Fletcher outside to retrieve WW.

"I signed on as first mate," grumbled Mr. Rooney as he watched the boy grab his jacket off the wall rack and head down the tiled hallway. "Not the goldarn captain."

The temperature was above average but still below freezing, and Fletcher slapped the sides of his arms as he called out tentatively, "Dad?"

There was no answer but the wind rattling the hooks and ropes of the flagpole. Fletcher stood there for a moment, shivering in the cold. He made a V with his fingers and held them to his mouth, inhaled, and blew out a trail of vapor. He tossed his imaginary cigarette and stepped on it, grinding it out with a little pivot of his foot the way WW did.

Where could his father be? Not wanting to disappoint Mr. Rooney by failing his mission, he decided to broaden his search by following the shoveled path around the building.

When he saw the stream of exhaust trailing out of the family's Chevy, he whispered uncharitably, "Cheater." If his father was going to take forty-five-minute cigarette breaks, he should take them outside, braving the elements the Boy Scout way rather than in the warmth of his idling car.

Crouching, he was suddenly Vince Shark, CIA secret commando, and he made his way toward the parking lot, reporting his progress to the chief of Interpol.

"We've spotted the suspect," he whispered into his cupped hand (which was equipped with high-frequency radio sensors). "If he refuses to come out peacefully, we'll force him out with smoke bombs, and if that fails we are prepared to shoot. Over and out."

To confuse any Russian spies following him, Shark ran in zigzags over the old, dirt-clotted snow. Making his way to the car, he tucked his right arm into his pocket and gripped his laser gun.

"Chief," he said, sidling up to the snowman that had been erected during the Christmas holidays and still stood, pockmarked and emaciated. "I'm going to need you for backup." He conferred with the snowman, making an elaborate diagram with his hands, before closing in on the enemy outpost.

He was ready to tell the suspect to "Freeze!" but instead he found himself obeying his own command, and all traces of Vince Shark, superspy, evaporated.

It was not the sight of his father that shocked him but the action his father was engaged in. It was definitely not smoking, although from the way the woman was bouncing on his father's lap, it did look to Fletcher like someone was trying to put a fire out.

WW's head was tilted back and on his face he wore a contorted expression of someone in great pain. The woman—Fletcher could see it was Miss Shirley, the Brownie leader—appeared to be screaming.

"Agent Shark—come back. We've got to help her!" whispered Fletcher, even though he was fairly clueless as to what kind of help he could or should offer. This wasn't a cut-and-dry Scout situation; this was not a paper drive in which a half-ton of newspapers needed to be collected; this was no old lady needing assistance crossing the street; this was Fletcher's dad hurting Miss Shirley!

Cold air rushed into the boy's lungs as he took a deep breath.

"Charge!" was his rallying call and warning as he lunged at the rocking car and flung open the driver's side door.

Branded into his memory cells were the pictures of his father's pants puddled around his shoes, his hands on the white and bare bottom of Miss Shirley.

There was a second that froze the features of all parties into masks of disbelief, broken by WW's bellow, "What the hell do you think you're doing?"

Mayhem broke loose as WW pushed his son back into the snow, slammed the door, and scrambled, along with Miss Shirley, for the lower halves of their clothing.

Dazed, Fletcher crab-walked backward a few yards before flinging himself over and scuttling to his feet. He raced around the community center and to its front doors. He leaned over, panting, thinking he might vomit.

He had never been taken aside and told the facts of life by anyone; there was no dry and awkward explanation from his parents (once, driving by a field in which a bull was mounting a heifer, Fletcher had asked his mother, "What are they doing?" to which Olive had tersely— and to Fletcher, logically—replied, "They're giving each other horsey back rides"). Nor had there been a fevered tell-all in a best friend's tree house (he had no best friend, let alone a best friend with a tree house). Here and there he had heard snippets of things going into things, of men planting seeds, but he had never pieced them all together. Now no one had to tell him; he understood perfectly what his father and Miss Shirley were doing in the front seat of the family sedan was *It*.

Fletcher's head was noisy with questions: *What should I do? Why would Dad do that? Will he kill me? Where should I go?*

He thought briefly of the kindly but exasperated Mr. Rooney who no doubt would have begun to worry about him, but Fletcher couldn't bear the thought of returning to a roomful of Scouts whose only worry was who was going to get the biggest Rice Krispies Treat during refreshments. He knew that even if he'd been able to concoct an answer to Mr. Rooney's question "Find your Pop?" his blushes and stammers and quite possibly tears would raise more questions than he could answer.

The idea of worrying Mr. Rooney was far less intimidating than facing his father, and so Fletcher, without regard to the twenty-one-degree temperature, began running. Running, running, running, slipping and sliding on the icy walks, falling twice, running through the dark night, running away from the sound of his father screaming, "What the hell do you think you're doing?"

"Fletch?" came his mother's voice from the living room as he tore through the front door and stumbled up the stairs.

"Fletcher?"

Olive Weschel sighed, not wanting to leave her cozy perch on the couch. She had been pasting recipes clipped from *Good Housekeeping* in a scrapbook titled "Household Hints." It was a vague title for a book that encompassed stain removal guides, fabric yardage configurations, and menu plans. As a reference book it was rarely referred to, but compiling it gave Olive satisfaction, somehow offering tangible proof that she was doing a good job as a housewife.

"Fletcher? WW?" When there was no answer, Olive allowed herself another aggrieved sigh, put down her glue pot and the magazine opened to "Down-Home Recipes That'll Have 'em Begging for Seconds!" and went off to scold her husband and son for not having the courtesy to come in and say hello.

She parted the living room drapes her sister had given her (Florence worked in Home Furnishings at the Montgomery Ward in Sioux Falls and was generous with her store discount), and when she didn't see the car in the driveway, her heart thumped. Maybe it wasn't Fletcher who had come through the door, but the Whistling Bandit of Yankton who'd been written up in the paper? Shaking her head, she reminded herself that she heard no one whistling.

"Fletcher?" she yelled at the bottom of the stairs. "Fletcher, you answer me this instant!"

Olive climbed the stairs two at a time, ready to give her son a piece of her mind.

Fletcher was bunched up under the chenille cowboy bedspread that his Aunt Florence had given him for Christmas.

"Fletcher, honey, what is it?" Olive sat on the edge of the bed, patting the quivering bump. "What's the matter? Were some of the Scouts mean to you?"

The quivering revved up.

"Fletcher, honey, is it your father? Where *is* your father?"

Lately, WW had been dropping the boy off after Scouts with instructions to tell Olive he had gone out for a nightcap.

"Be sure to tell her," he had said last time, "that you boys would drive Carrie Nation to drink." Then, leaning across the seat, he opened the door for Fletcher and practically pushed him out, the need for a nightcap apparently so pressing he didn't have time to answer the boy's question, "Who's Carrie Nation?"

Fletcher's quivering was now at full throttle, and Olive swallowed a bubble of fear that fissured in her throat. With considerable effort— it was like trying to strip the peel off an unripe peach—she pulled the bedspread away from him and then spent several more minutes trying to turn over the hunched-up ball that was her son.

"Fletcher," she said, pulling the rigid boy into a sitting position. "Fletcher, you must tell me right now what's going on."

The tight white line that was Fletcher's mouth suddenly cracked open and he wailed.

"For crying out loud, Fletcher, what's the matter?" said Olive. Torn between fear for and of her son, she shook him, trying to dislodge the answer as if it were a half-swallowed mint.

"He was in the car, Mom." The boy sobbed and then spit out the words as if they were terrible to the taste. "He was in the car with

Miss Shirley, the Brownie Mother, doing It! She was sitting on his lap, Mom, and neither one of them had their clothes on! At least not the bottom parts."

Fletcher would have gone on with his horrible story, but Olive had clamped her hand over his mouth, not wanting to hear anymore. She began keening and they both sat on the bed, making their own particular distress signals.

Later that night, Olive received a phone call in which WW simply stated that he wouldn't be coming home. A letter arrived several days later. It was three parts accusatory—*Why did you always have to nag, nag, nag?*—to one part vaguely apologetic—*Sorry, Olive, but it just wasn't working out for me*—with a P.S. thrown in—*Say, how's about sending my good suit over to the office?*

Sitting in the bed she had taken to since WW's departure, Olive cried over the letter until her tears rendered it a blue blur, but it didn't matter—she had memorized it anyway. He was running away with Shirley, *a woman who understands what a man needs.* He was going way out west where *a man has room to dream,* and he wasn't coming back. He'd send money when he could, and would Olive mind explaining things to the boy? He signed his whole name, Wendell Vernon Weschel, as if it were an official document, which, concurred Olive, a Dear Jane letter certainly was.

When it was clear WW wasn't coming back, Fletcher burned his Scout uniform out in the trash barrel, and it was both smoke and emotion that made his eyes water. Olive ranted about "that weasel Weschel" to God and anyone within earshot, and Fletcher knew instinctively that to defend his father was to strike a blow against his mother. Still, one afternoon when she sat in her bed littered with soggy tissues and Licorice Nibs wrappers, claiming what a bastard WW was, Fletcher said solemnly, "Yes, but he was our bastard."

He hardly recognized the woman who emerged from under the bed covers weeks later.

"It's a new day," said Olive, brushing her hands together like a villain concocting an evil plot. "And time to figure out what to do with it."

The knot of prematurely graying hair she wore at the base of her neck was sacrificed to sable black dye and a bubble cut. She became the Avon Lady's best customer and created a new face for herself featuring black silverfish eyebrows and coral lipstick that matched the ovals she rouged onto her cheeks.

"If I'm going to be a career gal, I've got to look like one," she told Fletcher. She enrolled in a real estate class, leaving Fletcher several times with Mrs. Pyle, the next-door neighbor who mounted competitive card games of War and Pinochle against him, all the while snapping the Beechnut gum she chewed by the packet and never thought to share. When Olive terminated the short-lived babysitting arrangement, Fletcher was thrilled; the card games were more a chore than an amusement, owing to Mrs. Pyle's compulsion to cheat.

"I've decided he's old enough to stay at home by himself," she told the neighbor. "He's very mature for a nine-year-old."

Fletcher felt proud and grown up hearing this assessment and had no idea that his mother's decision had anything to do with Mrs. Pyle's request for payment.

For nearly two years, WW sent checks totaling just under $3,000, which seemed to fulfill his sense of obligation, for they stopped with a postcard that read, *This is the end of the line—you should be on your feet now!* And Olive was. She was on her way to becoming if not a real estate dynamo then a woman licensed and capable of selling residential, farm, and commercial properties.

"I've got a showing," became Fletcher's least favorite words, for they meant his mother was not going to be home—not when he came home from school hungry for a snack and a sympathetic ear; not at suppertime, when the note she left for the TV dinner's heating instructions would be the only thing at his mother's place setting; and sometimes not when he went to bed.

If the bullies who already picked on him didn't know of his loneliness, they sensed something was the matter with Fletcher and cranked up the teasing to a degree that would have sent weaker victims tattling to the principal's office. Fletcher didn't revel in mistreatment, but at least it was some kind of attention, some nod to his existence, and so he bore the slings and arrows like a good soldier who was technically 4-F but willing to go out on the battlefield anyway.

2

"That couple from Vermillion wants to see the house at night," said Olive. "If they love it as much in the p.m. as they love it in the a.m., I've got a sale!" She dragged the coral lipstick around her mouth and pursed her lips at Fletcher. The air was charged with her peppery scent; she mixed Old Spice with Jean Naté to make what she called her Eau de Take Me Seriously cologne.

"There's a pot pie in the oven," she said, patting her helmet of hair as she limboed slightly to check her reflection in the gilt-framed hall mirror. "I'll be eating out later with the PLC."

The Professional Ladies Club was a group of modern working women who got together weekly to enjoy dinner and drinks at the Rumpus Room by the Capitol building. Olive Weschel claimed her fellow members gave her support and sanity, but all Fletcher knew was that she came home from these meetings reeking of gin and giggling as she apologized to the pieces of furniture she bumped into.

Her standard phrase as she careened into his room after a PLC night was, "Fletchie, honey, wake up and unzip your old mother."

Fletcher would snore to buttress his sleep act, but his mother wasn't worried about disturbing him, weaving her way to his narrow twin bed and sitting on it so heavily the springs squealed.

"Come on, Fletchie—help me out of this thing!" she'd say, bouncing on the bed to further rouse him.

Fletcher would groan as if he were being pulled from a deep sleep and reach out from under his cowboy bed covers to pull down his mother's dress zipper.

She would sit on his bed, the back of her dress sliced open like an outer crust, revealing the soft dough that spilled over the back of her slip and bra. Fletcher could hardly breathe, afraid of his gin-smelling mother and her opened dress and the long sighs that made her round shoulders rise.

Her final decree was always, "Aw, Fletchie, life is hard," before she would lurch off the bed and stumble out the door, holding her arms in front of her as if she couldn't see.

For a long time, Olive's social life orbited only around her PLC friends.

"I don't know," she told her sister Florence during their weekly long-distance telephone call. "The idea of having another man around the house sort of sickens me."

Seeing the disheartened look on her son's face as he overheard that particular remark, Olive decided it might be time to devote a little extra attention to Fletcher and, willing to make great sacrifice, designated Friday as their "date nights."

They sat next to each other on the nubbly beige nylon couch, Pyrex bowls of popcorn nestled on their laps. Olive was the type of disinterested cook for whom TV dinners were invented, yet her popcorn was blue-ribbon. There was rarely an old maid or burnt kernel in the batch, and she was liberal with the melted butter. That Fletcher was allowed to drink cream soda out of the bottle was one more bonus to these date nights, although the big attraction was the Hollywood Late Show, which wasn't so late, starting as it did at 10:00 p.m.

"You can't tell me there's a couple that had more chemistry than Myrna Loy and William Powell," Olive would say, as they watched *The Thin Man* on the RCA console.

"I don't know," said Fletcher, who loved the old movies as much as his mother. "What about Fred and Ginger? Bogie and Bacall?"

"You got me there," she said, clinking his pop bottle with her tumbler of gin and tonic. "Gad, why was there so much glamour back then, and how do we get it back?"

Wrapped in a chenille robe so soft and old that its ribbing was worn off at the elbows, and with her face scrubbed of all its black and coral makeup, Olive was a different woman on their movie nights. Stripped of all the scary armor that made her a PLC member, she was just his mother, and it was the easiest, most comfortable time Fletcher spent with her. They were two movie fans, enjoying the luxury of bantering back and forth without anyone in surrounding rows shushing them.

"I think Errol Flynn is a better actor than he's given credit for."

"I think you've got a crush on him, Mom."

"Well, what woman in her right mind wouldn't?"

"Is that Rita Hayworth?"

"No, that's Ann Sheridan. They do look alike, though."

"Bette Davis is kind of scary."

"Oh, hon, that's only because she doesn't take anyone's baloney."

Their date nights ended when Fletcher was eleven and the Hollywood Late Show was cancelled and replaced with World Wide Wrestling.

"It's the end of the world, Fletcher," said Olive, snapping off the television dial after they'd tuned in out of curiosity, already knowing there was no way they could summon the same enthusiasm for the Manchurian Mauler and Clyde the Crowbar as they did for Nick and Nora Charles.

It was just as well for Olive; Nanette Dickie, a dental hygienist and founding member of the PLC, had introduced her to her brother Alden, and the two had hit it off.

"I'm not saying I'm going to marry the guy," Olive told Florence, "but at least he doesn't make me want to puke."

After his mother left with Mr. Dickie for their first Friday night date, Fletcher went to the hall closet and put on the old fedora and raincoat his father had left behind. His chin trembled as the weight of abandonment bore down on him, but catching a glimpse of himself in the gilt-framed mirror, he knew there was no way this guy could cry. He straightened the lapels of his coat and, tipping his hat to his reflection, said, "Deke Drake, ladies man." He gave a rakish half-smile and a wink before ambling over to the kitchen, to see if Ava Gardner or Hedy Lamarr had stopped by to make him a sandwich.

———

As the years passed, Olive filled her calendar with business and social dates and Fletcher accepted his loneliness in the same way he accepted his cowlick and double-jointed thumbs. On the nights his mother was at home, she was distant, having usually drunk herself into a state a few degrees from stupor. Most often she was out showing properties, or wining and dining with the PLC or one of her boyfriends, none of whom was around the house enough for Fletcher to get to know.

Fletcher amused himself in the empty house by saving the world from communist, nuclear, or Mafioso threat as Vince Shark, world's craftiest spy, or riding the range that rose up in between the living and dining rooms as Hip Galloway, Texan cowboy, or by entertaining ladies, stealing jewels, and winning high-stakes Monaco roulette games as his newest alter ego, international playboy Deke Drake.

But it was being Fletcher Weschel in the real world, where there were no governments to overthrow, no shoot-outs in which to lend a deadly, accurate aim, no Miss Kuala Lumpur to escort to after-pageant parties, that was the real challenge.

His misery in junior high school was somewhat tempered by seeing how miserable everyone else was; when he broke out in pimples, he felt less anguished than part of the acne-spotted majority; when another boy's voice fluctuated between bass and soprano in the span of two syllables, Fletcher wasn't so mortified by his own oral gymnastics.

By high school, he'd lost his baby fat but not his lowly status. He joined the only organizations that he felt comfortable in, the Audio/Visual and Chess Clubs. Members were a small band unto themselves—boys with thick glasses and out-of-date crew cuts, boys who wore white socks and buttoned the top button of their short-sleeved shirts. These boys were usually ignored and sometimes picked on as they traversed the halls, shielding themselves with their stacks of books wrapped in homemade, brown grocery bag dustcovers.

The girls that the group attracted, when they attracted them at all, were similarly ostracized by the popular kids for the same deeply shallow reasons: they were too fat or too skinny, too homely or speech-impedimented, too brainy or too seriously involved in a pursuit that didn't qualify as cool. (Valerie Jerde, for instance, was doubly jeopardized by virtue of her 6'1" height and her passion for the bassoon.)

Several times a week, as a release from the prison of his lonely self-consciousness, Fletcher would drive out of town, radio blasting, stopping to get out of the car and dance in a farm field. On weekend nights, while his classmates were drinking in basement parties or out on La Framboise Island, he earned money by sitting with the ninety-four-year-old father of a PLC member. It was an easy job; Ossie Swanson slept the entire time he was there, only waking twice, and on both occasions he called Fletcher "Billings" and reminisced about the time they took their girlfriends to the Chicago World's Fair.

"Remember that damn Ferris wheel, Billings? First Ferris wheel in the whole G.D. world! Remember how we were going to wait until we got all the way to the top with the girls and then kiss them good, only Maude got sick and poor Annabel"—

Mr. Swanson died in the fall of Fletcher's senior year, never revealing the fate of poor Annabel. He didn't know Mr. Swanson enough to mourn him, but with his weekends now free he did miss having an excuse as to why he didn't have a social life.

Even within his own circle, Fletcher's presence was noted with the same interest as his absence, and it was true—in many ways Fletcher felt invisible. He had personality, even a flair, but his shyness and self-censorship kept that a secret from everyone but himself. He could be suave and witty, flirting with the '30s and '40s movie stars of his black-and-white fantasies, but he could not even summon a "Hi" to the local girls of the Class of '68 who were too real, too *in color*. He was resigned to be the Invisible Man as far as his female classmates went—until he was invited to the Sadie Hawkins Dance by Connie Yarborough.

"What?" he asked dully after she approached him at his locker to ask him.

"I want to know if you'll go to Sadie Hawkins with me."

"With you?" Fletcher's conversational skills were pre-remedial.

"Yeah. With me." Connie Yarborough smiled, her big rectangular teeth framed by a mouth that shimmered with lip gloss.

"I guess," said Fletcher, a watered-down version of what he wanted to say, wanted to shout: *Of course! Are you crazy? To the top of the world, baby!*

Sadie Hawkins was a dance modeled after the event held in comic strip *Dogpatch*, everyone dressing like Pappy and Mammy Yokum or Li'l Abner and Daisy Mae. Taking the boys' burden for the night, the girls paid for the tickets and provided transportation.

Having been resigned to the idea that she might be the only one ever dating in the family, Olive Weschel was breathless with excitement as she waited with Fletcher for Connie's arrival.

"I hope you gave her good directions," she said impatiently, the ice cubes clicking as she swirled her nearly empty glass of gin.

"Ma, Pierre's not exactly Hong Kong. I'm sure she'll find her way."

"Well, you'd be surprised how dense people can be about directions—your father, for instance, couldn't find his way out of the garage unless he had two maps and an atlas." Olive surveyed her son, chuckling. "Oh, just look at you—your first date and you have to dress like a hillbilly."

Fletcher wore tattered jeans with two pairs of suspenders and a gingham shirt Olive had patched with calico squares.

"Maybe this spring we'll be able to get you into a formal tux for the Senior Prom, hmm? Maybe one of those fancy powder blue ones."

When the doorbell rang he and his mother froze, their eyes wide, as if they'd heard gunshot.

Olive was the first to snap out of her trance, patting her sable hair and smoothing her skirt as she headed to the door. Fletcher stared after her, the tension in his stomach tightening into a knot.

He heard their murmured greeting, then his mother's loud voice.

"Fletcher, honey, your date's here!"

Dragging Connie in from the front hallway, Olive planted her in front of Fletcher like a gardener proud of the exotic specimen she had cultivated in her hothouse.

Hoping his ears weren't as red as they felt, Fletcher swallowed hard and then pulled out a dazzling conversational nugget from his repertoire. "Connie?"

There was a flash Fletcher would hold on to for years, an antidote against the absolute certainty that he was doomed to eternal loneliness, for in perfect synchronicity, they grinned, both of them displaying blacked-out teeth. It was a moment of connection that would have made Fletcher gasp if he hadn't already been laughing.

"Well, aren't you two something," twittered Olive, clapping her hands.

"Nice outfit," said Connie, and Fletcher, noting her bloomers under a dress fashioned out of burlap, said, "Likewise."

Smooth as a gigolo he poked out his elbow and Connie Yarborough placed her hand in its crook, and Olive leaned against the plaid recliner for support, watching them waltz toward the front door, waving the banners of youth and confidence that would never again unfurl for her.

In the gym, under a ceiling festooned with swags of twisted crepe paper, Fletcher gave himself to the music, moving his feet, hips, and shoulders the way he did when he danced out in the fields.

"Wow, you should be on *American Bandstand!*" shouted Connie over the music and Fletcher acknowledged the compliment, as Deke Drake might have done, with a wink and a spin.

Watching as she tried a spin herself, Fletcher thought, *She's beautiful.* It was not a word generally used to describe Connie—her face was wide and broad-featured but her brown eyes flashed with intelligence and her smile, while toothy, was friendly. She wore that smile now, and even though several of her teeth were blacked out, Fletcher found it dazzling. He was on cloud nine—for him, a most unusual perch.

They danced through the band's set and then, sweaty and loose, stood in line for Kick-a-Poo Joy Juice (lime punch) and Dogpatch Oar-Dervs (Ritz crackers topped with a swirl of Cheez Whiz). They sat with their backs to the gym wall, eating and drinking and chatting with anyone who sat down near them.

It was all so easy! Just teenagers sitting around having a good time, and for once Fletcher was a part of it, even earning a few laughs when he guzzled his punch and pretended to feel its potent effects.

When the band started its next set with a slow song, Fletcher pulled his partner to him as if she were a favorite sweater.

"Connie," he said, breathing in the peachy smell of her hair. "Connie, thank you for asking me."

"Asking you what?"

"To the dance. To Sadie Hawkins."

"No prob. My pleasure."

Fletcher held up her hand and spun her under the arch their arms made.

"But why did you ask me?"

"Because you look so handsome without your glasses."

"Pshaw," he answered in Dogpatch character. He had recently saved enough money to buy contact lenses, and he was thrilled someone finally noticed his new look.

"I asked you because I like you, Fletcher. You're different from other guys. And I like your accent in class."

Thanks to Miss Halprin, a newly certified language teacher who had lived two whole years in Milan, Fletcher and Connie were students in the first-ever Italian class taught at Central High.

"Grazi, grazi," said Fletcher, sounding more Italian than Marcello Mastroianni, and he dipped his *bella signorina*.

When he pulled her back up, he wondered for a moment why she was patting him on the back so insistently until he realized the pats were coming from the policewoman next to him. Not an official cop, but Mrs. Debby Purdy, the English and drama teacher, dressed up as one of Dogpatch's finest.

"I'm a-takin' you to the clinker, pal," she said, grabbing his arm.

"On what charge?" asked Fletcher, so genuinely confused that Connie laughed.

"Fletcher, it's a Sadie Hawkins thing. The guys get thrown in jail and the girls have to bail them out."

"It helps pay fer the victuals and the Best Costume ay-wards," explained Officer Purdy.

"Don't worry," laughed Connie. "I'm on my way to the bail bondsman now!"

It was a short, sulky trip out of the gym and to the slammer, a flimsy plywood and chicken wire structure built for extra credit by wood shop students.

Mrs. Purdy opened the gate and pushed Fletcher inside, directly into Dodd "The Bod" Beckerman.

"Fletchie!" said the massive boy, enveloping him in his big hairy arms. "Lookit, everybody, it's our old pal, Fletcher Weschel!"

Beckerman's cologne of Hai Karate and sweat was augmented by the smell of rancid hair oil, and Fletcher nearly gagged as he pushed himself away.

When both boys were in the eighth grade, Beckerman had moved into Mrs. Pyle's house after the gum hoarder went to live with her daughter in Rapid City, ensuring that the bullying that went on in school would continue on Fletcher's own block.

In the makeshift jail, three other boys sat on folding chairs, and with a cursory glance Fletcher could see he was not among allies. This was not an unusual predicament, but usually he had a means of escape—a hallway, a staircase, a bathroom stall.

Resigned, Fletcher sat on a folding chair across from his cellmates, Beckerman standing at his side.

"So Fletchie's got a girlfriend," said Beckerman in singsong. He put his bare foot on Fletcher's chair. "Big Dyke Connie Yarborough."

Blood roared in Fletcher's ears. He had long ago taught himself to ignore the slander served up by his next-door neighbor, but this was different: this was slander directed at the most wonderful girl in the world.

"Yeah," said the wrestling co-captain, nudging his big toe so that it pressed against Fletcher's thigh. "Yarborough's a dyke. Everybody knows it. They know it the same way they know you're a—"

One reflex launched Fletcher out of his chair, another propelled his fist into Beckerman's stomach. It was a hard stomach, conditioned by the wrestler's daily quota of three hundred sit-ups, and when contact was made it was Fletcher who cried, "Ow!"

A second later, Fletcher's head was in the crook of Beckerman's arm and he realized he was in a fight.

"Get him, Beckerman—get the dyke lover!" said a boy wearing a union suit.

Fletcher flailed his arms but they made such ineffectual contact with Beckerman that the wrestler laughed.

"Ooh, you're killing me, Weschel."

"Let go of him, Beckerman."

The boy's laugh was high for someone so big. "Oh, look, Fletchie, it's your dyke girlfriend come to save you."

"Let him go, *Peckerman*."

"That's right," chirped Mrs. Purdy. "Down, Dodd."

The wrestler unceremoniously let go of Fletcher, who stumbled out the door Mrs. Purdy held open. As she closed it, she looked at the unclaimed boys still in jail.

"I don't know what's taking yer gal pals so long to pay your bail," she said, waving the counterfeit Dogpatch bills Connie had given her. "Maybe they is all standing you up!"

Fletcher felt like a convict being transferred to another jail, not thrilled to be leaving, not thrilled to be staying. A trickle of sweat rolled over his lip as he walked down the school hallway and he struggled for breath as he pushed through the door. The evening air was bracing as a slap in the face.

"Fletcher, wait up!" said Connie, but her request had the opposite effect on her date, who broke into a trot. He ran down the steps and the wide sidewalk and made it to the curb before Connie caught up with him, grabbing him roughly by the arm.

"Fletcher! What's the matter with you?"

Biting his lower lip, Fletcher stood hunched for a moment, his whole body feeling like a condemned building caving in from the inside. He sat down heavily.

Connie sat next to him and he turned to the face he thought he had been falling in love with.

"Are you—are you what they say you are?"

Connie stared at him as if she were on the outside of an aquarium and he was a whiskered, walleyed sea creature floating before her.

"A dyke?" she said finally, and Fletcher, miserable, nodded. Connie wrapped her arms around her knees. "Those guys are talking about a . . . an . . . incident that happened last year. Between me and Paula Kleiser. You didn't hear about it?"

"I'm . . . I'm not exactly in the loop."

"Well, it was nothing, really, it was just a little . . . kiss . . . in the locker room. I don't even know if it meant anything but, boy, we were the talk of the town. You really didn't hear?"

Fletcher shook his head, staring at his palms.

"So are you—"

"—I don't know, Fletcher. Like I said, it was just a kiss. Geez. 'Course if I'm supposed to like slobs like Beckerman, then maybe something is wrong with me, 'cause the guy makes my skin crawl."

"So why'd you ask me to this stupid dance? Was it just some big joke?"

"It wasn't anything like that, Fletcher. I thought it would be fun to go to a dance with you, that's all."

Suddenly, to Fletcher's great surprise, Connie Yarborough wrapped her arms around him and pressed her lips—Fletcher couldn't imagine softer, warmer lips—against his. He was as buoyant as a helium balloon.

"Cinnamon," he said after their kiss. "Your lips taste like cinnamon. Your hair smells like peaches and your lips taste like cinnamon."

"It's my lip gloss," said Connie. "And my shampoo."

"I like it," said Fletcher, but as he leaned forward for another kiss, Connie leaned backward. Defeated, he put his hands in his lap.

"Fletcher—"

"Never mind."

"Fletcher, do you want to get a hamburger at Bunnie's?"

"No, no thanks."

"So . . . should I take you home?"

Fletcher stood up and brushed the dampness from the seat of his overalls. "Nah . . . I'll just walk."

"Are you sure? I mean, I don't want to leave my date in the lurch."

"Nah . . . I'll be fine. Thanks for everything, Connie."

He offered his hand and they stood under the streetlight shaking hands as solemnly as parting pallbearers.

"You're home early!" Olive stated the obvious from her perch on the living room couch. Her tumbler of gin sat like a king on the throw pillow she hugged to her lap.

"It's not that early, Ma," said Fletcher, poking his head into the room, which was lit only by the television screen. "Good night."

"Oh, Fletcher, you're not getting off the hook that easily. Now you come sit by your old mother and give me all the gory details."

And so Fletcher did. He didn't know what possessed him—he was a boy who had learned not to share confidences with his mother—but he enjoyed watching her face change. Expectation made her look almost young, but by the end of the story she was slack-jawed and haggard.

"Good heavens, Fletcher, what on earth made you think I wanted to hear to a story like that?"

"You asked me to give you all the gory details—"

"—a figure of speech, Fletcher! A figure of speech! I wasn't looking for something smutty—I just wanted to hear how well my boy had done, how many girls had asked you to dance, how you were the belle—well, the beau of the ball!"

"I would have liked telling you that story, too," said Fletcher wistfully, and by the time Olive figured it might behoove everyone if she said, "I'm sorry," Fletcher was already upstairs, lying on his bed and staring at the ceiling, his hillbilly boots folded over on their sides in the corner of the room where he had kicked them.

3

Fletcher went away to college, to the University of North Dakota at Grand Forks, but it was not the liberating experience it can be for other adventurous students. His roommate, a sullen boy from Minot, subsisted on a protein diet of peanuts in the shell and considered the wastebasket too bourgeois to bother with, resulting in a floor that was as littered as a shoreline after high tide.

His roommate's breath, farts, and sweat smelled of peanuts, and the gag reflex was one that was visited on Fletcher every time he opened the dorm room door.

"Geez," Flecher would complain, "it's like the monkey house at the zoo!"

His roommate had two responses at the ready: either he'd mimic a chimpanzee—"Ooh-ooh-ooh"—and fling a peanut shell at Fletcher's head, or he'd tell him, "Get bent, Weschel," and fling a peanut shell at him.

Olive was also a problem, calling her son every few days to tell him how much she missed him, how lonely the house was without him, and asking if all the men in her life were always going to abandon her. Fletcher tried to console and comfort her during these phone calls, a hard enough thing to do without the distraction of a boy shelling peanuts not ten feet away and reading aloud from his psychology textbook.

"Do you mind?" Fletcher once asked, cupping the receiver with his hand.

"Ooh-ooh-ooh," said his roommate, flinging a peanut shell at his head. "At outset, euphoria and a feeling of invincibility signal a manic episode."

Fletcher, by sheer tenacity, lasted his freshman year but had his credits transferred to South Dakota State in Brookings, bringing him closer to home by more than two hundred miles. Olive scolded him that he could no longer use distance as an excuse not to drive home every weekend, and on his first visit home she flung her arms around him, sloshing a good portion of her afternoon cocktail on his shoulder. At that moment, Fletcher knew he should have stuck with the flying peanut shells.

In Olive's boozy embrace, Fletcher saw his destiny rolled out like the braided carpet runner before him, and even as he screamed internally, he stepped right onto it.

———

Directly after graduating with a degree in accounting, Fletcher began his career at Mid Summit American Life. He had some sense of achievement in landing the first job he interviewed for (it wasn't his new suit his Aunt Florence had bought with her Montgomery Ward discount that swayed the interviewer but his high grades and willingness to accept, without haggling, the first salary figures that were quoted), but it was overshadowed by the tiny whisper in his ear that asked, "What the hell are you doing?"

These little voices—his own private hecklers—nagged him constantly about his choices or lack of choices. Vince Shark reminded him that the world was imperiled and needed his crack code-breaking skills or ability to wrest confessions out of diabolical counterspies with simple mind control; Hip Galloway told him that there were wild horses to be broken in the red canyons of Utah and fillies of an entirely different persuasion to lasso at the local saloon; and Deke Drake whispered that the Mediterranean was beautiful this time of year and had he ever captained a yacht bare-chested, wearing nothing but a beach towel borrowed from Yvette Mimieux?

When the voices rambled on in their fantasy mode, Fletcher was a rapt audience. Listening to his alter egos was like taking a minivacation, but of course Fletcher never went further than listening; after all, he was, as Olive put it, practical as white paint.

Fletcher felt he was a man not of his time. In college, he sidestepped the be-ins, the sit-ins, the antiwar protests that were the extracurricular activities on campuses across America. The few times he went to parties, he got headaches from the incense and pot smoke and loud music. He wondered what the point was of possessing a wild heart if it was ultimately harnessed by a timid soul. Others were capable of the adventure he yearned for—he read in the Central High Class of '68 update letter that Connie Yarborough was working with Vista, and that Perry Bringley, who'd played clarinet in the fifth hour jazz band, was now playing in a real off-Broadway production and was a dues-paying member of the musicians' union. Two classmates had gone to Vietnam, and one didn't come back. Fletcher had been lucky to have a student deferment as well as a high draft number, unlike Dodd Beckerman, who hadn't gone on to college and had a low number. Luck didn't completely abandon The Bod, though; he was shipped only as far as Frankfurt, serving out his tour of duty on a base in southern Germany. Fletcher could picture his former neighbor in a rathskeller, natty in his dress uniform, blowing beer suds at a dimpled and smiling *Fraulein*. As much as he thought Beckerman a cretin, he couldn't help but admire him, couldn't help but admire anyone who wasn't afraid of a little dazzle, a little risk in their lives. Anything had to be more glamorous than living with his mother and wearing a Montgomery Ward suit to work every day.

"You've got a fine job," Olive liked to remind him, cigarette smoke streaming out of her mouth. She had taken up smoking while Fletcher was at college; she said it strengthened her serious businesswoman image, and now their house smelled of smoke *and* opened gin bottles.

"It stinks like a bar," Fletcher complained. "All we need is a dart board and hard-boiled eggs in a jar."

"That's cute, Fletcher," said his mother. "But it's not my problem you're overly sensitive to smells. I can't hermetically seal the whole house, can I?"

"You could at least open a window."

"Oh, quit complaining. Honestly, you complain about everything—the smell of the house, how hard it is to be a professional in the insurance business—complain, complain, complain. You're a broken record, Fletcher." Smoke leaked out of her flared nostrils. "Now, listen, there's a TV dinner in the freezer—Salisbury steak, your favorite—don't tell me I don't cook what you like—and there's some Neapolitan ice cream for dessert. Just don't touch the strawberry part—it's Laird's favorite."

Laird, a furniture salesman, was the latest in what Olive hoped would pan out to be a love interest and what Fletcher knew would be a passing fancy.

Like a dog straining against a leash, Olive stretched as far as she could to get nearest a hand that might pet her.

You're too needy, he wanted to counsel his mother, but what on earth qualified him to give advice related to matters of the heart?

———

Fletcher's first sexual experience had been with a girl who had a proprietary relationship with his homework, asking for his notes after every econ class, a rapacious girl named Helen who one day demanded that he come to her dorm room that evening.

"Believe it or not," she said by way of greeting, "I'm a virgin. I don't think I'm wrong in assuming you are, too. Thus, my invitation."

Fletcher, who had no inkling she wanted to change their partnership from one of study to sex, was shocked mute. He would have loved to respond by taking her in his arms and kissing her artfully, showing her that she had indeed come to the right man. Instead, waiting for his heart to stop pounding, he pretended to take an interest in the stack of books on her desk.

"Oh," he said finally, "so you like Ayn Rand."

"I think Objectivism as a philosophy and a practice is the only thing that can save us. 'Every man must exist for his own sake!'" Helen picked up *The Fountainhead* and practically shoved it in Fletcher's face. "Have you read this?"

"Actually, I—"

"—you could really learn a thing or two from the protagonist, Howard Roark," she said, pressing the book to her breast. "He's like . . . he's like the intellectual superman. Now take off your clothes."

The last line was delivered bossily, but that it was even delivered was enough for Fletcher.

It was an awkward but ultimately satisfying experience for him and, he thought, for his partner—considering the noises she made— and lying next to her afterward, Fletcher reveled in a postcoital bliss, feeling like an explorer who'd finally found what he was looking for.

It was a short-lived happiness, Helen turning away and groping for their clothes, piled next to the bed.

"You'd better go now," she said, and as she tossed him his shirt and pants, his belt buckle banged his kneecap. Her words were muffled as she pulled her SDS sweatshirt over her head. "And FYI, this probably won't happen again, comprenez?"

"Why did it happen at all?" Fletcher asked, truly curious.

Helen pulled her lank hair into a ponytail. "Look, Fletcher, I hope you don't overanalyze this because, really, it was just a simple, hassle-free business transaction. I needed something from you, and it's obvious you needed the same thing from me."

As he was leaving, Helen had the gall to ask for his notes for the upcoming test on supply-side economics.

Thinking how gladly he would have honored the request had she been just a little *nice,* Fletcher instead nodded toward the shrine of books and said, "I don't think Howard Roark would approve."

———————

He had read in advice columns that if a man was polite, gainfully employed, and kept himself relatively clean, dates wouldn't be a problem; he was often tempted to write "Dear Abby," asking, *You wanna bet?* It was true, he probably could go out with those mousy women who were as lonely as he, but Fletcher hadn't quite grasped the concept that beggars can't be choosy. *He* was, with a preference that ran toward pretty, vivacious young woman like Cindy Dahlberg, Mid Summit American's blonde and blue-eyed goddess receptionist. Prompted in fact by the overheard comment that "she'd go out with anyone," Fletcher had once muscled up the courage to ask her for a date. As she coughed into her fist and shuffled the pages of her desk calendar, a blush passed over Cindy's face like a pink cloud, and without looking up at him once, she said, "Ah, gee, Fletcher, I'm pretty busy the next couple months, but why not try me some other time?"

He knew she was only trying to be kind and the last thing she wanted was another invitation, but still, false hope was as useless to him as counterfeit money. It would sit in his pocket, always a temptation but too dangerous to spend.

For a week he took a convoluted route to the water cooler to avoid passing her at her desk, but the following Monday he decided it was better to risk embarrassment and humiliation than deprive himself of a simple glance at the comely Cindy.

She hardly noticed him, used as she was to a parade of men skulking by, smiling, winking, and pulling at their ties as they passed. She encouraged seven-eighths of them and froze out the remaining fraction, of which Fletcher was a part. He wasn't an obvious pervert like Lou Eisler in Annuities, who stuck his hand underneath his suit lapel and rubbed his nipple every time he walked by. No, Fletcher Weschel was just too ho-hum bland, thought Cindy, and not worthy of a hot-cha-cha girl like herself who was going places in a hurry. Besides, that little whorled cowlick of his bothered her; it looked as if someone had pressed a thumb to his hairline, leaving a fingerprint.

When Fletcher completed his associate-level actuarial examinations, his boss presented him with a cake, crowded with icing that spelled, "F.W.'s Own Personal Actuarial Table—50 Yrs with MSA!"

When he completed his fellowship examinations, he was taken out to lunch at the Rumpus Room and highly encouraged to drink the mai tais that were continually brought to the table in response to his boss's snapping fingers. Fletcher spent the rest of the afternoon in an uncharacteristic fog, suffering a headache that pulsed a bass rhythm through his head while his boss fell asleep in his office, covered by the Triple A blanket he kept in his closet for such liquor-induced naps.

There was a modest party planned (donuts and coffee at afternoon break) for his twelfth anniversary with Mid Summit American, but the celebrant missed it, holding as he was the withered but manicured hand of his mother as she breathed her last breaths on earth. Olive had suffered a stroke while showing a young couple a house that was far too expensive for them but one the wife thought fitting for her husband, who was recently elected to the county commissioner's office, and if she had anything to say about it, was headed for the eventual governorship or a senate seat.

"The floor's brand new," said Olive, who suddenly seemed transfixed by the red brick pattern of the linoleum. The couple stood politely, waiting for her to further elaborate on the age of the refrigerator or the grain of the kitchen cabinets. After a minute passed, the wife nudged the husband who asked, "Mrs. Weschel?" a second before Olive's knees buckled and she sank to the floor.

She lived only three more days, and because the stroke stole her ability to move or speak, she was deprived of saying good-bye to her son in a way he could understand.

She telegraphed through her eyes, *I love you, my selfless son who stuck around when no one else would!* but all Fletcher saw was vacancy: slate-blue eyes that couldn't focus on the finger he held up, eyes that wandered in the sockets as if a tethering nerve had been cut.

When Fletcher cried on his mother's chest, feeling through the thin hospital blankets the ridge of bones against his cheek, Olive's first impulse was to holler, *Get off, you big lug—you're crushing me!* but as her mouth couldn't voice this impulse, Fletcher held her tighter. How she wanted to pet her son's head, to twirl her finger in his cowlick, to kiss his sweet forehead . . . *to push him off her!* She managed a low groan and Fletcher quickly sat up.

"Was I hurting you, Ma?" he asked and Olive felt more burdened by guilt than she had of his body pressing against her. She had had the chance to let her son hold her and now, even dying, she had batted him away.

I love you, Fletcher! You're the only man I've ever known who wasn't a bastard to me!

"Oh, Ma, what will I do without you?" asked Fletcher, tenderly smoothing a section of her bangs whose gray was seeping in at the hairline. This action triggered a violent need for communication in Olive.

Fletcher! She hollered silently. *I need a dye job! If I don't pull out of whatever this is, don't send me to my grave without a dye job!*

Fletcher had been enlisted for years to put on plastic gloves and shampoo the gray out of his mother's hair with Black Sable #2, a hair dye that made his eyes water and his throat burn, but now he was oblivious to the state of his mother's hair, only wanting it off her fore-head so he could see her whole face.

I mean it, Fletcher, begged Olive. *I don't want all my clients and my PLC friends walking past my casket and whispering how bad I look!*

A tear fell from her son's eye and splashed on Olive's cheek, which shamed away her vanity, making her want to concentrate on bigger issues.

Fletcher, I love you! It was hard for me to show it—I had to make a living for us, didn't I?—but honestly, Fletcher, you were a prince among sons. A prince! How did a gentleman like you come from a cad like your father?

Olive could have easily ranted on about WW but knowing her death was more imminent than not (dang, she'd never get to wear that fox-trimmed car coat she'd just ordered from the Spiegel catalog!) gave her more strength to ignore the topic she had already wasted years brooding over.

Fletcher! Fletcher! It's a lousy world most of the time, but it has its moments! Make use of them! Get out more! Make some friends! Take an Arthur Murray class! For God's sake, Fletcher, get on the bus! Don't let everything pass you by!

Fletcher, this isn't for my sake, it's for yours! she screamed. *Start living! Start fucking living!* She laughed, remembering the shock her son had registered when he first heard her swear. There had been no ice in the bucket and Olive had said, 'Shit.'

"Did you just say what I think you said?" Fletcher had asked, his eyes round as bottle caps.

"Oh, Fletcher," Olive had said, swirling her gin and tonic with her baby finger. "You can't be out in the business world, in the *real* world, without parlaying a little French."

Olive often wondered how her son got to be such a fuddy-duddy; it seemed his hang-ups grew in direct proportion to her own loosening inhibitions.

But I digress, she thought in her hospital bed. *I shock you, Fletcher, because I want to wake you up! Wake up and join the parade! Do you hear me, Fletcher? Here, I'll squeeze your hand, and if you can hear me, squeeze mine back!*

At that moment, Fletcher lifted his head, which had been bowed in sadness. A rattle had escaped from his mother's chest, a desolate sound like a dog scratching the door of an empty house, and he let go of his mother's hands to touch her face again, to feel her shallow breath against his fingers.

She died on a Wednesday, and Mid Summit American magnanimously gave Fletcher the rest of the week off to bury his mother and deal with her affairs.

He must have sighed, "Oh, Ma," a dozen times while looking through her Lane hope chest. It appeared Olive Weschel took the furniture's name literally—instead of filling it with extra sheets and blankets, she had planted within it tiny seeds of hope, seeds that never sprouted.

Fletcher dug out the top layers of weeds that had overtaken the garden; Rumpus Room and the River's Edge Supper Club matchbooks with notations made on the inside: *8/13/66—dinner with Howard Troy; I welcome in the New Year with Gordy Tummler, 12/31/ 74. Al Offenthaler—2/4/76—the less said, the better!*

"Oh, Ma," said Fletcher.

Next in the hope chest were framed certificates of merit, honoring Olive in fancy calligraphy for her excellent sales records.

But it was when Fletcher reached the bottom layers that he burst into tears, for this was the hope buried long ago, in what must have seemed like good black soil and what had turned out to be dust.

Carbon copies of the many letters she typed to WW filled a manila folder; there was no corresponding file filled with letters from him, only empty envelopes in which WW had mailed checks. Another small pile held unopened letters addressed to WW and returned to Olive marked "Return to Sender, Address Unknown."

Under these dead flowers were the earliest seeds of hope, the photos from Olive's courthouse wedding to WW in which the newlyweds stood with their respective hats askew, dazed and smiling, as if they'd survived a train wreck.

A souvenir from our honeymoon in the Badlands! read a scrap of paper tucked inside a miniature birch teepee inscribed with the inked message W+O.

There were certificates commemorating their marriage and Fletcher's birth; Fletcher's faded-blue baby book; and an album recording his *School Days*. Fletcher opened to the page announcing *Grade 3* and read: *Our Fletcher is an excellent student. He can add and subtract like an adding machine, and he reads above his grade level. Mrs. Knupfer claims he tends to be a bit of a dreamer, but I say, what's wrong with that?*

Fletcher grimaced, remembering the way Mrs. Knupfer used to knock—hard—on his head, asking, "Anyone home?"

It was a rose-scented envelope titled "United" that really got to Fletcher. It contained three locks of hair in varying textures and color, tied together with a curly ribbon and a poem, also titled "United":

BLACK HAIR, BROWN HAIR, BLOND!
THREE COLORS FORM OUR BOND,
DAD, MOM, AND BABY BOY,
WHO WITH US MAKES THE GREATEST JOY.
UNITED.

He examined the hair, surprised that his own had been so fair as a baby, and then the words "Oh, Ma" were expelled not on a sigh but a sob, and he gathered up the pile of dead hope Olive had tended for all those years and dumped it back into the cedar-smelling chest where it fell in no particular order.

Fletcher inherited a modest stock portfolio—Olive was a businesswoman, after all—and the house. He briefly toyed with the idea of holding an estate sale, thinking it might be healthy to do a major housecleaning, but the idea of neighbors and other strangers picking through Olive's things made him slightly queasy, and he only got as far as writing the headline of the ad he planned to place: "Fine Collectibles from Years of Sophisticated Living!"

"So, gonna turn the old homestead into a swinging bachelor pad?" asked Dodd Beckerman.

"Did you?" asked Fletcher.

Beckerman's own mother had died several years earlier, and Dodd had returned home after world travels that included a military tour, one unraveled marriage, and two cases of crabs.

The men were talking in the coatroom of the funeral home; that Beckerman had made an appearance touched Fletcher deeply, even though his neighbor seemed incapable of saying anything that might be considered thoughtful or comforting. At the casket, for instance, he had said, "Man, she's as orange as a basketball."

It was true, Olive's skin looked as if it had been swabbed with Mercurochrome, but still, did he have to mention it? Fletcher felt bad enough already for not instructing the mortician to give Olive one final dye job; he felt certain that his mother would have wanted to go to her grave with all traces of gray washed away.

Olive Weschel lay in her casket with her gray roots showing and a scowl on her orange face, which Fletcher could have sworn was a comment on her last public appearance.

"Did I turn the old lady's place into my own swinging pied-à-terre?" asked Beckerman, hopping a little as he put his arms into his coat sleeves. "You betcha. Haven't you ever seen it, Fletcher?"

When Fletcher shook his head, Beckerman laughed and punched him in the arm. "Well, consider yourself invited, old man. In fact, why don't you come on by after everything's all over? You could probably use some cheering up."

And Fletcher could. After the private internment at the cemetery, and seeing off his hiccupping Aunt Florence at the bus station, he knocked on Beckerman's door with the urgency of a town crier, announcing an approaching wild fire.

Lurching into the front hallway, the door hadn't closed behind him before Fletcher burst into tears.

"I know what you mean, man," said Beckerman. "It's rough losing your old lady."

With a big hand on Fletcher's shoulder, he steered him into the living room as well as into a bend in the conversation. "Whose the lame-o who started using *old lady* to mean girlfriend anyway? I'll bet it was those damn hippies. I hated those hippies, man." Beckerman pressed his hand harder on Fletcher's shoulder, a signal Fletcher took to mean, "Sit." He sat, on a slippery black couch.

"I'm sorry I'm such a wreck," said Fletcher, wiping his pink nose on a sodden handkerchief.

Beckerman held out his hand like a traffic cop. "Don't apologize, man. I know exactly how you feel. They throw the dirt over that coffin and you think—hey, that's my old lady in there."

Fletcher nodded so deeply that his chin grazed the knot of his tie.

"Us only children—we got it bad, man. No brothers or sisters to cry with. Mothers who couldn't keep their paws off us—always kissing us and hugging us, so of course we start believing all that shit they feed us about being king of the world."

Fletcher nodded as if he knew exactly, man, what Beckerman was talking about, until a sob snorted through his nose betrayed him.

"I'm sorry," he blubbered, saturating his handkerchief with facial fluids, "but my mother never really made me feel like I was the king of the world."

"No shit," said Beckerman, scratching one of his bushy black sideburns. "I thought all mothers did that."

"My mother did a lot for me," said Fletcher, feeling disloyal. "But she was busy with her career and . . . well, she didn't have a lot of time for me."

Beckerman's finger trolled over to his other sideburn. "That explains a lot," he said, nodding. "A lot about you."

"It does?"

Beckerman pressed his big hands against his thighs, using them to give himself a little boost before he stood up. "I think we need some beer," he said, walking toward the kitchen. Judging from the matted path beaten through the brown shag carpet, it was a popular route. He returned, carrying four bottles, the necks of which were propped between his massive fingers.

"Salut," he said and they clinked bottles. Beckerman's long draw half-emptied his bottle. "Ahh. Nothing like good old American beer. You know, I've had beer in Amsterdam and it's good—but it's Dutch. I've had beer in Munich and it's good—but it's German. Hell, I've even had beer in Singapore and it's good—but it's . . . Singaporean, I guess. I'm telling you, nothing beats the taste of good old American beer."

"So," said Fletcher, less interested in Beckerman's nationalistic beer reviews than in his theories as to Fletcher's arrested development. "You were saying something about my mother's behavior explaining a lot about me—"

"—oh, yeah." Beckerman finished his first beer and started his second. "It's classic. Cold, unaffectionate mother, runaway father. What chance does the kid have?" He took another long draw and shook his head. "None."

He leaned back on the couch and smiled, proud of his astute psychological analysis.

"See, you take a guy like me—mother who thinks he can do no wrong, a father who'll throw a football around with him for hours—man, when he bit the dust, that hurt—well, then you're pretty much bound to be a popular, well-adjusted guy."

Fletcher could have blamed what he said next on a drunk's loss of inhibition, but the fact was, he wasn't drunk. His forehead had started to pound in protest of cold beer too quickly consumed, but even a nondrinker like himself had a higher tolerance than inebriation from a half-bottle. No, what compelled him to ask the question was simple curiosity.

"Then why were you such a bully?"

Beckerman jerked his head, his eyes wide.

"Bully? What are you talking about? Me?"

Fletcher fiddled with the knot of his tie, finally unloosening it. There was something in Beckerman's voice that advised him to recant what he had just said, but already beat up emotionally, Fletcher thought he may as well get punched in the face, too.

"I asked why you were such a bully. I mean, your parents sound great, but still, you weren't very nice to people."

"Fletch, I am seriously wounded," said Beckerman, holding a splayed hand to his chest. "I have no idea where you get off saying such a thing."

"Please. You were always picking on me. In the eighth grade I couldn't walk to school without you ambushing me by the Jensons' peony bushes, taking my lunch money."

"Peony bushes," said Beckerman, shaking his head. "Only you would remember the Jensons' had fucking peony bushes."

"From the time you started wrestling in ninth grade, you liked to show me the holds you were working on—without my permission, of course. And in twelfth grade, right in the middle of the lunchroom, in front of everyone, you gave me the Biggest Spaz Award."

Beckerman laughed. "Oh yeah, I do remember that. A bunch of us made up awards out of tin foil and gave 'em out to all the class losers."

Fletcher shook his head at the memory. "Real nice."

"But you *were* the biggest spaz, Fletcher. I was only the messenger on that one, buddy."

"What about all the other things?"

"No memory of 'em, pal. If you ask anybody from Central, they'll tell you what a great guy I was."

"Would Connie Yarborough say that?"

Beckerman's shapely black eyebrows squiggled over his eyes. "Connie Yar—oh yeah, big dyke Connie Yarborough! I remember her."

"She was not a dyke! And don't use that word!"

Shaking his head, Beckerman got up and made his short walk to the kitchen and refills. He came back with two bottles, which he set in front of himself.

"You know what they say time does to memories, Fletcher. Distorts 'em. I'm a nice guy, always have been a nice guy. I'm sorry if I called you a spaz, but you were. Still are, if you don't mind me saying so."

"I mind you saying a lot of things—especially that my mother was cold and unaffectionate. Because even if she didn't think I was king of the world, she probably thought I was at least a duke or something."

Beckerman stared at Fletcher for a long moment.

"You are really too much, man," he said, but not unkindly. He stretched his arms to the ceiling and then brought them down, resting his clasped hands on top of his head. "So what do you think?"

Fletcher blinked. "Of what?"

"Of my pad. I ditched all the doilies—I'm telling you, the old lady loved her doilies. I junked all the little braided rugs that I was always tripping on and smashed to hell every little glass Hummel thing. Man, I hate those Hummel things."

Hippies and Hummels, thought Fletcher. *What else did Beckerman hate—hide-a-beds? Habadashery? Hackensack?*

"I mean, it's cute for a seventy-six-year-old woman, I guess, but a guy can't live in all that shit, right, Fletch?"

"Right." Realizing he wasn't about to get a belated apology for years of bullying, Fletcher decided he may as well go along with whatever conversation Beckerman wanted to pursue. It beat going back to his own empty house.

"So I got all this furniture—it's vinyl but it looks like leather, doesn't it?—at this warehouse sale in Sioux Falls, and the paintings are from a lady friend of mine."

There were four paintings—one for each wall—and each one contained a topless woman on a motorcycle. While the women looked identical in each painting, each motorcycle was a different make—a Harley, a Triumph, a BSA, and a Norton—and all intricately detailed.

"She's not a lady you'd want to mess with," said Beckerman.

"I guess not," agreed Fletcher.

The men sat back, nursing their beers in silence that to Fletcher was growing more companionable. He was beginning to relax, thanks to Beckerman's American beer, and quick fantasies flitted through his head of himself and Beckerman watching Sunday afternoon football games on TV, fishing in the Missouri River, or shooting pool together. That Fletcher didn't follow football, didn't fish, and had never chalked a pool cue in his life was immaterial; if he was going to be Beckerman's friend, he'd better learn!

During Fletcher's reverie, Beckerman stumbled off and returned with more beer and a small box.

"Here," he said, lobbing it at his guest.

"For me?" asked Fletcher, fumbling it.

"Geez . . . it's not a present, Weschel. It's just something I want you to see."

Fletcher struggled to sit up straighter on the slippery vinyl couch, and when he opened the small box he sat quietly, staring at its contents perched on a layer of cotton balls.

Presently he said, "It sort of looks like an ear."

Beckerman hooted, slapping the meaty thigh that strained against his creased dress jeans. "It is an ear! A real live, gen-u-ine ear!"

Fletcher's stomach churned and he snapped the box shut and dropped it on the coffee table as if it were hot to the touch.

"Why . . . what do you have it for?"

Beckerman took the box and opened it. "It's a war souvenir. I won it in a game of poker in Oberammergau. Won it from Captain "Killer" Ackerblade—guy had been in the Big One, in Korea, and just finished a tour in 'Nam. He was doing a little sightseeing—wanted to see the *Passion Play*—before he went stateside."

Fletcher wondered how on earth he could have thought he and The Bod might become friends.

"He couldn't tell me whose ear it was," said Beckerman, an odd glint in his eyes as he gazed at the box's contents. "All's he said to me was, 'Son, could be a Kraut ear, could be a Jap ear, could be a Gook ear. When you've killed as many of the enemy as I have, you can't really keep track."

"Well, then," said Fletcher, sliding off the couch to stand. "If anyone asks you to lend an ear, you'll be all set." He brushed the lapels of his suit as if something had spilled on them and headed, his path slightly crooked, toward the door. "Thanks for the beer, Dodd."

The former wrestler and private first class followed him. "It's just an ear, Fletcher. And it's not like *I* chopped it off or anything. Don't be such a baby, man. I hate babies."

"Why would you hate babies?" asked Fletcher. "And while we're on the subject, why do you hate hippies?"

"What? What the hell are you talking about?"

"I myself think hippies were on track about a lot of things. Peace and love and that sort of thing."

Beckerman looked at him as if he were speaking pig Latin *in* Latin.

"As for Hummels," Fletcher continued, "I really have no opinion."

Beckerman opened the door and with his hand on Fletcher's back gave him a hearty push out. "You're weird, man."

————————

The shell Fletcher had been in since boyhood was now a virtual sarcophagus. His days passed with little variety; it was work and sleep with a few evening hours reserved for household and yard maintenance, television, reading, and lonely amusements like solitaire and crossword puzzles.

Window monitoring also became something of a pastime.

Fletcher knew Mrs. Wilde across the street never cleaned up the messes her Airedale made on everyone's lawn but her own, and that every morning at seven Old Man Helger did isometrics in his boxer shorts while watching *The Today Show*. He also knew that gut or no gut, women still saw The Bod in Dodd's brawny body; there was much female commotion in and out of Chéz Beckerman.

Now a butcher at the Food Palace, Beckerman was in the enviable position of dealing with women every day. He was a big flirt—handing the lieutenant governor's wife her T-bones and reminding her that "the rarer the steak, the better the *amour*," and sending pregnant Nancy Bowser home with a fryer chicken, musing aloud to her why it was that breast meat was the most tender in all species.

He had recently had a pork chop tattooed on his bicep and made the friendly overture of showing it to his neighbor one evening when Fletcher was doing his weekly shopping.

While pricing ground beef, Fletcher heard a tap on the small window in the wall behind the meat counter and looked up to see Beckerman waving, meat cleaver in hand.

Laughing, the butcher came through the swinging door, dapper in a bloodied white coat and jauntily angled paper hat.

"Hey, stay away from the ground beef, Fletch. Clipped a couple of my fingernails into it today."

Fletcher dropped the cellophaned package back into the refrigerator case, despite Beckerman's claims that he was kidding.

So, you've seen this?" Beckerman asked as he let his white coat slip past the straps of his ribbed T-shirt. He tensed his bicep and the pork chop bulged.

"Nice," said Fletcher.

"Well, it sure beats what I've got tattooed on my ass."

Fletcher was saved from asking what that might be by a woman who nudged him aside with her cart, asking where the sweetbreads might be, and he scurried off, not particularly wanting to hear the butcher's answer.

In the summertime, Beckerman threw barbecues in his small square backyard and once, while weeding his tomato patch, Fletcher listened to him regale the assemblage of bikinied cashiers and sunburned stock boys gnawing at fatty Food Palace spareribs.

"The guy next door," Beckerman was saying in his loud voice, "guy's name is Fletcher Weschel, can you believe it? What kinda name is that? Sounds like a German specialty wine, if you ask me." He cleared his throat. "Ya, my frient here vill hef za Leibfraumilk und I vill hef a glass of za Fletcher Weschel."

The partygoers laughed, enjoying the sophisticated humor that some of them didn't quite get. On his knees in a slug-infested vegeta-

ble garden and hidden behind the lilac bushes that divided their properties, Fletcher sighed, wondering why he ever thought he might be
more to Beckerman than the butt of his jokes.

At thirty-seven, the edges of Fletcher's hair and the swirl of his
cowlick were faded brown, just on the verge of gray, but his face was
still boyish and unlined—unmarked, he thought, by experience. He
had just celebrated, in a manner of speaking, his fifteenth year with
Mid Summit American Life. Consciously, he hadn't the heart to
declare himself a lost cause, doomed to a life of loneliness, but his subconscious was well aware that Fletcher Weschel was a loser and sent
out subtle messages to that effect every day.

———————

He was savoring a cup of warm Ovaltine after his regular Monday
night supper of meatloaf and creamed corn, unscrambling the daily
word puzzle in the paper. It was a cold November night, a night when
the wind ran howling down the avenues like a mischievous ghost,
yanking leaves off trees and tossing them into roof gutters where they
would rot into muck and interfere with drainage.

Suddenly the fun of unscrambling words like *unratt* (truant)
and *kceifl* (fickle) was interrupted by a voice in his head, urging him
to do something about those pesky window drafts. It was obvious
that the *Farmers' Almanac* extended weather forecast was wrong, and
that maybe it wasn't going to be an unseasonably mild winter after
all. He hadn't planned on executing his winter insulation duties until
that weekend, but thinking, *What the heck?* he carefully cut putty strips
and tamped them into the window seams. Later, as he sat on the edge
of his bed, lining up the toe of his slippers with the blue stripe in the
rug, he chuckled at his spontaneity. It wasn't often that he fiddled with
his schedule, and it made him feel reckless and bold. He even set his
alarm clock to go off fifteen minutes later than usual, but eventually he

calmed down and changed it back to 5:45. He began to recite chrono-
logically the presidents and their terms of office, getting up to James
Buchanan, 1857–1861, before he fell asleep. Three hours later, his room
was filled with aliens.

Dear Readers:

*Please forgive this intrusion, but we (whom you will get to know shortly)
feel a need to express to those who have been so kind to come along on
Fletcher's journey thus far: Sorry.*

*It is now evident that what is about to happen to our hero is beyond
usual earthly conventions, if one subscribes to the idea that earthly conventions are, in fact, usual. We suspect you do not; advanced and lit-
erate earthlings like you (yes, flattery is a tool plied in any dimension)
are willing to suspend disbelief when faced with the irrefutable wonder
and mystery that exist in such depth, scope, and volume on your planet.*

*Still, you might have preferred the trajectory of Fletcher's story to
follow a less wild arc, perhaps something transformational, but more
along the lines of a career change, or an act of heroism, or the meeting
of a soul mate. At this point, we're certain Fletcher would also opt for
these more traditional choices. No one, however constrained their present life may be, is prepared when that life is tumbled, jumbled, tossed,
spun, jerked, and turned upside down. We do not presume to think that
a story can take such a sharp left turn without some sense of being jostled. We hope nothing was spilled.*

*And now, we request your patience and a willingness to go with
what is decidedly a very unusual flow.*

. . . Imagine how Fletcher feels.

4

He was in the middle of a dream featuring Cindy Dahlberg. A contestant in the first beauty contest of the civilized world, Cindy was playing the marimba in the middle of the Coliseum, wearing only a few well-placed Roman numerals. Her audience, men who looked like Peter Ustinov in *Spartacus,* sipped wine from goatskin pouches and bribed judges with their filthy lucre. Cindy was a crowd favorite, especially when the lively rhythm she played unhinged the X covering her left breast. Fletcher's unconscious mind was a pancake, pleasure pouring over it like warm syrup.

To be rudely awakened by thin luminescent space creatures was one thing, but to be deprived of a dream featuring Cindy Dahlberg as Miss Appian Way was downright mean.

"What on earth?" sputtered Fletcher, sitting up in his bed.

The aliens tittered, as if he had said something funny.

One stepped forward and said in an electronic monotone, "Take me to your leader."

Again the aliens laughed (Fletcher assumed it was laughter coming out of the turned-up slits that were their unattractive mouths), nudging each other with rubbery looking arms.

"Who are you?" asked Fletcher in a small voice, not certain at all that he wanted an answer. Feeling cold sweat begin to bead along his hairline, he drew the blankets over his chest. His Adam's apple bobbed above it like a buoy.

"We are what you call aliens," said the one who had spoken earlier. He gestured to the small group in the corner of the bedroom before pointing to a metallic emblem embedded in his shiny Lurex bodysuit. "Lodge 1212. Brother Charmat at your service." He gave a jaunty salute with one finger—the only finger—of his right hand.

"Lodge," said Fletcher. "You're a lodge member?" His panic was rising like swamp gas, but he couldn't help but respond to the absurd things the absurd-looking space thing was saying.

"All aliens are lodge members. It's a way of making us feel a little less, well . . . alien."

A tree branch, tossing in the wind, clicked against his windowpane. Under the covers, Fletcher pinched his thigh, and when he felt the quick zip of pain his analysis of the situation was gravely disappointing: this was no dream, what was happening was really happening.

Recalling a story he'd read in one of the tabloid magazines Cindy Dahlberg stocked the break room with, he asked, "Are you . . . are you going to conduct medical experiments on me?"

The half-dozen or so aliens laughed again.

"Good heavens, no," said Charmat. "That's Lodge 527's thing. They can't go anywhere without dissecting someone or something."

"You mean they're not harvesting genes or implanting tracking devices or something like that?"

"Lodge 527?" Charmat rolled his bulbous, opaque eyes. "They're nothing but scavengers, out to steal a few human souvenirs. First they'll raid your refrigerator, then they decide, 'Why not take home a jar of testosterone or a couple bile ducts while we're at it?'"

"They raid refrigerators?"

"They claim they can fuel their galaxy trams with a mixture of green salsa and RC Cola, but then why must they hoard the frozen waffles and the Hershey's syrup?" A pink light pulsed in Charmat's twelve-inch forehead as he shook his head. "They are *not* doing their jobs."

Fletcher gulped. "Jobs?"

The alien leader sat at the foot of Fletcher's bed and absently began

LORNA LANDVIK

to pet the coonskin hat that hung like a flea-bitten opossum on the bedpost. "We all have jobs to do. You don't think we make these house calls for fun, do you?"

Fletcher swallowed down the rock of fear that filled his throat and shook his head.

"Then you'd be wrong!" shouted the alien, leaping up.

Fletcher gasped, pulling the covers completely over his head. Crouching under his tent of sheets and blankets, he smelled the Ovaltine in his hot panicked breath. Hunkering there, he listened to the high-pitched hum of alien laughter, and when he felt himself being jostled, he lifted a square of sheet and peeked out. The circus had come to town.

Two aliens, their spindly legs gripped around each other's waists, were swinging from the small domed light fixture in the middle of the ceiling. Another did backflips up and down the side of the wall. Still another jumped on Fletcher's bed, gaining enough altitude to execute several graceful somersaults.

"Tandala, dance with me!" said Charmat, grabbing an alien. In seconds they were dancing a slinky tango with each other, their bodies pressed together like hands in prayer.

Fletcher pleaded with himself for some inner instruction but in this crisis state his mind was a weak receiver, able to pick up only the signals, *Bolt!* and *Excuse yourself to the bathroom!* Instinctively, he knew that he could not outrun these athletic aliens, but might they not be sympathetic to a man in need of a toilet?

"Excuse me." His voice wavered like a loon's. "I have to go to the bathroom."

"Bathroom?" asked one of the aliens on the light fixture.

Charmat dipped his partner one last time and sighed.

"Remember, Revlor, we covered this in our Good Neighbor seminar: humans void. Their waste products are not disposed of internally."

Fletcher's fright did another strange arabesque with curiosity. "And yours are?"

"Of course," said Charmat. "And in fifty thousand years or so, you'll catch up to us. You earthlings will have disposed with the need of disposal."

The aliens tittered at what Fletcher thought a rather weak play on words.

"But please," said Charmat, bowing slightly, "be our guest."

Fletcher slipped out of bed, pushed his feet into his waiting slippers, and made a dash across the room and to the bathroom down the hall.

He pushed the little button lock inside the knob and sat down on the toilet, where he began to shake convulsively, to the 4/16 rhythm of his chattering teeth.

Think! was his panicky order. *Think, think, think!*

He obeyed himself; an idea sprung to his mind as soon as he looked up at the small window above the hamper. Hours earlier he had stood at it, carefully sealing the seam where the sash and the sill met.

Wait a second, he thought, *was I somehow trying to keep these aliens out? Did a part of my brain know my home was about to be invaded by spacemen?*

Despite his terror and disbelief, he began to snicker. The idea that he, Fletcher Weschel, practical as masking tape, was clairvoyant tickled him.

He went to the window and saw that the lights were still on at Beckerman's house. Earlier that evening he had seen a young woman carrying a Food Palace grocery bag (containing her negligee, surmised Fletcher) storm out of the house while Beckerman, his velour robe opened to reveal leopard briefs, pleaded with her to "come back, Trudy, I was only joking!"

Beckerman's house offered something he needed at the moment— refuge—all he had to do was climb out the window and scamper across the lawn. Aliens wouldn't mess with a 220-lb. butcher with a pork chop tattooed on his bicep, would they?

Fletcher thought not, but he remained standing, staring out at the rectangles of yellow light shining through Beckerman's windows. *Have they hypnotized me?* he wondered as, to his great surprise, he found himself turning his back toward possible escape. He used the toilet, washed his hands, and brushed his teeth, scrubbing away the scent of Ovaltine.

He stood in the hallway, trying not to make the floorboards creak as he tried to pinpoint the strange sensation that had come over him. He snapped his fingers—of course! He was feeling what he had when WW announced he was going to lead the Cub Scouts—the anticipation that something wonderful was about to happen.

Fletcher sighed and shook his head as the memory of his father banging away in the Bel Air with Miss Shirley came into his head, reminding him of how it really was.

At his bedroom door, he squared his shoulders, took a deep breath, and opened it. Disappointment was as stinging as a slap on the face: the room was empty.

Fletcher turned around helplessly, feeling as hurt as a host whose guests run out of the party while he's still in the kitchen refilling the bowl of onion dip.

He sat heavily on the bed, wondering what terribly boring thing it was that caused them to roll their bulging eyes and telepathically plead with one another to "ditch this joint." He cocked his head to listen; perhaps they were at Dodd Beckerman's right now, whooping it up with the bodacious butcher, dancing with lampshades on their heads to music Fletcher had no idea existed. (He hadn't seen fit to change the radio dial from the station his mother listened to, a station that might as well have aired public announcements for war bonds and ration cards for all the big band music it played.)

Fletcher couldn't understand why he felt like crying: he should be thrilled, he told himself, that the aliens were out of his house—hadn't he nearly been scared to death?

"Awwww."

Snorting in surprise, Fletcher looked up to see the aliens slowly take on form as they emerged out of the walls.

"I thought you were gone! I thought you'd gone to Beckerman's!"

"We had," chuckled Charmat. "We short-sheeted the dweeb. While he was downstairs, watching *Cagney and Lacey*."

The aliens nodded, twittering as was their fashion.

"You short-sheeted him?" repeated Fletcher. He'd been thrown for so many loops, he felt limp.

"That's right," said Charmat, sitting next to him. "He'll get into bed feeling like the least popular boy at camp."

"But why? What did he ever do to you?"

The other aliens sat down around them, folding their Gumby-like legs underneath themselves.

"He bothers us," said the lodge leader. "We don't like how he treats people—particularly you."

"Wow," said Fletcher. "I'm not used to people sticking up for me."

"We're not people," said Tandala, the alien who had tangoed with the alien leader.

"Remember I told you we all have jobs?" asked Charmat. "Lodge 527 likes to scavenge—"

Fletcher nodded. "And conduct the occasional scientific experiment."

"That's right," said Charmat, pleased at his quick study. "Now take Lodge 809, they're partial to landscaping. They're the ones responsible for those strange patterns in British cornfields."

"But I thought two guys owned up to doing that," said Fletcher. "It was on the news—it was all a big hoax."

Charmat's eyes glowed. "The hoax is that those guys are Brother Zoltan and Brother Yadlac of Lodge 809!"

"They're aliens? But I saw those guys on TV! They looked as normal as . . . as I do!"

"Fletcher, please, give us some credit. If we're able to come to earth, if we're able to disappear—"

On cue, Revlor faded into a blank space, waited a few seconds, and reappeared again, looking exactly like Albert Einstein.

"If we're able to do all that," said Charmat, smoothing Mr. Einstein's wild white hair with his finger, "don't you think we might be able to transform ourselves into a couple of nondescript-looking farmers . . . or a descriptive-looking scientist?"

It took a moment for Fletcher to regain the ability to speak.

"I guess so. I just never thought about it much."

Albert Einstein shimmered away, and as Revlor resumed his alien form, a scowl appeared on Charmat's thin mouth.

"That's the trouble," he said. "The pond of human thought is a shallow one—most of you just don't think."

Fletcher felt himself began to sag—now he was being insulted by an alien—but a flash of anger flared in him, straightening his spine. "Hey," he said, defending his species, "we think!"

A furrow appeared on the alien leader's ample and browless forehead. "About what?"

Fletcher leaned forward and his bedsprings gave a little squeak. "About a lot of things! About . . . about aliens, for instance."

The room vibrated with the aliens' humming laughter, but Fletcher was not about to be cowed.

"We've done a lot of thinking about you guys. We've created books and movies with aliens who look *exactly* the way you look, who wear the same funny jumpsuits you do, whose names—Zoltan, Relvor—"

"—Revlor," corrected the alien.

"—are even like yours! That's pretty good thinking, if you ask me!"

The single finger of Charmat's right hand stroked his chin. "The thing about human thought is that even though it's often in the ball park, it's usually way off base. Don't you think we might have reconfigured ourselves into beings that are consistent with your limited imaginations? Do you think as evolved as we are, we seriously would look like this?"

Feeling baited, and not willing to be knocked out of Round One in Universal Debate without a fight, Fletcher said, "So you guys went with the cliché? You didn't think I—with my limited imagination—could handle anything more than that?"

Suddenly the room went dark, but the deepest blackest darkness was inside Fletcher and he moaned, sadness like a death grip around his heart.

In a flash, the lights returned and the aliens clustered around Fletcher.

Fletcher groaned. "Oh, my. What was that?"

"That was us," said Charmat. "In another configuration."

"You can be feelings?"

"We can be anything we want."

"Despair," said Fletcher. "That's what I was filled with and it was awful."

"Sorry," said Charmat. "But we don't like to be called clichés."

"I apologize as well."

There was an awkward moment of silence that sometimes follows apology, and then with a wave of his one-fingered hand Charmat drew the other aliens to him.

Like a benched player, Fletcher strained to hear what was being said in the on-field huddle.

"You're right, Fletcher," said Charmat as the small group broke up.

"We should have presented ourselves in a manner more befitting the mission of our lodge."

The aliens' rubbery luminescent bodies began to shimmer and within seconds they had reconfigured themselves into forms that made Fletcher gasp . . . again.

"That's a fine welcome for a ghost, but we were maybe expecting applause," said one of the six Groucho Marxes wiggling his grease-paint eyebrows and flicking cigar ash on the bedroom floor.

"I have had a perfectly wonderful evening," said one, "but this wasn't it."

"A man's only as old as the woman he feels," said another.

"I never forget a face, but in your case I'll be glad to make an exception."

"Is this more to your liking?" asked the Groucho Fletcher presumed was Charmat.

"Actually, I—"

Another paced in front of the bed. "Marry me and I'll never look at another horse."

"Actually," continued Fletcher, "this . . . this is a little disconcerting. The way you were before was just fine."

The half-dozen Groucho Marxes shimmered away and were replaced by the aliens in their original, albeit clichéd, form.

"That was really . . . something," said Fletcher, and at that moment the absurdity of aliens taking on the body and the bon mots of Groucho Marx struck him, and he began to laugh.

As he was to find out, the manners of Lodge 1212 of the Delphinus Constellation insisted on responding to any laughter with equal or greater laughter of their own. And so Fletcher Weschel's boyhood bedroom, with its pilly cowboy bed linens and rickracked curtains, with its dusty album covers and movie star pictures and baseball pennants thumbtacked to the wall, rocked with laughter. And when Fletcher had laughed so hard he complained of an aching stomach, the aliens claimed that yes, their bebobs hurt, too, and rubbed a flat curveless part of their body.

"Wait a second," said Fletcher, "your bebobs are your rear ends? It's your rear ends that ache when you laugh too much?"

"Remember, this is an alien incarnation to us," said Charmat without apparent irony. "We've formulated ourselves to make it easier for you to see us. And as it's obvious our backsides lack the curvature of those belonging to earthlings, we've created our own word for them."

"Oh, that's priceless," said Fletcher. "P-riceless." Glee made the atoms of his body bounce off one another; he was a flat soda that had been charged with a burst of effervescence. He felt he had been given a wonderful gift, and innately gracious he invited everyone into the kitchen for the homemade cranberry bread he had baked the night before.

After nearly unanimous compliments (only Revlor said tartness was a better concept than a flavor), the conversation returned to jobs. They made Fletcher explain his three times.

"People actually sit in small windowless cubicles?" asked Charmat.

"Calculating statistical risks?" asked Revlor.

"To figure our premiums?" said Tandala.

"Excuse me, but I had to study hard to become an actuary," said Fletcher. His voice lost its defensiveness before he finished his sentence and he sighed. "You're right. It's not really my true calling."

"What is?" said Charmat, a light pulsing in his forehead.

"I guess I haven't figured that out," said Fletcher, uncomfortable under Charmat's intense, glowing gaze. Refilling the aliens' milk glasses, he said, "Now, you—tell me more about Lodge 1212."

"Our jobs," said Charmat, flicking cranberry bread crumbs off the table with his finger, "our jobs are to be goof-offs." The aliens nodded and tittered and, as if to underscore the point, Revlor pulled the corners of his mouth in a ghoulish grin and stuck out his tongue, thin as a viper's.

A low wave of resignation rolled over Fletcher.

"Don't feel bad," said Charmat, reading his thoughts, "not everyone gets visited by Lodges 103 or 720." The alien leader didn't wait for Fletcher to vocalize the question in his head. "The brothers and sisters of Lodge 103 are the healers. You can't be in the same room with them without being cured of whatever it is that ails you."

"But then," whispered Tandala in a voice Fletcher found oddly attractive, "you smell like baked-on oven grease."

"They've been trying to iron that bug out for light years," said Charmat. "If you're cured by Lodge 103, you're going to smell like baked-on oven grease. The two go hand in hand."

"What about Lodge 270?" asked Fletcher.

"720," corrected the alien leader. "They're the spiritualists. They claim that one visit from them and you can never doubt the existence of God."

"Gosh," said Fletcher, "have you been visited by them?"

"Oh sure. Every year at the annual Interplanetary Mixer."

"All they do is pass out pamphlets," scoffed Revlor. "Pamphlets and little memo pads that say, 'Eternally Yours, Lodge 720.'"

"We don't believe in their particular God," said Charmat with a little shake of his big head.

"Do you . . . believe in any God?" asked Fletcher.

"Certainly. According to our belief system, God is fun, laughter. After all, isn't that when you feel the most holy, when you laugh?"

"I don't laugh much."

"So you'd say you're an agnostic."

"No! I . . . I like to laugh. It's just that things haven't struck me as funny lately."

"So tell me about the God you believe in," said Charmat.

"Well, He's—"

"Oh, so he's a he. Does he have a penis?"

Fletcher blushed. "That's not a very nice question to ask."

"Why not?"

"Because . . . because it's sacrilegious. A person doesn't go around talking about God's privates."

The aliens tittered.

"We're not laughing *at* you," said Charmat kindly. "Well, maybe we are. But in a loving way."

"720s hardly ever laugh," said Tandala. "That's why we tend to doubt their claim of having a free pass to the Great Beyond."

"The Great Beyond," said Fletcher. "What's the Great Beyond?"

"Nobody really knows. Although it's where we're all headed, eventually."

"Where is it?" asked Fletcher, hugging his knees to his chest.

Charmat pointed his finger toward the window. "It could be out there past the Galilean moons or"—he pointed downward—"it could be underneath your bed. We know as much as you do on that one, good buddy."

Feeling overwhelmed and not sure what to do with all this strange information, Fletcher said, "Shouldn't I call a news station or something? This really should be shared with a wider audience."

The aliens tittered.

"You humans endear us with your need to share," said Charmat. "But your world isn't ready for such knowledge. Our philosophy is to work like the Mayans—one brick at a time."

Leaning back against his pillow to quell a wave of dizziness, Fletcher said, "If the world isn't ready for 'such knowledge,' what makes you think I am?"

"He may have a point," Revlor said to Charmat.

"Fletcher, in this case, don't ask why so much. Try *why not* instead."

"So let me figure this out. You're not here to show me that God exists or to heal me of some disease, but to . . . "

The silence was long and deafening.

"Well," said Charmat, "we really haven't figured that out yet."

"We're usually the last of the Lodges to be told anything," said Tandala.

Fletcher concentrated on digging out a sliver of putty from under his fingernail.

"Oh dear," said Charmat, "you're starting to feel insignificant. You're feeling as if goof-offs are the bargain basement of the alien world."

"No, I'm not," stammered Fletcher. He rolled the piece of putty into a tiny ball. "Yes, I am."

"For heaven's sake—and I mean that in the literal sense," said Charmat crisply. "Here you get an alien visit—how common an occurrence do you suppose that is?—and you're sulking because you're not being visited by what you consider a more elite Lodge!"

"No, I'm not, I . . . " hemmed Fletcher, fiddling with the skin between his nostrils, a nervous habit.

"And quit picking your nose," said Revlor.

"I'm not!"

Charmat's homely android face suddenly moved in a swirl of color. Fletcher yelped in surprise; everything was in motion, transmogrifying into bends and turns of yellow, pink, lavender, and red. He closed his eyes, feeling nauseated.

When he opened them, he was on top of a mountain. He squinted his eyes at the bright sunlight that was reflected in a wide swath of sparkles on the hard white snow. Feeling the tickle of a light breeze against the back of his body, he looked down and saw with horror that he was wearing nothing but ski boots and skis.

"Oh, my gosh, I'm naked!"

Shouts and whoops of laughter resonated through the canyon like a round of fire, and Fletcher realized with even deeper horror that he was not alone.

At least a dozen skiers appeared from the crest of the hill, all of them dressed in regular skiwear.

"Way to go, Fletcher baby!" shouted a woman whose nose was white with a triangle of zinc oxide.

"Talk about your hot dog on skis!" shouted another woman.

Fletcher was in a zone of mortification so deadly he was certain death by stroke or coronary was close at hand. What was he doing under this dome of blue sky, on skis at the top of a mountaintop, naked? Who were these strangers applauding him and calling him by name?

None of these questions was answered as some demon possessed Fletcher. He lifted his chin up and after howling like the lead wolf in a partying pack, bent deep, pushed down hard on his poles, and was off.

Wind and flying snow pelted him with force and song—or was it his motion, swooshing, soaring, flying that made the music that was filling his head? Music that sang of a hundred thousand reasons to be happy, that yodeled a million assurances that he was utterly, thoroughly, deeply alive.

Pine trees passed him in a blur of green and then, with an innate sense more attuned than any ear, he heard them say, "Wow" and "Bye" and "Good ride, neighbor." The pine trees spoke to him! Fletcher had never known the speed that was pushing him down the mountain like a projectile, didn't know that snow could be sky, could be a place where one could fly.

"Oh joy!" he shouted above the noises of nature singing, above the bliss of his naked body gasping with sheer, awed pleasure. His skis angled through the snow in tight zigzags.

"Way to go, Fletcher!"

He became aware of the voices of his fan club as he twisted to a stop at the bottom of the hill, the edges of his skis throwing up tiny avalanches. He fell sideways and his naked body, hot as a race car engine, sizzled as it met the cold shadowed snow.

Fletcher opened his eyes.

"Good, wasn't it?" asked Charmat, sitting next to Fletcher on his boyhood bed. He turned to his fellow aliens. "I don't mean to brag, but that was good."

"Although an après-ski drink would have been nice," said Revlor. "Something along the lines of a buttered rum?"

"Ooooh!" said Fletcher. "No fair—take me back! Take me back to that mountain!"

"If you went back you'd be arrested for indecent exposure," said Charmat. "We want you to be a goof-off, but avoid entanglements with the law whenever possible. They're usually not fun."

Fletcher leaned against the headboard, his eyes glassy with the memory of what had just transpired.

"That really happened, didn't it? It wasn't some kind of mind-control thing, was it? I really skied in the buff, didn't I?"

"Yes," said Charmat. "You really skied—Aspen, as a matter of fact—and yes, you were in the buff."

"It was . . . transcendental," whispered Fletcher, using a word that never had occasion to pass his lips.

"That's what we mean, Fletcher. Our way is but one way . . . one fun way. Welcome to the Lodge, brother."

Fletcher felt a sudden rise of pain, as if an out-of-season bee had lowered itself and sunk its stinger into his chest. He unbuttoned his pajama top, wanting to squish the venomous insect, but imbedded in between his sparse growth of chest hair was not a wasp or bumblebee, only a small shiny medallion that read *Lodge 1212*.

"How . . . how am I worthy?"

"Actually," said Revlor, "you're not. We drew your name out of a hat."

Throwing Revlor a scolding look, Charmat said, "Fletcher, we've long admired the way you got through your childhood—not the toughest, by any means, but not the easiest either."

Fletcher stared at the alien as if unconvinced.

"You have a certain . . . quirkiness that drew us to you. We're great fans of your vivid fantasy life."

Fletcher gulped.

"Sometimes a person's only retreat is their imagination," said Tandala softly.

"You mean you've been able to spy on my fantasies?"

"On occasion we would tune in to some of your childhood ones," said Charmat. "I'm quite a fan of Vince Shark and Hip Galloway, I must say. But your adult fantasies, umm, generally not of interest. They so often trade mystery and delight for simple-minded sex."

Fletcher breathed a sigh of relief. He would have been mortified to think the aliens were aware of some of his more simple-minded fantasies featuring Cindy Dahlberg.

"When you used to dance by moonlight in the wheat fields . . . ," said Tandala, with a little sigh.

"Could we get on with things?" asked Revlor. "There's that galactic cannibalism party—we're betting on what planet gets eaten—"

"Silence!" bellowed Charmat with such power the room shook and a Chicago Cubs pennant lost most of its mooring, swinging alongside the wall by one remaining thumbtack.

Fletcher had no idea Charmat was capable of such temper, and his shocked gasp was followed by first silence and then the humming laughter.

"Oh, you were kidding!" said Fletcher. "You were just kidding!"

"Of course I was," said Charmat. "Bad temper is something we've been able to excise out of our benetic code."

"Benetic code?"

"As opposed to your genetic code. You see, we're not composed of genes but beans."

"We're full of beans!" chorused the lodge members.

Fletcher joined the laugh spree not because he found the word play so amusing but because the aliens' delight was irresistible to ignore.

Finally, Charmat hummed a high C, a gesture Fletcher assumed similar to clearing one's throat. The room was quiet.

"Fletcher," said the alien leader, "we feel privileged to have made your acquaintance and welcome you as our honorary lodge brother, but the saying, 'All good things must come to an end' is not only applicable to earthlings."

"We haven't quite gotten our oxygen calibration down pat yet," explained Tandala.

"You're leaving?" asked Fletcher, his voice as desolate as a canyon wind.

Charmat nodded. "Yes, we have to make tracks, as they say."

"We don't want to miss curfew," joked Revlor.

"But you haven't explained anything!" said Fletcher. "What am I supposed to do—"

There was an odd flurry then, a convergence of unseen matter. Fletcher's heart raced as most of the aliens shimmered into disappearance, leaving only the three spokesaliens. They were, Fletcher noticed, becoming a little too transparent for his liking. Their green skin, or covering, or whatever it was, had begun to blur and vibrate.

"Please don't go!" Fletcher begged, scrambling off his bed.

"Have faith, Fletcher," said Charmat. "We're goof-offs, but serious goof-offs. We wouldn't send someone on such an important mission without believing he can do the job."

"Mission—what mission? And what job? I can't do the job! I don't even know what the job is!"

"All will be revealed, Fletcher," said Charmat. "We hope."

"What do you mean, *hope*?"

The alien forms were nearly erased in an indistinguishable shining blur.

"We were given instructions to find someone who embodies our beliefs," Charmat. "That person is you."

"But for what purpose?" shouted Fletcher.

"We believe the universe is at a crossroads," came Charmat's faint voice. "Traffic's heavy and there are no signal lights."

"What's that supposed to mean?"

The green shimmer sounded like a power plant. The noise ground into him and Fletcher thought he might faint from anxiety and fear.

"Don't go! Don't leave me!"

Feeling lightheaded, Fletcher was on the verge of making one final plea or passing out (he couldn't tell which) when Tandala's voice was in his ear. Or her presence was in his head. Somehow she communicated to him.

"Fletcher, it will be all right. It will be more than all right. I'll help you."

"You will? How?"

But his questions were never answered because the vibrating green shimmer was gone, leaving in its wake a light wind that rippled through the rickrack-trimmed curtains and over the newest member of Lodge 1212, who was lying in a heap, passed out cold.

———

What on earth? thought Fletcher as he woke up on the floor, with a crick in his neck and his right arm numb and prickly from having been slept on. He stayed prone for a moment, gathering his thoughts, which were as scattered as the seeds of a wished-upon dandelion.

Let's see. He had weatherstripped the windows, and then there was that dream about Cindy Dahlberg he wanted to remember, and then, oh yeah, the alien visit. Fletcher eyes opened wide. *The alien visit.*

He got up off the floor as if a bomb had been planted and any false move would set it off, looking behind his shoulder as he tiptoed to the bathroom.

He studied his reflection in the mirror, pulling his lips to check his gums, lifting his eyelids to examine his eyeballs, bending his ears forward and his nose upward. He didn't know exactly what he was looking for—clinical incisions? Recording devices? The mark of depravity?

No. They weren't here to hurt me.

As if to slow his racing heart, he held one hand to his chest and then, feeling a small rise underneath his palm, he yanked up his pajama top. His breath stopped as he touched the puckered disc of skin that, if one didn't look too carefully, looked like a vaccination scar. On closer inspection, however, one could see in the sheen the tiny imprinted numbers "1212."

"Oh, my," said Fletcher, and not knowing exactly what to do with the proof of an alien visit, he scratched it.

5

Fletcher felt jittery as he got off the elevator on the third floor and stepped into the small maze of cubicles in which Mid Summit American Life had situated its Upper Midwest office. Had he been a coffee drinker, he would have attributed his nervousness to one too many milligrams of caffeine, but Fletcher drank nothing but grapefruit juice in the mornings, with the exception of V-8 on the weekends.

"Well, look at you," said Cindy Dahlberg as he skittered by her desk. "You look like something the cat brought in."

Fletcher smiled weakly and gave what he thought was a jaunty little wave, which from Cindy's vantage point looked like he was scratching his eyebrow.

Weird-o, thought the receptionist, and then noticing Mike Finnegan coming toward her, she straightened up, patting her frosted blonde hair. She was determined that this be the day the handsome up-and-coming underwriter asked her out.

Into his middle drawer Fletcher put the bagged lunch he'd made the night before, just hours before his life had been turned upside down by aliens, and, as was his habit, lined up any desk accessories the cleaning crew might have jostled. A thousand butterflies were battering around in his stomach, and running a finger along the inside of his collar, he felt a thread of sweat.

"Gee, Weschel, you look terrible," said Marv Gates, popping his head over the cubicle wall they shared.

"That seems to be the consensus," said Fletcher.

Marv took a sip of coffee from a mug that read, "Accountants Go Forth and Multiply."

"Say, Weschel, I was wondering if you could help me out with the Stephenson account—I can't seem to make the numbers jibe."

"Sure," said Fletcher. "Put it on my desk."

Marv Gates's trouble with numbers was well known to Fletcher, who was called on with great regularity to help him make his figures jibe. Although he often worked overtime to unsnarl the messes Marv created, there was little compensation given for his good deeds, other than Marv's gratitude, which manifested itself once a year in the form of roasted nuts, presented to Fletcher at Christmas. Marv's wife worked for the Greely Nut & Candy Company, and Marv passed out dented tins of cashews and almonds to anyone at Mid Summit American Life who had been or might be of service to him.

Fletcher plunged immediately into work as Marv, relieved of his burden, ambled off to join the others at the water cooler, eager to recount how the Vikings had creamed the Packers over the weekend.

His concentration was scattered, a rare occurrence for Fletcher, who added, subtracted, multiplied, and divided with a sharp, precise mind that locked out all wandering thoughts and wisps of daydreams. But now he stared at the columns of numbers before him, tapping his pen against his desk and his feet against the floor. He pulled at the skin between his nostrils. He probed at a back molar with his tongue, wondering if it was loose. He licked his forefinger and tried to flatten his whorled cowlick.

His ticker, which pre–alien visit had been as steady as Big Ben, was again racing in his chest, and Fletcher thought he was going to pass out and throw up; he just hoped it wouldn't be in that order.

"Oh, my," he said, standing up. Just as quickly he sat down. Anxiety was a bug, an army of bugs, crawling up and down his pant legs, his sleeves, under his shirt, and into his scalp. Fletcher clapped a hand over his mouth, certain he was about to scream. He sat back down in his chair and on the stiff plastic runner rolled backward toward the cubicle wall and forward toward his desk, back and forth, back and forth, back and forth.

"Waschel!" barked a man with a brush cut as he poked his head in the doorway. "You're going to melt that chair mat!"

Fletcher's old finger-snapping boss had recently retired to McAllen, Texas, replaced by Ralph Rockman, who never snapped his fingers at anyone, believing he commanded attention and respect because of his size. He was of average height, but he spent a lot of time in his garage with his barbells (his wife suggested he try to bench-press her once in awhile), and he had the upper body and swagger of Popeye.

Fletcher got out of his chair to greet his boss.

"Sit down, private, sit down," said Rockman, who had never served in the military but had adopted its lexicon in his workplace.

"Not to worry, ace," he continued, "I'm not here checking up on you—I wish all my employees had the dedication and company loyalty of Fletcher Wischel—"

"—Weschel."

"Whatever, boy. Whatever!" Rockman slapped him on the back. "I'm only here, you son-of-a-gun, to introduce the latest enlistee to our platoon. Fletcher, meet Ms. Tandy!"

Ralph Rockman stepped aside to allow into the small doorway a woman whose outrageous curves threatened the integrity of her dress fabric. Ever the gentleman, Fletcher rose and stepped forward to greet the female, whose dark skin and braided beaded hair branded her as "not from here."

"Oh, Fletcher!" the woman gushed, pronouncing his name "Fletch-aire." "I am so thrilled to get this assignment!" She played with vowels in a way a Midwesterner did not and pronounced *this* as *dees*.

"Well, then, I'll let you two get acquainted," said Ralph Rockman, dashing off and karate chopping the air in a salute. "Let's all bivouac in my office at 10:00 hours."

Immediately after his boss's departure, the woman clamped her arms around Fletcher in a fierce bear hug and the hugged man quickly realized that *flabbergasted* was to be the emotion of the day. His arms pinned against his sides by her iron grip, Fletcher wondered how he could possibly extricate himself from a woman he wasn't sure was merely excitable or a tiny bit nuts.

"I'll assist you any way I can!" said the woman—at least that's what he understood her to say. Her face was buried in his neck and her words were slightly muffled. "We shall make the greatest team!"

Worried that the woman's grasp was getting tighter, and exhausted from trying to hold in his stomach, Fletcher peeled her arms off him and scrambled to his chair, behind the safe haven of his desk.

"Miss . . . Tandy, isn't it?" he said, scraping his desk blotter with his thumbnail, afraid to look at her. "I appreciate your enthusiasm, but please refrain from such displays—"

"—oh, put a sock in it, Fletch," said the woman in her Caribbean accent. "Don't be so uptight." She began to approach him, not so much by walking as by slinking, and Fletcher couldn't help noticing that if she were in a race, the first thing to cross the finish line would be her very large breasts.

"I assure you, Ms. Tandy . . . ," he began.

"And who is here for assurances? I seek bigger things."

Fletcher wished desperately for an alarm button under his desk, one his knee could nudge against and summon security, or at least Ralph Rockman. His boss, after all, kept a saber belonging to General George Custer's first lieutenant in a display case above his desk, and if ever Fletcher needed a weapon, it was now.

Miss Tandy must have seen the panic in Fletcher's face, for she stopped abruptly and put her hands, heavy with jewelry, on her pillowy hips.

"Oh, Fletcher, I'm not going to hurt you. I'm just so excited to be with you at the start of your brand-new life."

"My brand-new life?" asked Fletcher and suddenly he understood who the woman in front of him was. He swallowed hard and whispered, "Tandala?"

The woman's broad face was taken up in a dazzling display of gums and teeth.

"Tandy for short. You like it, mon? I had to think fast when I introduced myself to your boss."

Light surrounded her and in the shimmer the alien transmogrified into her old familiar green form, before changing back into the smiling black woman with the braided beaded hair.

"Don't worry," she said as Fletcher gaped, clutching his chest. "No one saw that. I measured my risk factors and they were only 20 percent."

"A 20 percent risk factor?" said the insurance man, his eyes bulging. "Don't you think that's sort of high?"

"You needed to see me in alien form," said Tandy. "You're still doubting what has occurred to you, and we of Lodge 1212 have no time for doubters." She smoothed her floral skirt and her bracelets jangled. "It hurts our feelings."

"I don't doubt you," whispered Fletcher, standing on tiptoes to look into Marv Gates's cubicle. "Thank goodness," he said, relieved. "He must be at the water cooler."

"What a good idea," said Tandala, and for a second Fletcher thought he was squinting at the brightness of her gummy smile. A second later he realized he was facing a hot tropical sun, and instead of sitting in a small office cubicle he and the alien were reclining on thickly padded chaise longues, facing a carpet of white sand and the flutter of ocean waves.

"What is it with you people?" asked Fletcher, realizing their states of undress. "What is this thing with naked bodies?" He tore off the lei around his neck and piled several gardenias over his genitals, looking from side to side for unwanted spectators.

Tandy laughed, passing him a frozen daiquiri. "You should see your face."

"It's not my face I'm worried about you seeing!"

Tandy laughed again, and because her laughter mimicked bells, or a chorus of songbirds, or the essence of happiness (Fletcher couldn't decide which), he had to laugh with her. Being whisked away from an insurance office to a tropical paradise was worth a laugh or two, at least.

He settled back in his chair, and with the scent of salt air and suntan lotion in each inhale, he felt nearly boneless in his complete relaxation.

"I must say," he said, after nearly finishing his very refreshing drink, "I do enjoy this extracurricular stuff."

"But do not get spoiled," said Tandy. "It's not as if we're going to zamoosh to vacation hot spots all the time."

"Zamoosh?"

"I'd put it into English if there were an equivalent, but there is not. Zamoosh! To skip across time and/or space in the blink of a human eye."

In the midst of all that Fletcher's mind was trying to absorb came the idle thought that the word *zamoosh* was certainly onomatopoeic.

A breeze intensified the scent of gardenias, suntan lotion, and salt air and blew forth the calls and songs of a dozen birds, and maybe one monkey.

"Okay, then—why did you choose to be a black woman with such, such—"

"Such what? Please, always say to me what is on your mind, Fletcher."

"Well, you're so curvaceous," said Fletcher, embarrassed. "So va-va-voom."

"The va-va-voom was not planned," said Tandy, better adjusting the blossoms of her lei over her pendulous breasts. "All I know is your boss had just this morning read a memorandum about the need to hire more minorities. I thought I would ride in on that directive."

"And your accent? Where are you supposed to be from?"

"I was born in Jamaica but became an American citizen on my thirtieth birthday."

"So you've got a whole history mapped out?"

After taking a lusty sip of her drink, she answered, "I guess so."

"You guess so?"

"Fletcher, look, Lodge 1212 is advanced but not so advanced that we know all the answers. Colors and zamooshes and auras are a piece of cake, but earthling transmogrifications and all that that implies . . . to tell you the truth, all I did was shut my eyes and dig into the grab bag of human identities and this is what I got."

"I was hoping for something a little more scientific."

Tandy sighed, and Fletcher, who didn't like disapproval from anyone—even aliens—was about to apologize for his snotty tone.

"I am sorry, Fletcher," said Tandy, beating him to the apology. "But to explain the hows and whys of my earthly presence would be to explain something your brain is not capable of processing. No offense, of course."

"No offense taken."

"And please remember that I'm new to this, too. I am certain there will be many situations for which I have no explanation."

Fletcher sighed, and the two nude tourists with their strategically placed gardenias reclined in silence for a moment. When Tandy spoke again, her voice was soft. "I must tell you, Fletcher, it took a lot of faith on Charmat's part to send me here."

Fletcher pondered this statement before asking the question he'd wanted to ask since the night before.

"Are you and Charmat lovers?"

Tandy let out her sweet musical laugh.

"Oh, Fletcher, if you mean has he been my sex partner, yes. But who hasn't? Lodge 1212 enjoys sex, Fletcher, and we should. After all, we're practically the only ones left in the galaxy that still have two sexes."

"Oh my. The others don't?"

Tandala shook her head and her beaded cornrows clattered.

"A few light years ago, the UHC—the Universal Head Council—decreed that we had become evolved enough to do away with the fuss and bother of the male-female thing. Lodge 4 Squared—they're the big eggheads—had come up with a method of reproduction that involved skin grafts and telepathy—well, that is the simple explanation. It's a bit more complicated, but we couldn't be bothered to look at the schematics. We couldn't be bothered to participate either. We upheld our right to sexual congress, to the beauty and terror of the yin and the yang, and most importantly, our right to have fun."

"And they agreed to that?" asked Fletcher, unable to imagine standing up to Marv Gates, let alone a Universal Head Council.

"Hoola, baby," said Tandy, as she blotted perspiration above her lip with one of the pads of her long-nailed fingers. "The way you humans purge liquids is really something." She looked down at the rows of sweat trickling down her chest. "Look, my mountains have little rivers running over them!"

Fletcher couldn't help but laugh at her childish delight, but still curious he asked if there'd been any repercussions over the lodge's rebellion.

"Oh, sure, we were gossiped about, disinvited to the Mind Games on Uranus. But we've never exactly been embraced by the intergalactic lodges. You know how it is when you're having fun—those who aren't resent you."

"I guess I've never really known that kind of resentment."

"Well, my friend, those days are over!"

He raised his glass to return her toast, but it vanished from his hands and along with it, the heat of the sun on his body and the smell of the tropics. He was sitting in his off-white office cubicle again, and never had off-white seemed so constraining.

"Why are you so abrupt with those transition things?" he asked, clinging to his desk as if it were bobbing in the ocean and he'd just been through a shipwreck. "I was just getting used to the idea of an all-body suntan."

"I only zamooshed us there to get your attention, Fletcher. You seem to be resisting our collaboration. We believe in you—the question is, do you?"

There was no harshness to her voice, no reproach, yet all of Fletcher's favorite nervous tics converged; he pulled at the skin between his nostrils, bit the inside of his cheek, tugged at his cowlick, blinked his eyes, cracked his knuckles, cleared his throat, sniffed, sniffed again, chewed a cuticle, and tapped his foot. Then, as if he needed reminding of how frightened he was, his testicles drew up like a window shade.

The little red light on his phone blinked and he lunged for the receiver, grateful for the distraction.

"Fletcher," said Cindy Dahlberg, "Mr. Rockman wants you and . . . whatever her name is in his office, stat."

Under normal circumstances, hearing the voice of the comely receptionist, however bored or accusatory, would be like a kiss in his ear, but these were not normal circumstances. He didn't appreciate Cindy's tone at all and said as much.

"Wha . . . ?" said Cindy, shocked by Fletcher's scolding.

"Her name's Tandy," he said, "and it's a shame your acquaintanceship with her might be limited, because she could teach you a lot about what it is to be a woman."

Cindy's words came over the line in sputters. "How dare you even—"

Fletcher hung up on her midstammer. The snide voice of the receptionist was a slap of reality in the unreality that had become his life, and even though the flesh and bone of his legs had turned to rubber, he managed to stand tall as he unplugged his computer and puts its plastic protective cover over it. Watching him, Tandy held her hands above the shelf of her chest and clapped them.

Off his desk, he picked up a photograph of himself as a boy with his still intact family, a spider plant that never flourished but would not die, and his clock, shaped like a pyramid, its hands little Egyptian pharaohs.

As he searched the room for something to pack up his valuables, Tandy handed him a nearly empty box of copier paper.

"Thanks," said Fletcher. He grabbed the half-ream of paper and flung it out of the box and for a moment the air was filled with confetti sized for a giant's parade. Something was happening to him, something was mixing in with the fear he felt—a truant's joyousness, an explorer's thrill.

"Hey, Weschel, what gives?" asked Marv Gates, looming above his side of the wall, watching the pieces of copier paper drift to the ground.

"Everything," said Fletcher, putting his semi-valuables into the empty box. "Everything gives," he repeated. "It's a discovery I've just made."

Marv Gates scratched his temple, releasing a sprinkling of dandruff. "What the h-e-double-toothpicks are you talking about?"

Tandy leaned closer to Fletcher's desk, eager to hear herself.

"I guess, Marv, what I'm trying to say is that if you butt up against something long enough, it'll give."

"So what," asked Marv as he watched Fletcher rifling through a file cabinet, "in your case gives?"

Pushing the drawer back on its casters, Fletcher stood tall, to his full 5' 9-¾" height. He smiled, and Marv later said to his wife, "It just lit up his face, Margie. I never even knew boring old Fletcher was capable of a smile like that. I wonder if he's on some kind of medication."

"Marv, I'm going to miss you," said Fletcher, snapping shut the latches of his briefcase. "I won't pine for you, but I'll miss you."

"I'll miss you, too," said Marv, totally befuddled, "but where are you going?"

"Yes, ensign, where *are* you going?" asked Ralph Rockman, who didn't get into his position of management without keeping his ears and eyes open as to what was happening in his office. "Just what the Sam Hill is going on?"

He stepped toward Tandy, giving her the once-over, and her breasts the twice-over.

"You," he said. "Miss Tammy, wasn't it?"

"Tandy."

"Sure," said Ralph Rockman. "Didn't I send you in here to get to know our friend Fletcher? I mean, seeing as you'll be handling the Dight Properties account together."

"You did, sir," nodded Tandy. "I believe that was the original intent."

"Then why does it look as if you're packing up?" said Ralph Rockman, with a smile so tense it seemed his teeth might crumble.

"Because I am," said Fletcher, taking a cursory look around the office to which most of his identity had been for so long attached. "I am packing up and moving out, skipper."

His mouth opened horizontally in a big grin while Ralph Rockman's mouth dropped vertically into an oval. So did Marv's and those of other curious employees who had gathered around, and the only thing breaking the silence was the white noise of fluorescent lighting and data-displaying screens. When Ralph Rockman recovered his power of speech, there was a tinge of meanness that most people only heard inside his closed-door office.

"Are you telling me that you're quitting?" He looked at the black woman and her double-D chest. "Is it because of her? Because I can let her go like that"—he snapped two thick ruddy fingers—"because to tell you the truth, I'm not exactly sure why I hired her in the first place. I hadn't *planned* on hiring anyone today." He replaced the look of bafflement that uncharacteristically skirted across his face with his usual stern, in-charge one. "Is that really what you're telling me, *Wushchel?*"

"I guess I am, *Rockhead,*" said Fletcher. "Although hiring Ms. Tandy was probably the smartest thing you ever did, and it would have been a privilege to work here with her. But the bigger privilege will be to work with her *away* from here."

"Whatever are you babbling about, boy?" snarled Ralph Rockman.

Handing Tandy his briefcase, Fletcher grabbed his box of personal items.

"Excuse me," he said, passing in front of his former boss.

"Where are you going, Fletcher?" said Marv Gates, and in his voice was the yearning unspoken question, *Can I go, too?*

"We're off on a mad adventure," said Fletcher. "Off to follow the fun."

"Don't you mean the sun?" asked Marv helpfully.

Ralph Rockman folded his muscular arms over his muscular chest. "Whatever you're following, it's not going to lead you back here, Watchell. You leave this office, you leave it for good."

"Thank you," said Fletcher pleasantly, and as he led Tandy down the hallway to the elevators, the only sound breaking the stunned silence was the snapping of Cindy Dahlberg's grape bubble gum.

———

A bell sounded and the elevator door opened onto the small lobby that smelled of the homemade beef jerky Frank the handyman kept in the breast pocket of his coveralls. For the last time, Fletcher passed by the radiator that wheezed in the winter and clunked in the summer, passed by the small mural of the Black Hills painted by WPA artists, and pushed Tandy through the door into the cold November day. He felt as light and unbridled as a paroled felon, his fear for now pushed aside by the specter of possibility, and he would have danced a jig on the street, if there'd been a street to jig on.

Instead he'd have to make do tripping the light fantastic in a shorn wheat field outside town.

"Jeepers, Tandy, you can't have us zamooshing right off Capitol Avenue and onto—" he looked around at the flat expanse of land that lay in all directions.

—"onto your old dance floor?" smiled the alien.

"Sheesh," said Fletcher, embarrassed to think Tandala had watched him do the Boogaloo, the Jerk, the Pony, the Twist, and all the other slick dance moves in what he had thought was a private arena.

"Don't be embarrassed," said the alien kindly. "You always put on an excellent show."

"I haven't been out here since high school."

The wind flapped Fletcher's pant legs as he slowly turned in a complete circle, surveying the view. Fields stretched out in all directions like a patchwork quilt made by a seamstress with an engineering degree, and other than a moving speck in the distance—a farmer picking up hay bales—he and Tandala were alone in the mown golden acreage.

"Practically every time I got the car, I drove out here," he said. "It's funny when a kid feels he can only be himself in a deserted farm field."

"But not 'funny ha-ha,' right?"

"Right. Funny strange. Funny sad."

"And yet you have good memories of this place?" said Tandy, burrowing her chin inside the pelt of the rabbit fur jacket she now wore.

Fletcher nodded. "My dad used to take me out to these fields.

Well, twice. Once was after a hailstorm and the other was after a fire." He inhaled sharply, surprised at the way his heart thrummed at the memory. "I was so proud of him—thrilled, really—these farmers had suffered such big blows, and there was my dad swooping in to make everything all right."

"What was he—a magician?"

"Better than that to a farmer who's got crop damage," said Fletcher. "An insurance agent."

The two days his father took him out to the fields were bright coins in the stingy pocket change of his memories. He had walked side by side with WW, his hands clasped behind his back like his dad, nodding his head like his dad, stopping when his dad stopped to squint out at the beaten-down corn or burned soybeans.

One of the farmers had stopped to mop tears off his red-leather face, and Fletcher had watched transfixed as WW patted the farmer on the back and told him in a gentle voice, "There, there, Anders. It'll be all right. You're covered—in fact, I'll bet you a hot beef sandwich at Bunnie's that next year's beans will be your best crop ever."

The farmer had leaned against WW for a moment accepting his pats and then, gathering his strength, took a deep breath and hitched his thumbs in the metal fasteners of his overalls and nodded.

"Thanks, WW," he said, standing tall now. "It's a comfort to know I'm in good hands."

Fletcher ached for the kind of manly tenderness his father so easily showed the farmer, but he'd gladly take (what choice did he have?) the second prize of bearing witness to it. Seeing that WW was capable of supplying aid and comfort made Fletcher vow to be the kind of son who would earn it from him.

He wouldn't have believed that the day could have gotten any better, but it did. Afterwards, they had stopped at Bunnie's themselves, not for a hot beef sandwich but for malted milks, and as WW flirted with the old and arthritic restaurant namesake, Bunnie giggled and said, "If I were thirty years younger, you'd be in big trouble, WW."

"You look taller, Fletcher," said Tandala.

"Huh?" Shaking the sweet memories from his head, Fletcher looked at the cornrowed woman standing so incongruously in the wheat field.

"I was thinking of going to a tavern for a send-off but think this was a far better idea. Although I wouldn't have minded a Harvey Wallbanger."

"What are you talking about?" Fletcher turned up the collar on his coat against a wind that was no longer playful but biting.

"I wanted to bring you to a place that might give you confidence for what's ahead. I expected to zamoosh into the Rumpus Room, but I can see from your stance, and your smile, that this is what you needed."

"Needed . . . for what?"

"Fletcher, things might get a little strange from now on."

"Might?" Fletcher's eyes bulged as if he were harnessed in one of Dodd Beckerman's chokeholds. "Might get a little strange? What are we going to do?"

"A little exploring."

Panic trickled down Fletcher's throat and into the pit of his stomach. He swallowed hard.

"What are we going to explore?"

"You," said Tandy, and in one great swoosh of wind, he felt himself in a race with the speed of light, and he was winning.

Part II

6

If Fletcher hadn't been wearing chaps, his landing on the scrubby ground of the high desert might have hurt a little more than it did.

In all that there was for his mind to process—the soreness of his right hip, the smell of hot dogs, the lilting notes of calliope music—the thought that asserted itself first was, *I'm wearing chaps!*

As he stood, brushing the dirt off his black leather–covered thighs, he saw he was no longer wearing his brown crepe-soled oxfords.

I'm wearing black-and-white cowboy boots!

"Hip!" The word was punctuated by a clap on Fletcher's back that nearly sent him sailing.

"You, sombitch, it's about time you showed your candy ass around here!"

"Aw, leave him alone, Stretch. Least he's dressed."

Resisting the urge to run screaming into whatever abyss was out there (and he was now convinced there were plenty), Fletcher instead examined the rhinestones glittering on the cuffs of his fringed jacket. When he looked up, it was into the faces of a tall man in a jean jacket and Stetson hat and a shorter, older man in a Stetson hat and a jean jacket.

"Geez, Hip, you all right?" asked the older man.

"Yeah, you look like you seen a ghost," said the tall man. "Or maybe you just looked in a mirror." With wide strides, he began walking and added, "Don't know which would be scarier."

Fletcher seemed unable to fire the neurons that would command his feet to move, and the older cowboy seeing he wasn't following them stopped and scooped air with his hand, urging Fletcher forward.

"C'mon, Hip!" he said. "Show starts in ten minutes!"

The only motion Fletcher was capable of was to pull at the skin between his nostrils, but his old nervous tic made him even more nervous, when he felt something he'd never before felt under his nose— hair, and lots of it.

I've got a mustache!

He didn't have to touch his head to know that he was wearing a cowboy hat, but he did anyway, knocking back the brim with his hand.

"Curly, tell Hip to move his ass!"

"Hip, c'mon!"

His brain, realizing its helplessness in making sense of a senseless situation, finally gave his feet permission to move, and Fletcher, rubbing his right hip, limped after the jean-jacketed pair, toward a tent.

During his gimpy hundred-yard jog, he took in all he could.

Cacti and stunted, gnarled trees sprouted haphazardly from the weedy ground and in the distance, set against an immense blue sky, the jagged peaks of mountains.

I'm in the desert, he deduced. Maybe Arizona.

A sign said otherwise: "The Twenty-Nine Palms Chamber of Commerce Welcomes You."

Fletcher, an armchair adventurer who had supplemented the Norman Rockwell reproductions Olive hung on the wall ("Gad, Fletcher," she had told him, "if only the world were a Rockwell painting") with maps of the world, knew where Twenty-Nine Palms was. California.

He was at a carnival in California. Children slalomed between adult obstacles, their fists clutching pink cones of cotton candy, braided lollipops, electric-blue sno-cones. A few rickety rides flung or spun riders in steel cages and a Ferris wheel made its creaky orbit in fits and starts. Passing a parking lot full of dusty pickups, Fletcher followed the two cowboys to a small trailer parked near the big top.

LORNA LANDVIK

"Well, don't just stand there like an idiot," said the tall cowboy when Fletcher stood shyly in front of the steel mesh steps. "Come on."

The trailer was littered with crumpled bags from Carl's Jr. and In-N-Out Burger, with flattened cans and tipped bottles of beer, with a fan of playing cards, a splayed paperback book, and folded sections of the *L.A. Times*.

"Hey," said Curly, picking up the newspaper. "There's my crossword."

Fletcher's gaze rode over the open page, then backtracked when he saw the date, 1977. He had gone back in time ten years.

Stretch opened the gray, pleated vinyl door of a closet and then shut it again.

"Aw, what the hell. Let's just wear what we got on, Curly. No sense givin' 'em anymore for what they're paying us."

"But everyone likes the rhinestones," protested the older man. "Don't they, Hip?"

Licking his lips with a tongue that seemed devoid of saliva, Fletcher nodded.

"Sure. Everybody likes rhinestones."

After rolling his eyes, Stretch took off his hat and sailed it the length of the trailer and onto the grimy folds of a blanket heaped on the built-in bed.

"Fine," he said, taking off his jean jacket. "We'll give the assholes rhinestones."

Minutes later, Fletcher found himself in an improbable position: atop a black-maned horse named Grazi, behind two fringed and rhinestone cowboys named Stretch and Curly, who were also on horseback.

Tandy, he begged for the tenth or twentieth or thirtieth time, *help.*

Fletcher had only been on a horse once before in his life, and that occasion had convinced him he wasn't all that anxious for an encore ride.

Bryan Ellis, a kid new to school, had asked every boy in the third grade class to his birthday party, the invitation requesting, "Come Dressed like a Cowboy or an Injun!"

Olive bought a feathered headdress from the five-and-dime and sewed a line of fringe along the side seams of her son's slightly outgrown brown corduroy pants and a brown corduroy vest and helped him paint bold strokes of war paint across his face and around his bare arms.

"For Christ sakes," said WW, watching as Fletcher posed in front of the mirror. "What exactly is he supposed to be, anyway?"

"Why, an Indian chief, of course," said Olive through tight lips.

WW laughed. "A frou-frou Indian chief, if you ask me."

The boys at the party did not seem overly impressed by his costume either.

"Hey, it's Chief Squints A Lot," said Ron Zimmerman.

———————

The Tug-o-War team he was on lost, and during the Wild Coyote Egg Toss he was the first to drop the chicken egg Gene Palmeter hurled at him. And when it was his turn to play Pin the Tail on the Li'l Dogie, a blindfolded and dizzy-from-spinning Fletcher staggered toward the picture of the calf affixed to the shed door and managed to tack the paper tail exactly where the Li'l Dogie's li'l penis would have been, causing the boys to laugh so hard that Mark Speege pleaded for everyone to stop because he was going to wet his pants. Fletcher stood off to the side, pretending to be greatly interested in the nest-building barn swallows who flew in and out of the hayloft; he had not learned the art of laughing at himself and in fact thought his only line of self-defense was not to.

After cake and ice cream, the boys gathered at the corral for the event everyone had been waiting for.

There were two horses inside, Bryan's spirited Appaloosa, Streak, and Mabel, a big gentle Morgan. Mr. Ellis took turns helping the boys on Mabel, after which they rode around the corral with the birthday boy and his horse. Only Ron Zimmerman declined the ride, claiming a sore knee. Fletcher was fairly certain that if he had used the same excuse, he would have been teased for being chicken, but he was not about to use any excuse; he couldn't wait to ride. Standing on the fence with the other boys, he joined in the whooping and hollering as Streak, responding to the orders given by Bryan, pranced and turned circles, and as Mabel and her rider carefully plodded by.

Fletcher was the last boy to ride, and when he stepped into the laced fingers of Mr. Ellis for his boost up onto the horse, every single part of his body issued a happy and contented sigh.

"You're a natural!" said Mr. Ellis as Fletcher took the reins—he was not about to hold onto the saddle horn as some of the other boys had done—and gave his horse a little nudge with his heels.

Howdy Mabel, he thought. *It's me, Hip Galloway, King of the Cowboys!* He had the strangest feeling that this was his hundredth time on a horse rather than his first, and Bryan, noticing his confidence, smiled at Fletcher in a conspiratorial fashion.

"Git," whispered Fletcher, and Mabel, responding to his command, picked up her pace and Bryan hooted and gave his own signal to Streak, and soon the two horses were trotting around the corral to the shrieks of the surprised and impressed boys on the fence.

Fletcher had taken off his feathered headdress for the ride, but the fringes on his vest and pants riffled in the breeze created by his speed.

"Yee-haw!" he shouted, just the way Hip would, and exalting in the thrum of the horses' hooves on the hard dirt he'd added a joyful, "Yippee-ki-yay!"

It was then that Ron Zimmerman took out the slingshot he

carried like a wallet in his back pocket and with careful aim let fly a small stone. He could forgive his own cowardice but felt duty-bound to punish Fletcher's lack thereof.

The pebble hit Mabel hard in her right flank and she let out a wounded whinny, rearing up against the stinging pain. As natural a rider as he might be, it didn't change the fact that this was Fletcher's first time on a horse and surprise caught him unawares, and before he could respond to the Hold On! reflex, he tumbled off Mabel as easily as a load of dirt off a dump truck. His glasses preceded him to the ground, breaking, and when he landed he heard a soft snap, and he knew from the pain that something inside him had broken, too. He got a new pair of glasses and his fractured arm would heal, but the new and exciting confidence he had felt on Mabel was shattered beyond repair.

———

"Ladies and gentlemen," came the announcer's voice, "let's put our hands together and give a nice Twenty-Nine Palms welcome to the Daring Desperadoes!"

As his horse followed the other two cantering into the small arena, Fletcher wondered just how many shocks a system could survive. He had an urgent need to tug at the skin between his nostrils, but he didn't dare let go of the reins.

Considering their circumstances—they weren't masked and armed and inside a bank vault but instead on horses inside an arena— Fletcher's assumption that the Daring Desperadoes were trick riders and not wanted outlaws was a fairly easy one to make. This was fortified by watching Stretch race to the center of the arena, rein his horse to a stop, and command him to sit, which the horse promptly did, allowing Stretch to slide off his back. A further indication was given by watching Curly, whose horse was walking with stiff legs.

"Ladies and gentlemen," said the announcer, "ever seen a horse do a prettier Spanish Walk?"

And then his own horse reared up on his back legs and Fletcher muttered a string of expletives that had never before passed his lips, at least not in that order or furor. There was no doubt he was going to get thrown—and this time harder than when he was as a kid—but to his complete and thrilled surprise he not only stayed on but spun himself around so he was facing the horse's back end, then spun again to face forward. When Grazi bowed on bended knee, Fletcher's surprise grew exponentially, especially when he dismounted by doing a somersault down the front of the horse.

Did I just do that? wondered Fletcher, looking into Grazi's warm brown eyes as he untucked himself and stood up to acknowledge the audience with a wave of his hat.

To the music of "The Tennessee Waltz" the three Desperadoes led their horses through a series of synchronized steps and rears and dips, after which they chased and roped calves, finishing off by dismounting and standing in a circle, each with their twirling lariats.

"Now let's see how these fellers do the Texas Skip!" said the announcer, and the applause picked up as the Daring Desperadoes jumped inside their spinning circles of rope, but waned when in jumping through each other's circles Curly stepped on Stretch's rope, deflating the sphere to a squiggle of rope on the ground.

This one mistake triggered several others, and by the time they got back on their horses to take their final bows, the applause was more polite than enthusiastic.

In their trailer, Stretch was irate.

"Way to step on my rope, Curly," he said, yanking off his cowboy hat and sending it across the room with a backhanded spin.

"It's not like I meant to," said the old cowboy after a weary sigh.

Stretch muttered something that neither Curly nor Fletcher could decipher, but words weren't necessary to communicate his anger and disgust. They were the complete opposite emotions of Fletcher, who was having a hard time not cackling with glee.

"And what do you got that smirk on your face for, Hip?" asked Stretch, yanking off his bolo tie. "My second question: do you need help wiping it off?"

"No, thanks," said Fletcher amicably, watching as Stretch tore off his rhinestone jacket and flung it at Curly, who seemed to be acting as his valet.

Stretch muttered as he took off his chaps, and thinking it might be time to take a little walk, Fletcher said as much.

"Ain't you gonna change?" asked Curly.

"I'm pretty comfortable as is," said Fletcher. Truth be told, he wasn't about to take off the sharpest outfit he'd ever worn any sooner than he had to.

"See you at Josie's, then?" asked Curly. "'Bout seven?"

"Sure," said Fletcher thumbing the brim of his hat as he backed out of the narrow, beer-and-old-socks-smelling trailer.

He wandered past the horse barn, the smile on his face so broad that an elderly fairgoer passing him felt immediate pity.

"Look at that poor feeble-minded fellow all dressed up like a cowboy," she whispered to her sister.

"I hope he's not lost," her sister whispered back.

If this is lost, thought Fletcher, *let me stay lost.*

He couldn't exactly define what he was feeling because it was so beyond the realm of his normal emotions, but giddiness was definitely wrapped up in there, with a shiny ribbon of awe.

A brawny man loaded down with games-of-chance prizes bumped into him and Fletcher bent to help pick up a stuffed panda bear, a stuffed tiger, an inflatable bat, and a cellophane bag of saltwater taffy.

"That's quite a haul you made," said Fletcher.

"Wish they'd give cash prizes, though, instead of this junk," said the man. "Guy like me could be a millionaire."

The fancy cowboy watched teenagers pass a joint to one another as they rode on the merry-go-round and then stopped to listen to a barbershop quartet whose bass sang with his chin tucked into his chest but still couldn't get his note to go quite as low as he wanted it to. Continuing down the small midway, the invisible leash that was the aroma of grease and meat pulled him to the corn dog stand.

As he stood behind a young couple whose hands were tucked in the back pockets of each other's jeans, there was a pink and violet shimmer and next to him, in a sudden burst of color, Tandala.

"Oof!" she said, stumbling into him.

Fletcher gasped as he caught her in his arms.

"Geez, Tandy! You mind giving me a little advance warning?"

"That's one thing you're going to have to get used to, mon," said Tandy. "Things you aren't used to."

"But you can't . . . just suddenly show up like that," he whispered, looking around furtively for witnesses to the alien's sudden appearance.

"Of course, I can, Fletcher. People see what they want to see. Or what I want them to see."

"What'll it be, bud?"

Fletcher was dazed for a moment, forgetting what this man in a paper hat and a five o'clock shadow wanted from him, and then he remembered his short-term goal.

"Uh, a corn dog, please." He felt a nudge in his side. "Uh, make that two."

At the condiment counter, the yellow plastic bottle Fletcher squeezed splatted mustard all over his corn dog.

"My goodness," giggled Tandy.

"Where were you?" he asked, unable to help the little whine in his voice. "You wouldn't believe what—"

"—oh, I would," said Tandala, with a big smile. "I saw you. You were really something."

Pleasure swelled in Fletcher's chest.

"Thanks," he said, and looking up and down, he took in the vision that was a busty, bejeweled, cornrowed woman in full cowgirl regalia: a red skirt and vest fringed in white, and cowboy boots, shirt, and hat of the same two colors.

"And you. You're really something."

After acknowledging each other's somethingness, Fletcher took a bite of his corn dog and sucked in air, surprised by the heat.

Tandala's bite was more demure.

"Umm." She dabbed at the mustard on the corner of her mouth with a long-nailed finger. "Mon, oh mon. Hail Mary. Hoola, baby."

She shut her eyes and under the brim of her cowboy hat Fletcher saw a quick pulse of light in her forehead.

"Tandy!" hissed Fletcher, looking around, checking again for onlookers. "What are you doing?"

"Charmat told me to share samples of earth's great pleasures, and this"—she held up her corn dog—"is one of earth's great pleasures."

"And so you . . . you just took a picture of it?"

"Took it and sent it in a memo," said Tandala. "But it's more than a picture—it's a taste. I think he might enjoy it as much as the daiquiri."

"You can do that?" said Fletcher, and even though he was surprised, he wasn't.

"Our cameras have a few more features than yours."

———

After finishing their corn dogs, they threw their sticks and yellow-stained napkins into the tilted pyramid of detritus that rose from the trashcan, and Tandy took his arm and bumped his slim hip with the big cushion of her own.

"My goodness, I had no idea what a talented horseman you were!" Fletcher felt loopy with pleasure, as if champagne were his venous fluid.

"Neither did I—and believe me, I was scared stiff when I found myself on that horse." He stroked his mustache thoughtfully (he was tickled to have a mustache to stroke, thoughtfully or not). "But then again, I'm not just Fletcher right now—I'm Hip Galloway, too."

"Try your luck!" invited a carnie standing inside a booth canopied with stuffed plush animals. "Try your luck and win the lady's heart!"

They walked past a stand that advertised Ice Cold Treats!

"How exactly does that work, anyway, Tandy?"

"How does what work?" She had stopped, her concentration focused on the blue slush floating in a sno-cone machine.

"How do I . . . how do I—as Hip—fit so smoothly in all this? I mean Stretch and Curly—they're the other two Desperadoes—act like I've been with them for years. And Grazi—that's my horse—well, it's like I'd been riding her all my life. How'd you pull off something like that?"

"Obviously, I can't exactly explain the mechanics," said Tandy as a flicker of disappointment passed over her face, realizing they weren't going to stop to sample any of the icy blue slush. "In simple terms, there's a time and space continuum that is beyond human understanding. And while some of your scientists have grasped the physics of physical motion, you haven't seemed to be able to understand those same laws can be applied to the mind. Thought has forward and backward motion; your fantasy can be multiplied and grafted into others' realities, your—"

"Mommy, there's that cowboy that was in the show!" A little girl in her own cowboy hat pointed her giant lollipop at Fletcher.

Fletcher smiled and lifted his hat in greeting. "Afternoon, cowgirl."

"Mommy—he called me 'Cowgirl'!" said the little girl, giggling.

"Well, however you did it," said Fletcher squeezing Tandy's arm, "thank you. I can't remember when I had more fun."

"And that is what it's all about, isn't it, Fletcher?" asked Tandy, and they walked into the music of the calliope, or else it was the music of her voice.

———————

Good cheer was not the prevailing mood at Josie's, a smoky bar on the edge of town that Tandala had zamooshed them to.

They stood in front of a curved banquette, whose upper cushion was worn and split, revealing the yellowed and mealy foam rubber underneath the brown vinyl. The Formica table held clusters of beer bottles and a Bakelite ashtray, scabby with burn marks and heaped with cigarette butts.

Tandy had introduced herself to Stretch and Curly as "the Daring Desperadoes' biggest fan," to which Stretch had said, with no show of politesse, "then how come we ain't seen you before? I mean, you're pretty hard to miss, Miss."

Tandy smiled her gummy smile, as if she had just been on the receiving end of a compliment instead of sarcasm.

"Well, I haven't had the pleasure of seeing you before today. But one performance—that's all it took. All it took for me to become your biggest fan."

"Gosh," said Curly. "Can I buy you a beer?"

"I thought you would never ask," she said, and as she and Fletcher joined them in the booth, Stretch rolled his eyes and Curly beamed.

"And where are you from?" asked Curly. "I detect an accent hinting of the tropics."

"Aw, geez," said Stretch. "Here it comes."

Curly slid away from Stretch and closer to Tandy.

"I myself think island-bred people have a certain joie de vivre that we landlubbers can't grasp."

"The blow hole's been officially opened," said Stretch, rising. "Which means you can find me in the poolroom."

Baskets of hamburgers and onion rings and another round of beer were ordered, and Fletcher settled back, happy to listen to the little wiry cowboy woo the soft curvy Jamaican.

"Your hair," he said, holding a beaded cornrow. "Your hair is such a delightful amalgam of braids and jewelry."

Curly took off his Stetson, revealing his sweaty bald pate underneath.

"Do not despair the lack of my own hair," he said, "for baldness bespeaks of a noble soul . . . and teeming virility."

The more Curly drank, the more florid he became, and seeing that Tandala didn't seem to have a problem with him, Fletcher decided he didn't either and settled back in the booth, eager to think back to the afternoon and what it had been like to be a Daring Desperado.

How did I do that? he wondered. *How did I know how to do a somersault off the front of a horse? How'd I know how to rope a calf? How'd we know how to do a Spanish Walk?* On Grazi's back—once the initial shock had worn off—he had been transformed; he was the easygoing, affable, yet highly skilled cowboy of his boyhood fantasies; he *was* Hip Galloway. He choreographed Grazi with the slightest pressure of his knee or his ankle—hell, hardly any pressure at all—and felt as if he and the horse were a team that had played together all its life.

His mind shifted for a moment back to his old life, wondering what the people at Mid Summit American Life were doing. Thumbing his mustache, he suppressed a cackle, imagining what Marv Gates or Cindy Dahlberg would think of the former actuary who had traded in his Robert Hall suits for cowboy gear and answered to the name of Hip!

"What's so funny?" asked Tandala as she dabbed her napkin in water and rubbed at a ketchup stain that had joined the mustard one already on her cowgirl shirt.

"Everything," said Fletcher, full of a child's happiness, a happiness as bright and promising as a box of new crayons. "Say, where's Curly?"

"He's visiting the little cowboy's room," said Tandy, her head wobbling as she nodded toward the hallway.

"Why, Tandala, I do believe you're a little tipsy."

"I do believe you're right." She offered him a wide, slightly uneven smile. "This is something I'm definitely bringing back with me." Her forehead pulsed light as she stared at the beer bottle in front of her.

"What, you don't have liquor in outer space?"

"No," said Tandy, opening wide her large liquid brown eyes as if she couldn't believe it herself. "We have many ways to emotionally transport ourselves, but none that transport us so . . . lightly."

"Keep drinking and the transport gets a little heavier," said Fletcher as Curly slid into the booth, with three bottles of beer.

"One for Hip," he said, "one for the Island Temptress, and one for me. Cheers."

Fletcher and Tandy obliged him by clinking bottles.

"Dang, I ain't had this much fun since the Texas days." Curly's features were outlined by the deep wrinkles his smile caused. "Hip, tell the lovely Tandala-whose-name-sounds-like-a-tropical-breeze here about the Texas days."

Fletcher sucked on his beer bottle because he didn't know what else to do.

"Curly," said Tandy, and Fletcher saw that simply by addressing the old cowboy, Tandy could cause a little quiver of his shoulders. "Why don't you tell me? I'm dying to hear all about the Texas days—and you're such a good storyteller." She looked at Fletcher. "No offense, Hip."

Fletcher put his bottle down. "None taken."

"Well, I don't like to monopolize a conversation," said Curly, drawing himself close to Tandala. "But I do like to oblige a lady's wishes."

A woman who'd stuffed her many curves and rolls into a silver tube top stood at the jukebox, punching in numbers. Fletcher had never listened to country-western music and couldn't identify the singer taunting someone about not being woman enough to take her man.

"Well, it's like this," Curly was saying, stretching his thin, hard-muscled arm across the back of the banquette until his hand dangled next to Tandy's right shoulder. "We were all young—well, I was younger; Stretch and Hip here were youngsters—and we were all hands on a ranch belonging to Jake Arnett."

He paused for a moment and repeated. "Jake Arnett."

Tandy picked up her cue. "Sorry, mon, am I supposed to know who this Jake Arnett fellow is?"

Curly's quick laugh was a burst that sounded like "Teeee" followed by "Ha!"

"He'd like to think so! Hell, Jake Arnett probably thinks the only people that ain't heard of him are Martians or something!"

Fletcher and Tandy's faces remained neutral, but under the table Fletcher's knee pressed against the alien's. Curly held his bottle of beer a half-inch from his lips, muttering something unintelligible.

"I beg your pardon?" said Tandy.

Curly took a long swig of beer that sent his Adam's apple surfing up and down his windpipe.

"You'd really be begging my pardon if I said out loud what I just said to myself." Curly set his bottle on the table with a little more force than necessary. "Suffice it to say, don't ever mention the name Jake Arnett to Stretch or most especially the name 'Jake Jr.'"

He looked meaningfully at Fletcher before glancing across the room and into the poolroom, and it was when he saw Stretch there that he felt it safe to continue.

"Arnett was one of the richest sombitches in Texas and the ranch was more or less a hobby farm to him, a place where he could practice being a cowboy and throw all sorts of barbeques and fund-raisers for all the hoi polloi from Dallas and Houston and Washington—that's D is for dumb and C is for corrupt, Washington!

"But even though he wasn't involved in the day-to-day, he needed hands that were, and so about a half-dozen of us worked there, tending his herd of cattle, keeping up the ranch maintenance and such. The pay wasn't all that good, considering how rich Arnett was, but we had a good cook and the bunkhouse was warm, and besides, that's where Hip and Stretch and I met, and we got on right off the bat, didn't we, Hip?"

Fletcher nodded. "Like peas in a pod."

"Let me tell you, as hard as we worked in the day, we were always up for hijinks at night."

"Hijinks?" asked Tandala.

"Well, mostly—we would figure out tricks and such, horse tricks and rope tricks."

"That's right," said Fletcher. "We'd take the horses out and try the craziest stuff."

An alarm rang in him: *How'd I know that?*

"See, I was fortunate to see Will Rogers as a boy—in person once, and then all his movies—I declare, that fellow could get on and off a horse in ways you could never imagine—and what I learnt from him, I taught Stretch and Hip here." The smile of fond remembrance softened the crags and gullies of the cowboy's face.

"Now I remember…" Curly's voice was like a lullaby, only it wasn't sleep Fletcher fell into but a dream, only the dream went way past the story Curly narrated. As he felt himself rushing back into the warm air of time past, he wondered vaguely, *I wonder if I'll be back before last call.*

7

"That's it! That's it, Stretch!" cried the older cowboy, slapping his thigh with his hand.

Why, Curly's got hair, thought Fletcher, and while there wasn't a lot of it, it was curly. *Well, wavy, but nobody calls a cowboy "Wavy."* It was his last conscious thought as Fletcher, and when he shouted, "Ride her, Stretch, ride her!" he was twenty-one-year-old Hip Galloway and had never been anybody but.

After executing a handstand on the back of a gray dappled paint, a younger version of the tall, slim cowboy that was Stretch laughed as he kicked his legs back and then forward until he was sitting on the saddle.

"Yee-haw!" he hollered. "Did you see that, Hip?"

"I saw it and I still can't believe it," said Hip. "How'd a stumblebum like you do something like that?"

"Stumblebum," said Stretch with a laugh. "If you were half the stumblebum I was, you might be able to do this."

He crouched on the saddle and quickly rose into a standing position. His horse cantered in a circle as if she were inside a corral, which she was not, and Stretch stood on the horse as if his boots were fastened to the saddle, which they were not.

It was a sweet Sunday morning in May, and the three cowboys, riding back to the ranch from church, had stopped alongside the creek. Here, away from the prying eyes of the other hands, the two younger cowboys practiced the tricks that Curly showed them. That church was a part of their regular Sunday habit would surprise people who knew them later, but at that time Stretch was a pious fellow who might have been a man of the cloth himself had the lure of horses and the open range not been so strong. But it was, and he figured God wouldn't make him love the life of a cowboy so much if He hadn't intended Stretch to be a cowboy, and so it was with an open heart and calloused hands that the young man joyfully accepted his lot in life, leaving the family's barely sustainable turkey farm in Oklahoma (eternally grateful to his older brother Lucas who had taken over its operation so he didn't have to) to do a cowboy's work.

The Arnett place was the first ranch he had worked on, and it was fancier than the ones he had imagined, equipped with indoor toilets and showers. Even better than the plumbing was the name given him by Curly, who upon seeing the young rangy cowboy enter the bunkhouse had greeted him with "Howdy, Stretch."

"Don't matter what name you come in with," said Hip, "if it don't sound like a cowboy's name, Curly here'll give you one. He's kinda like a branding iron, only it don't hurt none—less of course you don't like the name he gives you."

Stretch immediately loved his; he felt his new name fit him like his old soft Levis, fit him better than his real name—Stephen—ever did.

"What's *Hip* stand for?" asked Stretch.

"Kid gets so excited about things," explained Curly. "It's like he's ready to break out in a cheer all the time."

Hip's smile was sheepish. "You know, like 'Yippee-ki-yay' or 'Hip hip hooray' or something of that nature."

Pudge rolled his eyes and The Mexican muttered something in Spanish, at which time Lefty stood up and said, "All in favor of getting drunk, follow me."

The bunkhouse was suddenly empty by half of the nicknamed cowboys.

"It's not that they ain't friendly," said Hip, after the three other hands had left.

"Yeah, it is," said Curly.

It didn't matter; Stretch only needed the friendship he forged with Hip and Curly, a friendship he especially valued when he learned that Curly was a veteran of countless rodeos.

"Can you teach me some tricks?" he asked casually, although he was willing to get on his knees and beg if need be.

"Why, surely," said Curly. "I'm already schooling Hip."

––––––––

He wasn't sure how much his friends appreciated the Sunday service he hauled them to (Hip did seem to nap quite a bit, but at least he didn't snore and Curly always enthusiastically lent his high, wavering tenor to the hymn singing), but Stretch understood that in any group of people, even a trio of friends, a leader was likely to emerge, and he was that leader. He was the idea man, and if occasionally his ideas were not ones the others would have embraced on their own, Hip and Curly followed along anyway. Church was tolerable to his friends because of what happened afterward in the rodeo lessons; in fact, the three often enjoyed themselves so much that they were late for the noon meal, an impropriety that Dash, the moody cook, took personally.

"I slave all morning making my five-alarm chili—at your request, Curly—and you bums don't even have the courtesy to show up on time?"

But on this particular Sunday morning that smelled of rich black earth and the first wildflowers to burst through it, Stretch suggested that they all take a break and help themselves to the coffee that Curly, a ten-cups-a-day man, always brought along.

As the horses nibbled on the tender green grass, Curly filled three tin cups from his coffee thermos and the men sat on the weather-beaten picnic table that still bore the carved intentions (CV—Marry Me?) of Jake Arnett's grandfather, the man who had long ago built the table and set it by the creek as a place to court his wife-to-be.

"You feelin' all right, Stretch?" asked Hip of his friend who normally didn't have time for coffee, wanting to practice tricks right away.

"All right but for this arrow in my heart."

"What?" said Hip, alarmed.

"I knew it!" said Curly, slapping his knobby knee. "I seen the way you looked at her!"

"Who?" said Hip, who had fallen asleep during the hymn "Come Ye Disconsolate" and didn't wake up until "Blessed Assurance." "What are you two talking about?"

"While you were sawing Zs," said Curly, "Stretch here was enjoying a certain view from a couple pews ahead of us."

"Wasn't she pretty?" asked Stretch. "Did you see her pretty little ballerina neck?"

"Oh, brother," said Curly.

"Was she," said Hip, trying to remember what he'd seen when he'd been conscious, "was she that brown-haired gal sitting up near the pastor's wife?"

She was, and Stretch's prayers that whole week were, *Please let me see her again, God.* The next Sunday, the Lord let Stretch know that He had heard his supplications loud and clear.

After the service, to the organist's perky rendition of "Abide with Me," Stretch was heading with the other congregants toward the door when he felt an arm on his sleeve. He had been rehearsing the charming and witty repartee with which he was going to introduce himself to the brown-haired gal with the ballerina neck, but to see her now, to feel her small pretty hand on his arm discombobulated him so much that all charming and witty repartee was rendered mute.

It turned out she had plenty of words for both of them.

"I love that you come to church on horseback," she said. "I would too if my Aunt Ludy weren't so fussy about how a 'lady' gets around on the Sabbath." She rolled her green eyes, further hypnotizing Stretch. "What I was thinking—maybe we could go riding sometime together? I'm staying at Ludy's house—she's kin to the pastor's wife—and well, gee, I think it'd be a lot of fun."

Trying to process everything—*She's even prettier up close! She wants to ride with me! That means she's got to like me!*—he could only offer a smile of such yearning that the brown-haired gal with the ballerina neck laughed.

"Well, I best be going—my aunt's waiting on me." She squeezed his arm before letting go. "My name's Penny—what's yours?"

"Stretch," he mumbled.

"Stretch?"

He nodded, and as she looked him up and down, she nodded her approval and said, "It fits, I guess."

The next thing Stretch knew he was standing in the gravel parking lot, blinking in the bright sunlight, feeling as fuzzy headed as if he had gone a round with Sonny Liston.

"Stretch, you all right?" asked Curly.

"She came up to me," said Stretch. "She came up and started talking to me."

"Who?" said Hip.

Curly rolled his eyes. "Who do you think, Hip? The brown-haired gal." He turned to Stretch. "She got a name?"

"Penny," said Stretch, with all the awe and wonder a miner inspecting his pan in an ice-cold creek might say, "Gold."

Their romance was fast and furious. No longer was Stretch available after a day's work to practice Roman riding, rope tricks, or Suicide Drags. Nor did the three cowboys get together after church to practice.

"Shoot," complained Hip to Curly. "You'd think seeing that brown-haired gal every night would be enough, but no—he's gotta court her after church, too."

Curly nodded. "Don't much see the point of going ourselves if we ain't gonna practice our drills afterwards."

"Me neither!" said Hip brightly, who preferred to sleep in his own bunk rather than a church pew. "So let's not!"

Stretch, once interested in the souls of his friends, didn't seem to mind their defection; now he rode over to Penny's after church, and let her Aunt Ludy serve the couple what she called her famous lemonade.

"Famous for what?" whispered Stretch to Penny, once his mouth unpuckered.

In the hours he spent working alongside Hip and Curly, he laughed and joked and seemed like the old Stretch, until he'd suddenly go quiet, as if listening to a song no one else could hear.

"I've had it bad myself a couple times," said Curly one evening.

After Stretch, splashing cologne all over himself as if it were water and he was on fire, raced off to pick up Penny, his two friends wiled away the evening, sitting out on the rusted lawn chairs on the worn patch of dirt that was their patio behind the bunk house. They watched the sun take its red bath in the west and, as cicadas pulsed their evening percussion, observed the first stars wink and sparkle in the broad night sky.

"A fella can have the strength of Samson," said Curly, "but it's all for naught when that special gal casts her spell over him."

Hip nodded, he hoped sagely. While he wasn't a neophyte in matters of love, he wasn't Casanova either. He had had girlfriends back in Tucson, and one of them had been fairly upset to learn he'd chosen to seek his fortune as a cowboy rather than a husband, but the kind of head-over-heels love that Stretch was tumbling in was a state Hip had not yet visited.

Curly tilted his head, directing his stream of smoke at the moon.

"Ah, Alice," he said, softly.

"Alice," asked Hip. "Who's Alice?"

He had known who Curly had voted for in the last election: "I could tolerate Nixon as Eisenhower's number two, but there was no way I could tolerate Nixon as America's number one, and besides, I thought Mrs. Kennedy was awful pretty"; had known Curly loved to read almost as much as he liked riding, and his two favorite writers were, not surprisingly, Louis L'Amour and, surprisingly, Jane Austen; had known he'd planned to enlist in the army on the day he turned sixteen only to have V-J Day precede his birthday by one week ("Can't say I wasn't disappointed but can't say I wasn't relieved either"); had known that Curly's real name was Howard and that his younger sister had been born with six toes on each foot ("Ma and Pa never had 'em removed either, and it's only that Rita's so pretty that it don't matter much"). In other words, he knew a lot about Curly, but he knew nothing about this woman named Alice.

The older man sighed a gust of cigarette smoke into the night.

"She and I were on the circuit together—her act was called 'Alice and El Diablo,' and a better trick rider you never did see."

Hip looked at Curly, whose sentence had ended in a little gasp. The older cowboy stared at his cigarette for a moment, before flicking it into the dirt.

"Oh, she was something else," he said after a long moment. "Long black hair that she wore in braids and a waist this big." Curly formed a circle with his hands. "She had the sweetest face, too, but that's as far as her sweetness went." His chuckle was low. "The horse should have been called Alice, because Alice was the real El Diablo."

"Is she still in the rodeo?"

"Nah. She got herself killed."

Hip flinched. "What happened?"

The cicadas chirped a whole concerto before Curly spoke again.

"Well, she took a fall."

"Off El Diablo?"

"Nah, off the steps of a portapotty of all things. Well, not even steps. A little palette that they had set it up on, not higher than a foot, I'd say, off the ground."

The older cowboy shook his head.

"Don't that beat all? Here was a woman who liked to take her joy rides on bucking broncos, who could ride bareback a horse most men couldn't ride tied into the saddle, and she goldarn meets her end stepping off a portapotty."

"How . . . how did that exactly kill her?"

Curly struck a match and Hip watched as the tiny triangle of flame jumped as it lit a new cigarette. He inhaled and his exhale was another smoky sigh.

"Well, see, it was one of them clumsy moves—even people who are pure grace like Alice make a clumsy move now and again, I expect. What happened was her ankle turned and it made her fall, hard on the ground, hurting her shoulder. Now a dislocated shoulder and a broken ankle ain't gonna kill nobody, but, man, was she mad! We were set up in Abilene for a big rodeo, and she come into the horse barn swearin' a blue streak, holding her shoulder and limping and lost her footing again—it's hard walking on a sprained ankle—and this time fell backwards, and wouldn't you know some of the day help they'd hired didn't know nothing about a horse barn and didn't hang up the rake and there it was, resting on a hay bale points up and when Alice fell on that, well, *that* killed her."

"Jesus," whispered Hip.

Curly dragged his big thin hand across his face as if it were a towel. "Yup," he said after he'd mopped his forehead, his cheeks, his chin. "Kinda put me in a bad place for a couple years." He took a long drag off his cigarette. "A man don't need drama like that in his life."

"Nope. He sure don't."

Curly's mouth bunched and he made a sound like he was trying to dislodge a bit of gristle stuck between his teeth.

"And that's what's got me a tad worried about Stretch," he said. "I feel like he's heading toward a whole lot of drama."

Live Field Report/Sense-O-Gram

To: Charmat
From: Tandala

Flowers, tamed and wild, carpet this parcel of Texas. Herewith a bunch of wild blue phlox. Simply inhale; it will make you a believer that out of Earthlings' five senses smell is king. Then again, taste could also reign. Check out this assortment of treats. My favorite is the bridge mix; a willy-nilly potpourri whose inventor must have thought, "Hmm—what can I dip in chocolate now?"

I trust that you're finding my work with Fletcher satisfactory; I also ask (somewhat belatedly) for your permission to continue independent study. I feel like a kid in a candy store times infinity.

Your faithful cut-up,
Tandy

Live Field Report/Reply

From: Charmat
To: Tandala

I was amused by your request for more freedom while on Earth; from here, it looks as if you're giving yourself permission to do whatever you like. To which I say, *Indulge!* While I think your presence provides security to Fletcher, I also agree with you that it's wisest to act as a good mother, protective when need be but willing to let the young one learn from his own mistakes. It appears Earth's treasure trove is deeper than we had ever imagined—I am still marveling at the scent of phlox. It seems such a communal flower, hundreds of those little purple stars bunched together on a stem, inviting one in with their sweet, cheerful fragrance. What were we thinking when we decided that the inevitable decay of flora and fauna, their resulting mess, was not worth their short but spectacular existence?

I trust you to run the mission as you see fit and in exchange for more tastes of Earthly life (Cracker Jacks—I was transported!), I shall do my best in finding out what exactly the mission is, anyway.

Hi-ho,

Charmat

Stretch was on Aunt Ludy's porch playing a game of Hearts with Penny and the old woman, trying to sip her lemonade without shuddering. He hated Hearts and the sour lemonade that made his balls shrivel, but he realized in courting Penny he was courting her relations, too. Besides, he knew as soon as the game was over, Aunt Ludy would button her ratty cardigan and comment on the chill of the night air and excuse herself to go inside and watch Lawrence Welk on the television. He and Penny would exchange looks then, knowing it wouldn't be long until they were out on Old Ranch Road, thrashing around in the back of the pickup truck.

Stretch had just taken a handful of the Spanish peanuts that were Aunt Ludy's signature appetizer when a cherry red Mustang convertible glided to a stop in front of the house.

"Who's that?" he asked, the papery skins of the peanuts molting in his warm hands.

Penny, who had already stood up and was running toward the car, didn't answer him, but Aunt Ludy did.

"Trouble," she said.

Stretch was 6'3" tall, but when Penny, flushed and excited, pulled the strange man by the arm out of the car and up the steps, he felt himself shrink, felt himself recede into a tiny inconsequential speck.

"Aunt Ludy, look who's here!" said Penny, as if she were announcing the King to the Court of St. James. "Stretch, let me introduce you to Jake Arnett."

Stretch stood, needing to show off his height (and prayed that it was still there, prayed that just because he felt he'd almost disappeared, he was in fact still the same size he'd been a minute ago), and he took the young man's hand in a grip that said, "Here I am, deal with it."

His brain belatedly registered the name by which Penny had introduced the man as he squeezed the man's knuckles.

"Hey," he said, "I work for Jake Arnett." He turned to Penny. "He's not Jake Arnett."

"Jake Arnett, Junior," said the man, giving his own hand a little shake after Stretch released it.

"He's home from school," said Penny to her aunt.

"Home for good, ma'am," said Jake, nodding to the older woman. "I graduated."

"Who'd a thunk?" said Penny, turning to Stretch, who couldn't help noticing she still held on to the guy's arm. "We've known each other forever," she explained. "When I was a kid, I'd visit Aunt Ludy every summer and Jake Jr. was one of my playmates."

"She was a chubby little thing," said Jake Jr. "If I'd of known what was under that baby fat then . . . "

While Stretch's preference was to smack this callow college boy right in the kisser, he chose to sit down instead and tipped back in his chair so its front legs were off the floor.

Aunt Ludy filled the lemonade pitcher, and Jake Jr. was urged to take a seat, and he did so gingerly, one leg unbending.

"Knee injury," he explained and then proceeded to update them on his recent graduation from SMU and his last season playing place kicker for the Mustangs.

"That's why I drive that," he said to Stretch, pointing to the red convertible. "I'm a Mustang driving a Mustang."

Penny twittered a little laugh.

"Fortunately, I busted up my knee on the tennis court when football season was long over. But you should have seen the other guy."

Penny rewarded this comment with another laugh, and Stretch swallowed down bile that had burned low in his throat. As Jake Jr. the college boy continued to regale his female audience, the other male present silently heckled him.

"I made the dean's list twice."

"Really?" asked Penny, impressed.

"Sure. Dean Brody was my roommate, and every week he posted a Who Drank the Most Beer list."

Asshole, thought Stretch.

"Now that I've got a degree in business, I figure you owe me a dollar and ninety-eight cents."

"How's that?" asked Penny.

"Well, remember that nickel I loaned you when you were ten? It's compounded 5 percent interest over the past nine years, plus several late fees, subject to my discretion, of course."

"Your discretion?" said Penny, offering her pretty smile.

I'll show you discretion, shithead, thought Stretch.

Taking a break in what Stretch could only call a performance, Jake Jr. took a sip of lemonade. He grimaced, his mouth frowning to expose all of his lower teeth.

"Got a little tip for you, Miss Ludy," he said. "You might want to turn up your ratio of sugar to lemons."

That Penny and her aunt laughed hurt Stretch's feelings all the more.

How come I can't tease her about her lemonade? he thought, and then as resentment built toward the one who could, he added words for which his pious mother would have scrubbed out his mouth with lye soap: *Son of a bitch! Bastard! Dickhead!*

"Stretch, Jake Jr. asked you a question."

"Huh?" said Stretch, the front legs of his chair thunking on the porch floor as he sat forward.

Penny gave Stretch a look he had never before seen on her face— one of exasperation and embarrassment—and he couldn't have been more shocked and hurt than if she'd karate-chopped him.

"I was asking where you went to college," said Jake Jr. amicably.

"Where I went to college?" said Stretch, as if answering the dumbest question he'd ever been asked.

Jake Jr. looked at Penny and shrugged.

Stretch wanted to jump between the two of them, to block them from any more of their cozy looks.

"Young Stretch here's not a college boy," said Aunt Ludy, her bony fingers scratching the hollow in the center of her collarbone. "Not every one is, you know."

"Ain't that the truth" said Jake Jr. "I sure didn't figure I was. Anyway,

I guess I'll be seeing a lot of you this summer—I'll be working on the ranch, too."

"Now won't that be fun," said Stretch, and rising, he held out his hand to his beloved. "Come on, Penny, we don't want to be late for the movie."

"Movie?" said Penny, "but I thought—"

There was no time to express her thoughts, for he had grabbed her hand and was pulling her down the steps and toward the rust-spotted pickup truck parked ahead of the cherry-red Mustang convertible.

———

Like a worm in an apple, anxiety bore its way into Stretch's courtship.

"He's just a friend!" Penny claimed, but her assurances had the effect of butter on a burn—they felt good for a second and then proceeded to make things worse.

"What does she mean by *friend*?" asked Stretch one day as the cowhands sat outside the bunkhouse, finishing their supper.

"I'd say that's what she means," said Curly. In the past week, he and Hip had watched their friend go from a dreamy, ballad-humming fellow in love to a nervous, short-tempered man, certain the arrow Eros had aimed at him was a poison one. "They've known each other a long time. They're friends."

"Ha!" said Stretch. "How many *girl* friends do you have, huh, Curly? I don't see you taking walks or sitting on a porch with no *girl* friend!"

"I had a friend back in Tucson," said Hip. "Girl by the name of Dawn. We both had BB guns and we'd target-practice together. Cans and stuff. She was a real good shot, and afterwards we'd talk about stuff like how Miss Henski, our teacher, had b.o. like a man, or who we thought made a better cowboy—John Wayne or Gary Cooper. See, we went to the Saturday matinees together too and—"

"—shut up!" said Stretch. "This ain't two kids talking about movie actors or some teacher who stunk! This is about—"

"—anyone want more?" asked Dash, emerging from the kitchen, pot in hand.

Hip declined, his mouth feeling nearly blistered, but Curly held out his bowl.

"Fill 'er up," he said, "and tell me, what other peppers am I tasting beside the New Mexico and the serrano?"

"You're a connoisseur, my friend," said the cook, scraping the last of the stew into Curly's bowl. "I might have thrown in a little poblano, a pinch of—"

"Jesus R. Jones!" said Stretch, pushing himself away from the table. "I'm watching the love of my life slip through my fingers and you guys are talking about peppers?"

He stomped off toward the bunkhouse as if he were trying to kill a particularly big and nasty bug with each step.

Curly spooned stew into his mouth and sat for a moment, considering.

"Ah, yes," he said presently. "A pinch of cayenne."

———————

It was with great relief that Stretch realized that what Jake Jr. meant by "working on the ranch" didn't mean working with the cowhands.

"Nah, the pantywaist is inside all day, working with the bookkeeper," said Stretch, repeating the news Penny had given him. "Guess he can't handle the life of a cowboy."

It cheered him to think of Jake Arnett Jr. being stuck inside attending to ledgers and phone calls from brokers and lawyers, while Stretch got to spend the daylight hours outside, either on a horse or near one.

"Yeah," said Hip, "so the guy can handle a pencil—I'd like to see him handle a horse!"

"Ha," said Curly, "not when his office chair is his saddle!"

Hip's eyes squinted in a gesture indicating thought.

"Not when his . . . not when his chaps are a business suit!"

That's right, thought Stretch, appreciating his friends' support as well as their humor. *Penny's in love with a cowboy, not a businessman.*

Only trouble was, Jake Arnett Jr. was both.

Live Field Report/Sense-O-Gram

To: Charmat

From: Tandala

Last night I "closed down the joint," which means I didn't leave the tavern until the bouncer told me I had to. It was Square Dance Night—Bow to your partner, Charmat! Bow to your corner! Now circle right! Smell the sweat and the hopeful cologne, contemplate the lacy petticoats and their peek-a-boo allure, notice the man in the turquoise shirt and how he struts like a rooster, unaware that his barn door's open. Feel that sense of harmony when everyone's in step with the caller, and the easy forgiveness when the short woman in the yellow dress messes up her Pass-Through. Hum the "Ozark Rag" without tapping your feet. I dare you.

8

After a week so heavy with heat that every living thing, from flora to fauna, was limp with it, the skies had filled and unleashed a morning's worth of rain, promising a clean, fresh evening for the big party.

It wasn't one of his fancy, raise-a-zillion-dollars affairs; this was the annual Fourth of July celebration, put on to show his employees, friends, and neighbors what a good guy Jake Arnett was.

It was easy for Stretch to feel benevolent toward his boss while cruising by the long table set out in the yard, laden as it was with all manner of barbeque, salads and side dishes, fresh fruit and grilled vegetables, baskets of corn bread and biscuits, and cakes, cookies, and a divinity the Arnett's cook was justly famous for.

"Hey, Dash—you responsible for any of this?" asked Stretch, waving his fork toward the food.

"Nah, they never let me cook for parties," said the cook. "Too many bland palates they've got to cater to!"

Stretch refilled his plate and took it over to one of the gingham-covered picnic tables arranged under the ash trees.

"Sweets for the sweet," he said, handing both Penny and Aunt Ludy pieces of the divinity they had requested.

Hip looked hurt. "So where's mine?"

His reflexes were quick enough to catch the short rib Stretch threw at him, and he attacked it like a rabid dog.

"Can't take him anywhere," said Curly to Penny.

"How 'bout a kennel?" suggested Aunt Ludy.

Jokes were passed around the table as easily as the pitcher of sun tea, and Stretch was filled with a contentment that made him feel almost buoyant. He put his arm around Penny; if he were going to float away into the blue open sky, he was going to take his pretty brown-haired girlfriend with him.

"Having fun?" he asked, his fingertips drawing circles on her ballerina neck and down the slope of her bare shoulder.

"Sure am," she said, offering a smile so sweet it could have been wrapped and sold at a candy store.

He wanted to take her by the hand and rush her into the empty bunkhouse.

"What are you thinking?" she said, leaning into him so that her breast flattened against his arm.

"I can't say it in polite company."

Stretch was ready to kiss her—to hell with Aunt Ludy sitting right across from them—when the warm yielding body that was Penny's straightened up, and she said, "Hey, there's Jake Jr.!"

For everyone else, the sun still shone high in the blue Texas sky, but for Stretch a dark cloud rolled in, casting a shadow across the entire day. Jake Jr. had been away from the ranch for nearly two weeks—traveling on business for his father, Penny had mentioned casually—and Stretch had gotten used to his absence. So much so that his presence made Stretch want to hit somebody—preferably Jake Jr.

"Well, how's everybody doing?" asked the young scion, sitting down to a table he hadn't been invited to. "I must say, Penny, you're looking even prettier than the last time I saw you."

Stretch's teeth clenched.

"That goes double for you, Miss Ludy." he said.

"Fast talker," said Aunt Ludy, trying not to bare her dentures in a smile.

Under the table, Stretch's fists clenched.

"And hey, Stretch," said Jake Jr., and Stretch thought it wouldn't matter what else the jerk said to him, he was ready to smack him but good.

"Ladies and gentlemen," came a booming voice, and Jake Jr. and Stretch held each other's gaze for a moment, knowing something had just been averted, before turning to face the ranch owner.

Jake Sr. was a big man, and although he wore a simple plaid shirt and jeans, there was no mistaking him for anything but Lord of the Manor. He had planted himself on a small rise of lawn, and taking off his worn Stetson, he thanked everyone for coming.

"I hope you've all had enough to eat, but not too much, because now it's rodeo time!"

Cheers went up from the crowd.

"Rodeo time," said Stretch to his friends. "What's he talking about?"

"It's a tradition at this party," Jake Jr. explained amicably, as if Stretch were suddenly his dearest friend. "Anyone who wants to participate can."

The black cloud was swallowed by the blue sky and Stretch was in the sun again.

"Well, shucks," he said, standing. "I'm in."

"Me, too," added Hip.

"Sounds good," said Curly, and then surprising everyone, Jake Jr. said, "Then let's go get on those horses."

"You're going to be in the rodeo?" asked Stretch.

Jake Jr. offered a smile enhanced by years of orthodontia. "Any objections?"

"Jake," said Penny softly, "what about your knee?"

"Knee's all healed," said Jake Jr. brightly. "In fact, I'd say now I'm good as gold." To prove his point, he did three quick squats.

"Yeah, but can you ride?" asked Stretch, and later he came to think it was the dumbest question he had ever asked.

"Oh my," said Fletcher, his voice buried in his folded arms.

Curly laughed. "Welcome back, Hip. Guess you're not the beer drinker you thought you were."

Lifting his head, Fletcher felt a sudden unspooling, as if someone had wrapped his head in cotton gauze and was now pulling it off. A gust of wind seemed to blow through his brain and he blinked twice, hard. When his eyes focused, he was looking into Tandala's face.

"I'm glad you woke up, Hip, because I was just telling your friend here that we should be leaving." Although her voice was light, a fierceness was telegraphed in her eyes.

"What?" said Fletcher, as groggy as if he'd been awakened from a coma.

"Guy can only take three beers," said Stretch, whose slurred voice suggested he had taken many more. "I know grade school girls who could drink him under the table."

As if an antenna had been fiddled with, the picture before him grew sharper and Fletcher realized he was back at Josie's. But there was something new here, a tension as thick as the indoor fog of cigarette smoke.

"So," he said, brightly, "how'd you do in the pool room, Stretch?"

"'How'd you do in the pool room, Stretch?'" repeated Stretch, his mouth twisted as he mocked Fletcher. "How do you think I did? I beat everyone's ass." He leaned into Tandy, flipping her beaded braids of hair with his pointer finger. "Except yours. Yours is an ass I'd really like to—"

"—say," said Curly, whose place next to Tandy had been stolen by Stretch while the old cowboy had been visiting the head. "That's enough of that."

His words, made sodden by alcohol, lacked authority, yet Stretch felt it necessary to shove his old friend and tell him to shut up.

"Now," he said, turning back to Tandy, "what do you say you come on home with me? Because I've never been with anyone with skin as dark as yours and I really like chocolate, and—my God!—your titties and that ass we were talking about are just about the biggest things I've ever seen, and I'd love—"

"—come on, Tandy," said Fletcher, gripping the alien by the arm. "You don't need to listen to this crap."

"That's right," said Curly. "Criminy, Stretch—where're your manners, anyhow?"

His previous shove might have been considered playful, but the one Stretch now gave was not, and Curly was knocked to the floor, despite grabbing the end of the vinyl banquette.

"Hey!" he said, his voice full of insult and injury, and Fletcher, using the distraction of Curly's tumble, pulled Tandy out of the booth.

But not quite fast enough.

"Let go of me!" she said as Stretch seized her other arm.

"Yeah, let go of her!" said Curly, who had staggered upright and now held an empty beer bottle in his hand like a club.

"What the hell?" asked Stretch, dropping Tandy's arm as he lunged at Curly. The table rocked forward, and empty bottles and a full ashtray cascaded down its surface and crashed to the floor.

The sound and fury got the attention of other patrons who weren't averse to perking up their evening by joining a bar brawl, and there was a sudden rush of bodies to the table.

Fletcher was shocked—physically and emotionally—by the fist that drove into his stomach. He was surrounded by men throwing punches and their beery, sweaty stench, surrounded by the sounds of knuckles meeting flesh. Dodging another curled fist, Fletcher heard Tandy yelp, and suddenly he was hurtling through space, as if he had been picked up and tossed by the world's biggest bouncer.

Knowing it was pointless to question the hows or whys of finding himself in a Cadillac DeVille driven by an alien who looked like a Jamaican cowgirl, Fletcher decided to focus on the relief he felt in getting out of the melee with nothing more than a dull ache in his stomach.

"Whoa," he said finally, rolling down the window and breathing in the cool desert air. "I have no idea what that was all about."

"I do," said Tandy, looking over her shoulder as she backed out of the parking lot. "It was about that vile man Stretch pinching and poking me and saying things like, 'If you've seen me ride my horse, just imagine how I can ride you.'"

"Aw, Tandy." Fletcher slumped, as if under the weight of Stretch's crudeness.

"And that was hardly the all of it! I kept kicking you under the table to wake you up, but you wouldn't, and meanwhile, he's saying nasty things about my skin color and my anatomy!"

Fletcher was quiet, filled with shame and guilt over his failure to protect the alien from his own kind.

"I of course had been warned of human men, but warnings are a piffle compared to the real experience! I tell you—nothing would give me greater pleasure than to flush that brute down a black hole!"

A single bump of laughter rose in Fletcher's chest.

"Or let him take a ride on an exploding nova!"

"Just punishment," Fletcher concurred, as a car passed them, mariachi music pouring from its open windows.

Tandy had driven through one intersection, turned right at another, and now they had left behind the street lights and were in the desert, driving a road lit by stars and a moon that looked over them like a benevolent chaperone.

"But this shouldn't be about me," Tandy said as the Cadillac cruised along like an ocean liner, the sand a calm sea on both sides of them. She took a deep breath. "I am fine now. This is about you and what happened when you went away in the bar."

"I did go away?" He was confused, unsure of the realities he had been in and out of. "It wasn't just a dream?"

"It was way beyond a dream, mon. So tell me about it."

Taking off his cowboy hat and setting it on one knee, Fletcher leaned his head back on the leather headrest and broke into a grin.

"Tandy, I was Hip when he was a young man!" he said, the memory of which was like yeast in him, filling him with a rising softness. "A boy, really. I was Hip when he first got together with Stretch and Curly—and Stretch wasn't at all like the jerk he was tonight!"

"I certainly would hope not," said Tandy.

Fletcher told her all about Jake Arnett's ranch, about Curly with hair, about the trick-riding practice sessions after church.

"I met Stretch when he was twenty-one—he used to drag me and Curly to church every Sunday, plus he never cussed!" Fletcher chuckled. "He didn't just think the world was his oyster—he thought the world was his oyster and he had the exact tool to pry it open!"

"*That* I can believe," said Tandala. "But what were you like?"

Fletcher shrugged. "I was a kid, too. More of a follower than a leader, I guess, and . . . and pretty happy. It was easy for me to be happy."

"That's a nice thing to know about yourself, isn't it?"

"Sure, but it's not really me-Fletcher we're talking about. It's me-Hip, remember?"

The cool night air was fragrant with sage, and like a dog Fletcher stuck his head out the window to gulp it in. The wind on his face brought tears to his eyes, and for a long moment he reveled in the speed, the sound of the car wheels on gravel, and the deep, dark, perfumed night.

"You know what Stretch told me once as we rode after church?" he asked, when he finally sat back in his seat. "'God holds all of us in his lap; our problem is we're like squirmy kids, always trying to get off.'"

A single pulse of light appeared on Tandy's forehead. "How did he go from saying something like that to the things he said tonight? You must tell me everything, Fletcher."

And he did. By the time he got to the part about the Fourth of July rodeo, Tandala had pulled off the road, past a sign that promised food and gas in fifty-four miles.

"The thing is, Stretch had grown up on a turkey farm," said Fletcher. "How did he ever think he could outride someone who'd grown up on a real ranch?"

Hip had been heartened when he saw Curly ride into the corral, sliding off one side of the saddle and pretending to run alongside the horse before boosting himself back into the saddle and then off the other side.

The audience had clapped and whistled, and when Curly draped himself over the side of his horse so that his head was nearly touching the ground, Hip thought, *No one can touch Curly. He's going to win the rodeo and everything will be all right.*

The older cowboy finished his routine by twirling his pistols while standing on the back of his horse, and as he rode out of the corral Stretch rode in.

"He started off big, bringing himself up into a handstand on the saddle," said Fletcher. "I'd seen him fall off his horse a million times practicing that trick, but he didn't fall now and the crowd was going nuts.

"Technically, Curly was the best rider out there, but both Stretch and Jake Jr. had youth on their sides. And both of them had a lot to prove." Fletcher explained the tricks Stretch had performed and how in his estimation Stretch had never performed better.

"When he was done, he rode out, waving nonchalantly, like he was taking a stroll past the crowd. The thing was, he was standing on top of a horse."

Fletcher's chuckle didn't last long.

"Then Jake Jr. rode out. And no, the jerk couldn't do his own routine—he had to humiliate Stretch by doing the exact same tricks. The exact same tricks, only better."

"If he did the exact same tricks," said Tandala, "how could he do them better?"

Fletcher chose to think the alien was not being sarcastic but was genuinely confused over the semantics of the language.

"Well, see, after he got himself up on a handstand, he had to take it further and do a *one-handed* handstand."

In a flash, Tandala was outside on the hood of the Cadillac, attempting to perform a handstand. Her skirt fell over her like a curtain, briefly revealing a pair of shiny pink underpants encasing a sizable posterior before the alien/gymnast collapsed into the windshield with a thump so loud Fletcher expected it to crack. In a second, she was back behind the steering wheel, brushing off her sleeves and breathing hard.

"Are you all right?" asked Fletcher.

"It seems my corporeal body is not as graceful as I would like," said Tandy. "Hoola, baby. And I was just trying a two-handed handstand."

Relieved that she hadn't hurt herself, Fletcher allowed himself to feel irritation.

"How many times do I have to ask, Could I please get a little warning before you do something like that?"

"Sorry, but I must act when the spirit moves me."

Fletcher put his cowboy hat back on and folded his arm across his chest, mumbling something about being shocked into an early grave.

"Don't worry, Fletcher. I will not reenact the other stunts. Suffice it to say, I can assume that when Stretch did a somersault, Jake Jr. did a somersault and a half."

"That's right. And when Stretch leapfrogged onto the saddle from the back of his horse, Jake Jr. leapfrogged onto the saddle and then sprung off the front. He'd had years and years more practice, and it showed."

Fletcher shook his head, remembering how Stretch had lost color, as if all blood vessels leading to his face had been cauterized.

The crowd's explosive applause designated Jake Jr. the winner, and after he dismounted, his father slapped him on the back, and congratulations were offered by all, including Penny, who offered an outstretched hand. Not satisfied with this paltry prize, Jake Jr. pulled her to him and kissed her on the lips with the force of an industrial-strength vacuum cleaner.

"I thought for sure there'd be bloodshed," said Fletcher. "But instead of going after him, Stretch just turned away. Turned away and walked back to the bunkhouse. He was packing his bag when Curly and I got there, and when we asked where he was going he said, 'Away from here,' and Curly said, 'Me, too,' and I said, 'Me, three,' and we left the ranch in Stretch's old pickup. Penny chased us, hollering, 'Honey, what's wrong? but Stretch wouldn't turn around. You wouldn't even know by his face that he was upset, unless you noticed the bone in his jaw twitching like a live wire."

Fletcher's thumb moved back and forth over his mustache.

"We stuck together, Tandy. We stayed for a while with Curly's sister outside of San Antonio—nicest lady—she was born with an extra toe on each foot—and she was married to an oilman who'd died in a rig accident and left her a wealthy woman. Anyway, she lent us the money to buy three horses, and we ultimately found ourselves on the rodeo circuit."

Fletcher sighed, his memories a warm bath he could have floated in forever.

"I sure did enjoy being a cowboy, and I—"

But he did not complete his thought, for in a wind that would have decimated the desert tumbleweeds he was suddenly blown into a bathroom with fluttering florescent lighting. Coming in for a landing, as it were, he braced the edge of the sink, feeling the wind of motion on his back. When he had steadied himself, he raised his head.

Every time he looked in a mirror, it was a sweet surprise for Fletcher to see Hip. Just as the twenty-one-year-old Hip had looked much younger than Fletcher had at that age (he shuddered to remember the pressed chinos and V-neck sweater over a shirt and tie that had been his uniform in the swinging sixties), Hip in his midthirties still had youth's hope and excitement animating his features.

And the mustache doesn't hurt, thought Fletcher, petting it affectionately with his thumb, as if it were a small furry animal that had come to hibernate under the shelter of his nose.

He posed in front of the mirror with his arms in half-circles at his sides, ready to draw; he turned and looked at himself over his shoulder; he cocked his head to the left and then to the right and wished he had a hand mirror to check out his back view, when Stretch burst through the swinging door.

"Jesus Christ, Hip, come on! The doctor's waiting to talk to us!"

Stretch's urgent plea answered one question for Fletcher, *Oh, so this is a hospital,* but it raised more, *Why are we in a hospital?* and most important, *Whose doctor is waiting to talk to us?*

"As heart attacks go, this one's fairly mild," said the woman whose badge identified her as Dr. Sayers. "We'll keep him a day or two and monitor his vitals, but on the whole the prognosis looks pretty good."

Hip felt a little funny, as if the soles of his boots were made of gelatin. "So he'll live?"

Dr. Sayers offered a smile composed of teeth so small Hip wondered if her baby teeth had ever fallen out.

"Yes, he'll live. For how long, I don't know. Could be a week, could be fifty years. But it might behoove him," she raised an eyebrow as she looked at Stretch—"it might behoove you all—to stay out of bar fights."

Live Field Complaint

To Charmat
From: Tandala

I am reminded far too often why Earth is such an underachiever. I cannot walk down a street, sit at a lunch counter or on a park bench without men whistling at me or yelling ugly things about my anatomy. Just minutes ago, a man in a mud-clotted pickup pulls up next to the curb and offers me money to suck something of his that I was not the least bit interested in sucking. I ignore his question, which he persists in asking, as if my not hearing him was the problem, until finally he calls me a "black whore" before gunning his engine and charging off. To earn this sort of treatment, I am doing nothing but being present in this world. It appears that to be a woman—especially ones whose bodies are round and curvy—and to have skin darker than many is to invite bad behavior.

P.S. Believe me, I'd rather be sending you a Johnny Cash and June Carter duet or hot fudge sundaes with extra pecans.

In his hospital bed, Curly looked smaller and older than when Hip had last seen him at Josie's. His skin was pallid and his bald pate, usually covered with a cowboy hat, now wore a film of sweat. His black eye didn't help his appearance any either.

"Curly," said Stretch, settling his lanky frame into a chair next to the hospital bed. "You look like hell."

"You wouldn't win no beauty pageants neither," said Curly, and it was true, Stretch's face bore a bruise on his cheekbone and a swollen lip. "Now cut the compliments and get me out of here, will ya?"

"Uh, we will," said Hip, watching the jagged range of lines on the monitor above Curly's bed and feeling his stomach lurch any time he saw an irregular peak. "Only it won't be until the day after tomorrow."

"The day after tomorrow?" said Curly, sounding like an old shut-in disappointed at the mailman's pronouncement as to when the Sears and Roebuck catalog might be delivered.

"I wish they'd keep you a whole week," said Stretch. "Give me seven less days to worry about you."

"You don't have to worry about me!" said Curly, and as Hip heard a renewed vigor in his voice, he also saw one of the peaks of the range on the heart monitor jump.

"Settle down, Curly, and don't let Stretch aggravate you. You know he's only kidding."

"Yeah," said Stretch. "I wish they'd keep you here *two* weeks."

Hip shot him a look but Stretch merely rolled his eyes and then turned his attention to the nurse entering the room.

"The doctor wants Mr. Briggs to get some rest now," she said, charging toward Curly with thermometer in hand. "You can see him tomorrow."

"All right," said Stretch, needing no further coaxing. "Let's hit the road, Hip, and let this bum get his rest."

"See you tomorrow," said Hip, squeezing Curly's shoulder again.

"Hey, bring me the book in the trailer, will ya? The one next to my bed, the Irwin Shaw, not the—" the old cowboy's request was lost as he was forced to accept the thermometer the nurse not so delicately shoved into his mouth.

————

In the lobby, Hip and Stretch stood to the side as the automatic door opened to let a family tethered by balloons squeeze by.

In their celebratory mood (*Must be a new baby,* Hip thought) no one noticed them but a little boy. As his mother pulled him along, he stared in wonder at the two cowboys and Hip smiled, ready to tip his hat, but Stretch mimed pulling a gun out of his holster and pointing at the little boy whispered, "Bang."

The boy's face crumpled in a wail.

"Geez, Stretch, what the—" began Hip, but Stretch grabbed his arm, pushing him out the door and into the parking lot.

"What is your problem?" asked Hip, wiggling out of Stretch's grasp.

"Next time Curly has a heart attack," said Stretch, letting go of him with a hard little push, "*you* be the guy who watches him fall to the floor, okay? You be the guy who calls the ambulance. You be the guy sitting outside the emergency room wondering if he's going to live or die."

"Hey," said Hip, unwilling to hold the burden of blame Stretch shoved at him. "Why don't *you* try being the guy who doesn't start the fight? Why don't you try being the guy who doesn't make a fool of himself hitting on Tandy? Maybe that's what upset Curly so much in the first place—"

"—Hip, I would shut my mouth right now if I were you," warned Stretch, his hands curling into fists.

"Well, you ain't," said Hip, tired of Stretch trying to be in charge of everything, including Hip's own anger. "So if you wanna get more jollies by hitting me, just try."

Like two bulls, the cowboys stood facing one another, pawing the ground with their hooves, snorting air out of their noses. Then the lanky cowboy dismissed the other with an ugly laugh and turned away, loping toward his pickup.

The engine roared to life, and Hip watched as Stretch careened around a line of parked cars, causing a nurse who had just gotten off work to grab her white cap with one hand and shake the fist of the other. He flew by Hip but just as he reached the driveway, he laid on the horn and summoned him with a sharp wave of his hand.

"I'm only stopping because I'd rather drink with an asshole than drink alone," he said, stepping on the gas as Hip jumped into the front seat.

————

"To the end of the Daring Desperadoes," said Stretch, raising his glass.

They had stopped at the first bar Stretch saw, sharing a serious gloom in the air with patrons who were all over the age of retirement and who nursed their drinks slowly, fully aware that a Social Security income didn't allow for unlimited boilermakers.

"What?" said Hip when the shock began to thaw. "What's that supposed to mean?

"Aw, Hip, you knew this day was coming."

"Come on, Stretch, we've had fights before! Sure, Curly never collapsed with a heart attack, but—"

"Hell, Hip, it ain't about Curly's heart—it's about mine." He scratched his throat with his knuckles. "It just ain't in it anymore."

Hip stared at him, his tongue working in his mouth to produce the saliva he needed for speech.

"Don't look at me like that, Hip. You know we've barely been making it—shit, the Gilroy Fair just canceled us!"

There was enough saliva in Hip's mouth to form two words.

"They did?"

Dumping the contents of his glass down his throat, Stretch banged the glass on the bar for a refill.

"I just heard yesterday—that's probably why I was in such a foul mood at Josie's. They decided to go with that brother-sister act out of Laredo." A drop of his voice in a glass of milk would have curdled it. "Seems we don't 'appeal to the crowd' the way those young punks do."

"Stretch—it's just one show. We've got other shows—there's

Oklahoma and then the jamboree in Yuma and what about Cowboys for Kids?"

"Damn it—I'm through, Hip! I'm so tired."

"Tired of what?"

"Tired of everything! Tired of wondering, Are the horses fed? How're we going to get to the next gig? What is the next gig? Are we going to get paid what we agreed on, or are we gonna get swindled? Did Hip pick up the jackets at the dry cleaners? Did he find the trailer hitch? Am I gonna have to break the news to Curly that he's gonna have to drop the Roman riding because he's getting too old?

"Don't get me wrong, Hip I loved being a rodeo cowboy. Had more fun than's legal. We had a good ride, but that ride's over!"

Hip watched Stretch's throat expand and contract as he guzzled down his drink and watched as his friend stormed out of the bar, leaving in his wake a half-dozen trembling old men—and the tab.

Live Field Report/Sense-O-Gram

To: Charmat
From: Tandala

The sun shines through yellowing blinds of this town's library, making stripes of light across my legs, and I am browsing through the Science Fiction section. From what I've read, they really—except maybe for Isaac Asimov—have no clue.

An elderly patron pages through *The Oxford Book of English Verse*, sighing every now and then.

Two eleven-year-old kids sit hunched, their thin little shoulders vibrating with the laughter they can't unleash in the quiet of the library. When they leave, I pick up that which has entertained them, something called *Mad Magazine*.

Oh, the riotous delight, Charmat! My civics receptors tell

me Alfred E. Neuman is not the president of this country, but he should be! And I nominate Dave Berg for Cartoonist Laureate!

In the past few years, amid the cancellations and lack of bookings that led to the breakup of the Daring Desperadoes, one date had remained that even Stretch felt duty-bound to keep. It was the Cowboys for Kids fund-raiser, an event spearheaded by Curly's sister, Rita. Not having kids of her own, Rita enjoyed sponsoring any number of charities that helped children and gave lavishly of her time and her dead oilman husband's money. The biggest event was the one that brought orphaned children and deep-pocketed Texans to her property for an all-day party. The Daring Desperadoes had been a part of Cowboys for Kids since its inception a dozen years earlier, and even Stretch was not about to disappoint Miss Rita.

"Remember, it's in two weeks," they had told Stretch the day Curly was released from the hospital. He had promised to be there, even as he reminded them the Daring Desperadoes were a thing of the past.

"Even if I weren't ready to see the group end," Stretch had said as the men gathered at a diner for their final breakfast together, "look at Curly here. He's in no condition to get back on a horse."

Curly continued dousing his eggs with hot sauce before setting the bottle down on the table. He waved a fly away, wiped a fork with his napkin, and poked the napkin into his shirt collar. Only when this business was completed did he look Stretch in the eye and in a voice that sizzled like the bacon on the grill behind the counter, said, "Listen here, you sombitch, the only thing my doctor told me I had to stop doing was smoking. So don't you worry about my condition—I'll be jumping off horses when you're watching soap operas in diapers."

A nervous giggle erupted out of Hip—he was used to Stretch giving him and Curly the what-for but not vice versa.

"It's fine you got your own reasons for quitting the group," said the older cowboy, "but I'll thank you to leave me out of your lame excuses."

With that, Curly jabbed a forkful of eggs and shoved them into his mouth, a trail of red dripping out of the corner of his mouth like blood.

"Okay, then," said Stretch, petulant as a scolded boy. "Geez."

The men ate their last breakfast together in a silence broken only by the clatter of silverware and gulps of coffee, and it was only after Stretch had pushed aside his plate and patted his mouth with his napkin that he spoke.

"All right, then," he said. "I guess I'll be seeing you two in San Antonio."

He stood up and offered his hand, which Hip shook. Curly did, too, only he didn't let go.

"You owe three and a quarter, Stretch," he said, picking up with his free hand the bill left by the waitress. "Matter of fact, better make it three-seventy-five with the tip."

His ears below his hat burning red, Stretch dug into the pocket of his jeans for his share of the tab, and only then did Curly let go of his hand so that Stretch could count it out.

9

The morning of Cowboys for Kids dawned pink and pretty, and Curly, sitting on his sister's porch watching the sunrise, wondered if he had been a fool to believe Stretch would come. It was true that in rating Stretch's personality there may be more marks in the debit column than in the assets, but historically he'd been a man of his word. Anytime Rita's phone rang, he'd look at his sister hopefully; anytime the postman brought out the mail, he'd watch her sift through it, but there was never word from Stretch.

"You all right?'" said Hip, nudging open the screen door with his elbow, his hands holding two mugs of coffee.

"Sure," said Curly, blinking back the tears that had filled his eyes as he'd watched the day begin in the east. Ever since his heart trouble, he'd become the biggest baby—a goldarn sunrise bringing him to near blubbering!

Hip handed Curly his coffee and sat down in the rocker next to his.

"I s'pose you didn't get no late-night call or telegram from Stretch this morning," said Hip and when Curly shook his head, he added, a little tease his voice, "If he knew who was coming, I know he'd show."

Blowing on his coffee to cool it, Curly squinted his eyes. "What's that supposed to mean?"

Hip shrugged. "I might have invited Penny."

"Yaow!" said Curly as he jostled his cup and coffee splashed on the knee of his jeans.

"Kind of a dumb thing to do, huh?" said Hip. "Although I checked with Miss Rita to make sure it was all right."

"No, no, it's a great idea," said Curly, rubbing at his knee with his handkerchief. "What'd she say—Penny, I mean?"

"Well, she was surprised to hear my voice, as you can imagine. But she knew all about this party and its good cause and all—she said she's good friends with the Ewings, who go every year—"

"—that's rich people for you," said Curly. "It's a pretty tight circle. So is she coming?"

"Well, she sounded pleased to get the invitation, but she said she'd have to check her and Jake's schedule."

"Don't tell me you invited that weasel, too."

"I didn't . . . but I reckon she made the assumption that I did."

———

The grounds of Rita's ranch were swarming with kids swimming in the pool, kids chasing each other around the lawn, kids heckling the clowns and magicians, and kids snitching slices of watermelon off the picnic tables. Although the invitation had suggested a cowboy-casual dress code, the gentry of Texas was easily identifiable from the orphanage's directors and staff by the diamonds and five-thousand-dollar watches tucked under their embroidered collars and cuffs. One of the subtly fancy couples was Penny and Jake Arnett Jr.

"She's still pretty, isn't she?" Hip asked Curly as the two walked to the horse barn. "Although I barely recognized her with that blonde hair."

"Couldn't miss that snake Arnett, though," said Curly. "He's still got that same old smirk."

"But he never used to wear pinky rings," said Hip. "Jeepers, he was wearing more jewelry than Liberace!"

This tickled Curly, but his laughter ended abruptly as Stretch stepped out of the barn door they were just about to walk into.

"I knew you'd make it!" said Hip, hopping around his old friend like a puppy.

"Did you bring your horse?" asked Curly, his voice gruff to disguise the catch in his throat.

Stretch pointed backwards into the barn with his thumb.

"She's in there with her old pals."

"Just like we are!" said Hip.

"Well, how in the Sam Hill did you get here without us seeing you?" said Curly, still gruff and maddeningly close to tears.

"Took the back road," said Stretch. "Didn't want to drive by all the fat cats on the front lawn. And . . . did I hear you correctly? That two of them fat cats are Penny and Jake Arnett Jr.?"

Hip and Curly exchanged sheepish looks.

"Yeah," Hip said finally. "I hope you're not sore."

"Why should I be sore?" said Stretch with an elaborate shrug of his shoulders. "That's all water under an old, old bridge." He pulled at the embroidered cuff of his cowboy shirt and then the other, and centering his Stetson on his head, he looked at two-thirds of the Daring Desperadoes and smiled. "So how're we gonna dazzle 'em today?"

———

It didn't take much to dazzle the crowd who were seated in the bleachers Rita had set up by the corral; the kids oohed and ahhed at the mere sight of cowboys on horses and the adults were happy to share in their delight. There were tricks performed—you couldn't get the Daring Desperadoes on horseback without throwing in a Suicide Drop or two—but the hit of the Cowboys for Kids event was letting the kids be cowboys, giving them rides on horses and showing them how to twirl a rope.

It was why, Hip was certain, that the burned-out Desperado that was Stretch agreed to come back. Getting a scared little kid onto the saddle and feeling him tremble, first from fear and eventually from glee, was a big treat for the cowboys, reminding them of why they themselves got up on a horse in the first place. It made everything new for a while—the excitement, the awe, and the pure love they felt for the beautiful beasts that so graciously offered their backs for human pleasure and purpose.

"We're going so fast!" said the little girl who was in the saddle with Hip now.

"Too fast?" asked Hip.

"No, let's go faster!" said the girl, the words bouncing on her laugher.

"When I grow up," said a redheaded boy riding with Curly, "I'm gonna get me a horse and be a cowboy."

"You don't say," said Curly, one of his arms a sash across the boy's scrawny chest.

"Yeah. I'm gonna get me a horse and I'm gonna name it Bullet 'cause it's gonna be as fast as one!"

"That's pretty fast," said Curly, and as he tightened his grip on the boy, he signaled his horse to rear up and walk on his hind legs, which caused the spectators to applaud and the little boy to cry out.

"You all right?" asked Curly, when Jigs was back on all fours.

The boy's head bobbed in a spasmodic nod, and when the ride was over and a worker from the orphanage helped him down, ready to load up another child, he looked up at Curly.

"Thanks," he said, solemnly. "That was the most fun I ever ever ever had in my whole life. Ever."

After every child who had wanted a ride had a ride, a dance band assembled on a small stage began to play "The Yellow Rose of Texas."

"You gonna at least say hello to her?" Curly asked Stretch as they walked the horses back to the barn.

"Who?"

"Oh come on, now. You know who. Penny."

"If I happen to run into her, I will." He said his words in a tone as aloof and bored as a French waiter, but Curly couldn't help noticing how Stretch's hand on the lead rope trembled.

Live Field Report/Sense-O-Gram

To: Charmat

From: Tandala

Two things: first, the game of tag, played with a group of kids under the age of ten. The giddiness when you dodge a hand about to touch you is positively rhapsodic. Best played at dusk, for an element of spookiness.

Second thing: garlic. They say it's life's elixir. Whether it's insomnia, anxiety, gout, dipsomania, fear of flying, indigestion, high blood pressure, low libido, or melancholia—your life's never the same when garlic comes to call!

I send you several bulbs forthwith in the hopes that they'll clear up your fear of alienation. Ha! By the way—you're It!

———

Having marveled, as he did every time he used one of Miss Rita's bathrooms, at the plush towels that felt more like velvet than terry cloth, Hip was walking down a back hallway when he heard a yelp and the sounds of a scuffle. That the noise was coming from the guest bedroom that he himself occupied surprised and irritated him, and he yanked the door open, ready to yell at the kids who were wrestling around—uninvited—in his room.

Two figures were on the bed, but they weren't kids, and they weren't wrestling, at least not in the conventional sense.

"Get off me!" said a young woman, trying valiantly to push off the bejeweled figure that was Jake Arnett Jr.

"What the—" began Hip.

"—help me!" cried the woman, and reflexively acting, Hip raced to the bed—his bed—and pulled the young woman out of the cage of Jake Arnett's arms.

The woman, whom Hip recognized as an orphanage employee, rushed to the door buttoning her shirt, and Jake scrambled off the bed, swinging wildly, in the direction of Hip's face.

"What the hell did you do to her?" said Hip, grabbing Jake's wrist before it made contact with his jaw.

"Nothing she didn't want! Now, let go of me!"

"My pleasure!" said Hip, giving Jake a powerful push.

The man fell to the bed but bounced back up, his arms swinging.

Hip stepped easily out of the range of both flailing arms but stumbled against the nightstand, and Jake was able to land a weak punch that glanced Hip's jaw. Had it not been for the pinky ring that broke Hip's skin, it wouldn't have hurt much at all.

"Hey!" Hip feeling blood on his jawline. "What'd you do that for?"

"Same reason I did this," said Jake, but Hip had regained his balance and not only blocked his opponent's next punch but was able to land a solid one of his own directly to Jake's midsection.

Arnett folded over like a broken chair.

Hip had a hundred things he could have said to the groaning man on the floor hugging his arms to his chest, but instead he pressed the toe of his cowboy boot into Jake's side—less than a kick but more than a nudge—before stepping over him.

The sun had ambled across the Western sky and was waving its goodbye to daylight. The band was playing "Crazy," the shouts and squeals of playing children providing a sporadic downbeat. Curly nodded to his sister Rita who was deep in conversation with a mayor, a three-star general, and the owner of a cosmetic company whose slogan was "Release Your Inner Tigress!" The heart that had given him trouble just weeks ago felt sure and strong, and watching his light, easy walk no one would suspect that arthritis had begun to seep into his knees and shoulders. Curly felt so goldarned good that it took him a moment to recognize, amid all the sounds of a good party, the cry for help.

Like a dog, he cocked his head, and locating the sound he raced toward it.

"Oh my God," a woman was screaming, "we thought all the kids were out of the pool! Oh my God, oh my God, oh my God!"

Well, shut your damn mouth and get him! thought Curly.

There was a rush of people now, alerted by the woman's keening, but Curly got to the pool first and dove in, toward the shadow at the bottom.

He wrapped his arm around the small body and pulled it through the water. When he burst through it, he flung himself and his cargo over the edge. His hands covered the entirety of the redheaded boy's chest, and when he pushed down, he prayed he wouldn't crush any bones. A crowd gathered around him, voices shouting for a doctor, and Curly pumped and pumped and pumped again, and the little boy turned his head and vomited a gush of water. Curly was glad there was already a whiff of piss from all the kids who had used the pool for their own toilet, because he wasn't sure he hadn't wet his own pants.

The boy struggled to his side and threw up again, and the crowd around him and Curly burst into applause.

"If I had to pinpoint a time," said Curly later, "it would be then. When I heard all that applause, I thought, 'Hey, they're clapping for me and my son.'"

———

"You're sure you want to do this?" asked Rita, as they sat inside the director's office of the Little Angels orphanage. It was a week after the near-drowning, a week after Curly had decided to adopt the little boy.

"More than anything," said Curly. "Me and Clint belong together, don't we?"

The scrawny little boy who sat on his hands nodded his head with such vigor that Rita worried he might get a brain bleed. She had asked Curly this question dozens of times—she didn't want to be a nag but she had to make sure a man in his midfifties understood the responsibilities of taking on a child—and his response was always a firm, "I'm supposed to be his dad, Rita."

Certainly his sister's decades' long support of the orphanage went a long way in greasing the wheels of adoption, and the day Curly took pen to the documents that made his paternity legal, he kissed not just his new son but his sister and the orphanage's director.

———

It had been one of Curly's rituals since he brought the boy home to sing him to sleep. The boy was so busy in the day learning how to be a cowboy himself that he was bushed by bedtime, and even as he struggled to stay awake, it usually took only one or two songs before his eyes fluttered shut one last time.

That night Hip had come in to add his voice to "Home on the Range," and the little boy—suddenly a music critic—had raised an eyebrow when Hip tried to reach a note he had no business trying to reach.

"Just a little frog in my throat," said Hip, making a big show of swallowing. "There. All gone."

"WHERE SELDOM IS HEARD, A DISCOURAGING WORD,
AND THE SKIES ARE NOT CLOUDY ALL DAY."

The little cowboy fell asleep during the second verse of "Red River Valley," and the big cowboys each got a beer out of the fridge and adjourned to Rita's porch. It was there that Hip told Curly he was leaving on Saturday, right after the ceremony.

"I was afraid this day was going to come," said Curly, scraping at the corner of the bottle's label with his thumbnail. "Who's gonna help me with the boy?"

Along with occasionally joining him in the bedtime sing-a-longs, Hip was helping Curly teach Clint how to ride.

"You don't need any help," said Hip. "This fathering stuff seems to come pretty natural to you."

A yip of a laugh escaped out of Curly's mouth.

"It does, don't it? Hip, I can't explain it, but I just knew that I was supposed to be this boy's daddy."

Deciding to play devil's advocate, Hip asked, "But what would you have done if Stretch had said, 'I made a mistake, let's keep the act going'?"

Curly tipped his hat back with one hand and with the other, palmed his bald pate.

"I would have said, 'Thanks but no thanks, Stretch,'" he said, with both resolve and surprise in his voice. "I would have said, 'That time came and went, and now's the time for me and the boy.'"

"I never figured you for a daddy," said Hip.

"Can't say that I did either. But Alice—you remember me talking about Alice, don't you, Hip?"

"'Course I do."

"I might not have told you exactly everything. Remember me telling you about how Alice died—you know, that awful accident in the horse barn?"

Hip grimaced.

"Well, what she had told me earlier that morning, before she fell off the portapotty steps, was that she was pregnant with our child."

Hip inhaled a short gust of breath.

"And you know what I had said to my Alice? I said, 'I ain't ready for no baby. Get rid of it.' Now I don't know if she ever would have—she pretty much made up her own mind about everything." Curly shrugged and drew his mouth up so that his lower lip nearly touched the tip of his nose. "And it's funny—even after she died, I can't say I really grieved the death of our baby right then. I guess it sort of built up through the years, the feelings of all I really lost." Curly's voice trailed off like a wisp of smoke in the wind. "And then this young scamp comes along."

Both men pondered the darkening landscape for a long moment.

"And something just clicked, Hip. Like a safecracker fiddling with the combination." He patted the left side of his chest. "'Click.' This door opened."

Live Field Report/Sense-O-Gram

To: Charmat
From: Tandy

This is what a little boy's faith feels like. Weightless, but stronger than steel. Hold on to it when you get too close to a black hole.

———

"You know I ain't much of a church man," Curly said, "but if Rita thinks a baptism is a good idea, who's it gonna hurt, really?"

"Remember how Stretch would drag us to Sunday services all those years ago?"

Curly nodded, and looking into the mirror, he drew his hand over his chin to make sure there weren't any errant whiskers he'd missed shaving.

"Remember how right away when he saw Penny sitting in the pew next to her aunt, he knew she was the one? Geez, you think they'll get back together, Curly?"

The older cowboy adjusted his bolo tie and admired its medallion, one Rita had a silversmith make up, one that had the initials C & C engraved in it, with the date of Clint's adoption.

"I don't know. Just yesterday Stretch said that if he were in his right mind, he'd forget all about Penny."

"Yeah, but he ain't in his right mind. He's driving all the way up to the Arnetts' to go with her to that meeting, you know."

Although the sweet brown-haired gal of his youth was now a platinum blonde with a drinking problem, a volcano of sparks flew at the Cowboys for Kids event when Penny had accepted Stretch's invitation to dance and their hands touched. Although Stretch could smell the whiskey on her, he assumed she was wobbly on her feet for the same shy and excited reasons he was, and it took more will than Stretch thought he possessed to keep himself from plastering himself to her body, to keep his lips off her lovely ballerina neck. Still, they kept a decorous distance apart while dancing, and Stretch was forever grateful to the couple who jostled them, giving them an excuse to press themselves together, so close they could feel each other's heartbeat.

Stretch was in a state he hadn't visited in years—bliss—and he wondered how he might signal the band to play the same song all night and into the next day.

"Oh, Stretch," said Penny, her head against his chest. "Why did you ever leave me?"

"I wish I could tell you a good reason," he said, leading her around the orphanage director dancing with the premier cowboy boot manufacturer who, oddly, was wearing loafers. "But there ain't none."

The song was nearly over and Stretch mourned the upcoming final notes, not wanting to let go of Penny.

"Come on, we're going home!"

One second Stretch's arms were around everything he ever wanted in life, and the next they were empty.

"Hey!" he said to Jake Arnett Jr.

"Come on!" said Jake, pulling Penny by the hand. "We're leaving!"

Penny's face, looking back at Stretch, was filled with the emotions that had worked as poison on Stretch for all their years apart: regret and apology and helplessness and a slow seething anger.

Minutes later, Hip showed up and explained why there was a Band-Aid on his jaw.

"Well, let's find that girl!" said Stretch. "Let's get her to press charges against that Arnett bastard!"

But the young woman, whose goodwill aim had been only to help raise money for the orphanage, quietly said the incident was over as far as she was concerned and there need not be another word said.

"Sometimes I'm sad I'm a man," said Hip.

"I know," said Curly. "We are most definitely part of a shameful lot."

———

The baptismal ceremony was simple, with Curly and Clint standing before the preacher in Miss Rita's parlor.

"How're you doing, sweetheart?" Stretch whispered to Penny.

"Okay," said Penny. She'd wished she could say "Great!" or "Never better!" but the fact was, it had been five days since she'd had a drink, and as much as she'd like to focus on what was happening in front of her, the larger part of her brain was fixed on Miss Rita's liquor cabinet in the next room, and the lineup of bottles it held.

One minute at a time, she said, modifying the saying to better suit her. *Concentrate on the good! You're finally divorcing your no-good, philandering, mean-spirited, poor excuse for a husband! So let's raise a glass—of Tab— to that!*

Miss Rita's cook had baked a lemon meringue pie and a chocolate cake for refreshments after the baptismal ceremony, and everyone gathered around her dining room table, trying to keep the mood light. As far as Hip was concerned, it was like playing badminton with a medicine ball, so he kept quiet.

"Clinton," said the preacher, "how's it feel to have a daddy like old Curly here?"

"It feels good," said the boy.

After one piece of chocolate cake and one and a half pieces of the lemon meringue pie, Hip put down his fork, realizing that the only thing he'd get by delaying his departure was a bellyache.

"Well," he said, pushing himself away from the table. "I guess it's time for me to hit the road."

Both Curly and Stretch jumped a little, the way people will when a loud noise goes off.

"We'll walk you out," said Stretch, his voice sounding a little higher than usual.

Hip hugged both Rita and Penny, thinking he wouldn't mind staying in their soft yet fierce embraces for, oh, maybe always, but then Stretch, his voice restored to its natural baritone, said, "Hey, Hip, let go of my woman," and everyone laughed, and the three big cowboys and one little one walked toward the door.

"Son," said Curly, clamping his hand on the little boy's shoulder. "Say your good-byes to Uncle Hip here."

"But I—" he began, but from the look on his father's face, he understood that he was not to argue, and he turned to Hip.

"Good-bye, Uncle Hip," said the boy, throwing himself into Hip's open arms. "Thanks for helping me learn how to ride. Pop says next time you see me you won't believe what I can do! I'll be able to do a Suicide Drop and the Texas Skip, and Aunt Rita says she'll buy me red cowboy boots if I do good in school this year and—and aw, don't go!"

———

Outside, the three old friends stood in a circle trying to figure out a way to say good-bye to one another. Curly scratched his chin. Stretch scratched the back of his neck.

"Well," said Hip, scratching his sideburn.

"You mean *Hell*," said Stretch. "As in 'Hell, as hard as this is to believe, I'm sure gonna miss you, you knucklehead.'"

"Likewise," said Hip. "You think . . . you think you and Penny'll get together?"

Stretch studied the toe of his cowboy boot.

"I . . . I hope so. It's gonna be a tough road for her, and I hope to be by her side . . . but you know me."

"I do know you," said Hip. "You're a son of a bitch, but you just might be there for her."

Stretch laughed. "Maybe I will be. Maybe I will." He patted Grazi's saddle pack. "So now you're gonna live the life of the Lone Ranger, huh?"

Hip shrugged. His plan was to live out in the open for a while and see what there was to be seen. Beyond that, the plan fuzzed up a bit.

Finally using his tongue for something other than pushing out the side of his cheek, Curly said, "Maybe you'll start a solo career, huh?"

"I doubt that," said Hip. "Wouldn't be much fun without you two."

After a series of throat clearing, Stretch said, "Well, you could, you know. You were the best all-around Daring Desperado, that's for sure."

Hip shivered, as if he'd drank something too cold too fast. He looked at Curly, wondering if he'd heard this crazy thing Stretch just said, but the old cowboy only nodded.

"It's true. I expect being a cowboy came the easiest for you because you loved it the most."

A month of silence passed among the cowboys.

"All right, then," said Stretch, walking in a zigzag to Hip. "We can't drag out this good-bye like a bunch of girls." He clamped his arms around Hip and gave his back a hard swat. "Good-bye, Hip. Keep your horse and your boots dry."

He stepped aside, staring at the ground with a sudden interest, allowing for Curly to step in. His embrace lasted a little longer.

"Happy trails, amigo," he whispered. "I'm gonna miss you."

Hip nodded hard, wanting but unable to respond. He nodded again, and when they stepped away from each other, Stretch's fascination in the scrubby ground had spread to all them.

Grazi pawed at the dirt as if to say, *C'mon, let's get this show on the road.*

Not knowing where he got his strength—he wanted to run back into the house, take his seat at the table, and ask for another piece of lemon meringue pie—Hip mounted his horse. He looked at his friends one last time, and because he still couldn't talk, he thumbed the brim of his cowboy hat, gave Grazi a little nudge, and rode off.

Curly and Stretch watched him until they couldn't see him any longer, and then they walked back to the house, Curly to his new son and Stretch to his long-lost love.

———

The afternoon air was baked hot, and after an hour's ride Hip rode toward a creek dappled with the light of the late afternoon sun. He got off Grazi and let his horse drink and cupped some of the cool water to his own mouth. When he stood up, a curvaceous black woman in a red and white cowgirl dress was standing beside him.

"I most surely could use a ride, mon," she said in a musical voice, and lacing his fingers together to form a step, Hip helped her mount the horse.

When he got into the saddle in front of her, Grazi turned her great head to look at him, as if to ask, *Hey, haven't I got a weight limit?* but Hip ignored her pained expression and told her to "Git!"

She began to trot, that beautiful horse who could do more than twenty-one tricks, and the woman behind Hip hugged him tight, and the three of them were one working speed and rhythm. The wind in their faces smelled like Texas Bluebonnets and the sound of Grazi's hooves on the dirt shoulder of the road sounded like drums alerting tribal members to a party.

"Hold on, Tandy," said the cowboy.

"I was about to say the same to you."

10

The chair on which Fletcher skidded forward was meant for bodies half his size. So was the desk, which broke his momentum.

"Holy moly," he muttered, and feeling a literal need to hold on to his hat, he did so. "Holy moly," he reiterated, looking around the classroom.

ABCs marched along the upper rim of the blackboard, in capital and small letters. On one side of the door, construction paper balloons with children's names on them—Katie! Matt! Bryan!—floated on a Helpers chart; from the position of Katie's balloon, it appeared she was one helpful girl. On the other side, stars rose on a Star Students chart and here Matt was shining a bit brighter than Katie. There was an upright piano against one wall and across from it a little library with a sign that read Reading Nook. A cage housing a gerbil and a small aquarium made up the Zoo Corner. A desk decorated with a papier-mâché apple and an in-and-out box made of Lincoln Logs was positioned front and center, and in front of a blackboard dusted with chalk swirls stood Tandy.

She wore wire-rimmed glasses and a rayon print dress whose fabric was making a valiant effort at containing her ample chest, and her wild hair was collected as primly as possible in a bun at the nape of her neck.

Even though he wasn't feeling particularly cheerful, Fletcher laughed at the transition the alien had made from flashy cowgirl to dowdy matron—but Tandy stared past him, as if he weren't occupying the tiny wooden desk at all.

Late afternoon sun warmed the room with an amber light, and even though Fletcher could hear the ticking of the clock, the purring motor of the aquarium, and the creak of a gerbil working out on its exercise wheel, the room was infused with the deep quiet of a classroom after school hours.

Fletcher sat waiting for Tandy to give him a sign—any sign—as to what the hell was going on. When the discomfort of sitting in the too-small chair got to be too much, he cleared his throat. This sound was ignored by Tandy, so in deference to his surroundings Fletcher raised his hand.

This was the correct gesture; Tandy broke out of her reverie.

"Yes, you in the second row there."

Fletcher cocked his head and tapped his chest.

"Yes, you. What is your question, mon?"

"Question? How about questions? How about, Where do I begin?"

"Shall we start then by reviewing your last assignment?"

Fletcher looked at the alien-cum-school-marm. He was both confused and taken aback.

"Are you serious? You brought me into this third grade classroom so—"

"—actually, it's second grade."

"Figures," grumbled Fletcher. "I've just been through the most mind-blowing experience of my life, and I'm supposed to 'review it' in a second grade classroom?"

"All I requested in the zamoosh was to land in a place of learning, and this"—she waved her hand, the nails now primly manicured—"is where we ended up. To be a second grader is to be on the cusp of great learning, Fletcher. Hoola, baby, if you were to color-image the brain of a seven-year-old and the brain of a rocket scientist . . . well, I don't have to tell you whose would show the most vibrant activity."

"So? What has that got to do with me?"

As he spoke, one finger traced the looping embroidery on the cuff on his cowboy shirt.

"You enjoyed being Hip, didn't you?" asked Tandala so kindly that Fletcher's petulance began to fade.

"Yes," he said, tearing up. "It . . . it might have been the best time of my life . . . or Hip's life . . ."

"Best Time of My Life," wrote Tandala on the chalkboard in a script so Palmer Method–perfect that those who care about penmanship and the orderliness and artistry it conveys about character would have wept. She turned to her pupil, chalk in hand.

"And why was that, Fletcher?"

"Because I was a cowboy! If you'd been around in Texas, you would have seen that! Where were you, by the way?"

"I was around—but in a backstage way . . . more of an emcee, Fletcher, than a fellow player. I introduce you to your fantasy but then for the most part hang out behind the curtain. But that doesn't mean I'm not aware of what's happening onstage." She tapped the chalk on the board. "Now continue. Why was it the best time of your life?"

"Because I got to ride Grazi! Because I had cowboys for friends—real friends—and because I was in rodeos!"

Each sentence struck him with a blow of sadness, and he sat back in his tiny chair, spent.

"Liked riding Grazi," Tandala wrote on the board. "Liked cowboy friends and rodeos."

Brushing chalk dust from her hands, she turned to find Fletcher glaring at her.

"Why do you look that way at me, Fletcher?"

"This is stupid," he said, pushing his chair back. "It's stupid that I'm sitting here in this kid's desk"—here he struggled a moment trying to extricate his legs from under it before standing up—"and what you're writing on the board is stupid. I don't need you to mock what I just went through—"

"I would never mock you!"

Considering this for a moment, Fletcher said, "You're right, I don't think you would." He sat down, but this time on top of a desk instead of behind one. It was a much better fit.

"Why, by the way, am I still dressed up like Hip but you've completely changed?"

"I . . . I don't really know," said Tandala, patting her hair in its neat bun. "It might be something deep, or it might be only that I really needed to get out of those cowboy boots—they pinched!"

Fletcher smirked.

"Well, it's true! And I never thought that cowgirl outfit flattered my figure. Not the way your cowboy clothes flatter you."

Fletcher accepted the compliment with a wistful smile.

"Thanks for letting it happen, by the way. But why *did* it happen? Why did I get to live my boyhood fantasy?"

"I really don't know, but it was fun, wasn't it?"

"Fun is hardly the word. Although seeing that it was *my* boyhood fantasy, Stretch sure had a big part in it. Sometimes it felt like his story overshadowed mine."

"That might be something you need to work on," said Tandy. "Being the star of your own show."

"Figures," mumbled Fletcher. "I'm the second lead in my own fantasy." He fiddled with the snaps on his cuff. "And why—logistically speaking—was I only Hip at certain points in his life? How come I never got to be Hip as a young boy—even though it seemed I knew his entire history? And how is it I had a fifteen-year history with the Daring Desperadoes, and yet I didn't experience all those years of being on the road with them?" He paused, feeling a lump grow in his throat. "I would have liked that."

"I know you would have, Fletcher," said Tandala, sitting down at the teacher's desk. "But providing you with Hip's whole life experience was not possible. You experienced the beginning and ending of your friendship with Stretch and Curly, and that you missed out on the middle . . . well, that's the way this particular ball has bounced."

Frustrated at her simple explanations, Fletcher rolled his eyes.

"But how did I, how did I as Hip fit so smoothly in their world, no matter what the time or place? How'd you make me fit into their lives so well?"

"Fletcher, I've tried to explain the vagaries of the time and space continuum, whereby thought has forward and backward motion—"

"—so what you're really saying is there is no real explanation that I can understand . . . other than 'That's the way the ball bounces.'"

"I would give the same explanation to your world's top astrophysicists," said Tandala kindly. "Because they wouldn't be able to grasp it either. But for now, Fletcher, all—"

"Oh, excuse me, I—"

Fletcher leaped off his desk and Tandala sprung from her chair, and they both gaped at the figure in the doorway. It was as if they were looking at a talking doll.

Wearing a red skirt and a blouse imprinted with apples, the woman was small and blonde and her cheeks were stained with two perfect blossoms of pink.

"I didn't know anyone was using my room . . . no one had—"

"—oh, excuse us," said Tandala, recovering her poise. "I had spoken to the principal. Didn't he—"

"—no, Mr. Everest didn't say a thing," said the woman, fingering the gold bug with little garnet eyes pinned on her apple-printed collar.

"Our apologies," said Tandala, walking toward her, hand extended. "I'm Miss Tandala Jones, of the Excellence 1212 program, and this is my colleague, Mr. Fletcher Weschel."

"How do you do?" said the woman politely, even as she looked wide-eyed at the grown cowboy in her classroom. "I'm Miss Plum—Wanda Plum—and I . . . the Excellence in 1212 program?"

"Yes, we're an independent foundation collecting data on those schools and teachers making a difference in our educational system, and Mr. Everest directed us to your classroom for our debriefing. We assumed you had left for the day."

"Well, I had," said Miss Plum. "I just forgot my Star Students list, and tomorrow is Recognition Day, and I, well, I want to make sure I don't miss anyone."

She race-walked to her desk and grabbed a folder out of the Lincoln Log inbox.

"I'm sorry to interrupt; please feel free to use my room as long as you need to, and . . . well, good-bye!"

Pulling the door open, she rushed through it, and Fletcher could swear he smelled apples in her wake.

"I suppose we'd better make tracks, hmm?" asked Tandala, and as she began to erase the blackboard, Fletcher said, "Oh no—you don't suppose she read that, do you?"

Wiping away the words "I Liked Being a Cowboy" and "Liked Riding Grazi," Tandala giggled. "If she did, she probably thought it had something to do with the Excellence 1212 program. Where I come up with these things I have no idea."

"Well, I feel like a dope," said Fletcher. "She probably thinks I'm some imbecile cowboy getting remedial training."

"She doesn't look the type to make such judgments. Now let's hurry."

"So that's it?" asked Fletcher, watching as her eraser mopped up the words "Liked cowboy friends and rodeos." He felt that for an assignment review, not much had been reviewed. "School's over?"

"For now," said Tandy, and Fletcher was abruptly a projectile, hurtling through time and space.

Part III

11

"B-5. B-5."

"Oh darn!"

"Did he say B-5 or G-5?"

"Melvina, can you spot me a dollar?"

As he felt himself settle in the leather wingback chair, the phrase "faster than a speeding bullet" from the *Superman* television series came into Fletcher's head.

No, a speeding bullet's a snail compared to the rate I just moved.

And unlike Superman, Fletcher didn't have to bother with finding a phone booth to change clothes in; looking down, he saw that in his rapid transit, he had shed his cowboy getup and was now wearing a sports coat and linen trousers. This clothing wasn't like his own mass-produced, machine-made suits; he could tell just by looking at his sleeve and the snow-white shirt cuff that edged out of it that this jacket was hand-tailored. He could tell by the way the fabric felt on his body that his trousers—never mind his jacket—cost more than the total of all the suits he had ever bought in his actuarial life.

"Deke, honey, are you going to thrill us all by staying for lunch?"

"I believe the question," Fletcher found himself saying, "is, 'Are you going to thrill me by allowing me to stay for lunch?'"

Titters of giggles filled the airspace around him like birdsong.

"N-31. N-31."

"Why, I believe you've got that, Aunt Edna." Pointing to the woman's bingo card, Fletcher was surprised to see how well manicured his—or Deke's—fingers were, and doubly surprised by the gold watch around his wrist. Fletcher didn't know much about watches (he'd received a Timex for his twelfth birthday and had remained loyal to the brand ever since), but he knew this one was fancy.

"Bingo!" shouted Edna, bouncing in her seat. "Bingo!"

"Excuse me," Fletcher said, gliding out of his chair as Edna began reading back her numbers.

He had no idea where the men's room was, but Deke did, and he was soon in it, standing before its mirror to see what exactly he looked like now. He looked at his own face, his own face made handsome, and he couldn't help grinning, especially when his reflection had such a nice smile.

A *dashing smile*, corrected Fletcher, and as he took a step back to get a bigger view, he saw that everything about him, from his finely cut navy sports coat, to his pearl pink ascot and matching handkerchief, to his mustache (not big and bushy like Hip's, but a narrow line above his lip) was either suave, or dashing, or both.

Wowie, thought Fletcher, palming the sides of his hair.

He had no question about who he was; this was Deke Drake, international playboy, gambler, and jewel thief. What he had no answer to was the question, What's a guy like Deke Drake doing playing Bingo at a senior citizen home?

But I suppose I'll find out, he thought, and as he winked at his reflection he wondered what the name of the cologne he was wearing was, because he was certain he had never smelled so good in his entire life.

Back in the game room, as the bingo caller thanked everyone for playing and an aide picked up the game cards and markers, Fletcher spotted the woman with the whipped confection of hair whose silver color held a definite tinge of blue.

"Oh, Deke," his aunt called, waving a hand heavy with jewelry. "Deke, honey—I've got to use the Ladies'—meet me in the dining room!"

Fletcher nodded, and as he watched the small blue-haired woman in the ruffly dress laugh and talk with the crowd of women who were also on their way to the Ladies,' he thought of Olive and how he wished she had lived to old age. But as he followed the elderly woman into the dining room, Fletcher and his memories receded until he was thoroughly, deeply Deke Drake, who was keeping a lunch date with his Aunt Edna.

———

"All right, my darling, I love your jacket—it sets off those big shoulders of yours so nicely—and your color's good, although how a busy man like you can find the time to sunbathe is beyond me—but I have one question to ask: six weeks? Six weeks since your last visit?"

"Edna, I told you I had to go to South America. I sent you—what?—a letter a week, plus postcards? And didn't I call you twice, even though long-distance from Bogotá costs an arm and a leg and a torso?"

The old woman waved her hand. "Since when can't you afford a torso?"

With her fork, she dug out a chunk of pineapple from the mound of chicken salad collapsing on top of a frond of lettuce.

"But I don't want to talk about me," he said, buttering a soft roll (stupid Americans—didn't they realize that bread should have weight and heft?). "I want to talk about you. How are you? How are they treating you?"

His aunt, who had more than enough resources to stay in Chéz Edna, had recently chosen to move into the Oceanside Manor senior citizen home.

"It's like a country club I never have to leave!" she had told Deke, "and I like to be around people my own age. People who voted for Roosevelt—Teddy Roosevelt!"

"They treat me wonderfully," said Edna, her fork rooting for more pineapple. "Don't tell Cook, but the chef here makes her Beef Wellington look like meatloaf."

"So, you won't ditch this joint and run off to the Greek Islands with me?"

"I'll go," proffered a woman across the table, whose chin barely cleared the tabletop.

"And I'd take you, Mrs. Orman," said Deke, "but there's your husband to consider."

"How many times do I have to tell you? Call me Melvina. And don't worry about my husband—he'd like it if I went away. It'd give him more time to sort his socks."

"Irving spends hours in front of his sock drawer," explained Deke's aunt. "Folding and refolding his socks, putting them in rows—"

"—he fights wars with them!" said Melvina. "I'll go in the bedroom and he's busy staging the Battle of the Argyles!"

Twirling her finger alongside her head, Edna mouthed, "He's crazy."

"Not crazy." Melvina looked at Deke and sagged. "Senile."

When he saw the spark of tears in the corners of her eyes, Deke reached across the table to squeeze her hand.

"I always remember how kind Mr. Orman was in his business counsel."

"He's still kind," said Melvina, and as she nodded, the drapery of skin under her chin quivered. "Even in his senility."

When lunch was over, Deke's aunt yawned, patting her mouth with her tiny, crocodile-skin hand. Each finger was studded with a ring, which in turn was studded with a different stone—a sapphire, an emerald, a ruby, a diamond.

"Dekey, I think it's my nap time."

"But, of course," he said, adding a Maurice Chevalier flair to his voice. "A woman like you needs her beauty sleep."

Tucking her reptilian hand in the crook of his elbow, she allowed her nephew to escort her to her room.

"So you'll be my bridge partner in the tournament tomorrow?" she said, eying her bed with an emotion close to lust.

"Wouldn't miss it for anything," said Deke, and tasting the sharp bite of hairspray as he kissed the air above his aunt's blue curls, he gently set her down on the piece of furniture she had been eyeing so covetously.

Outside the senior home, he strolled to a gleaming red 1962 Alfa Romeo Spider, hopped in, and within minutes was cruising down the coastline at a brisk eighty miles per hour, a speed that normally would have inspired the highway patrolman on duty to give chase, but seeing the delinquent driver was Deke Drake, the officer merely tipped his hat. Deke returned the salutation with a toot of his horn.

Having once been part of the motorcycle escort that led Adlai Stevenson into town and having been a drinking buddy of Totie Fields's cousin, the patrolman was no stranger to celebrity. Still, watching the blur that was Deke Drake's speeding Spider convertible, he felt touched by greatness.

Intergalatic Memo

To: Tandala
From: Charmat

Do not doubt your methods (or lack thereof). I think you are correct in having Fletcher be "Fletcher" at the outset of each new experience and when interacting with you. I believe it makes him better understand the situation before he is completely absorbed by his alter ego, and at least one of you should understand the situation—ha!

Revlor ran into a Head Council member while tanning on

the Celestial Equator and tried in his sly way to extract information as to what the meaning of this mission is. Suffice it to say the UHC member did not appreciate Revlor's inquisitiveness (they are so uptight on that board!) and consigned him to Contemplative KP. He is now wiping up spills in the Milky Way.

As to that After-Eating-Cowboy-Stew-Fart you sent, I hope you know that in opening that particular Sense-O-Gram, several nearby stars extinguished themselves.

Ames, the butler, welcomed the lord of the manor into the palatial great hall of High Palms, the grand beachfront estate Deke had grown up in.

"And how is Miss Edna today?" asked Ames.

"Quite well, thank you. Still the belle of the ball, no matter the circumstance."

"She's a lady like no other."

Deke looked through the stack of mail—equal parts invitations and bills—set aside for him on the marble-topped side table.

"She thinks highly of you, too, old chap. Just today she asked, 'And is old Ames still mooning after the laundry girl?'"

"I'm so glad my love life—or lack thereof—amuses you and Miss Edna," said Ames, his dour expression unchanging. "Cocktails on the terrace, sir?"

"Excellent idea. Right after my swim."

The lord of the manor loped up the grand curving staircase, and if standing by the butler there had been a movie director whose objective had been to capture grace and athleticism and style, he would have called into his megaphone, "Cut. Print it."

While Deke's extracurricular career at Princeton had been colorful and sometimes rash (he had run a gambling operation that depleted the funds of two senators' sons and had an affair with his comparative literature tutor, who also happened to be the daughter of the dean of the English department), he had been a serious and circumspect member of the swim team, setting several Ivy League records in the freestyle and butterfly. Now, only three pounds over his college weight, he dove into the water, and with his arms and legs moving with the precision of a factory machine he swam the length of the pool and back again. He swam for thirty minutes, altering his strokes every few laps, and when he stepped out of the pool and into the terry cloth robe Ames held open for him, there was waiting for him on an ironwork table a martini shaker, a glass, a small crystal bowl, and in the chair next to it a black woman in a tight pink uniform.

"I told her you'd speak to her later in the kitchen," whispered Ames, "but you know how pushy she can be."

"Why don't you bring another glass?" said Fletcher, who upon seeing Tandala had regained consciousness of his own self.

Pursing his lips, the butler walked stiffly into the house.

"Well, well, look at you," said Fletcher, his palm flat on the front of his robe so it wouldn't gape open as he sat down.

"Yes," she said in her Caribbean lilt. "My Earth culture receptors have informed me that I am a maid. A person hired to clean up the messes of others?"

"Well, the messes that *can* be cleaned up."

"And you," said Tandala, watching as the man shook the martini canister. "Who are you?"

"Deke Drake," said Fletcher. "Deke Drake, international ladies man and jewel thief?"

"Ahh, yes. The man no woman or diamond can resist."

"But how old am I—I mean, is Deke?"

"I would say he's a year or two older than you, Fletcher."

"But we're back in the early '60s, aren't we? I mean, I'm driving a '62 Alfa Romeo—sweet car, by the way—that looks brand new and the fashions—"

"—you must remember: there are a lot of variables to time travel, Fletcher. Signals get crossed, sound and light waves bend in unexpected ways. My guess as to why we're spending time in the early '60s is because we're returning to the time when you as a boy began acting out so many of your fantasies. Then again, my guess could be absolutely wrong. In the end we land where we land."

"It might behoove Lodge 1212—" said Fletcher, but seeing Ames open the French doors, he stopped his scolding and said, "So what exactly can I do for you, Miss Tandy?"

"I'm speaking for Helena," said Tandala, not missing a beat. "And on behalf of her, I am requesting a raise."

"If Helena needs a raise, don't you think she should come to me herself?"

"Helena is shy, Mr. Drake. And I—I am not."

"No, you are not," agreed Fletcher as Ames set an empty martini glass in front of him.

"She is the best laundress I have ever seen," said Tandy as Fletcher took a skewer of olives out of the crystal bowl and put them in the glass. "She can get stains out like nobody's business, and the creases she irons are sharp enough to do damage."

"Well, you've certainly sold me," he said, passing Tandy the filled martini glass. "A raise will be reflected in her next paycheck."

Beaming, Ames asked his master if there'd be anything else.

"I think we're quite well taken care of. Why don't you relax, Ames; I shan't need you until dinner."

"Very good, sir," said the butler with a crisp little bow.

Watching him leave, Fletcher laughed softly.

"Can you believe I said the word *shan't* in a sentence? By the way, very clever way to endear yourself to old Ames."

"Everyone knows he fancies Helena." Tandy sipped at her drink and made a face. "Isn't it funny that he can be bewitched by a woman even more foreign than I am?"

"That's a bit of an overstatement. Helena's from Poland—you're from outer space."

"I am talking about this incarnation," said Tandy, waving her hands in circles around her face and chest. "As my dark and bounteous Jamaican self! Your butler can fall for someone who has a different native language, but he has no time for me!"

"What do you mean?"

"He's said things."

"What kind of things?"

The look of anger on her face was softened by hurt. "Yesterday I was going into the kitchen and he told me to 'move my big black ass.'"

"Ames? He must have been joking."

"Is that funny to you?"

"No. Truly . . . I'm truly shocked. He's always been nothing but an absolute gentleman to me."

"He's your butler," said Tandy. "That's his job. And of course you're a color he approves of. Believe me—'big black ass' is not the worst thing he's said to me!"

"Then I'll fire him."

"Fletcher, I'm not here to disrupt things—well, at least not intentionally." She sighed. "Officially, I'm here to observe. And what I've observed . . . Hoola, baby, to dislike someone for the mere piffling fact that their outside coloring is a little different!"

"Tandy, it's ignorance, pure and—"

"—*ignorance* is not the word! Can't you humans see how your many misguided hatreds are so restrictive . . . so earthbound?"

"We've got to stay earthbound. Because of the gravity and stuff."

"I know I am what you call 'preaching to the choir.' So I shall stop." She tended to her drink as Fletcher looked toward the beach and the mild surf.

"How about this view?"

"Yes," agreed Tandy. "Earth is not chintzy in its beauty."

"Even though its inhabitants rank at the bottom of universal life forms?"

"That's the great heartbreak! You've got all this beauty, but there seems to be a perverse need to match it with ugliness."

"Ouch," said Fletcher, studying the row of palm trees whose garish wigs of leaves poked above the tiled roof of the guesthouse. "So we're doomed?"

"Fletcher, you must remember we Lodge 1212 members are the eternal optimists."

"I thought you were the fun seekers."

"One and the same." She swigged down the rest of her drink and dragged the last olive off its skewer with her teeth. "I must run. Clarence and I are going to the movies tonight."

"Who?"

"Clarence. The chauffeur you, Mr. Drake, never use because you like driving yourself."

"Ahh," said Fletcher, nodding. "*That* Clarence. Say, are you and he—"

"—I have no idea what we are. Remember, I'm as new to all of this as you are."

"And now what am I supposed—"

"—Fletcher, I am your alien sidekick, not your babysitter. My guess—judging from history—is you'll find out."

Fluttering her fingers in a wave, she scurried alongside the pool, the orbs of her behind bobbing under the thin skirt of her pink uniform, and by the time she was gone Fletcher, for all intents and purposes, was too.

Live Field Report/Sense-O-Gram

To: Charmat
From: Tandala

Several gifts from Florida: spray from an Atlantic Ocean wave. Feel the adventure and longing. A walk through an orange grove. Pick the heavy fruit that drips from the trees like round orange tears. The smell of the Okefenokee Swamp. I wonder if Earthlings know how many secrets are buried in that dank ooze? Lastly, a fried plantain I bought from a Cuban street vendor. A food that makes you want to move your hips.

———

It was a much younger Deke Drake who found himself in a bedroom that embraced swank and didn't let go. Here, velvet was an accent fabric, supporting silk, the obvious boss of the room. Silk covered the settees and divans that were arranged in small intimate collections, silk draped in great soft pleats from windows tall and wide enough to drive a Rolls Royce through, silk covered the duvet and the dozen pillows of a bed whose four posters were spiraled in carved flowers and curlicues.

———

The vanity and armoires, dressers, and end tables had first been used by French royalty centuries past (carved on the inside of one drawer were the words *Martine aime le roi*) and among the portraits of ancestors were several small paintings—a Manet, a Monet, and one by the niece of the bedroom's occupant. It was odd that this watercolor of limp daisies should engross Deke Drake, a connoisseur of fine art, but looking closely one would see that it wasn't the artistry of the painting that intrigued him but its more utilitarian purpose. The painting served as a door opening to a safe, a safe that was being successfully cracked.

Party music from a small combo rhumbaed up the wide staircase and slunk under the bedroom door as he turned the lock.

He had decided he was not going to be a jewel thief to work by cover of darkness; at this moment light from a central chandelier and two bedside lamps lit his efforts. An invited guest of the party downstairs, he hadn't yet announced his presence, instead slipping in through the servants' entry and up the back staircase, walking softly to Marjorie Allen's bedroom.

Ah, Marjorie, he thought, admiring the dowager's taste as he took a string of pearls that had been scraped out of the shells of dozens of discriminating oysters and a cuff necklace containing eight rows of diamonds that seemed to sparkle and wink at Deke in conspiratorial delight. There was a ruby ring and emerald earrings, and the thief filled the false bottom of his doctor's bag with all of them, and when his pillaging was through, he shut the safe door and closed the hinged painting of the flaccid daisies.

Not ready to have his relatively new career foiled by a moment's carelessness, he looked around the room as he padded across the cushiony carpet, making certain no monogrammed handkerchief or cigarette lighter had fallen from his pocket. Passing an ornately framed mirror, he ignored his handsome, youthful reflection and slipped down the servant stairs and out the back door, walking to his car where he safely locked the doctor's bag in the trunk of his Dusenberg.

Briskly he walked back to the mansion and into the party.

"Why, Deke, you're late!" scolded Marjorie Allen, sidling up to him as soon as he reached for a flute of champagne from a passing waiter.

"Sorry, I had some last-minute business to attend to. A crisis in Cairo."

"Oh, Deke, you work too hard."

"And that's why I play as hard as I do."

The elder woman's smile was filled with coquettishness and paper-white dentures. "Then I must invite you into my sandbox soon!"

Deke wiggled his eyebrows and they shared a laugh, and then Barbette Thigpin of the Thigpin Box and Crates fortune asked Marjorie if she'd pretty-please sacrifice Mr. Drake for one moment so that she might dance with him. She spilled a little of her champagne on Deke's dinner jacket but made up for it by pressing her breasts, sheathed in baby blue taffeta, against his chest, and whispering that Deke could choose whatever fine she must pay for her clumsiness.

Hmm, he thought, *how about the entire contents of your parents' safe?*

Out loud, he said, "Well, I do have a penalty box in my bedroom."

"Ooh," said Barbette with a giggle. "Do I have to sit in it?"

"If you'd like. But I'd prefer you recline."

Barbette purred into his ear like a contented cat, and Deke pulled her tighter as he led her in a cha-cha around a couple whose bank account contained much more fluidity than their dance steps.

———

"Enjoyed yourself, hmmm?" said Aunt Edna, pouring coffee from a silver service.

"And good morning to you," said Deke courteously, settling himself into his place at the breakfast table. Dressed in the tuxedo he had put on again after leaving Barbette's apartment, he tried not to lunge as his aunt passed him the china cup and saucer—he needed coffee and he needed it bad.

"When are you going to realize you don't need to dress for breakfast?" said Edna, trying to suppress a smile. "A nice shirt and cardigan would have been fine."

"For you, I'd consider anything less than a tuxedo an insult."

"Like hell you would." Chuckling, she clamped a sugar cube with tongs and dropped it into her nephew's cup. "Now, seriously, Deke, why waste your mornings with women left over from the night before?"

"Auntie, I should think you would have learned something about rationing from the war: leftovers are patriotic."

Coffee and laughter had an unfortunate coalescence in Edna's sinuses, and she sputtered a laugh, waving the air with one hand and dabbing at her nose with her napkin.

Deke, ever mindful of his aunt's comfort, was out of his chair and at her side, patting her on the back and asking if she was all right.

"How many times have I told you?" she said after a moment, blinking rapidly against the tears that had risen up in her eyes. "Don't make me laugh when I'm drinking my coffee!"

Deke slunk like a kicked dog back to his chair.

"You're trying to make me laugh again!"

Sitting down and rearranging his napkin on his lap, Deke looked at her mournfully.

Edna refused to take the bait.

"Now, certainly, amusing your aunt is . . . nice, but it's hardly a pastime, and certainly not a vocation."

Deke looked up at the ceiling and began to whistle.

"Now Larry Watling has said all along there's a place for you at his firm, and of course the same thing goes for Irving Orman."

"Aunt Edna, I don't want to work for the stock exchange. Nor do I want to work in banking."

"Well, Deke dear, you've been home for nearly three months. Isn't it about time you set your course and follow it?"

I already have, he thought, and then time spiraled further backwards into his not-too-distant past, and he found himself gasping for air in a bed sodden with wet sheets.

Terror gripped him as he flung himself up, gulping like a fish on a dock. He sat against the headboard, his eyes wide, the damp blanket pulled up under his chin, and gradually his racing heart slowed and the panic simmered to a low boil, and he said out loud, "You're okay, Deke. You're all right."

He looked around the room. As his eyes adjusted to the dark, he made out the shape of the dresser, the small chair, the curtains drawn across the window.

"I'm in my room," he said, orienting himself. "In my room at Mrs. Bozell's in Clapham Common, London, England."

He got up, shivering in his soggy pajamas, and put another pence into the electric heater that spit out warmth in stingy bursts.

The bear of panic that had squeezed all air out of him had backed off now, but not far. He felt it skulking in the corner, a stinking, matted-fur beast, waiting for him to show a twitch, a hiccup of fear so that it could once again pounce.

With a shaking hand, Deke reached for the robe hanging from the painted metal hook on the door. Belting it, he felt the bear move up on its haunches, but Deke gritted his teeth, ignoring it, and went into the bathroom to take a piss, to wash his face, and to brush his teeth, normal things that would push the bear back into its cage.

12

Deke Drake had been raised by his Aunt Edna, who took him in after his parents died in separate freak accidents—his father first after falling down the stairs of a New York speakeasy and his mother two months later from an infected blister she'd gotten while playing tennis.

His widowed aunt did not hesitate to claim him, taking the six-year-old to her palatial home in Palm Springs, Florida, and it was her kindness as well as the home's proximity to the vastly engrossing ocean that went a long way in patching the little boy's holes of grief and confusion. Edna answered every question he had about his parents: "No, they'd never return, but they'd always be with him." "No, they didn't die because they didn't like him—they had *loved* him." And "Yes, she would look after him for what she hoped would be a long, long time."

He made little-boy promises to honor his parents—he would never go into a speakeasy and never play tennis—but when he was twelve, the daughter of a woman in Edna's bridge club invited him to play and because he thought this girl was just about the prettiest he'd ever seen, he accepted her invitation, demonstrating in tennis an immediate, natural affinity. Lessons followed and through the years, he was always up for a game, becoming everyone's opponent or doubles partner of choice (always meticulously checking his feet for blisters after each game). As far as his first promise, by the time he came of age speakeasies were long a thing of the past, and he hardly saw it a display of disloyalty to patronize nightclubs.

He was a smart, considerate young man, and the icing on the already fine cake was that he was as handsome and stylish as a movie star.

"He looks like Tyrone Power," a member of Edna's garden club opined, "only without that awful widow's peak." "Oh, no," said another, "Deke is the spitting image of Ray Milland, only with dimples."

He had promised his aunt that he would finish college before enlisting, and so as World War II raged, he was playing football, taking exams, and dating girls from nearby Rider University and the Westminster Choir College. A week after he collected his diploma from Princeton, when he had sobered up from all the graduation parties, he joined the army, grateful the war had lasted long enough for him to play a part in it.

Edna had the highest hopes for her nephew and was convinced that the loss of his parents protected him from further tragedy and that his good fortune was innate and inviolate, even on a battlefield. She sent him off after throwing a party that featured better brands of alcohol than the graduation parties, an eight-piece band, and at least three tearful women pledging to be faithful to Deke while he was off fighting the Nazis.

He was shipped out in the fall of 1944, and while intellectually the young soldier knew that war was hard and bloody, he could not conjure the depth of the difficulty or the blood.

He was in Belgium in December when Slater, a convivial cutup able to amuse his fellow soldiers with dead-on impressions of Jimmy Durante, Jack Benny, and Ma Kettle took a bullet in the neck. A moment before, Deke had been immersed in a conversation about holiday meals with him and Kendricks, a welder from Pittsburgh whose forearms were bigger than most men's calves.

They had debated what side dishes best complemented a Christmas dinner and were on the subject of turkey dressing.

"Chestnut's the only way to go," Deke had said.

"Like hell!" answered Kendricks. "There's nothing like cornbread. Nothing like the cornbread stuffing my mother makes."

"You men are such simpletons," said Slater, "when everyone knows it's sage and onion." These last words he had sung à la Al Jolson, on bended knee, arms outstretched.

Seeing the look of outraged surprise on Slater's face, Deke had laughed, assuming it was part of his friend's act, but there was nothing funny when his friend fell to his side, a geyser of blood spurting from his neck.

"Sniper!" shouted Kendricks, as they dove behind a snow bank, and as gunfire filled the air with its pops and zings and whistles the world Deke Drake thought he knew was riven apart, and he fell into Hell.

Live Field Report/Sense-O-Gram

To: Charmat
From: Tandala

I hesitate to send you this, but you need to feel this vice of fear that squeezes these men in war. Not just a vice, but a vice with teeth, stabbing them as it chokes the air out of their lungs. Whatever mission Fletcher and I are on—this shouldn't be a part of it. Should not be a part of anyone's.

———

Peace had been declared, but not in the hearts and minds of soldiers like Deke Drake. His dreams were stained with the sights and sounds of war; with Selby, calling for his mother; Peterborough, hiccupping bubbles of blood; Brewer's frozen body being dug out of the snow, his tongue as blue as a plum. Awake, he felt assaulted by the slightest noise—a dropped book in the library, a child dragging a stick along a metal fence, a dog barking. His heart stopped with each of these noises and he'd duck or run for cover or, if he were out in public, strain against the impulse to do so. Once, drinking in a pub, he had been seized with fear when a drunk, flopping off his stool, knocked it over. The fact that he made eye contact with another customer whose face registered the same fear did not offer him consolation but embarrassment, for himself and the other serviceman, for their weakness.

What's wrong with me? Where've I gone—the easy, affable guy who could charm his way in and out of any situation, anyone's arms? Why had I thought that charm had been important? What kind of empty shell am I?

He spent hours—whole days—walking London's streets, his arms folded tight in front of him like a shield, his head down, asking himself these questions. Sometimes, looking up at a crosswalk, he'd notice passersby looking at him strangely, and he'd wonder if he'd been asking the questions aloud.

What did they die for? Slater and Selby and Peterborough? Brewer and Borris and Mellom?

The bear of panic waited at the corner, massive, clawed paws ready to grab him. Deke crossed the street, reassuring himself: *They died to save the world. They died for our freedom.* But he couldn't help his postscript: *What about theirs?*

———

His aunt wrote him chatty letters about engagements and parties and reminders to look up this Earl or that Lady, all old friends from Edna's extensive and international address book.

"Everyone here's in a celebratory mood, dear, of course, how can we not be? The war is over! That awful man Hitler is gone! I'm tremendously proud of you, Deke, for doing your part in our glorious cause, but when are you coming home? It's a question the young women keep badgering me with . . ."

Deke couldn't help his dry, cynical laugh. "That awful man Hitler"? *Now there was an understatement. And "our glorious cause"? Who did she think she was, Aunt Pittypat from* Gone with the Wind?

His own letters were jam-packed with trivia about the weather ("They're not kidding about the fog!") the food ("Bangers and hash—sounds like a car repair business rather than a breakfast staple, doesn't it?"), and his pension owner ("Her Cockney's so thick I can hardly understand her, so whatever she says, I just nod"). He never answered his aunt's questions about when he was coming home because he himself had no clue. All he knew was that he wasn't ready to go home to pretty, intact America; he needed to be in a city ravaged by war, needed to walk past jagged shells of buildings, past piles of bricks, needed to be in a place that was like him, damaged but still alive. It gave him, in a strange way, hope.

So did Millicent Preuve-Bailey.

"Of course, all my friends call me Millie," she said, after he had thrown her onto his bed in his room at Mrs. Bozell's.

Normally he wasn't the type to throw anyone onto his bed—everyone in past experience had gotten on and into his bed willingly—but if he were to throw anyone onto his bed, a woman like Millie wouldn't be the type. For one thing, she was thin as a boy (Deke preferred curves to straight lines, hills to prairies) and homely, with acne-pitted skin and deep-set eyes ringed in dark circles.

He wasn't inclined to call her Millie either but, rather, "Thief!"

"Forgive me, sir, for my confusion; I thought this was the flat of my friend."

The woman's posh accent was not one he'd expected from a burglar.

"Then what's my watch doing in your hand?"

"I was only checking the time, sir."

It was as if a switch had been turned off and all the anger that had pulsed through him was stilled.

"Is that right?" he said amicably. "Then you probably don't mind showing me what else is in your satchel."

The woman clutched the battered leather bag to her chest. "Really, sir, the contents of a woman's handbag should be considered private."

Deke laughed at her effrontery.

"In normal circumstances, I'd agreed with you. But these circumstances aren't normal." He held out his hand. "My cufflinks, please."

"Your cufflinks?" she asked quizzically.

Deke nodded, waggling his fingers.

A trace of a blush colored the woman's thin, scarred cheeks, but she smiled as she fished in her bag.

"Imagine my surprise at finding these in here," she said, depositing the cufflinks in Deke's open hand.

"Imagine."

He couldn't explain it, but a lightness of spirit had overtaken him, an invitation to take a bite of life's deliciousness. It had been a long, long time since he'd felt anything like it.

"Say, Millie," he asked, "are you hungry?"

Uncertainty briefly puckered the woman's forehead before she smiled.

"Why, a morsel or two might be to my liking."

Deke laughed again and taking the thief's hand pulled her off of his bed.

———————

After watching the thin woman eat her way through a bowl of vegetable soup, a shepherd's pie, and a plate of fish and chips, Deke said, "Excuse me, but if that was a 'morsel or two,' I'd like to see what you consider a full meal."

The woman finished the last remaining inch in her pint of Guinness and patted her mouth with a napkin.

"Weren't you ever told it's impolite to comment on a lady's eating habits?"

Deke looked around the pub. "Is there a lady here?"

"Oh, sir, you wound me."

Deke smiled at the woman and nodded to the barkeep, indicating yes, another round of Guinness.

"So, Millie," he said, clinking his pint against hers, "tell me a little about yourself. What do you do when you're not burgling?"

"I make no confessions without the presence of my solicitor," she said, and her smile, although revealing teeth in obvious need of cosmetic dentistry, was nonetheless beguiling.

"I'm sure you'll make an exception for me," said Deke, his smile offering its own beguilement. "Now, how did you come to choose me as one of your marks?"

"Convenience. I noticed the front door of the pension opened, and that's all an invitation I need."

"You make your own invitations."

"A person like me has to."

The bar girl set down two more pints and Millie waited until she left.

"It's obvious I'm not a member of the ruling class, even though I have more brains than most of those who are. Unfortunately, I live in a time and place where bloodlines are far more important than brains or imagination."

"So you became a thief because your options were limited?"

"Sometimes one's options are that limited," she said seriously. "Look at me. Even if I were the type to put my body up for sale, I hardly think I'd get enough takers to feed, let alone clothe, myself. There's always scullery work, but a maid's life has never held much appeal for me. My feeling is that it's much more fun to break into homes than to clean them."

"How is it that you sound like Greer Garson in *Mrs. Miniver*?"

"Oh, guv'nor, it's just a ruse, a course. By way of entertainin' meself."

Deke laughed—it felt so good to laugh! "I suppose you could do a fair job imitating me."

"I can imitate anyone my little ol' heart desires," she said, exaggerating Deke's slight drawl. "I'll swipe yeh accent and yeh wallet!" This sentence was said like a Brooklyn native.

Deke listened to Millie, enthralled as she told him stories of her life in crime that began when she was a little girl, abandoned by her father and trying to help her mother put food on the table.

"There wasn't a greengrocer in a two-mile radius who wasn't subject to my brother's and my fast and crafty hands."

Deke's enthrallment ended when she told him how she volunteered in a veterans' hospital during the war and stole from the patients and patients' visitors.

"I don't like hearing that," he said gruffly. "Some people are off-limits. Soldiers are off-limits. They were putting their lives on the line so they could come back home and be burgled by you when they were in the hospital?"

"It's a jungle out there," said Millie with a shrug of her narrow shoulders.

Anger heated the blood pumping through Deke's circulatory system.

"You have no idea what those men went through! You had no right to prey on them when they were at their most helpless!"

"Relax," said Millie, patting his hand. "I chose them wisely. Only the meanest, most cowardly were the beneficiaries of my light touch."

"Who are you to determine cowardice? Have you ever been to war?"

Millie stared at her pub mate for a long moment.

"No, but I've seen the aftereffects in a war hospital," she began, her voice low. "And that's the cowardice I was speaking about—the babies who cry and moan about a broken arm or leg—something that'll heal—whereas you don't hear a peep from chaps like my brother, who was lucky enough to come home, but whose legs weren't!"

Deke was the first to break their stare; he looked away as the sadness that Millie's company had made him forget sidled up to him again.

"Believe me, I've got my morals," said Millie. "I wouldn't do a job without approval from Gerry."

"Gerry being your brother?"

Millie nodded. "He spent nearly two months in hospital when he came home. That's why I started working there. I saw all the soldiers who needed company and thought, 'Oh, I can do that. I was able to make them laugh—and the ones who'd lost their sight thought I was a knockout too."

"Millie, I'm sure—"

The woman held up her hand. "I appreciate the effort, but don't even bother. I do have my sight, Deke. I've looked in mirrors. Now let me tell my story."

Deke dipped his hand, motioning her to go ahead.

"All right, so two beds from Gerry was this bloke named Henry—we were supposed to address them by their rank, but I never did; when you're in hospital you need all the friendliness you can get. Anyway, this Henry is a real bugger, always complaining"—Millie's cultivated accent was fading into an earthier one—"always yelling at the nurses, throwing his food, a right baby.

"Wasn't even hurt much—he'd taken some shrapnel in the chest and shattered an elbow, but bloody hell, at least he was whole!" She took another sip of beer and wiped her mouth with a knuckle. "His sister would come visit him—she was always decked out to the nines and as posh as could be, her nose in the air, treating everyone as if they were her and her brother's personal servants.

"So one sunny day, the sister decides that instead of sitting there complaining about how her chauffeur asked for a raise, she's going to take her brother for a walk, and the stupid cow leaves her coat and bag behind! Right there on the chair next to her brother's bed!

"'Take a look,' says Gerry. 'See if she carries around anything valuable.'

"Now I'm sneaky, remember—I've had a lifetime of sneaking around—so I pull up the chair what's got all the goodies on it and pretend to chat up the soldier who's on the other side of Henry's bed. 'Course the fellow—Reggie, I believe his name was—is sleeping; Reggie probably spends about two hours a day awake—but I carry on a conversation as I'm rifling through Sis's bag and pockets.

"The old bat had about seventy quid in her purse, but I only took a couple fivers, thinking she might not notice those. And she didn't. That was my modus operandi at hospital—never take everything, but just enough—"

"—to make a statement?" asked Deke.

"Sure," said Millie with a grin. "I like to put it to the ol' buggers. But mostly, well, I used it to buy little treats for us." She leaned toward Deke, looking at the watch he'd put on after she had tried to purloin it.

"Blimey, I'm late. Must run."

"May I come?" asked Deke.

Millie had been wriggling into her coat but stopped for a moment, one arm held out as if she were signaling a left turn.

"What—to see Gerry?"

Deke finished his last smooth sip of beer and nodded.

Buttoning up her coat, Millie stared at him and then with a shrug, said, "Fine by me."

———

Had Deke Drake ever drawn up a list of influential friends, the Preuve-Baileys would have been at the top. During his months in

London, he was a regular visitor to Gerry's flat, which was attached to his smaller locksmith business.

"I've legitimized my illegitimacy," said Gerry, showing him around the small shop.

"Yea," said Millie. "First I break into their homes, and then they come to Gerry to get new locks made!"

"I wish that's how we operated," said Gerry, who like his sister could speak in all sorts of accents and whose default one was a high-toned dialect that belied his roots. "But yes, occasionally the circumstance arises whereby both our talents come into play."

The first invitation to visit had led to a second and a third until Deke fell into a habit of having tea with them, sharing scones and hardboiled eggs and tinned-meat sandwiches. But it was the sustenance of their company that allowed him to thrive, their easy banter and quick wit, their particular worldview. Deke admitted to himself an attraction to this criminal side; he'd known cheaters and swindlers back home, but they never admitted to their cheating and swindling.

"Our mum always said there was no excuse for stealing," Millie said one evening, pouring Deke a second cup of tea. "But me and Gerry; we thought a little differently."

"Yea," said Gerry, cranking up the Cockney. "Empty stomachs got a way of excusin' a lot of iffy behavior. Not that a swell like you'd ever know what that's like."

Millie and Gerry teased him just as they ribbed each other, and rather than taking offense Deke was flattered by their willingness to treat him as an equal.

"Come on, the two of you could be as rich as the King of England and you'd still plot to break into the U.S. Treasury."

"You're probably right about that," said Gerry with a laugh.

Sometimes Deke would visit Gerry in his shop in the mornings, chatting with him in idle moments and working on self-appointed tasks when the locksmith was busy with customers or Bridget, the nurse who came round twice a week to assess his condition.

"Oh, rot," said Gerry. "Except for the fact I'm missing a pair of legs, I'm fit as a fiddle. Why don't you spend your time attending to people who need you?"

"Because you fancy me so," said the nurse as she pumped up Gerry's blood pressure cuff. "And I know you live to gaze upon my lovely face every Tuesday and Thursday."

"That's exactly what he tells me," said Deke, who was refining the rather crude backdoor ramp to make it better accessible for Gerry's wheelchair. "Your lovely face is what makes him carry on."

The two men enjoyed each other's company, having lively conversations about everything from the news of the day ("That Truman's not as dumb as he looks!" Gerry asserted) to childhood stories to jokes. They had only once talked about the war and only to ask where the other had served.

"The Argonne."

"Italy."

They were silent for a long time, Gerry sitting in his wheelchair and Deke leaning against the counter, each thinking thoughts that couldn't rise up into words, couldn't get past the many gates and doors each man thought were better kept locked.

Finally Gerry sighed and whispered, "Bloody hell," and Deke nodded, and the little bell on the door jingled, signifying a customer.

———

One evening, as Deke was leaving after a nice tea and a few games of gin rummy, Millie walked him outside and said, "I've got a little job tomorrow night—fancy coming along?"

"Sure," said Deke, surprised and excited by the invitation.

"Good. Meet me outside the Crest Hotel in Mayfair. Seven o'clock. Black tie."

"Black tie?"

Millie nodded. "You have a problem with that?"

He didn't, buying a tux the next morning. Time didn't allow a custom fit, but he had the lean, muscular body that didn't need much extra tailoring, and when he walked into the lobby of the Crest Hotel, there weren't many women whose eyes didn't linger on the fine figure that Deke Drake cut. But more than his pulchritude, his obvious kindness was admired—just look at the way he so carefully escorted the poor blind woman at his side.

The poor blind woman was Millie, dressed like a grand dame in a gray wig, fur coat, and gown. She wore dark glasses and carried a cane in the hand that wasn't resting on Deke's arm.

"Act like you belong here," whispered Millie.

"Well, I do," said Deke, and as he led her through the champagne-drinking crowd, he nodded and said things like, "Lovely to see you, "How're things?" and "Good evening."

Millie led—for despite the picture they made, it was she who was doing the leading—them to the elevator and when they stepped on with a small group of people, she told the operator, "Six, please."

On the sixth floor, Millie found the stairwell and said to Deke, "Now we'll go down a couple flights" and when they got to the fourth floor, Millie walked briskly to room 406 and extracted a hairpin from her small handbag. After a few slight maneuvers with it inside the keyhole, the lock opened.

"There we are," she said, once they were inside. "Now you check for anything they might have left lying about, and I'll try my hand at the safe."

"Whose room are we in?" whispered Deke.

"Work now, talk later," directed Millie as she opened an armoire and set about turning the dial of the safe within it.

Later, with a zippered pocket in the lining of her fur coat holding a substantial jewelry booty, she and Deke enjoyed a glass of champagne as they moved through the lobby crowd and enjoyed another in the bar at Claridges.

"To Lord and Lady Westerbrook!" whispered Millie as they toasted to their caper.

"So what was your motivation for this robbery?" asked Deke. "Was Lord Westerbrook a war profiteer? Did Lady Westerbrook consort with the enemy?"

"Simple ease is all," said Millie. "I read in the paper they were hosting a reception at the Crest, and I thought, 'Exactly what I like—a piece of cake.'"

"How'd you know what room they'd be in?"

"First lesson, my dear Yank: keep your eyes and ears open." She took a sip of champagne, smiling as the liquid fizzed inside her mouth. "See, a couple years ago, I had a friend who was a maid at the Crest, and she'd always go on and on about how mucky-mucks left the dirtiest rooms."

"So our Lord and Lady really are filthy rich?"

"Ha ha. 'All except for Lord and Lady Westerbrook,' she'd say. 'They hardly need me, they keep their room so clean, which is surprising, considering they always stay in room 406, which is puny compared to the other suites.' So my subconscious, deviant mind, never knowing when it might need something, stored that useful bit of information—room 406." Millie shrugged. "They must stay there for sentimental reasons. It's probably where he popped her cherry, back in the dark ages."

"Your sense of romance is a beautiful thing," said Deke.

"Thank you. Now, anything else you want to know?"

It turned out Deke wanted to know a lot, and under Millie and Gerry's aegis, he learned it. He struggled with the technical side of thievery, sitting for hours and hours in Gerry's shop, practicing lock picking.

"It's about listening and feeling," schooled Gerry, but Deke was clumsy at sensing tumblers and pins engaging.

"You might never have Gerry's instinct or his light touch," said Millie, watching him one afternoon as he struggled to pick a padlock. "But you've got what most thieves would kill for."

"What's that?" said Deke, banging the stubborn lock on the table.

"Charm and accessibility."

"That's right," said Gerry, who'd been doing a crossword puzzle at his perch behind the cash register. "What's a four letter word for 'needle case' again?"

"*Etui*," said Millie.

"Right" said Gerry, filling in the answer. "Quite right."

"See, Deke," said Millie. "Your station in life and your good looks will always allow you easy access into the world of the wealthy. No party crashing or dressing up in costume for you."

"And the charm part?" teased Deke.

"Well, that's really the key—no pun intended," said Gerry. "Because what is charm but the art of engaging someone? Of making a person feel special. And that someone, fully engaged and feeling special, is often willing to reveal information the charmer seeks."

"People like to talk," said Millie, "especially to someone who listens—and a charmer likes to listen. Listen and learn."

"Care to elaborate just a bit?" asked Deke.

"Well, take combination locks, for example," said Gerry. "Often people will assign numbers to them that are meaningful. So your job might be to, oh, find out their birthday—"

"—or their children's," said Millie.

"Or if they're newly married, their wedding anniversary. A good thief is really like a good doctor, always listening for clues that might help his case."

———

Deke's bear still visited, in his blood-drenched, scream-filled dreams, and in his waking life, grabbing him suddenly when he'd been doing nothing more than buying cigarettes in a tobacco shop or sitting and watching curtains of pigeons descend from the sky at Trafalgar Square. The panic would squeeze him while images played and replayed in his head: of Slater doing his impersonation of Al Jolson and the next moment spraying blood; of Mellom valiantly trying to push his own guts back into his body, a wry smile on his face; of Selby's smooth eighteen-year-old face and the sadness in his eyes as he looked at Deke, fighting for breaths that he knew would soon be ending.

"Mama?" said the teenaged soldier. "Mama?"

And the bear, nearly suffocating him with memories, would remind him of the two tears that had slid down Selby's face and how the poor boy had whispered, "Sorry." That skewed apology—it was Selby who was owed one, who shouldn't give one—taunted Deke, who felt the seismic weight of it and how it would shudder across continents and into the home and heart of the family Selby talked about: his parents, his brothers and sisters, his pregnant girlfriend.

———

"You mind if I ask you something?" Deke asked Gerry one afternoon, when rain had sliced through the air all day, cutting it up into cold, wet pieces.

Gerry looked up from behind the counter, his face wary.

"I might."

Deke nodded, knowing that he was about to cross a line both he and Gerry had drawn a long time ago.

"Do you have terrible dreams?" he asked, looking at his hands. "And do your bad dreams ever seep into your real life?"

"Yes," said Gerry simply, "and yes."

Deke raised his head, waiting for Gerry to go on, but now it was the other man's turn to stare at his hands.

"A couple of days ago," said Deke after it was clear his friend was not going to elaborate. "I was at Temple Church, just doing a little sightseeing, but then, there in the rotunda is a young American couple, laughing about what it would be like to have a wedding in a place like this instead of city hall, and the man—a kid, really—looked just like a guy in my unit who died in my arms. Just like him! For a moment I was so happy, thinking, he didn't die! and I called out, 'Selby!' as I approached them, but I must have looked crazy, because they took off as if I were a madman. And I stand there and see that the guy was probably a foot taller than Selby and had a different color hair, and I'm getting so dizzy I can barely stand, and I'm thinking, 'I'm not even safe in Temple Church.' If I can't even be safe in a fucking church, where can I be?"

Gerry didn't answer his question, his head bowed.

"And then yesterday—some guy whistles for his dog and the sound reminds me of that whining whistle of bullets. After that first terrible day, after that crazy zing of bullets had passed and my sergeant said it was okay, I could get up now, you know what occurred to me, Gerry? *I'm in a fucking slaughterhouse!*—only it wasn't cows or pigs that were being butchered but men!"

Deke felt his stomach clench at the horror of the memory, the awful realization that although this abattoir wasn't a series of pens and chutes he was trapped nonetheless, trapped in a winter-white forest, where in sane times a guy might take his girl for a sleigh ride and kiss her warm lips in the frosty air, a place where a group of friends might cross-country ski and drink beer in a cabin as they played cards and fed the fireplace with logs they'd chopped themselves. But in this forest, the snow was trampled and bloodied, and among the sprawled and crumpled bodies a soldier lay on his back, arms and legs spread the way a child's are when making a snow angel, but the bullets had stopped all movement that would have allowed the making of the angels' skirts, of its wings.

"Are you driven crazy with these kinds of thoughts, Gerry? Or is it just me who's going crazy?"

"It's not just you," said Gerry finally, his voice rusty with emotion. "But I can't speak about any of it with you. I can't speak about any of it with anyone. It took me a long time to grow the scab, and if I pick at it . . . well, you know. I can't risk bleeding to death."

His clear blue eyes met Deke's and in their stare the two men saw the other's pain, as well as their own, reflected. In that small narrow room with its cubby holes filled with all manner of locks and picks, it occurred to Deke that maybe Gerry knew more than he did, maybe there were things better left unopened. So on that cold afternoon with its weeping skies, he decided that he would have to strangle his nightmares by neglect, and that his bear would be wrestled in silence.

Intergalactic Memo

To: Tandala
From: Charmat

I appreciate your trying to send the English toffee and scones, but they were crushed under the weight of war. Even contained in a simple Sense-O-Gram, those sights and smells of that abomination were enough to cause an eclipse. And you're right; both sides die the same. I can't shake those lullabies—sung in English and German by their moms and their muttis—that lulled those dying boys into their final sleep. Please, for the sake of your Lodge brothers and sisters, refrain from sending us any more war.

13

"Oh, my God." In his cupped hands, Fletcher caught the words as they came out of his mouth, and to him it was almost as if he had vomited, so bitter and acrid was the taste in his mouth.

"Oh, Fletcher," said Tandala, and when her hand pressed against his back, Fletcher felt himself sag.

"Tandy," he whispered, "why did you make me go through all of that?"

The alien, in her housemaid dress, tsked. "I am so sorry, Fletcher, but you assume I have more power than I do. I just give you the ticket to your story—I don't tell the story."

"But my Deke Drake was a simple jewel thief! He was debonair, charming, rich—not a veteran nearly done in by war!"

She sat next to Fletcher at the wrought-iron table near the pool.

"I think," she began, "that Deke Drake is all that you say, including a veteran nearly done in by war."

"I thought this was going to be like make-believe! I wanted jewel heists—not battle scenes! Tandy, this was so horrible . . . horrible. I thought you guys were about fun!"

"Fletcher, if I had my way, you would only know the life of a circus clown, an acrobat, a regular comic on *The Ed Sullivan Show*! I don't know why you just went through that—I can only think that we can't control the fantasy when it meets reality."

"If that's reality—" began Fletcher, but then his material world swirled, and on its speed and colors he rode it into a cobblestone street in the Knightsbridge section of London.

Deke was running, and from his breathlessness it was clear that he'd been either running for a while or running at a very fast pace. Odd too was the fact that he was wearing a tuxedo and patent leather slip-ons and that Millie, breathing just as hard, was running slightly behind him.

With a quick nod toward a stone fence, he was able to communicate to her their next plan of action, and veering to the left he gracefully hurdled the fence and then helped Millie, whose long evening gown and fur wrap did not lend itself to graceful, or successful, hurdling.

"Aw, blimey!" she said, as Deke pulled her off the stone fence onto the narrow strip of ground that separated it from a hedge. "I've ruined me dress!"

"That's the least of your worries now," whispered Deke, and before she had time to brush the leaves and dirt off her skirt, he crawled through a break in the hedge.

"Follow me!" he ordered. "Hurry!"

She obeyed, dirt and pebbles collecting in the nap of her fur wrap and smearing and tearing at her gown. No sooner was she on the other side of the hedge, panting, than the two heard shouts and the approach of footsteps on the street.

"I'm sure they went this way!"

"Maybe they've gone into the park!"

"Bloody hell!"

The voices trailed off as the footsteps clattered away, but Deke and Millie lay on the ground for a long time, making sure their pursuers weren't coming back.

"Sorry," Deke finally whispered.

"Well, you get an E for effort," whispered Millie back. "But an F for execution."

"I don't know about that," said Deke, holding up the purloined wallet he still carried, and his laugh ignited one in Millie. For several long minutes, they lay on the cold ground, their laughter fed by excitement and relief.

Back in Millie's flat, they examined the wallet's contents.

"Two hundred quid!" said Millie with a low whistle. "These blokes weren't just drunks—they're rich drunks!"

"Look at this," said Deke, handing Millie an actors' guild card.

"Theo Jeffries! I thought he looked familiar! I saw him in *Two Gentlemen of Verona* at the Old Vic!"

"Now I feel bad that we robbed actors," said Deke, taking the wad of cash out of his wallet.

"You wouldn't if you'd seen his performance," said Millie, counting bills. "I'll bet they were headed to Angela Park's party, too."

Several days before, an item in the paper had alerted Millie to the reception honoring "Britain's favorite comic actress and her Saudi Arabian fiancé."

"We're going to this," she told Deke, showing him the news article.

"And I suppose you have an invitation?"

"Invitation," Millie scoffed. "Invitations are for amateurs."

They had been on their way to the Knightsbridge mansion, with the goal of relieving the actress of some of her heavy burden of jewelry, but two blocks from their destination, Millie had ordered the cabbie to stop.

In response to Deke's question as to what they were doing, she nodded to a trio of men across the street.

"This is our warm-up act."

Two of the men were fighting and both of them had piled their coats on the arm of their friend, either because they didn't want to dirty them or they wanted to better their slugging range of motion. It was obvious from their wild flailings and the laughter of the coat holder that liquor had been ingested and ingested freely.

She and Deke crossed the street, and feigning concern Millie asked the coat holder if he needed any help.

"Naw," said the man, weaving. "They're both too drunk to land a punch, and even if they did, they're too drunk to feel it."

"Bloody bastard!" said one, as he missed his target and stumbled forward.

"See what I mean?" asked the convivial coat holder before he stumbled backwards to avoid collision with the clumsy pugilist.

Staggering, he dropped one of the coats, which Millie graciously picked up.

"Here you are," she said, returning to its holder the coat but not the wallet inside its pocket.

Seeing this larcenous exchange, Deke became emboldened and decided to explore the pockets of the other coat for a wallet or money clip, but he was not as graceful as Millie.

"Hey," said the coat holder. "Just what the hell are you doing?"

His outrage was enough to make the drunken fighters release their grips, and they turned to look at Deke, who stood holding a wallet he had just plucked out of the pocket of the coat the man still held. Under the glare of accusation, he stood frozen and no doubt would have been the new target of the amateur boxers' blows had it not been for Millie's directive to run.

Deke followed Millie, who was following her own advice.

It was a wild chase, and at one point Millie was only an arm's length away from the coat holder, but in lunging for her he stumbled and fell, his mobility affected by his earlier visit to the pub.

Still, adrenaline burned off enough alcohol to make the three drunks viable pursuers. But with no liquor to burn off and with the additional fear of getting pummeled, Deke and Millie held the advantage, and by the second block they had a good lead. When they turned down a back street, Deke thought they might have lost them altogether. Still, it seemed prudent to jump the fence and hide in the hedges.

"This probably worked out for the best," said Millie, putting on the teakettle. "Even if we had gotten in—and I'm sure we would have—I'll bet the sultan had pretty tight security." She rummaged through a cupboard above the stove. "I know I have some biscuits somewhere in here."

"Four hundred and thirty quid altogether," said Deke, putting the bills in a pile. "Maybe I should go into acting."

"All good thieves are actors," said Millie. "Only at the end of our performances, we get to spend our applause."

———

Despite Gerry's tutelage, Deke never became adept at lock picking ("I'd be better off hitting my intended victim over the head with this," he said once in exasperation, waving the torque wrench with which he'd been unsuccessfully practicing), but he became quite good at picking pockets, which was, according to Millie, "the bread and butter of our profession—well, that and simple burglary." He realized if he were to be successful in the fine art of jewel theft, he'd have to hone the skills Gerry and Millie were convinced he had in spades—his charm and his ability to listen.

He began to look up those high-placed friends of his Aunt Edna's. Introductions led to invitations, and soon Deke was in and out of his work uniform—his tuxedo—and on the party circuit, mingling with British and American elite. He was invited into nearly as many beds as parties, and before he returned to America, he had successfully wrested away several necklaces, bracelets, and rings from an international group of victims.

"I want you to have this," he said, on his last visit with the two he considered his only real friends.

He poured a long pearl necklace into Millie's hand.

"And Gerry, this is for you." He gave his friend an onyx men's ring and matching cufflinks. "Courtesy of Sir Rutherford."

"Sir Terrance Rutherford?" asked Gerry, and at Deke's nod he chuckled. "Well done! I heard that prick on the radio once, going on about how he wished he could go to war but for his 'debilitating case of flat feet.'"

They had a final tea and a final game of gin rummy—Gerry beat them both—and when Deke held Millie to himself in a long good-bye hug, he was surprised to find himself teary-eyed.

Millie was not.

"Good heavens, Deke," she said, pulling away from him. "You Yanks are such bloody pushovers."

Live Field Report

To: Charmat
From: Tandala

Have a little motion sickness from all this time travel. The pastel colors and bright sunshine of 1960s Florida have been a real tonic compared to London and its gloom, which is not helped at all by the shroud of war that still covers it. Any insight as to why I am not able to penetrate the terrible layers of Fletcher's fantasies and be there with him physically? I want to fight off that bear that haunts him; it has mauled me, too! Honestly, Charmat, I don't know how against all this darkness light still shines. That's a lesson I can hardly believe: humans still find reason to laugh when they've earned every single right to never smile again.

After leaving London, Deke moved in with his Aunt Edna, who was thrilled to have him back home, even as the weeks passed into months. She realized that he needed time to assimilate back into civilian life, and when he turned down offers of employment from her friends, she tried to keep her disappointment and nagging to a minimum. When he finally told her of his plans to begin a financial consulting service, she felt her prayers for her nephew had been answered and again offered her friends, this time as clients.

He used her connections and provided them with perfectly constructive, often judicious, and always legal financial consultation, and it was through these contacts that he was able to expand on his alternative—and much more satisfying—vocation. From associations with clients, he learned any number of things about them and their associates and was able to use information about vacations, birthdays, safe locations, special occasions, and so on—to his highly profitable benefit. His base grew to an international one and his jewel thievery grew exponentially. His "profits" were fenced by the same Scotsman Millie employed, and for several years he lived and loved a self-described life of "larceny, luxury, and sex." It was a life he was perfectly happy with, but one night in Rome, after attending a party of a friend of a friend and liberating the contents of a luggage company heiress's jewelry box, he fell asleep in his own hotel room only to be visited by his long-absent bear.

He was yanked out of the peace that he had forged for himself after his long-ago talk with Gerry by a nightmare of bloody brutality, one that didn't come from the dark and twisted imaginings of a subconscious mind but worse—was an exact recounting of his first day of battle. Awakened with a jolt, with his mind and body filled with one loud and agonizing shout of "No!" he sat up in bed with such force that the headboard thumped against the wall.

His breathing ragged, he stared out wildly and felt nausea creep under his panic, for there in the corner, next to the hotel divan, crouched his bear.

"What do you want?" he said, his voice a hoarse rasp.

"More," said the bear simply.

Like a child trying to convince himself that the monster would go away if he couldn't see it, Deke closed his eyes as tightly as he could and sat frozen against the headboard. Gradually, the muscles around his eyes relaxed, but he still did not open his eyes for several minutes more. When he finally did, he nearly groaned with relief, for he was alone.

From Rome he flew to Paris to visit a client and almost did not take advantage of a party invitation, still too rattled by the bear's reappearance to concentrate on a potential mark, but when his client mentioned a particularly comely Folies Bergère dancer who was to be in attendance, Deke rallied himself and in fact not only managed a rendezvous with the French dancer in the wine cellar but appropriated the money clip of a drunken Swiss industrialist as well.

The first part of his walk back to the hotel had been cheerful—it was a balmy summer's night and the French dancer had been wonderfully acrobatic—but by and by he realized he was being followed. He knew it was neither the dancer begging for an encore nor the industrialist demanding the return of his money—but his bear.

He sped up his pace, thinking he might out-walk the beast before it jumped on him and had nearly broken into a trot when a figure suddenly appeared from the recessed doorway of a shuttered shop. Deke put on his brakes, but still he collided with the man, knocking him down.

"Sorry," said Deke, helping him up and hearing the man mutter in French, he added, "Désolé."

With great dignity, the man brushed his right sleeve with his left hand and Deke noted, with a gasp, that the sleeve was swinging, empty, and before he could censor himself, he asked in his rudimentary French, "Étiez-vous dans le guerre?"

The one-armed man nodded, answering that yes, yes, of course he was in the war, and as the bear lurked near enough for Deke to smell his breath, the American veteran reached into his pocket and stripped off a bill from the wad of Swiss francs encased in the money clip.

"Pour votre service," said Deke, and realizing he sounded as if he were giving the man a tip, and a cheap one at that, he thrust the entire wad of money into the man's hand.

The Frenchman's mustache stretched toward his ears as he smiled.

"Merci, monsieur, merci," he said and turned abruptly, before his benefactor could change his mind. But Deke didn't change his mind, and as he crossed the street, he plunged his hands into his much-emptier pockets and began to whistle, and the bear lumbered away into the shadows of the Parisian night.

Thus began his tithing, only it wasn't ten percent of his day-job income that he handed over to his church, but thirty, fifty, and sometimes one hundred percent of his night-job income, after his *agent's* (he preferred the word to *fence's*) commission.

He sent anonymous checks to VFWs around the country, to veteran's hospitals, and sometimes, after reading a story in the paper, to a veteran himself. Then he began sending anonymous checks to the Quaker Friends and other pacifist organizations. It didn't assuage his guilt over stealing—he had no guilt over stealing—rather, it lightened his heart to imagine the war-ravaged sergeant puzzling over an envelope's return address (Deke always wrote simply, "Pax") before opening it and finding a cashier's check for five thousand dollars inside. It tickled him to imagine the congregants after a Friends meeting, abuzz about a ten thousand dollar check tucked inside a piece of paper that said, "End war!" It outright made him laugh to think of the administrative secretary working in a VA hospital who opened her boss's letter containing a check for twenty thousand dollars and the message, "Buy each patient a steak on me!"

Fed now, too, the bear stayed away.

After an afternoon game of bridge, Deke was strolling through the reception area of Oceanside Manor.

"Mr. Drake," said Tina who sat at the front desk. "Miss Griggs would like to see you in admissions."

"Uh-oh," said the man for whom Tina would have left her husband of thirty-two years (at least for a weekend). "Am I being kicked out?"

"Hardly," said Tina, thinking, *How could any woman anywhere kick you out of any place?*

In Miss Griggs's office, Deke thought his knees might buckle, and it wasn't in reaction to the admissions officer's decorating taste, which celebrated cows, in figurines carved of wood, forged of metal, blown in glass, or molded of clay.

"Millie!"

"I was going to surprise you at your house," said the small woman, rising from her chair to embrace Deke. "But your butler said you were visiting your aunt, so I had the driver take me here."

"Millie!" said Deke again, holding her tight.

"Miss Preuve-Bailey tells me you were friends years ago in London," said Miss Griggs, in whose round brown eyes and wide mouth one could understand her affinity toward things bovine.

"Yes, " said Deke, holding her in front of him. "Dear, *dear* friends."

"We were, weren't we?" said Millie and something in her use of the past tense worried Deke.

"Gerry," said Deke, "Gerry is . . . ?"

"Yes, dead," said Millie simply. "Last year, actually, but he outlived all his prognoses by years, and in the end he was ready to go."

"Millie, I'm so sorry."

And he was. After he had left England, he had kept up with Millie and Gerry, flying over for biannual visits, but the past few years had been so busy, what with settling Edna into the home, and he'd let things—important things, like friendship—lapse.

"And how . . . ," he began.

"How did I find myself here?" asked Millie. "Well, with Gerry gone, I'm a little freer to come and go as I please, and in the middle of a cold, damp winter, I thought, why not visit my old Yankee pal?"

"Maybe you can talk her into putting her name on our waiting list," said Miss Griggs. "In the event she'd like to spend her senior years in our establishment."

"Which I just might," said Millie. "I think it would be peaceful spending time around so many cows."

Miss Griggs beamed. "They're calming figures, aren't they?"

"Quite."

———

Out of Miss Griggs's office Deke took Millie's hard, thin arm and led her outside before they let loose their laughter.

"Oh, Deke," said Millie, "did you see that huge porcelain Guernsey next to her chair? It was as big as a cat! And those little teeny glass ones that look like they're grazing on her desktop? Good God—there must by more than a hundred cows in there!"

"Two hundred and eighteen: I counted," said Deke. "The very first time my aunt and I were in there, she looks around and says, 'Don't you ever get cowstraphobic?' and honestly, I thought Miss Griggs was going to refuse her admission. You do not joke about those cows." He took Millie's hand in his. "I'm thrilled to see you, Millie. Thrilled, but surprised."

"I'm glad. I meant to thrill and surprise you."

"Now where are you staying?"

"I checked into the Breakers Hotel."

"Well, let's check you out then. You're staying with me."

Live Field Report/Sense-O-Gram

To: Charmat
From: Tandala

This is a kiss. And we thought meteor showers were a big deal.

————————

Millie had been visiting for more than a week but was hardly overstaying her welcome. She was a wonderful companion: partnering with Aunt Edna, she played crafty hands of bridge that always beat Deke and Melvina; attending two parties with her host, she entertained the hoity-toity folks of Palm Springs with tales of Deke as a dashing young man footloose and fancy-free in London (failing to mention, of course, both his internship as a thief and what postwar suffering he had shared with her); lounging poolside with him, she had no worries other than whether she needed more suntan lotion ("I'm already peeling like an onion," she complained) or when Ames was going to serve the next round of gin and tonics.

"It's quite a life you got for yourself here, Deke," she said, lapsing into the Cockney that liquor seemed to invite. "'Cept I thought there might be a Mrs. Drake by now."

"It may be I've got quite a life for myself," said Deke, "precisely because there is no Mrs. Drake."

"Tandy," said Millie to the maid who was bringing a pile of towels to the cabana, "don't you think it's a shame our Deke has never made an honest woman out of anyone?"

"Perhaps Mr. Drake is not interested in honest women," said the maid.

Millie hooted. "You hear that, Deke? Even your maid can see through you!"

"Oh, Tandy," said Deke after she had made her towel delivery and was on her way back to the house. "Before you leave for your date with Clarence, tell Ames to lay out my dinner clothes, will you please?"

Tandala mumbled, "Yes, sir," and walked briskly back to the house, not bothering to tell Mr. Drake there would be no date with Clarence that evening.

———

That morning as she'd been emptying the trash into the bins, Clarence had come out of the garage looking so sheepish Tandy wondered for a minute if he'd had a fender bender with Deke's favorite Alfa Romeo.

"Are you all right?" she asked, putting her arms around the chauffeur.

"Fine," he said, but as he wheeled out of her embrace she knew she wasn't going to be.

"Clarence, are you breaking up with me?"

"Tandy!" said the chauffeur, and his face seemed to pale and blush at the same time. "Of course I'm not breaking up with you."

"I am sensing you're doing something."

He wanted to kiss her then, and tried to, but she stepped back and made him miss his target.

"I'm not breaking up with you, but I am breaking our date tonight."

Tandy picked up the empty wastebasket and held it to her chest. "Why?"

"Because I have to see my mother. She's not feeling so hot, and I can't get out of it."

Tandy studied his face for a moment and then, not seeing any signs of lying, she said, "Then I'll come with you! I would love to meet your mother—I could bring some of Cook's chicken soup."

"No, no," said Clarence, his head shaking in a barely perceptible motion. "No, I don't think so, Tandy. I don't think she's ready for a woman like you."

She flushed, thinking at first Clarence was paying her a compliment, but seeing the shame and embarrassment in his face she realized he was not.

"Because of how I look?"

At Clarence's nod, Tandy turned and walked toward the house.

"Tandy, my mother's old, and old-fashioned! She still thinks the Confederacy will rise again! You know I don't feel that way!"

He grabbed her arm and she dropped the wastebasket. Picking it up, he put it over his head. "You know how I feel about you, don't you?" His voice was amplified and muffled at the same time.

She suppressed a smile. "I hope so."

"We'll go out tomorrow," Clarence promised, taking the wastebasket off his head and handing it back to her. "We'll see a double-feature!"

And so that evening, instead of going out with Clarence to the drive-in movie theater as was their Friday night routine, Tandy locked herself in her room. She knew there was something wrong with Clarence's mother that she would automatically dislike her because of her color, but still, it wounded Tandy deeply, and she slipped into bed, muffled sobs and sniffles the sad little lullaby that finally put her to sleep.

She awakened a little past ten, ravenous with an appetite fueled by self-pity and loneliness. She padded to the kitchen, imagining building the Dagwood of all Dagwood sandwiches, when she heard a thump above her. This thump came from Miss Edna's room and was not a welcome sound, as she was alone in the house: Ames was out with his laundress Helena, and Cook with her butcher, and Mr. Deke with Miss Millie.

There was another thump, and even as Tandala's heart thumped louder, she grabbed out of the refrigerator a bottle of RC Cola (*Lodge 527 might use it for fuel,* she thought, *but I'll use it for a weapon*) and made her stealthy way up the stairs.

It's probably just the wind, she reasoned, and it might have been because she aired out Miss Edna's room twice a week. That day, however, had not been an airing-out day.

Tandala was a big woman, but she moved up the staircase and down the hall as quietly and deliberately as a big cat after its quarry. As she neared Miss Edna's room, she slowed, moving along the wall like a shadow, and when she got to the slightly opened door, she tightened her grip on the pop bottle, held her breath, and looked through the three-inch crack.

She clamped her free hand over her mouth to stop the gasp that rose in her throat, but the speed of sound is faster than even the quickest hand.

Miss Millie stood frozen, one clenched fist drooling gold chains.

"Tandy!" she said as brightly as a truant running into the school principal in a pool hall.

"Millie!" said the maid, not as brightly.

"Seems you've caught me at a rather inconvenient moment," said Millie, dropping the jewelry into a black velvet bag. "Well . . . good-bye then."

Tandala was so shocked by the woman's gall that she was paralyzed for a moment, even as Millie made quick haste toward the bathroom, which had an exit door into the hallway.

Snapping out of her inertia, the maid commanded, "Not so fast!" but the thief ignored her, dashing toward the bathroom.

She was fast, but an enraged Tandala was fast and powerful, and after several loping strides across the room, she jumped on the bed and after one bounce on the mattress sailed toward Millie, who was almost to the bathroom door but not quite.

Tandy flattened her as if she were a fly on a tabletop.

"Owwwww!" came Millie's muffled cry. "Get offa me, you big ox!"

That this so-called friend of Mr. Deke was stealing from him enraged Tandy and the name-calling only amped up her anger.

"Big ox, eh?" she bellowed, tossing Millie on the bed as easily as if the Englishwoman were her baby doll. As quickly as Millie tried to scramble off, Tandy held her down, gathering Millie's hands behind her back and encircling them with her own bathrobe belt.

It was this scene that Deke, on his way to his own bedroom, came across.

"Tandy?" he asked. "Millie?" Confusion, amusement, and alarm all played in his voice. "What's going on?"

"Your maid is mangling me," said Millie.

With her hands on Millie's back, Tandala pushed her hard into the mattress and said, "You might ask why!"

Deke leaned against the doorframe, a magazine model of elegance in his white dinner jacket and untied bow tie.

"Why is Tandy mangling you, Millie?" he asked, crossing his arms.

"Because she's a big brute! Because she's unhinged! Because she's—"

Another push into the mattress cut off her last explanation.

"And you're a lying thief!" said Tandy. "Take a look at this, Mr. Deke!"

She held up the velvet bag she had wrested from Millie's hand. "How is it that your aunt's jewelry got into this bag of hers?"

As Deke looked quickly to the alcove where his aunt's opened wall safe was, dismay and shock deflated his posture.

"Millie," he said, his voice heavy with disappointment.

"You're going to believe this big baboon?"

As soon as she heard the word *baboon,* Tandy slammed her hard again into the mattress.

"Deke, tell her to get off me!"

"Tandy, you can let go," said Deke softly. "She won't be going anywhere."

Millie thought otherwise, for upon Tandy's release she tried to hurl herself off the bed, but her progress was stopped by four hands.

"Please, allow me," Deke said to Tandy, who dropped her grip.

With great courtliness, as if escorting an arthritic octogenarian across the street, Deke gently walked Millie across the room.

"Mr. and Mrs. Manthey were so sorry you had to leave before dinner was finished," he said amicably. "Has your headache cleared up?"

Stopping in front of his aunt's safe, he looked inside, and seeing the opened jewelry box half empty of its contents, he said cheerfully, "Looks like you did a good job of cleaning out her cash, Millie, but how could you miss this?" He plucked a diamond brooch from its satin compartment. "And this?" He held up a sapphire ring.

"Deke, you've got it all wrong!" said Millie, struggling to loosen the bathrobe tie that tethered her hands behind her back. "The maid did it—it was I who caught her breaking in!"

Not so gently this time, Deke led Millie to his aunt's vanity table and pushed her onto the velvet-cushioned stool.

"Why'd you do it, Millie? Was this why you visited me in the first place—this is what you planned to do all along?"

"I tell you, I didn't—" began the accused, but seeing Deke's face in the vanity mirror, her denial faded like a far-off church bell. Dropping her head, she stared into her lap, and Tandy was glad to see the thief finally expressing what looked like shame. But Millie's moment of ignominy was broken with a snort of laughter that tipped back her head.

"Aw, Deke, come on," said Millie, speaking to his reflection. "It's what I do."

"To friends?" asked Deke.

"When opportunity presents itself," she said with a shrug, "one forgets about things likes friends."

"Things like friends," repeated Deke slowly, and a flush spread up Millie's neck.

"Oh, right. *You* can take a woman to bed and then steal the jewels she's left on the bedside table, but I help myself to an old woman's safe, and suddenly there are different standards?"

"Friends don't steal from one another."

Millie snorted again. "I didn't steal from you! I stole from your aunt!"

The two thieves with a different code of ethics stared at one another in the mirror, Deke's eyes full of disappointment, Millie's defiance.

"So what are you going to do?" she asked.

"Call the cops!" offered Tandala.

Deke still held Millie by the shoulders, but now his grip softened, and he began to rub her shoulders. Millie looked to his reflection and was inspired to smile, feeling as if this tender massage signaled they would be able to work out this misunderstanding without the bother of calling in the law.

Deke smiled back, but it was the wistful smile of someone remembering something long gone and never to be found again. Millie bowed her head in real shame, knowing that he wasn't going to turn her in but he was going to turn her out.

"Mr. Drake, don't let her get away with—" began Tandy, but her words were lost in a convergence of speed, light, and sound.

14

In the zamoosh, the debonair facade of Deke Drake remained, but it was definitely Fletcher who slammed into the small classroom chair. He sat for a moment until the sensation of swirling stopped, and then with a small groan he stood up, took a deep breath, and brushed off the sleeves of his dinner jacket.

"So it's back to the pinnacle of higher learning," he said, looking at the ABCs above the blackboard, the balloon chart near the door. He stretched to the left (it had been a particularly rough zamoosh) and stretched to the right. He watched as the minute hand of the big wall clock ticked forward and then spasmed back half a space before settling onto the mark it would stay on for its full minute. He noticed the achievement charts near the door, seeing that Katie's Helper balloon was still the highest and her star had overtaken Matt on the Star Students list.

"Tandy," he said aloud. "Where are you?"

Trying to convince himself that he was restless rather than worried, he walked up to the blackboard and wrote 17 under the neatly written problem 6 + 11 = ___. At the windows, he looked out at the empty playground before pulling down and then releasing the ring of a canvas shade. He said hello to the gerbil in the Zoo Corner, tapping on the glass wall of its cage. He sat at the piano and with two fingers battered out a version of "Chopsticks." He played the simple melody over and over, until in a gust of wind Tandy was slammed against the end of the piano, the bass notes making a loud bark of protest.

"Uhhnn!" she grunted and taking a step forward rubbed her posterior, which had made hard contact with the keyboard. Although her hair was gray and collected in a bun and she wore the wire-rimmed glasses she had worn as the leader of the Excellence 1212 program, she was still wearing her maid's uniform.

"You planning on doing a little cleaning?" asked Fletcher.

Tandy looked down and smoothed her apron. "I . . . I . . ."

"Say, are you all right?"

"Why, yes . . . I," she began, looking around the classroom as if for the first time.

"Tandy," said Fletcher, gently taking her hand and pulling her next to him on the piano bench. "What's the matter?"

The alien stared at the keyboard, her hands folded on her lap.

"It was just harder than I thought."

"What was?"

As tears sparkled in her eyes, Tandy offered Fletcher a shy smile.

"Saying good-bye to Clarence."

It took Fletcher a moment to synthesize this information.

"Clarence, Deke's chauffeur?"

"Do we know any other Clarence?"

"You don't have to snap at me."

Tandy's brow remained wrinkled for a moment before easing into smoothness.

"I'm sorry, Fletcher. It's just that Clarence was so . . . unexpected. And so nice." She sighed a big sigh that lifted her epic chest. "You Earthlings really do know a thing or two about courtship."

She struck a note on the piano, and then another.

"Clarence would take me for drives in that convertible of yours," said Tandy. "Along the ocean with the radio playing." She reached up the keyboard, striking a few more notes, a sweet high tinkling. "Fletcher, Lodge 1212 can move at the speed of light, but honestly, I never felt more transported than I was in the open car, smelling the sea breeze and listening to Eartha Kitt and Tony Bennett and Peggy Lee."

Fletcher whistled. "That sounds like a heck of a radio station he tuned in to."

"Your music," said Tandy and Fletcher heard a quaver in her voice. "Hoola, baby—I was not prepared for your music."

"I'll take you to a symphony. And an opera. And maybe a Temptations concert."

"You're a nice man, Fletcher," she said, squeezing his arm. A second later she blew air through her generous lips and shook her head. "But as usual—I digress! It's you we must be focusing on. So tell me, how would you rate your Deke experience?"

Fletcher pressed his thumb against middle C and dragged his finger down two octaves and back again.

"Well," he said slowly, "my Deke never had all these complications. My Deke was all dash and intrigue . . . a guy having a great time living the high life. I never imagined him getting betrayed by the woman who taught him everything—"

"—Millie never should have done that—"

"—or going to war."

Tandala shook her head. "I did not expect that either. And I'm so sorry I couldn't—"

A loud clatter made her gasp, and Fletcher popped up like a slice of toast. But after this initial burst of action, he was stymied as to what to do next. The small blonde woman emerging from the cloakroom, armed with an umbrella, did not suffer from such inertia.

"Who *are* you?" she asked, jabbing the air with her umbrella. "Why did you come back to my classroom?"

"Miss Plum!" said Fletcher, his relief tinged with an odd sense of elation. He sat back on the bench and took a deep breath. "How are you? Remember us?"

"Shh!" she hissed, waving her sword-umbrella. "Now I am going to ask you once more, and you *will* give me an answer. Who are you?"

"Why, we're the staff of the Excellence 1212 program," said Tandy smoothly. "We met earlier, remember?"

Miss Plum banged the tip of her umbrella against the floor. "Don't give me that baloney! I've been in the cloakroom the whole time! I heard your conversation!"

"You should have made your presence known," suggested Tandy.

"You're the ones who invaded my classroom!"

If ever there was a time to reassure the second grade teacher, it was now, but all Fletcher could think of to say was, "I like your top."

Miss Plum started. It was true, it took a lot of time and effort to create the signature fruit blouses she knew delighted her students—the fabric of the one she was wearing now was imprinted with cherries—but she hardly thought it was the time and place to comment on it. Still, good manners were important enough to her that she felt obliged to say a quick thank you.

"But don't think you're distracting me from getting an answer! I need to know what you're doing here!" She had put her hands on her hips, the umbrella handle looped around her wrist, but her face suddenly did not match her authoritative body language, slackening as it did into fear.

"Oh my goodness," she said, as a shocking new idea occurred to her. She raced to the bank of windows and looked out. "Is this a worldwide invasion? Are we under alien attack?"

"Miss Plum, there's no worldwide invasion. There's no invasion at all, there's just—"

"—stay back!" warned the armed teacher, waving her umbrella as Tandy stepped toward her. "Do not underestimate me because of my size!"

I wouldn't think of it, thought Fletcher.

Tandy stood by the Reading Nook, her arms outstretched, her palms facing the ceiling. "I am not trying to underestimate you; I am only trying to reassure you."

"Then stop with the lies! I heard your conversation! Tell me what you're doing on my planet!"

"It's my planet, too," said Fletcher, stepping toward her.

"You sit!" ordered Miss Plum, pointing with her umbrella to desks near the front of the room. She cast a severe look at Tandy. "You, too!"

Tandy and Fletcher meekly squeezed into two second grade chairs, and seeing the difficult feat it was for the medium-sized man and the voluptuous woman, Miss Plum amended her order. "You may sit on top of the desks if you're more comfortable," she said, seating herself where she felt the most comfortable, behind her own teacher's desk.

Folding her hands and resting them on her blotter, she leveled a gaze at Fletcher.

"You say this is your planet, too?"

Fletcher nodded his head vigorously. "I'm an Earthling! I was minding my own business—sleeping in my own bed, as a matter of fact—when suddenly a whole pack of aliens were in my room!"

Tandala made a huffing sound. "A *whole pack*. You make it sound like we're wild animals, Fletcher."

"Shh!" directed the teacher and, chastened, Tandy pressed her lips together.

"When was this?" said Miss Plum.

"When?" asked Fletcher. "Well, it seems like years ago, but—" He looked at the neat writing on the top of the blackboard. "Is that today's date?"

The teacher craned her head to look at the board behind her and nodded.

"Then it was just days ago." He looked at Tandy. "Wow, time really does fly."

"I won't argue with that," agreed the alien.

Miss Plum rapped her knuckles on the desktop.

"I'm going to ask you what I ask my students when I need to get to the bottom of something: start at the beginning."

Tandy and Fletcher exchanged looks and resigned shrugs and proceeded to do exactly as the teacher ordered.

————

"Why, I never . . . ," said Miss Plum after Fletcher and Tandala had told their tale. Finally, she was successful at speaking aloud; she had opened her mouth three times with the intention of verbally communicating but had shut it just as many times when words failed to materialize. The fourth time proved the charm. "Who would have . . . well, all I can say is thank goodness I stayed after school to clean out the cloakroom!"

"Really?" asked Fletcher, his heart suddenly beating faster. "You're glad?"

"Of course," said Miss Plum. "I always teach my students to be open to new learning experiences—and you can't deny an alien encounter is a new learning experience!"

"Unfortunately," said Tandy, "this particular experience is going to have to end. Fletcher and I have other business to attend to."

"Oh," said the teacher, her pretty lips pouted in disappointment. "May I ask what other business?"

Rising, Tandala shrugged. "We really have no idea."

Miss Plum frowned. "If it were my mission, I think I'd like a bit more of a lesson plan."

Seeing Tandy bow her head as if scolded, Fletcher couldn't help his blurt of laughter, which made the teacher color.

"I don't mean to criticize," she said.

"No, no, I understand completely," said Tandala. "I would have liked a bit more of a lesson plan, too, but Lodge 1212 always—oh, what is your saying?—flies by the seat of its pants."

"Well, now you've got Mr. Weschel to consider," said Miss Plum, folding her hands primly in front her. "And maybe flying by the seat of your pants isn't the best method of transport for his comfort and safety."

Fletcher felt as if he had just had a medal pinned on him by a five-star general.

"Looking to history," said the teacher, writing on a pad of paper, "we could presume that you're off to another one of Fletcher's boyhood fantasies." She looked up at Fletcher. "That's also presuming you had more than two fantasies."

Fletcher blushed. "You would be correct in that presumption."

"So," said the teacher, regarding Tandy. "Is that what you're doing, exploring Mr. Weschel's imagination? And if so, for what purpose?"

The alien scratched the nape of her neck and then, with a look of concern, looked down at her shoe, as if it had caused her sudden pain.

Miss Plum was familiar with stall tactics from her students but she was abashed that the alien used them.

"You really don't have a clue, do you?"

"One does not necessarily need a map to travel."

The teacher wrote something down and clicked her pen before setting it down.

"I guess one way or another, things will be revealed."

"Exactly!" said Tandala, appreciating the young teacher's graciousness. She looked at Fletcher. "Are you ready?"

"This is so exciting!" said Miss Plum, standing up. "I've always been a fan of science fiction, but to witness science *fact*—my goodness . . . it's just so hard to believe."

"Ha!" said Fletcher. "Imagine how I feel."

The blonde teacher stared at him for a moment, her brow furrowing as if she were displeased at him, but when she broke into a smile, deep dimples flashing, Fletcher's stomach rode a little elevator.

"Like you've been through a cosmic wringer, I'll bet!"

Fletcher returned her smile, thinking, *That's it exactly.*

Part IV

15

Fletcher plunged into water and a minute later bobbed up, gasping for air from both the shock of the cold and the shock of his new circumstances. To go from bathing in the delightful attentions of Miss Plum to this plummet into glacial waters was the most jarring—and unwelcomed—zamoosh thus far.

"What's the big idea?" he sputtered, assuming Tandala was near enough to respond, but before he could see or hear her, he was yanked out of the water with such force that he cried out.

Fletcher had never tried LSD, but he imagined that what his mind was trying to process right now would make an acid trip seem like a mild caffeine rush. Speed. Water. Blue. White. Speed. Maniacal laughter—his own! Shouts. A boat. A boat ahead of him. He looked at his hands—small fat hands attached to short fat forearms—which held a triangular plastic handle attached to a rope, attached to a boat, in blue and white water, going fast. He was waterskiing.

Remembering his very first zamoosh on mountain slopes, he looked down to see if he was naked again. He couldn't see over his big belly, so he leaned forward and saw that thankfully the practical jokers had at least allowed him the modesty of swimming trunks.

"You're doing it, Shark! Way to go, Shark!"

Straightening up, he looked at the boat ahead of him and returned the waves of several boys whose heft matched his.

"Why are they calling me 'Shark,' Tandy?" Fletcher said, but he heard no answer and his skis jumped in the boat's wake as it cut sharply to the left. Losing his balance, Fletcher fell into the water with a resounding splash, and when the boat circled around and the man at the helm asked him if he was all right, it was the eleven-year-old boy nicknamed Shark who said, "Sure, Bear—but can I go around again one more time, please?"

Intergalactic Memo

To: Tandala
From: Charmat

We are hearing stirrings that there is some sort of big competition afloat and that Fletcher is key in this competition. Because Lodge 1212's tendency is not to worry, we're not worrying.... Still, if I were a member of another Lodge who was paranoid (I'm specifically thinking of those of #448 who think that wherever they are Orion's arrow is aimed at them), I'd think that you might wish to be more engaged in Fletcher's life/lives, as your extracurricular activities might harm our chances in winning whatever prize there is to be won.

But far be it from me to counsel you to do anything but party on!

Intergalactic Memo/Reply

To: Charmat
From: Tandala

I'm engaged, Charmat, hoola, baby, am I engaged.

As for Fletcher, I marvel at his adaptability and independence.

In the attached Sense-O-Gram, enjoy the moonlight stroll down the pier, and when an ocean breeze picks up, the soft grateful smile you feel when a sweater is placed across your shoulders by hands you trust.

The stated mission of Camp WoogiWikki, located on the banks of the pristine Vermont lake from which its name derived, was To Turn Your Overweight, Idle Child into a Slim, Active One! It gave hope and relief to parents of means from all over the country who responded by sending their children to its eight-week sessions. The camp was at its capacity from its inception.

"Man, I never realized there were so many rich fat kids," said one counselor to another as they watched the very first group of children disembark from assorted chauffeured cars.

"Shh!" warned Miss DuBarry, the founder, who had herself been more than pleasingly plump as a youngster. "*Fat* is not a word we allow at Camp WoogiWikki!"

I only calls 'em like I sees 'em, thought the new State College graduate with a degree in physical fitness.

It was that small exchange that gave Lucille DuBarry one of what she called her Eureka Flashes.

"We're going to give every child a nickname that will give him or her a sense of strength," she told her counselors. "A name that unlike their real one has nothing to do with how they see themselves currently."

Now in its twelfth successful year, it was Camp WoogiWikki's tradition to have its counselors, after the Camp Welcome, Camp Song, and Recitation of the Camp Pledge, conduct a New Identity Ceremony. The first year, a counselor thought names inspired by weather, like Storm, Hurricane, and Hail, denoted energy but had to rethink one moniker when the boy he called Wind tearfully told him the sort of teasing he was being subject to.

Mac (short for McKinley), a counselor who conducted his Oak cabin workouts like a drill sergeant, gave himself and his charges names of mountains—Teton, Sierra, Shasta—although one year when he had a particularly lazy camper, he often thought, *Even I can't move this mountain.*

In the Birch cabin, Shark tried to convey the thrill of waterskiing to his parents, in his biweekly letter:

I was going so fast, and it's not like it's not bumpy on that water, and I just couldn't help laughing! This boy named Cheetah nearly stayed up as long as me but not quite!! Our counselor who I hope you get to meet because he's the greatest says I might just be a natural! Well, I guess I should go now because we've got lunch and then it's the big volleyball match!
Your son, Vince (otherwise known as Shark)

It was an intense and insular eight weeks. Originally, there had been more interplay with the girls, whose weight-loss camp Miss DuBarry had situated on the other side of the lake, but the dance was dropped after its second year (the kids were so self-conscious that it seemed more a punishment than a reward), and two years later, for the same reason the coed opening and closing ceremonies were withdrawn.

Miss DuBarry tried to subvert the rivalry among the four cabins that made up the boys' camp by grouping some classes and games by age rather than cabin, but loyalty to the cabin prevailed.

In the dining hall, it was obvious that Aspen didn't mingle with Oak, who had nothing to do with Birch, who hadn't the time of day for Fir. (The cabins were already named when Miss DuBarry bought the camp, and rather than bother with repainting the signs or taking them down she kept them the way they were.) Each cabin held boys ranging from ages eight to twelve; this, thought Miss DuBarry, was a way for the older boys to inspire the younger boys and the younger boys to teach responsibility to the older ones. That hopeful scenario seemed to work itself out in public, but away from adult supervision inside their cabins little fiefdoms were constructed in which the older boys made all the decisions and used the younger boys primarily as their personal servants.

"Oaks, how many times do I have to tell you—chew your food, don't inhale it!"

Listening to Mac bark orders at his campers, Shark helped himself to another carrot from the relish tray, thinking how lucky he was to be a Birch, with a nice counselor like Bear. More than once, he had seen Oak boys vomit or cry or both from the strenuous workouts Mac put them through.

"Come on, Teton, you can't tell me you can only do thirty-two sit-ups!"

"One more time around the track, Allegheny, or it's no dinner for you!"

Now as Mac continued to berate his Oaks, Shark gave what he hoped was a reassuring smile to Zebra, the youngest member of the Birch cabin. Even as they had entered the second week, the boy was still homesick, crying himself to sleep after Lights Out. Shark could see that Mac's harsh tone affected Zebra, who was beginning to tear up.

"Don't worry," he whispered, knowing that it was one thing to cry in the dark privacy of your own bunk and a different thing altogether to cry in the dining hall, in broad daylight. "They say people who talk the toughest are really the biggest wimps."

This brought a bashful smile to the eight-year-old's face.

"You think he'th a wimp?" he lisped.

Shark nodded. "I heard him cry like a baby when Bear beat him in a swimming race."

"Really?" said Zebra, who snuck a sidelong glance at the counselor who was now reminding another boy that just because the relish tray held "free food," it didn't mean he was allowed to empty it.

"Oh, it was pathetic," said Shark.

Zebra chortled at this, and as he happily returned to his own lunch, Shark decided he was finished with his. There was still a quarter of a canned peach slice and at least two tablespoons of cottage cheese remaining in the partitions of his plate, but he was done. He had never been able to leave food on his plate—whether he liked it or not—and the act of doing so filled him with a sense of control he had never before felt. As he savored his water, he looked around the dining hall at his competition.

There were two boys from the Aspen cabin he'd have to watch—in the first week, Eagle had lost the most weight of any of the eleven-year-olds and Tern had done well at both weigh-ins, but Shark had seen them buying candy on a field trip into town last Saturday. It wasn't as if one Butterfinger or a Mars bar would torpedo everything, but still, Shark was not going to take any chances.

Absently drumming his fingers on the brim of the baseball cap in his lap (hats weren't allowed indoors), he coolly eyed the Fir table, where Copper was dabbing his mouth with his napkin. The biggest boy at camp, Copper couldn't walk ten steps without his shorts riding up and bunching in places they weren't supposed to bunch. He was always the last in a race or on a hike, having to stop to ingloriously dig his shorts out from his hindquarters. Shark had heard that his father was a nuclear physicist who had been lured to America from Austria before the war; at the last Tuesday Night Talent Show, Copper had sung German songs, wearing a pair of lederhosen for whose construction a very large cow had sacrificed its hide. He had a high sweet voice, which Miss DuBarry appreciated but which didn't do much in the way of impressing his peers.

Still, Shark sensed in Copper a steely resolution, one that would serve him well even as the rest of the kids made fun of him.

It was in Rocky at the Oak table that Shark saw his biggest rival. After the first weigh-in, he realized the two were the exact same weight—212 pounds. They were about the same height, too, although Rocky carried himself as if he were the tallest person in the whole camp, adults included. Shark thought that because they shared the same weight, they might also enjoy a cross-cabin friendship, but his first words to Rocky as they walked out of the Weigh Station—"Do you wanna—" were interrupted by an adamant "No!"

Since then, Shark had adapted Rocky's own cool-toward-every-one-but-his-own-cabin-mates demeanor.

I'm not here to make friends, he'd remind himself when he wanted to look at Hawk's marbles or play darts with Iron and Steel. *I'm here to lose weight. And win the contest.*

The contest was what was helping many of the boys stick to the rigid diet and exercise program.

"Can you believe it?" Cheetah, Shark's closest friend in the cabin, asked. "Isn't that the best prize ever?

"I know," said Shark. "I can't wait to win it!"

Jack Parrish was a former bodybuilder who had parlayed his muscles, killer smile, and thick black hair into a movie career. His movie *Agent of Impossibility* had been a huge hit, arriving the same week as *Dr. No.* Two months later, it was still number one in theaters.

"Ha!" a major film reviewer had reported. "Seems our American Jack Parrish is smoother, smarter, and better looking than Great Britain's Sean Connery!"

By a stroke of outrageous luck, Lucille DuBarry had grown up next door to Mervin Phillips, who as a child had been ridiculed for his weight as well as his black curly hair, which his mother liked to keep longish just because it was so pretty. In the neighborhood they grew up in, it was thought that the two eldest Phillips sons were the ones to watch, and not the little fat kid with the ringlets.

There were lowered expectations for the DuBarry girl, too, because of her weight, and it was this shared burden that brought Lucille and Mervin together. While the other children swam and played kickball and climbed trees, Lucille and Mervin played games of jacks and Tiddlywinks and Parcheesi or wrote plays they acted out for themselves, in which they were the beautiful princess and the handsome prince, who rather than getting picked on were revered.

The Phillips family had moved away when Mervin was twelve and Lucille was fourteen, and the friendship had died out after the two exchanged a few letters, until Lucille read an article in *Look* magazine about the actor who was about to star in a major Hollywood espionage movie.

Miss DuBarry had been drinking tea (she found it staved off hunger pains) and nearly spit it all over the pages of the magazine.

"Good heavens," she said, after swallowing hard. "That's Mervin Phillips!"

Indeed it was, although the obese boy with the black curls was now Jack Parrish, a tall and sculpted man whose musculature was shown off in several very flattering photographs and whose curls were now controlled by Brylcreem.

She wrote him immediately, in care of the magazine, and got a reply back two months later.

"So nice to hear from you, Lucille! Of course I remember you—you were my best friend!"

The letters continued, and there were even several long-distance phone calls, and when Lucille got the Eureka Flash to ask Jack (he explained gently to her that Mervin Phillips was dead and gone as far as he was concerned) if he'd ever consider doing anything "for my campers who're in the same shape you and I were in once," he couldn't have said yes faster.

"And now," Miss DuBarry had said on opening day, after the New

Identity Ceremony, "let me tell you what very special prize awaits the boy who loses the most weight."

This got the boys' attention—there was even a bigger prize than their name joining past winners on the brass plaque in the Great Hall? The nostrils of Miss DuBarry's long narrow nose pinched shut as she inhaled deeply and flared with her mighty exhale. "This one very special, hard-working boy," she said, "will be rewarded with a one-on-one meeting here at camp with Mr. Jack Parrish!"

A gasp snatched at the air—there were a few children who hadn't seen *Agent of Impossibility* yet, but they all had heard about it and knew the name of its red-hot new star.

"That's right, the day after the final weigh-in, Mr. Parrish, whom I knew as a child"—the campers traded looks and elbow jabs, the strange, skinny camp director's stock suddenly rising—"and who had something of a weight problem himself, will come to our camp and have a healthy lunch with everyone and then meet the winner for a private conversation while riding in his limousine!"

The prize had its desired effect on the children; every boy vowed to himself, "I'm going to win!"

"All right, men," said Mac, after a quick blast of his whistle. "Now we've got to get down to business. We've got a volleyball tournament to play, so after you bus your tables, get yourselves out on the north lawn pronto."

———

Shark tugged at the brim of his baseball cap and wiped his hand—again—on the seat of his shorts. The heat had colluded with his nerves to produce unending perspiration.

I'm like a fountain! he thought, tucking the ball against his hip so he could wipe his other hand.

"Come on!" yelled Rocky on the other side. "Serve the dang ball!"

Holding the ball on his sweaty palm, Shark made a sweaty fist with his other hand. Trying to visualize where he wanted the ball to land—right in between two Oak players—he announced the score, "One—seven," and hit the ball.

He was happy that it made it over the net—barely—but not so happy when Rocky jumped up and smacked the ball, not just over the net, but directly at Shark, who fought his impulse to step aside and instead tried to return it. He was unsuccessful, the ball bouncing off his forearm and sputtering into the net. The Oak boys cheered the play and Shark tried to avoid the looks of his fellow teammates.

He felt heat on his face and stared at the ground as he rotated to his new position in the front. Back home, he was the fat kid chosen last on every team, but among his peers here, these overweight and clumsy boys, he was one of the better athletes—able to hit a baseball with a bat or shoot a basketball into a net or throw a football with a fair aim—but today he was incapable of doing anything worthwhile with a volleyball.

"C'mon, Allegheny, burn it in there, burn it in," shouted Rocky as his teammate prepared to serve.

"Okay, back row," said the Birch's counselor from the sidelines. "Move back and cover your positions."

Shark wiped his hands on his shorts again and crouched into what he thought was a more prepared stance.

Pyrennes smiled at him through the net, the sort that didn't invite a return smile but that inferred, *I look forward to your annihilation.*

"Seven-one!" shouted Allegheny, striking the ball with his fist. It sailed over the net and landed in between Cheetah and Cougar, who shrugged at each other helplessly.

Even though the ball, surprisingly, was in play a few times back and forth over the net, the score continued to mount in the Oaks' favor—eight-one, nine-one, ten-one.

"Way to go boys, way to go," encouraged their counselor, Mac.

"Just keep your eyes on the ball," countered Bear.

A sudden flare of desire rose in Shark; he *would* keep his eye on the ball; he would do good by his counselor, whose belief in his Birch campers never seemed to flag. He would show Bear he was worthy of his belief; he wasn't some fat pathetic kid who couldn't hit a ball if it was right in front of his face—

Thwack! Reflexively, he'd held up a fist against the ball coming at him like a targeted bomb.

It streaked over the net like a meteor and right into an Oak player's face.

"Owwww!" squealed Rocky, blood spurting out of his nose.

Shark stood slack-jawed. It had been thrilling to hit a ball with such force, but that it had landed in the middle of Rocky's face was an extraspecial bonus.

"I think it's broken!" wailed Rocky, through cupped and bloodied hands.

"You broke his nose!" shouted Andes.

Shaking his head as if he couldn't believe one of his men had been felled by a mere volleyball, Mac put his hand on Rocky's shoulder.

"Come on, let's get some ice on that," he said, and as he led the boy off the volleyball court, Rocky stopped blubbering and turned to offer a warning to Shark.

"I'm going to get you!"

Nervousness caused an inappropriate response in Shark: he laughed.

Live Field Report

To: Charmat
From: Tandala

We may be able to defy the laws of gravity and time and space, but that we gave up crying seems to be a big step backwards. Charmat, I have cried more tears than I thought I had bodily fluid, yet after each jag I think, I needed that; I am cleansed and now ready for what's next. Clarence and I had a fight (a stupid one—my fault), and now everything makes me cry: Doris Day singing "Que Sera Sera," the awkward, flapping pink cloud of a group of flamingoes taking flight, the smell of toast in the morning. I didn't know love involves so many tears. I only know I'm willing to cry them if it means I get to keep loving!

Instant Reply

To: Tandala
From: Charmat

To quote our Cosmic Evolutions professor: *"The flip side of love is not hate but loss. The emotional entanglements of the human race are what prevent them from acting with sound clarity—imagine trying to retain equilibrium when scaling the peaks of love and plunging into the depths of a love lost."*

It's hard for me to scold you for insubordination when insubordination is one of the precepts on which our Lodge is based. Still, you seem to be falling into territory so strange and unfamiliar I am unsure I can help you escape! I urge you to step back and remember your responsibilities are to Fletcher; being more a part of his life at this moment would be more helpful to our mission, him, and you. If you're unable to do that, please send more calamari and a couple bouquets of frangipani.

———

LORNA LANDVIK

That night in the Birch cabin, Shark heard from his cabin-mates what he could expect from Rocky.

"He's gonna cream you!" said Jaguar.

"He's gonna murdalize you!" said Cheetah.

"Yeth," said Zebra. "He'th gonna cream you *and* murdalithe you!"

"It's not like I meant it," said Shark. "I didn't aim for his nose."

"That would have been so cool if you did," said Cheetah.

"Yeah, but even if you didn't," said Jaguar, "the fact is you still hit him. And he's going to want to hit you back."

"Juth ignore him," said Zebra, offering advice his mother gave him when dealing with all the kids who teased him about his weight or the way he talked. "Ignore him and thay out of hith way."

At Lights Out, the predictions of violence about to be perpetuated against him played on and on in Shark's head, an anti-lullaby shouting away sleep.

Why did I have to play volleyball today? Why couldn't I have missed that ball—like usual? Why did I even have to come to this stupid camp?

Moonlight shone through the cabin windows, and from his bottom bunk he looked at the shadowy figures in the beds across from him.

That's why, he thought sadly, seeing the hump of Jaguar's belly, the big round mass that was Cheetah's backside.

He threw his camp blanket off and rolled out of bed. He grabbed his robe (every boy brought a robe; it was good camouflage) and tiptoed across the wooden floor, taking the big flashlight on the shelf by the door.

Shark would have ignored Nature's call if he could have; the walk to the outhouses was not far from the cabins, but any distance in the dark was far enough. It wasn't as if he was afraid of the dark; he just preferred to have company in it. He race-waddled, wagging his hand back and forth on the path so that the streaking motion of light from his flashlight would scare away any mountain lions or armed-and-dangerous escaped convicts who might be hiding out at a weight-loss camp for kids in Vermont.

His relief, as he stood urinating into the hole in the small wooden outhouse, was both physical and mental. The trip there had been non-eventful and gave him confidence that the return trip would be the same. Opening the outhouse door, he began to whistle, but softly, so as to not wake up his fellow campers. The whistle froze on his lips as he stepped off the wooden steps.

"Oh, you scared me!" he whispered hoarsely to the figure standing in front of him, and the boy's shock swung into the man's surprised recognition.

"Tandy!" said Fletcher.

———

They rocked gently in the canoe, as if they were in a cradle in the water.

"So where've you been? I thought you would have been here days ago! Don't you know—"

"You are so cute," said Tandy, reaching across to poke him in his soft belly.

Fletcher swatted away her hand. "I am not cute! I'm an obese eleven-year-old boy! And if you think it's fun—it's not!"

Tandy had started talking on their walk down to the lake, but Fletcher had shushed her, telling her he'd get in trouble if he were caught outside so late at night.

"Especially with a strange woman," he whispered, adding to himself, *If only they knew how strange.*

Now that they had paddled out past the diving raft, he thought it safe to converse but reminded her to keep her voice down.

"And why are you still in your maid's uniform? Shouldn't you be dressed like a camp counselor or a grounds keeper or something?"

"I'm still under the employ of Deke Drake."

"But how can that be? I'm Deke!"

Tandy shrugged. "In my world, Mr. Drake is on a business trip to Shanghai."

"But I'm Deke!" Fletcher whispered fiercely. "Or was!"

Crossing her arms, Tandy looked him up and down. "So you're not enjoying experiencing childhood again?"

"No!" Fletcher whispered fiercely. "I mean, I was mildly chubby as a kid, but nothing like this!" He opened his robe and grabbed his chest. "This is fat! My Vince Shark was a suave and debonair spy—and this, this kid Vince aka Shark needs a training bra!" He pulled his robe around him again and folded his arms on the shelf his big belly made. As happy as he was to see Tandy, he also had an urge to smack her. "And you, for one, should not tease someone about their size."

"And what, mon, is that supposed to mean?"

"Well, look at you!" Fletcher regarded the alien with a look of disapproval. "You're like a caricature—I mean, speaking of bras, what's your cup size? A triple E? And you have to admit you're riding a pretty big caboose."

"Fletch-aire, that's mean."

"You're right, it is. Almost as mean as making me this kind of Shark."

It seemed a possibility that the canoe might sink under the weight of their mutual hurt feelings until Tandy made the effort to bail out the resentment.

"Oh, Fletcher," she said, leaning toward him and putting a hand over his. "I really am sorry you're not happy with this version of Shark. But how many times must I tell you—I have nothing to do with who and what you become. I'm just along for the ride."

"Only you haven't been! One minute I'm with you and Miss Plum and then I'm practically drowning in this very lake and you're nowhere to be found! I haven't seen you for more than two weeks—and now I find you're hanging out in my old fantasy!"

Fletcher frowned at the pout in his voice. It was bad enough having the body of an eleven-year-old; did he have to sound like one, too?

Tandala's deep breath was one that inflated her chest, and Fletcher couldn't help but chuckle.

"What?" asked Tandy eagerly, wanting to share in the joke. "What's so funny?"

"Actually, I think I spoke too soon. You look thinner to me, Tandy. Here I am at fat camp, and *you're* the one who's losing weight."

"I . . . I guess I hadn't noticed," she said, pulling at the fabric of her uniform.

They sat for a moment, the dark water gently slapping the sides of the canoe, the sky above them a celestial Vegas, welcoming its convention of stars.

"Tandy," he said softly, "are you crying?"

The face of the alien, as dear to Fletcher as a sister's might have been, was puckered in sadness and a line of tears zipped from each eye down her cheeks as if in a race.

"It's just . . . ," her hands opened. "Hoola, baby . . . all of this."

"All of what?"

She drew her head back, and he heard the click of her beaded braids. "Are you kidding? Oh, Fletcher—everything! This water!"

In an instant, without a splash, they were out of the canoe and in the lake.

"Tandy!" Fletcher gasped. "Give a guy a little warning!"

He realized as the water swished around him like a soft fabric that he wasn't wearing his robe . . . or his pajama bottoms.

"You just can't get enough of nudity, can you?"

The alien laughed. "It's just so nice to feel things on your skin."

Fletcher had to agree; it was like a submersion into cool liquid silk.

Tandy flipped over to float on her back and Fletcher followed suit, the darkness hiding their nakedness, which was completely inconsequential to both of them anyway.

"It's so different from the ocean," said Tandy, and her voice in the middle of the lake seemed as if it were the only voice in the world. "I was scared to go in the ocean—those big foamy waves crashing!—and then I learned how to body surf! I rode waves like they were an animal!"

"When did you, who showed you how to—"

"But this water. So calm, so clear . . ." She brought the fingers of one hand to her mouth. "And absolutely no taste of salt. Isn't it funny, Fletcher, that the ocean tastes like tears?"

The ocean tastes like tears, thought Fletcher, filled with an odd sense of serenity and sadness.

"We knew about water, of course," continued Tandy, "we know it's one of humans' basic necessities—but it's so much more talented than food or oxygen!"

Fletcher chuckled, knowing he'd probably never hear again water described as talented.

"Think of it—you can't swim in food or oxygen!"

"No, you can't," agreed Fletcher.

"But not only can you swim in water, you can submerge yourself in it, can water-ski on it, or . . . or skate on it when it's frozen—not to mention crush it up for those lovely tropical drinks. And you can get rained on by it—water literally falls from the sky!"

Laughing with delight, Tandy flipped over and began to breaststroke toward the drifting canoe. Fletcher followed her.

"To be out on this quiet lake, Fletcher—first floating on top of it on a boat and now in it swimming! And look! Look at how the moon shines on the surface." She jabbed her chin toward it. "Look how the light looks like a white ribbon you could walk on. Imagine—walking across a lake on moonshine!"

"I can imagine stumbling on moonshine, or throwing up on moonshine . . . "

Ignoring his play on words, Tandy said, "Only let's not imagine, let's do it!"

Appropriate clothing materialized on them as they rose.

A local fisherman, convinced that trout bit best in the middle of the night, had almost decided to leave his sleeping wife and go on a late-night trout expedition. Had he gone through with his plans, he would have seen an exotic-looking woman in a silver gown and a fat boy in a silver tuxedo walking on water on a path of moonlight. Fortunately for the fisherman and his sanity, he decided the warmth of his wife's body was the bigger lure, and he snuggled close to her, dreaming dreams far more pedestrian than what was happening on the surface of Lake WoogiWikki.

I don't want to make a cheap joke about this being a religious experience, thought Fletcher, *but it is.*

He couldn't describe the feeling; it was as if he were walking on water woven thicker by more water, his feet shattering a buoyancy that was immediately recovered with each step.

And the light! The cool silvery light of the moon!

"It's so beautiful," he whispered and then, getting one of the best ideas of his life, he said, "Tandy, let's dance."

The alien turned to him and took his other hand and there, down the glittering strip of moonlight, the couple danced. It was a waltz, and the pine trees, huddled like chaperones across the lake, began to hum. An owl hooted a soft bass and a squirrel chittered some percussion. Tandy towered over Fletcher, but they were beyond grace, and the water splashed up sparkles of applause.

"We always thought your planet was the poor relation," said Tandy, her head held at an elegant angle. "So backward, but it's . . . it's almost . . . too much."

"Tandy," whispered Fletcher. "Don't go."

She hadn't given any indication that she was going to, but Fletcher knew it to be true.

"I have to, Fletcher. You're doing fine here."

His boyish petulance rose up quick as a fist at a riot. "No, I'm not!" he said, letting go of her. "I'm about to get pulverized by this kid named Rocky! I have to exercise all the time and—"

Tandy had begun to shimmer.

"No! Don't! I need you. Where are you going?"

"Back to Florida."

The outlines of Tandy's body had completely disappeared but he could still see her face in the sparkle and light.

"Back to love," she said and smiled, her old smile—gummy, huge, and bright.

"Love?"

What remained of Tandy's face nodded, and then the pink and purple shimmer swallowed up her vast smile, and abruptly Fletcher, back in his robe and pajama bottoms, was plopped down in the canoe.

"Love?" he said, louder than he had intended, and he sat still for a moment, half expecting to see cabin lights go on. When none did, he began paddling back to shore, and by the time he had tied the boat to a stake and run back to the cabin, Fletcher was gone, and it was Shark who quietly opened the door and tiptoed to his bunk so as not to wake his fellow Birch mates.

Intergalactic Memo

To: Tandala
From: Charmat

The heavens are humming: from Alpha Centauri to Groombridge 34 there is much activity and we are a big part of it. Tandy, I am being sent signals that something big is underfoot. Do not lose focus—remember that it is Fletcher who should be first and foremost in your attentions.

You're right—the smell of suntan lotion is something that could inspire citizens of Venus to finally write that truce with Mars—but I reiterate: focus!

Intergalactic Memo/Reply

To: Charmat
From: Tandala

I was given a gardenia to tuck behind my hair, and later the lead singer of a bar band announced, "This one's for Tandy," and played "When I Fall in Love" as Clarence and I danced to what we decided was "our song." We drove along the beach afterward, and yes, I saw you winking at me. You and a billion stars.

By week four, the resolve of about half the boys was compromised by tepid weigh-ins—if they were going to all the trouble of practically starving themselves *and* having to exercise, shouldn't they lose more than a lousy two or three pounds a week?—and temptation. Eagle and Tern, whom Shark had once considered rivals, had turned their attention away from losing the most weight at camp to making the most money, a goal they worked diligently toward by selling the candy bars Tern's brother sent in packages. It was as flourishing and furtive a business as drug dealing, and both boys enjoyed the money as well as the power; discovering everyone was your friend when they knew you had Milk Duds or Almond Joys for sale.

Unfortunately for Shark, Copper was not temped by candy bars sold at a 100 percent markup and was proving himself a worthy rival, having lost weight consistently each week.

"He never rests during Rest Hour," whispered Shark to his friend Cheetah, as they sat in the Great Hall watching the weekly weigh-in. Miss DuBarry didn't believe in privacy; she figured since the main goal of the campers was to lose weight, they should share in each other's successes and failures.

Standing on a stepladder, she stood at the blackboard and wrote 237 in the box that met with the horizontal row with the heading *Copper* and the vertical one reading *Week 4*.

"Wow," said Shark, "he's down five more pounds."

He himself had already weighed in and had been happy with his loss of two-and-three-quarters pounds, until he saw how much his Fir rival had lost.

Stepping off the weighing stage, Copper bunched his mouth into a repressed smile, careful not to look any other campers in the eye. He got picked on for too many things already and knew that gloating would only exacerbate persecution.

Despite his discretion, someone made a loud farting noise as Copper walked by. It was Rocky, sitting with his friends Andes and Alps, whose laughter was the mirthless, gruff laughter of bullies.

"What a bunch of jerks," whispered Cheetah.

"No kidding," said Shark. Since the volleyball incident, Rocky had failed to deliver on his threat to get him, but Shark was convinced it was only because of his own tireless effort to stay out of his tormentor's way.

"Let's get out of here," said Shark. He took one more look at the blackboard, visualizing his total weight loss—the biggest number of all—written into the final square. "Shoot some baskets or something."

"Hah," said Cheetah mirthlessly. "You forgot. We've got Feelings."

"Oh man," said Shark, pulling down the brim of his baseball cap so it half-covered his face. "Don't make me barf."

16

Another Eureka Flash for Lucille DuBarry had occurred several years ago while she was getting her hair done.

"So how's the battle of the bulge going over there?" asked Ruby, squishing her Pall Mall in a sand-filled ashtray before she began Lucille's shampoo.

Ruby didn't actually smoke while she worked on clients, only before and after. Lucille wasn't about to complain; since the Classy Coif was the only beauty salon in town and Ruby was its proprietor, her choices were somewhat limited. Besides, no one could tame Lucille's frizzy mane the way Ruby could.

"The girls are fairly easy," explained the camp director, who divided her time between the two camps. "Girls I understand. But you know boys ... no, I guess that's my problem—I don't know them! Boys keep *all* doors closed!"

"Well, break 'em down," advised Ruby, dousing Lucille's hair with a spray attachment.

"How ... how am I supposed to do that?"

"Listen, Lucy, you know I've got a couple boys of my own, and after their dad—the bastard—ran off, they shut down. First, I liked it—yahoo—peace and quiet! But then I realized that just because they were quiet didn't mean they were staying out of trouble. Hell, no!"

"So what did you do?" asked Lucille, wincing as the hairstylist massaged her scalp a little too vigorously.

"Well, after Danny got suspended for fighting in school—and Danny was my 'good' boy—I set all three of 'em down at the kitchen table and told 'em, 'Look, you've got problems, you talk about 'em to me. And if you can't talk about 'em, write 'em down.' So that's what they did—they wrote down what had got 'em steamed or sad, and they put those pieces of paper in a little coffee can, and every Friday night I'd dump it out and we'd talk about what they'd written."

"And how did it work out?"

The steel trap of Ruby's fingers loosened for a moment.

"Well, Tom has got a good job with the creamery and just got married, and Mark drives truck for a big cross-country outfit, and Danny—well, my Danny graduates from UVM next spring!"

"You must be very proud," said Lucille, smiling, her eyes closed.

"Way I see it," Ruby said, beginning to rinse, "is them fat kids are just as sad and mad as my boys were, only they don't show it by breaking windows or skipping school. Nope. Instead they shove food in their mouths. So get 'em to talk—at least talking, they can't be eating!"

I'll make a game of it, thought Lucille, *just like Ruby did,* and when she left the salon, she tripled her usual tip, which was already more generous than any of the other Classy Coif clients gave.

———

"My favorite song is . . . ," Miss DuBarry said, throwing the ball at a boy.

Tern caught it, his misery and embarrassment evident by his red, red ears.

"No stopping to think," said Miss DuBarry. "No judging what another boy says. Just say the first thing that comes to your mind and then throw the ball. Speak and throw."

"'Row, Row, Row Your Boat!'" said Tern, flinging the ball at Iron.

Rocky and his friend Pyrennes laughed, but the other boys standing in a circle did not, knowing that when it came their turn, they might just as easily come up with as dumb an answer.

"'The Theme from *Agent of Impossibility!*'" shouted Pyrennes, and every boy and Miss DuBarry broke the rule of judging and nodded their approval; that was a good song.

Pyrennes threw the ball as hard as he could at Copper, who, surprising many, didn't drop it.

"'Für Elise!'"

One or two of the boys who had had piano lessons recognized the song, but the others didn't; nevertheless, because it was spoken by Copper, it was assumed it was a lot more stupid than even "Row, Row, Row Your Boat," but Copper hurled the ball so fast at Rocky that the impulse to laugh was cut short.

Rocky caught the ball and glared at Copper.

"Speak and throw!" reminded Miss DuBarry.

A smile came over Rocky's face, and as he fondled the ball he turned his head to direct his stare at Shark.

"Speak and throw!"

This game was one Lucille DuBarry had culled from her background in theater (she had nearly majored in it in college); its object was to get everyone loose and in the moment. Holding on to the ball and giving dirty looks to fellow players was not part of the game, and she did not like this blatant lack of cooperation.

"Speak and throw!"

"'Big Bad John!'" shouted Rocky and threw the ball as hard as he could.

Shark's hands stung, but he had caught it.

"'Sixteen Tons!'" He could be as tough as Rocky, he thought, throwing the ball at Hawk.

When all the boys had a chance to catch and throw the ball and reveal their favorite songs, they switched to men they admired.

"President Kennedy!"

"Chuck Conners from *The Rifleman!*"

"Beethoven!" (This was Copper's.)

And when they were done with that, they switched to naming their least favorite foods.

"Baked squash!"

"Liver!"

"And onions!"

Finally Miss DuBarry showed mercy and blew the whistle around her neck.

"Good job, men, now let's all take a seat. Shark, put the ball in the bin, please."

As they sat down in a circle, energy drained out of the boys like water through a sieve. If Feelings were an elective, the Great Hall would be empty.

"Men, I know this is not your favorite camp activity," said Miss DuBarry, which made more than one boy wonder if she was a mind reader, too. "But if one fails to master one's feelings, one isn't a master at all."

Ignoring some of the ruder boys' smirks, Miss DuBarry continued.

"Now, we're going to count to eight twice. Starting with you, Iron."

"One," said Iron, with the enthusiasm of a robot with a failing battery.

Steel said, "Two," and they went around the circle until Hawk said the second and final "Eight."

"All right, then," said Miss DuBarry briskly. "Will the Ones please line up over here?"

Warily eying one another, Iron and Cheetah followed instructions.

Miss DuBarry directed the rest of the groups to join the line.

"And now," she said, her voice trilling with excitement, "shake hands with your partners."

Shark looked at the other boy who was a Four and wished hard that the floor would open and swallow him up, but the rough wooden planks did not relent. He reached out his hand, and as Rocky took it in his, squeezing it as hard as he could, Shark wondered how many bones were fractured.

"Yeah, and I'm happy about this, too," he said through a clenched smile.

"I see none of you is with your cabin-mate, which is what I intended," said Miss DuBarry, pacing the line. "Because new friendships can teach you new things. And that's what we're about to discover today."

From a leather pouch hanging on a hook on the wall, Miss DuBarry took out eight rolled tubes of paper and gave them to each twosome.

"Behold Camp WoogiWikki's Treasure Hunt!"

After unrolling the mimeographed paper, several boys held the paper to their nose and inhaled.

"Let me smell that!" said Allegheny to his partner, Hawk.

"Boys! Attention! *Please!*" Miss DuBarry pushed her cat's-eye glasses up the bony ridge of her nose and clasped her hands. "Now. At each destination shown on the map, you'll find a task. Complete the task and move on to the next one. You've got until three o'clock!"

"What about lunch?" asked Tern. "We haven't even eaten lunch yet."

"There are bagged lunches for you waiting on the picnic table outside. You may eat them there or you may eat them on the run. Remember, first team back wins!"

"Wins what?" asked Lynx, who was partnered with Copper.

"Well, that's for me to know and you to find out!" said Miss DuBarry, who in truth had been so excited creating the game she had neglected to think of a prize. "But let me just say that although the first boys back to the Great Hall will be the *technical* winners, merely by playing this game, you'll all be winners!"

"Yeah, right," muttered Rocky under his breath.

"Oh, and you'll need these," she said, giving each pair a pocket-sized notebook and the short pencils golfers use to keep score. She looked harried, but certain she'd gone through all pertinent instructions she said, "Now on your mark, get set—"

She blew the whistle she wore on a lanyard around her neck, and sixteen big boys thundered out of the Great Hall and toward the picnic table. Two nine-year-olds, heading for the lake with towels yoked around their necks, scurried off the path, hoping to avoid the stampede.

Most of the boys grabbed their lunches and raced off in the direction of the beach.

"Why aren't we going?" asked Shark, as Rocky seated himself at the picnic table and began unfolding the top of a brown lunch bag. "Come on, everyone's getting ahead of us, let's—"

"Will you shut up?" said Rocky, polishing an apple on the front of his T-shirt.

"But everybody—"

"I don't give a shit about everybody. I'm going to eat my lunch." He chomped into his apple, juice spraying.

I'd like to smack you in your big fat mouth, thought Shark as he reluctantly sat down across from his partner.

"Can I at least see the map?" he asked, "so I can see where we *should* be going?"

His cheeks bulging with apple, Rocky reached into his back pocket and slapped the squished roll of paper on the table.

"Eshytee—"

"I can't understand you," said Shark crossly, "with your mouth full."

Smoothing the map out on the splintery wood tabletop and looking at the various locations, Shark traced the distance between them with his finger. Rocky gnawed away at his apple, and when it was almost down to the core, he threw it at one of the randomly placed geranium plants Miss DuBarry thought perked up the landscape.

"He scores!" he said, as the core thwacked against the stems of the plant and landed in the pot. He unfolded the wax paper from his sandwich and regarded Shark.

"What I had started to say was, every team needs a captain, and guess what, doofus—I'm ours."

"My name's Shark."

Rocky sighed. "Okay, Shark, but get this straight: I make the rules, I decide how we're gonna operate, okay?"

Shark tugged at the brim of his baseball cap and shrugged his reluctant approval.

"All those idiots," said Rocky, nodding toward the beach and the fading shouts of their competitors—"are just getting in each other's way. They'll stop to eat sooner or later—and meanwhile, we've already eaten. They'll all have left the boathouse by the time we get there—we avoid the crowd and get our stuff done easier. We'll make up our time like that." He snapped his fingers and gave Shark a self-satisfied smile. "It's all about strategy."

Shark nodded, torn between being impressed by Rocky's cool thinking and loathing the guy. He surveyed the map as he absently chewed his sandwich.

"Well, if we're thinking strategy," he said, "why don't we just go to all these places backward?"

"What do you mean, *backward?*" Rocky asked sharply.

Shark pointed to the seven destinations on the map.

"Look, each place is numbered, but it doesn't say anywhere that we've got to go to any of these places in any order."

Not particularly fond of input from his subordinate, Rocky's forehead creased.

"See, we could really avoid the crowd if we didn't go to each place in order. We could do it backwards, go to 7 first, then 6."

Rocky surveyed the map. "But what if the clue at the first spot leads to the clue in the second spot?"

Shark idly picked a shred of turkey out of his teeth and flicked it on the ground.

"Miss DuBarry didn't say *clues*. She said *tasks*." He pointed to 1, the boathouse, and at 2, the camp library on the map. "I'd bet one place has nothing to do with the other."

Crumpling his empty milk carton in his hand, Rocky stood up.

"All right, but if you're wrong, I'll kill you."

"That might get in the way of us winning."

"Funny," said Rocky, standing up. "And remember, I'm still the captain, and what I say goes."

Shark got up to follow him but not before quickly collecting his own garbage as well as the lunch detritus Rocky left behind and depositing it all into the big waste receptacle that sat five feet away from the picnic table.

"So where are we headed?" he asked, chasing Rocky up the path.

"To number 7, stupid! We said we're going backwards."

Shark pushed Rocky's shoulder in what could have been an affectionate gesture but wasn't.

"Hey!" said Rocky.

"You call me *stupid* again and I'm out," said Shark. "I'll drop out and we'll be disqualified, got it?"

Rocky stood on the path, his hands balled up into chubby fists.

"You ever touch me again and I'll drop out, after I kill you."

"Good," said Shark, glad his voice didn't crack. "Then I guess we understand each other."

Live Field Report/Sense-O-Gram

To: Charmat
From: Tandala

Today, as I was polishing the silver, Clarence came into the kitchen with a present.

"A rose," he said, handing me the long-stemmed flower. "Some say, 'A rose for a rose,' but in your case I have to say, 'A rose for someone ten times sweeter, twenty times more lovely, and thirty times more beautiful.'" Who wouldn't swoon at that romance? And yet it is the everyday gesture that makes me feel so cherished: the unasked-for back rub after a long afternoon of ironing . . . turning the radio dial to my favorite station, even when the ballgame's on another . . . slipping out during the movie previews to buy me the Jordan almonds I said I didn't want but really did . . .

Intergalactic Memo/Reply

To: Tandala
From: Charmat

Frankly, your ellipses frighten me.

You must wrap up all this earthly folderol as quickly as possible. Finally, thanks to a little bribe (he promised her a ride on a gravity wave), a UHC member told Revlor what exactly the Lodges have been in competition for.

This is big, so wrap it up!

———

When they reached the weight room, both boys were panting with exertion, and when Rocky flung open the door, he shouted, "There it is!"

Following behind him, Shark saw a piece of paper thumbtacked

LORNA LANDVIK

to the bulletin board that usually posted instructional photographs on how to lift weights.

Rocky read aloud, "Do fifteen squats, ten bicep curls with five-pound weights, and five push-ups. Then tell each other what your favorite movie star in your favorite movie is, and remember to write it down in your notebooks!"

"This is stupid!" said Rocky. "I'm not going to do it! Or better yet— I'm not going to do it, but I'll say I did!"

"Well, I'm not a cheater," said Shark, and he got down on the floor and began to do his push-ups, counting off each one.

"One!"

"There's a difference in being a cheater and a sap," said Rocky.

"Two!"

"Nobody's gonna do these!"

"Three!"

"Oh, all right," said Rocky, and he joined Shark on the floor and began his own set of push-ups.

Getting up to do his squats, Shark noticed that Rocky was doing his push-ups the modified on-your-knees way (Shark had done all real ones), and he couldn't help feeling smug, although he was smart enough to feel smug internally.

Squats were not the easiest exercise for either boy, but neither laughed when the other teetered off balance.

"How many of these stupid things are we supposed to do?" said Rocky, struggling to rise and squatting down.

"Fifteen."

"I'll bet Du-DuBarry really got her jollies thinking of these stupid things."

Shark snorted a laugh at his partner's joke.

Finishing the squats, they staggered to the weight rack, and Rocky took the eight-pound barbells, doing his bicep curls faster than Shark, who had the five-pound ones.

"You're good," said Shark.

Nodding his thanks, Rocky did ten more than required.

"So who's your favorite movie star and what movie did you like him in?" asked Shark, sitting down on the weight bench and opening the notebook.

"That's easy. Jack Parrish in *Agent of Impossibility*."

"Mine, too," said Shark.

"Well, you can't use my answer."

"Hey, you don't own Jack Parrish," said Shark.

"I don't own him, but I'm gonna meet him—when I win the contest."

17

A few clouds had started forming in the summer sky, but it was still hot as the boys headed toward 6 on the map—the camp's laundry facilities.

"I sure hope that old hag isn't there," said Rocky. Each boy had to bag his dirty laundry and deliver it on assigned days to Gertl, a small, wiry woman from Albania whose nearly toothless grin and unfamiliarity with the English language frightened the younger campers and embarrassed the older ones.

"Where your dirt stuff?" said Shark, imitating the woman's signature phrase. "Give to me dirt stuff!"

Rocky allowed himself a little laugh and said, "And then the way she always pokes you in the chest when she talks—man, every time she does that, I want to grab her finger and break it right off!"

Shark had felt the same thing when the old women jabbed his collarbone with her finger, but he never would have said it out loud.

They were both relieved to find the laundry cabin empty of Gertl the Poker.

"Twenty sit-ups," said Rocky, reading the instructions taped over one of the washers. "And then we're supposed to use the clothesline post outside to do four chin-ups."

Shark groaned; he was terrible at chin-ups.

"And then get this—we're supposed to tell each other about our favorite birthday."

The laundry room smelled pleasantly of bleach and detergent, but both campers, afraid that the Albanian laundress might appear at any time to attack their collarbones, decided to do their sit-ups as well as chin-ups outside.

Again, each boy showed their particular strengths—the sit-ups were easy for Shark while Rocky huffed and puffed and grunted through his. When it came time to the chin-ups, Rocky was a machine cutting through the air while it seemed an earthquake had its epicenter in Shark's arms as he pulled himself up to the bar for the last two times.

Hiking to the Arts and Crafts cabin, Shark said, "So do you want to tell me about your favorite birthday or should I tell you about mine?"

"This whole thing wouldn't be so bad if we didn't have to do this feelings crap," said Rocky. He sighed. "Go ahead."

"Three years ago, my grandpa died."

"Your favorite birthday is when your grandpa died?"

"No!" said Shark, suddenly on the verge of tears. "My grandpa, he . . . uh, he was a great guy."

"So why were you happy when he died on your birthday?"

"I wasn't! He didn't! Will you just let me tell the story?"

"Sheesh. Go ahead."

Both boys increased their pace as if rushing away from their discomfort.

"Well, he . . . ," began Shark, wondering why he had ever opened his big mouth at all. "He . . . never teased me about the way I look, he liked to do stuff with me, he laughed at my jokes." Shark focused on the clouds gathering in the sky, not daring to look at his partner. "He'd take me into his office and tell everybody, from the shoeshine guy in the lobby to the elevator guy to his secretaries, 'This is my grandson, Vince.'"

Rocky's laugh was like a bark. "We're not supposed to tell each other our real names, Vince!"

"Sorry," said Shark, and he was—sorry for revealing so much of himself, sorry for sharing the memory of his grandfather with this clod who couldn't care less about him. He increased his pace.

"Well, go on," said Rocky after a long moment. "Cripes."

Shark would have just as soon turned around and run back to his cabin, finished with this stupid game and his stupid partner, but the remembrance of his grandfather's affection gave him the courage to finish his story.

"The stuff we did doesn't sound like a lot of fun—we didn't go fishing or to the movies or anything 'cause he was always so busy working, but like I said, he'd take me to his office sometimes or we'd go out for lunch. Anytime I was with him, he made me feel . . . like I was important." Shark's mouth went through a strange series of configurations—he pursed his lips, pressed them together, then blew out a stream of air—before he continued.

"Then he told me for my ninth birthday he was going to take me to Yankee Stadium."

"Who were they playing?"

Sounds of an argument rose up from the basketball court where a game between the twelve-year-olds was under way, an accusation of cheating and a counteraccusation of playing like babies.

"The Red Sox," said Shark. "I was so excited . . . but then two weeks before the game, he had a heart attack."

Rocky inhaled a little gasp.

"Right in the middle of the stockholders' meeting, my mom told me. He was in the hospital for three days before he died and I . . . I felt like I'd been robbed or something."

The boys kept walking, the incline of the path was rising, and they were breathing harder.

"On my birthday, I felt so . . . lonesome, and then my dad says, 'Come on, we've got a ball game to go to.' Turns out, in the hospital, my grandpa told my dad the tickets were on his desk and to take me if he didn't make it. Turns out he did some other stuff, too."

"What?"

Shark cleared his throat; he had a powerful thirst.

"Well, my grandpa was sort of a big shot, I guess, although he never acted like it, and well, not only did I get to go to the game, I got to go in the clubhouse afterwards." He took off the cap that was rarely off his head and handed it to Rocky. "Whitey Ford gave this to me. It was the hat he wore during the game."

"Wow," said Rocky, stopping in his tracks. "I didn't know this was the real thing." He fingered the signature and set the cap on his own head, and a tiny explosion of panic detonated in Shark's chest.

"Don't worry," said Rocky, taking it off and flinging it at Shark. "It's not like I was going to keep it or anything."

Ashamed at how transparent his feelings must have shown on his face, Shark settled the hat back on his own head while his cheeks singed with color.

There was a bench in front of the Arts and Crafts cabin and Rocky sat down on it.

"So I'm supposed to write this down, right?" he said, taking out the little pencil he'd put in his shorts pocket. He took the notebook his partner gave him.

"Shark got to go to a Yankees game," he said aloud as he wrote. "He got Whitey Ford to sign a hat for him." With a hard poke of his pencil he added the period and then handed the notebook to Shark, who didn't know whether to be hurt or grateful for Rocky's brevity.

"The best birthday party I ever had was my last one. We had a big party for my relatives, and I saw my cousin Susie's tits."

"Really?"

"Yeah. She was changing in one of the spare bedrooms—only I didn't know it. I was just trying to find my cousin Leonard. Anyway, I walk right in—and boom," here he curved his fingers, as if holding imaginary melons, "there they were."

Shark couldn't help himself; he laughed.

"How am I supposed to write something like that?"

Rocky thought for a moment. "Just say once I got a really good present from my cousin Susie."

Leaving their fourth stop, the camp library, they ran into two other boys.

"Hey, where've you guys been?" asked Bronze.

"Yeah, you get lost or something?" asked Condor.

"We'll see who's lost," said Rocky.

"Yeah," said Shark. "We'll save a place for you at the finish line."

"Ha!" said Bronze.

Other competitors they passed said the same things: "Where've you been?" "Do you know you're going backwards?" "Are you lost?" to which the boys answered back with any number of insults.

"We're going to win, you know," said Shark after they had passed the last of their competitors.

"'Course we are!" said Rocky, and after a moment with an uncharacteristic lack of bluster asked, "But how do you know for sure?"

"Bronze and Condor are ahead of all the other guys, and we ran into them coming into the library."

"So?"

"So we were coming out. We were already done with 4 and they were just coming in. So we're like one step ahead of them."

Rocky thought for a moment. "Yeah, but maybe the tasks are harder and longer at the stops we haven't been to yet."

That was a possibility Shark hadn't thought of.

"In that case, let's run."

And they did. By the time they were at their last destination—the boathouse—they had jumped rope, sprinted around the Dining Hall, and had done any number of lunges, side-twists, and toe-touches. Shark had learned Rocky's favorite book was *Robinson Crusoe* and that his best family vacation was to Disneyland.

"Although my sister made us ride those stupid little teacups about a million times," he said.

Rocky in turn learned Shark's favorite book was *Where the Red Fern Grows* and that his favorite vacation had been to Yellowstone.

"We saw four black bears in camp and one grizzly bear up in the mountains."

What Miss DuBarry would be most pleased to know, of course, was that each boy had also learned that his partner wasn't so bad after all.

And isn't that the crux of successful weight—nay, life—management? she wrote in her journal. *By getting in touch with feelings, others' and one's own?*

Live Field Report/Sense-O-Gram

To: Charmat
From: Tandala

This is what a warm hand caressing your face feels like. And this, the depths of looking not into someone's eyes but their very souls—well, I'm still swimming in it!

Live Field Report/Reply

To: Tandala
From: Charmat

Enough with the fooling around: report back to the Lodge immediately. And when you do, bring me an ice cream sandwich.

———

Humps of dark clouds had slowly gathered on the horizon like a herd of bison, and a stiff wind ruffled the surface of the lake.

The boys' last task was to paddle to the diving dock and circle it three times before heading back, but as they put on their life jackets, Shark said, "I don't know if we should go out there, Rocky."

His partner's answer was to push the canoe out into the lake, and Shark scrambled after him.

The wind was like an invisible hand pushing them backwards, and Shark wished he'd been brave enough not to get into the boat.

"Can't you go any faster?" asked Rocky.

"I'm going as fast as I can!"

"Cripes, we're hardly moving!" said Rocky, his voice nearly swallowed by the wind.

Both boys' arms moved like pistons and they were on their second trip around the dock when he saw the first lightning strike.

"Hey! Hey, did you see that, Rocky? We've got to get off the lake now!"

Rocky laughed. "What, are you scared of a little lightning?"

"Yes! Now come on, let's get back!"

Big splats of rain began to fall.

"We've gotta go around one more time," said Rocky. "You're the one who said you didn't want to cheat."

A low rumble of thunder crescendoed in a loud crack.

"Rocky, we've got to go back, *now!*"

When they rounded the dock, Shark began paddling hard, steering toward shore, but Rocky paddled in opposition to him.

"Rocky! *Rocky!*"

The boy's laugh was almost maniacal as he leaned toward Shark and pulled off his baseball cap.

"Now maybe you'll listen to the captain, huh?"

For a moment Shark was stunned into muteness, staring through the rain at Rocky as he put his cap on.

"Give me that!" he said, lunging toward Rocky. The canoe rocked.

"One more time around is all," said Rocky, leaning back and pushing his paddle through the water.

Lightning zigzagged above the pine trees and the following thunderclap was almost immediate.

"We've got to get off the lake now!"

Rocky continued paddling in the direction he wanted to go, and as much as Shark fought the motion, Rocky was stronger than he was, and it appeared the canoe would once again round the diving dock.

But not with me in it, thought Shark.

He jumped out of the canoe, nearly upturning it, and began swimming toward shore. The rain was now hard and fast, slicing through the sky. Behind him Rocky screamed at him, reviving his old names and calling him some new ones.

"You stupid shit! Fat ass! Come back here, you chicken shit!"

Shark staggered up the shore just as Rocky paddled up, and after jumping out of the canoe he gave chase, tackling Shark near the boathouse.

Lightning lit up the sky and thunder made its accompanying crash.

"Get off me!" shouted Shark.

"How'd I get such a pansy for a partner?"

Intergalactic Memo

To: Tandala
From: Charmat

Tandy—can't you see Fletcher needs your help? Tandy? Tandy, shake the sand out of your receptors and answer me!

———

The two boys rolled in the grass, pounding each other as the rain pelted them. Shark had just about pushed Rocky off him when he was yanked up onto his feet.

"What the hell is going on?" cried Bear, his counselor, and holding on to Shark with one hand, he grabbed Rocky with the other, and the three of them began to run.

The lightning and thunder chased them as they raced through the heavy drapes of rain. When they got to the nearest shelter, Bear pulled them up the stairs and pushed them through the doors of the Great Hall.

Miss DuBarry and the rest of the eleven-year-old boys, seated around the fireplace, gaped at them.

"Goodness, you boys are soaking wet!"

After stating the obvious, the camp director pointed to the closet next to the door and said, "Bear, get those boys some blankets. Thank goodness we've got a fire built!"

Shark accepted the blanket Bear draped around his shoulders and ran his fingers through his wet hair, gasping at what was not there.

"Where's my hat?" he said to Rocky.

His partner shrugged elaborately. "It probably came off when I was beating you up."

He smirked at his friends, but Pyrennes and Allegheny did not offer any laughter.

"Wait a second," said Bear, grabbing Shark as he turned back toward the door. "You're not going anywhere."

"I've got to get my hat!"

"Not in this weather," said the counselor. "Now sit down." He pressed on Shark's shoulder so that the boy was forced to sit on one end of the semicircle. "Rocky," he said pointing, "you sit over there."

"Yes, yes, both of you boys get close to the fire," said Miss DuBarry. "I don't want anyone catching pneumonia on top of everything else." She pushed up her glasses. "Honestly, you boys know better than to stay out in a storm like this. Didn't you hear the weather bell?"

"We didn't hear anything," said Shark, who huddled under the blanket was still trying to stop shivering. "We were out on the lake."

Miss DuBarry's pale face lost even more color.

"Out on the lake—why would you be out on the lake?"

"Because that's what the task told us to do!" said Rocky.

Confusion flickered in the camp director's eyes.

"Task? The first task was at the lake. You boys should have finished that one long ago."

"They did the tasks backwards," offered Tern. "They started at the weight room and ended at the boathouse."

"Why would you do that?" asked Miss DuBarry.

"Because it was good strategy!" said Rocky. "Nobody else got to all the places and did all the stuff, did they?"

"We almost did," said Steel. "We were on the way to the weight room when we heard the gong."

Lightning flashed in the windows like a strobe light, and several boys jumped at the crack of thunder.

"All right, then," said Rocky, pulling his blanket more tightly around himself. "We did everything. We won the game."

"Well, I don't know," said Miss DuBarry, clearly flustered. "You played the game backwards—"

"You didn't say we had to go in any order!" said Rocky. "You can't penalize us for that!"

"Well, that's true . . . but you were out on the lake in violation of camp policy." She wagged a finger. "No one is to be on the water during a storm."

"So what exactly are you saying?" asked Rocky, anger propelling him to his feet.

"I don't like your tone, young man," said Miss DuBarry. "Sit down.

"Now, I think it's safe to say that because of Mother Nature, who does manage to assert herself without regard to the plans of man"— her smile was not returned by anyone—"it may be that no clear winner can be announced. However, I—"

"No clear winner!" said Rocky. "We won! We did all the tasks!"

"No, we didn't," said Shark, who had been sitting hugging his knees, holding tight the volcanic rage and anger that roiled through him.

"Yes, we did," said Rocky, the sneer on his face audible in his voice.

"We only went around the dock twice."

"That's because you were such a chicken! That's because you jumped out of the boat! That's because—"

"And we didn't answer the last question," said Shark. Knowing how important winning was to Rocky was like a weapon for him, and he felt as still and composed as a tiger ready to spring onto an antelope. "We didn't tell each other who the person we most admired in the world is."

"Well, it sure isn't you!" said Rocky. The blanket dropped from his shoulders as he leapt up and charged toward his partner.

But Shark was ready, and unlike the nosebleed he'd accidentally given Rocky during the volleyball game, this one was bestowed with full intent. The thunder that cracked just at the moment his fist met Rocky's nose was a perfect sound effect.

The day after the big Feelings competition fiasco, Shark had paced the lakeshore, and Copper, who had planned to spend his free time swimming, decided to instead help him look for his hat.

"It stinks that you lost it," said Copper. "It was the coolest hat ever."

Because of the rainstorm and the subsequent brawl, the boys hadn't been able to share the stories they'd learned about their partners with the rest of their group. Copper had no idea of what had been lost until Shark told him the story of his grandfather.

"Oh, boy," said Copper. "That really stinks."

From then on, he spent every Morning Free Time partnered with Shark, a two-man search party.

"You don't have to do this," Shark had said on the second day.

"We should look over there," said Copper, pointing to a clump of cattails.

On the third day, Copper suggested that Miss DuBarry should force Rocky to help them look for the cap since it was his fault it was missing.

Shark shook his head. "The less I see of Rocky the better."

Copper considered this for a moment. "Yeah, I guess I'd feel the same way. Hey, why don't we go look in the woods? Maybe the wind blew it there. Or a bird could have carried it up and dropped it."

Shark valued his easy friendships with Cheetah and Zebra and other members of the Birch cabin, but as the days passed, it was Copper to whom he confessed his rage and sadness.

"I know that I'll always have my Grandpa, you know, here." He tapped his chest and fought the tears that often seemed only a blink away. "But that cap was just . . . I don't know, it was like . . ."

"Like him still being with you?"

Shark nodded. "Yeah. There was no way I could wear that hat without remembering how much he loved me."

"I've got a picture of my grandfather," said Copper. Armed with sticks, they poked through the weeds that grew alongside the path. "Everyone says I look a lot like him . . . although he wasn't fat."

"You never met him?"

Copper shook his head. "No, he died before I was born . . . in the war."

Shark remembered hearing about Copper's family having emigrated from Austria before the war, and suddenly the plot of the story was spiked with intrigue.

"Was he . . . was he a Nazi?'

Copper beat back a clump of weeds before tossing the stick aside. "No, it was the Nazis who killed him."

———

LORNA LANDVIK

"And so that's how I went from this," said Jack Parrish, pointing to the photo of a young, curly-haired obese boy projected on the screen, "to this."

Miss DuBarry, operating the slide projector, clicked the next picture forward. It was a publicity photo of Jack Parrish wearing a tuxedo and holding a revolver, and the air was softened by all the little sighs issued by campers wondering if ever they might look as dashing and dangerous.

"Now it wasn't easy—as you well know—but guys, you've taken the first step, a *big* step in deciding you're the captain of your own ship. And you don't want to steer a big, bulky ship, do you, boys?" Jack Parrish walked through the beam of light projected on the screen as he paced across the floor. "You want to steer a streamlined ship that'll take you anywhere you want to go, in no time flat!"

He pumped his fist in the air and the boys burst into applause.

Miss DuBarry turned off the slide projector and raced up to the stage, clapping her hands like a seal begging for a treat.

On stage, she hugged her childhood friend, feeling woozy in his embrace.

"Wasn't he wonderful, children?" she asked, after he (she could have held on forever) ended the hug.

Most of the children needed no prodding; nearly everyone was on their feet, stomping and clapping and whistling.

Rocky, however, chose to stay in his seat in the back row, arms crossed over his chest, frown lines crossing his forehead.

The applause lasted a long time, until it was finally cut off by Jack Parrish's hand gestures.

"As much as I'd like to stay," he said, "I've got to be back in California tomorrow." He cupped his hand to the side of his mouth and stage-whispered, "I'll be screen-testing several actresses who'll be working with me on my next motion picture."

The boys, thrilled to be in on this bit of Hollywood gossip, clapped and whistled some more.

"Maybe I should tell the director to take a look at Miss DuBarry, hmm?" he said, holding his hand out to the camp director, who was struck dumb that the kindness and sensitivity Mervin Phillips had displayed as a boy was still intact in the movie star.

"Well, I'm sure Camp WoogiWikki needs her even more," he said and promptly kissed Miss DuBarry's hand. Then, glancing at the Swiss watch his agent had given him (and whose engraving read, *BBO!* for *Boffo Box Office!*), he said, "But now the time's come for me to meet with a certain winner of a certain contest. Will the winner please step up onstage so that I may escort him to my limousine for a ride around the lake?"

There was not the sort of wild applause the boys gave Jack Parrish, but it was enthusiastic and sincere enough, and Copper flushed with pleasure as he mounted the stage.

Shark clapped as hard—probably harder—than anyone, truly feeling that for a change the best man *had* won, the boy who had become his trusted friend.

"What's this?" asked Jack Parrish, accepting the folded note Copper handed him. After reading it, he held a brief whispered conference with Copper and then stood for a moment, scratching one eyebrow with a thumbnail, an affectation at least a dozen boys in the Great Hall would thereafter pick up.

"Well, now," he said to the boys, "Copper has asked me to read this to you."

An excitable murmur rose from the boys, and Miss DuBarry craned her long neck, trying to read the words on the paper.

"All right, settle down," said the movie star. "Here's what Copper writes." He clamped one hand on the boy's shoulder and began reading the note. "'Losing weight is a good thing, but what my friend Shark lost wasn't so good, and that's why I'd like him to win the prize of a private meeting with Jack Parrish.'"

There was a moment of silence before the room erupted in gasps, and then applause. Rocky shot out of the room like a runner hearing the firing pistol, but as fast as he departed it was a turtle's pace compared to the velocity in which Shark exited.

Part V

18

It was such a light drizzle that it appeared the rain didn't fall to the ground as much as it shimmied in space. Miss Plum had the lights on; she thought there was almost nothing cozier than a classroom lit up against darkening, rainy skies. The weatherman had promised a snowy holiday but for now it was still above freezing.

Humming "Turkey in the Straw," one of the songs the children had sung in that morning's all-school Thanksgiving pageant, she chuckled to herself, thinking of little Raymond Erk, who played the very important part of the vegetable that had brought the pilgrims and Indians together. Encased in a green tube on which candy corn had been glued, the kindergartner forgot his line and stood mute under the spotlight, nervously twirling the crepe paper tassels of his gold cap while the children playing Indians hissed, "Maze! Say, 'I'm Maze!'"

Miss Plum's class was taught good manners, but when the bell rang their teacher allowed them the excitement that precedes a holiday, an excitement that manifested itself in the children jostling at the doorway, some breaking away from the knot to throw their arms around her in a hug, others shouting "Happy Thanksgiving!" as they pushed out into the hallway.

She had declined the offer of Mrs. Bryers, the other second grade teacher, to join her and her family again for Thanksgiving; at last year's dinner, Mrs. Bryers's husband and her brother had gotten into such a heated argument about taxes that Miss Plum had heartburn even before she had digested the lumpy potatoes and oversalted green bean casserole. That the pumpkin pie—Miss Plum's favorite!—slumped in an undercooked crust and was served without whipped cream was another disappointment, but it was the confession of Mrs. Bryers's brother that he'd voted against the school referendum that convinced the teacher that this would be her one and only Thanksgiving with the Bryers.

"That referendum," she had said sweetly, dabbing her pretty mouth with a paper napkin imprinted with cartoon pilgrims, "allowed the entire school district to upgrade their math and science text books. Do you really consider that a waste of money?"

Mrs. Bryers's brother had offered a smile oilier than the gravy and said, "Heck, yeah—unless the periodic table has suddenly changed! Unless two and two equals something different from four now!"

Yes, this year Miss Plum would be perfectly grateful spending Thanksgiving all by herself, and furthermore she was going to buck tradition and make lasagna, the leftovers of which she would enjoy all week.

Humming "Bless This House," she was almost finished with cleaning her classroom, taking down the construction paper turkeys and cornucopias that decorated the windowpanes.

Admiring the care with which Katie Charbonneau had fringed the edges of her paper turkey's tail feathers, Miss Plum held the fowl by its head and pulled up, carefully unpeeling the rectangle of tape off the window. She had now a clear view to the empty playground, only it wasn't empty, and her gasp was as loud as if the paper turkey in her hand had gobbled.

Seeing a figure curled up next to the slide, she grabbed her raincoat and raced down the hallway and out the side door, remembering to put the wooden block between it and the doorjamb, as she knew the janitor along with everyone else had already left for their long holiday weekend. Her assumption had been that the figure was a child who'd hurt himself and so was surprised as she drew nearer to see that this was not a child but a man curled up in the fetal position. When she knelt beside him, she immediately saw who it was and she gasped again, loud enough to rouse Fletcher.

He groaned, and accepting the arms that pulled him up, he leaned on her as she led him into the school and to the nurse's office. Several times she staggered under his weight, but determination gave muscle to adrenaline, and she was successful in reaching her destination.

Miss Plum leaned him against the door's height chart and as he stood there, slightly weaving, his eyes closed, she told him to stand still so she could take off his wet clothes. Although her hands shook as she gently pulled off the wet Camp WoogiWikki T-shirt and the khaki shorts, her voice nonetheless betrayed no nerves as she calmly spelled out for him what was happening: "Now I'm setting you on the cot, Fletcher. Now you're lying back on it. Now I'm getting some blankets out of the cupboard.

"There, there," she said, sitting next to the cot on Nurse Pam's wheeled stool. "There, there. You just rest now."

They were probably superfluous words; from the moment Fletcher lay down on the cot he had fallen into a deep sleep. She hoped it was sleep and not a coma, and she was nervous that she didn't know how to tell the difference between the two.

Darkness crept into the office and Miss Plum leaned backward to turn on the lamp on the nurse's desk. It cast a warm soft light, and as the clocked ticked she stroked the slope of Fletcher's shoulder back and forth, back and forth, until she felt nearly hypnotized.

She was just thinking she might doze off herself when the patient opened his eyes and looking into hers asked, "Am I in Oz?"

Miss Plum smiled, and seeing the deep dimples in her cheeks Fletcher knew at least who he was with, if not where.

"You're not Auntie Em," he said, "you're Miss Plum!"

"Yes, but please, call me Wanda."

"Okay . . . Wanda," said Fletcher, liking the shape his mouth had to make to say her name. "But Wanda . . . where am I?"

"In the school nurse's office. I found you outside on the playground."

"Oh, no! I hope . . . I hope I didn't cause you any embarrassment with your—"

"Everyone's gone. For the Thanksgiving weekend."

"Is that why you're wearing pumpkins?" asked Fletcher, looking at her blouse.

"Actually, they're gourds. I do have a pumpkin blouse—well, jack-o'-lanterns, really—that I wear on Halloween."

"And Tandy?" said Fletcher, suddenly sitting up. "Is she here yet?"

"I just found you."

Clutching the blanket to his chest, Fletcher looked around, knowing that if the alien were with him, her presence would be quite obvious in the small narrow room. He saw a growth chart and a small cabinet, a step-on scale, and hanging by two hooks his damp Camp WoogiWikki T-shirt and shorts.

"You found me in those?"

Miss Plum—Wanda—nodded. "I take it you were at a camp?"

"A camp for fat boys. Which is why I could probably still fit into those as a grown man." Fletcher pulled at the skin under his nose before confessing, "I'm a little nervous. I don't really know what to do until Tandy gets here."

Decision making was one of the many areas in which Wanda Plum shone.

"We'll wait for her . . . at my house."

"But she doesn't know where you live!"

The petite blonde enjoyed the release of laughter.

"Your aliens seem pretty resourceful. And I am in the phone book."

Still wrapped in the school blankets, Fletcher rode to Wanda's house in her Volkswagen Beetle.

"Where are we, anyway?" he asked as they drove through the dark rainy streets.

"Aberdeen."

"Aberdeen!" said Fletcher. "Aberdeen, South Dakota?"

"Well, lad, it's not Aberdeen, Scotland," said Wanda, in a fairly good brogue.

"You're kidding me! Out of all the places Tandy could have brought me to for our debriefings, she brings me to Aberdeen?"

"It's not Paris, but it has its charms. Why, the Brown County Fair is top-notch, and our community theater has been compared to—"

"I'm thrilled that it's Aberdeen," said Fletcher, touched by her boosterism. "I mean, you're just 125 miles from Pierre!"

"You're from Pierre?" asked Wanda, and when Fletcher nodded they both laughed.

"Small world," she said.

"Well, not so small," said Fletcher, gesturing skyward. "But certainly strange."

———

The house was neat and pretty like its owner, the walls of the living and dining room painted a soft peach and decorated with paintings and chintz-upholstered furniture and a fireplace with an unusual hearth and mantle.

"Wow," said Fletcher, looking at the glazed ceramic squares on which titled portraits of women were painted. "That's Eleanor Roosevelt!" He squatted to his knees, to better view the 5"x5" likenesses and read the names written below each one in fine script. "Sojourner Truth. Sacagawea. And look at Amelia Earhart!"

"I don't think I got her nose quite right."

"You painted these?" asked Fletcher, bobbling a little in his squat.

Wanda nodded, bending down next to him. "For our American

History unit, we did a Hall of Fame portrait project in class, but instead of drawing pictures I wanted the children to decorate a household object with an American who'd made a difference in the world. The idea was to bring history into their everyday lives. So sure enough, I got a lot of portraits painted on coffee mugs, but I also had Jennifer Erlich cross-stitching a picture of Abraham Lincoln on a dishtowel, and Brian Lindvall painted one of his dad's golf balls with a picture of George Washington." She sighed. "Most of the kids did presidents, although there were two astronauts and a Thomas Edison, but only Katie Charbonneau drew a woman."

"Who?" asked Fletcher.

"Laura Ingalls Wilder. Katie's nuts about the Little House on the Prairie series, and she made a portrait of the author out of felt pieces and glued it on her book bag. It was a clever idea, but still, it was dispiriting out of a class of twenty-two students only one thought to honor a woman."

"But you," said Fletcher, surveying the portraits that framed the fireplace. "You've got all women here."

"That's right," said the teacher crisply. "Someone's got to give us the attention we deserve."

After soaking in the hot bath Wanda drew for him, Fletcher joined her in the living room. A fire crackled in the feminist fireplace, and the rescued time traveler, who had every intention of having a nice long conversation with the gracious and interesting teacher, felt so at home that he promptly fell asleep.

He woke up on the couch, warmed by a patchwork quilt that smelled of lavender, a tender morning light, and as he remembered where he was, a sense of contentment. He smiled, remembering the sound of Wanda Plum's laughter as she told him about her father, whose pajamas he now wore.

"He and Mom live in New Mexico most of the year," she had said the night before. "Right next door to my aunt and uncle. But they come to stay with me every summer. Dad's convinced he needs"— here she lowered her voice—"at least six weeks of South Dakota sense to immunize him from the insanity of the rest of the country." Wanda laughed. "Dad's quite a character."

And so are you, Fletcher thought, stretching his arms above his head. He wondered if she were up yet, what fruit or vegetable print she might be wearing, what they might have for breakfast. He would have liked to focus his thoughts on his hostess, but worry nipped at him like a badly behaved dog.

Where's Tandy? Is she all right? What was going to happen now?

————

Fletcher stood in the dining room entryway watching as Wanda scattered autumn leaves on the table.

"Wow," he said. "Did you make that?"

The centerpiece of Wanda Plum's Thanksgiving table was a two-foot tree branch on which small amber votive candleholders were glued.

Wanda nodded, fully taking in the sight that was Fletcher dressed in her father's clothes, which she had laid out for him. "Sorry about Dad's taste."

"And I thought I looked dapper," said Fletcher, striking a pose in his checked polyester pants and pale pink golf shirt.

"So does Dad," said Wanda. "That's his problem."

Fletcher watched as she finished her leaf placement.

"A gold doubloon for your thoughts," said Wanda.

"Huh—and all this time I've been accepting pennies."

"No, really," said Wanda, as she considered a yellow leaf, moving it a quarter-inch, "tell me what's on your mind."

"Nothing deep," said Fletcher. "I was just thinking about the big ugly turkey candle my Aunt Florence used to set in the middle of the table every year at Thanksgiving. First the flame put a big indentation in the head, and gradually the whole head melted down, and then the wattle melted into the chest—eventually it became this brown blob—until one year, my mother threw it away, saying if she wanted to look at a cow pie while she was eating, she'd go out in the field."

"Your mother sounds like she has a good sense of humor."

"Had," Fletcher said, feeling a catch in his chest. "Yeah, I guess she did. Anyway, I sure like your centerpiece. It's very . . . creative."

"A teacher's salary forces creativity," said Wanda. "Plus I enjoy making things."

"I've gathered that. Like your fireplace, like your fruit and vegetable blouses—which, by the way, I notice you're not wearing today."

Wanda blushed. "Oh, that's just a silly thing I do for the children."

"I think it's nice. I had a teacher named Mrs. Lake, and I can tell you, that old crab never did anything fun with *her* name."

"What should she have done—come in soaking wet?"

"Yeah, and dripping weeds and old fishing line."

When they were done sharing a small laugh, they stood at the dining room table staring at one another.

"Well!" said Wanda, laying one last oak leaf under her centerpiece. "What kind of hostess am I? Dinner won't be ready for hours—let me get you some breakfast."

Tulips bloomed on the white cupboards in the yellow kitchen.

"Did you paint those?" asked Fletcher.

"Sometimes I go a little crazy," said Wanda. From the small kitchen table, she pulled out a white chair also sprouting tulips.

Fletcher was served coffee and warm banana bread, and had his sense of taste and smell been so armed it would have offered a twenty-one-gun salute.

"I never had homemade banana bread as a kid," he said, thinking of the toasted hot dog buns spread with margarine and sprinkled with sugar that was Olive's dessert bread. "I don't think I ever had any homemade bread of any kind. It's probably why I started baking it myself." He took another bite, closing his eyes as he chewed. "Only mine never tastes anything like this."

Wanda cut another slice and put it on the china dish in front of him. After refilling his coffee cup, she folded her hands on the tabletop and regarded him gravely.

"Fletcher, I can't begin to imagine what you've been through, but I know it's a lot."

Hearing the seriousness in her tone, Fletcher wiped his mouth with the snowy cloth napkin and folded his own hands in his lap.

"Oh, sorry," she said. "Sometimes I use my teacher's voice and I'm not even aware of it." She waved her hand. "Please, keep eating."

Happy to comply, Fletcher took a big bite of banana bread.

"I wanted your . . . your reentry, for lack of a better word," said Wanda, "to be as easy as possible, and to that end I thought we should just get to know each other a little bit as fellow human beings."

Fletcher chewed quickly and swallowed. "I think that was a good idea. I've enjoyed getting to know you."

"And I you. But of course, I can't help notice how worried you are."

"I thought . . . I thought I was covering that up pretty good."

"I'd say more than pretty good. My goodness, I think most people would have had nervous breakdowns in the first zamoosh."

That Wanda Plum should remember the word *zamoosh* caused a zip of pleasure to ride Fletcher's spine.

"And although I remember Tandala's tardiness in getting back to you in my classroom, that she's been gone this long is cause for some concern."

"It is, isn't it?" said Fletcher, feeling as if a door had been opened and a cold draft skittered inside.

"So, Fletcher, if you don't mind, before I start our Thanksgiving dinner—and it's going to be lasagna, I hope you don't mind—why don't you tell me everything that's happened since I last saw you? If you're up to it."

Fletcher nodded. He was up to it and glad that she was.

"Well, if you remember," he said, taking a sip of coffee—it tasted the way commercials claimed their coffee tasted but never did—"the first time I was Hip Galloway, rodeo cowboy? Then I was brought into Deke Drake's life—ladies' man, war vet, jewel thief?"

Wanda nodded, her eyes shining, as if she were listening to her favorite story.

"Well, this time—boy, they've really got a weird sense of humor—they brought me to a fat camp."

"Right," said Wanda. "Camp WoogiWikki, like it said on your T-shirt."

Fletcher nodded. "And my real name was Vince, I guess, but my nickname was Shark because all the kids in camp had nicknames."

"I'm not following you."

"Vince Shark was one of my alter egos when I was a kid," he explained. "Only my Vince Shark was an international spy."

"So did you . . . did you do any spying in camp?"

"No," said Fletcher. "I can't figure out what my Vince Shark and the kid I was at camp had to do with one another. I think it was all just sort of a joke."

"Hmm," said Wanda. "Maybe instead of international espionage, you were trying to solve some other mystery."

"Ha," said Fletcher. "Like how cottage cheese helps you lose weight?"

"What about Tandala—was she a counselor there? Or the camp cook?"

"No, she wasn't around for this experience. In fact, I only saw her once—and she was still Tandy the maid from Deke Drake's life."

"Strange," said Wanda, refilling his cup. "Tell me more."

He told her all about his time at Camp WoogiWikki, and when he got to the part about losing his baseball cap, he teared up.

"I'm sorry," he said, his smile sheepish, "it's just that that damn hat meant so much to me."

"You don't have to apologize. Anyone would be upset about losing a symbol like that. It's like losing a wedding ring, I'd imagine." She thought for a moment. "No, more like a war widow losing a wedding ring."

Fletcher took her small hand and squeezed it, grateful for the depth of her understanding.

"So I want to understand this exactly," said Wanda. "You're not reliving your own life at all, but living out the lives of your fantasies?"

"Except that I really hadn't mapped out whole lives for them—I mean, they were just fantasies, you know? This is great coffee, by the way."

The look on her face was not typical of one who'd just been complimented; in fact, alarm rounded her eyes and mouth as the air shimmered with colors before solidifying into the form of Charmat.

Wanda said, "Oh, my!" with all the awe and disbelief to be expected when finding a thin, green, bulbous-headed, Lurex-bodysuit-wearing alien in one's kitchen.

"Charmat!" said Fletcher. "What are you doing here?" A tiny blast of fear detonated in his stomach. "Where's Tandy? Is Tandy all right?"

"We'll be seeing her momentarily." His voice was as calm as if he were suggesting a stroll around the block, and it reassured Fletcher enough that he was able to smile at Wanda in an *Isn't this something?* sort of way.

The teacher sat with her hands clutched under her slack jaw, and Fletcher remembered his manners.

"Wanda, this is Charmat, head of Lodge 1212. Charmat, meet Wanda Plum."

"Pleasure," said the alien, nodding.

"Likewise," she said, her voice small, but excited. "May I get you some coffee?"

"Under usual circumstances, yes, but not these." He turned to Fletcher. "We must go now."

"Where?"

"The Universal Head Council meeting."

Another blast of fear—but this one sending out a trickle of ice through every vein—was unleashed in Fletcher.

"Will Tandy be there?"

"Very nice to have met you," Charmat said to Wanda, and as he reached for Fletcher, Wanda grabbed the lone finger of the alien's other hand.

"I'm going, too."

"Miss, I can't allow that."

"You'll have to," said Fletcher simply, suddenly not wanting to go anywhere without the second grader teacher.

Charmat looked first at Fletcher and then Wanda, his eyes darkening and his forehead pulsing. Wanda didn't look away or let go of his hand.

"Oh, all right," said Charmat finally, and as Mrs. Bryers stuffed her turkey with store-bought dressing and Katie Charbonneau colored a pilgrim for the newspaper contest and the Plums watched the Macy's parade on TV, their colleague, teacher, and daughter, respectively, broke all known rules of time and space and dimension.

19

The first sound Wanda became aware of was the low roar of ocean waves.

"Fletcher!" she whispered, after plunking down on something that felt like sand. They were in such deep darkness that the only way she knew she was with Fletcher was that she felt his hand in hers. "Fletcher, I think we're at the ocean!"

"You're right," came Charmat's voice. "I am receiving the coordinates as approximately eighteen degrees, fifteen minutes, zero seconds south, and thirty-five degrees, zero minutes, and zero seconds east. Putting us in Mozambique."

"Mozambique," said Fletcher the geography buff. "Then that must be the Indian Ocean."

"The Indian Ocean," said Wanda. "Oh, I wish it were daylight so I could see it!"

As if her words were a cue, the darkness parted like a stage curtain and they found themselves under a moonlit sky.

The alien leader pointed to a bonfire several hundred yards away.

"Over there!" he said, pulling up the humans, and together they ran along the shoreline, next to the white-capped waves unraveling like old lace and toward the orange glow.

Near the fire, a woman appeared to be sleeping. She was wrapped in a blanket and sitting on a low-to-the-ground lawn chair, her legs extended, feet crossed.

Kneeling in the sand next to her, Fletcher took her hand and whispered, "Tandy?"

For a long moment, there was no sound except for the tumbling of the ocean waves, and then with a snort Tandy awoke.

———

"Why is he here?" she said, her voice sharp. "There's no time for this!"

"No time for what?" asked Fletcher. "What's going on?"

"The UHC is about to make its decision," said Charmat.

"Yes, and you'll blow it all if you're late!" said Tandala, and regarding Fletcher in his pastel finery, she asked, "Are you in some fantasy?"

In the eerie flickering glow of the fire, Fletcher could see that Tandy's dark skin was ashen and her eyes sunken, but he did not want the panic he felt reflected in his face, and so he forced his mouth to turn upward.

"Nope, I'm just me," he said lightly. "These are Wanda's dad's golf clothes."

"Hi," said Wanda, offering a small wave as she stepped into the light of the fire.

"Oh," said Tandy, "you brought the teacher! Miss Plum, isn't it?"

"Call me Wanda," she said, leaning toward Tandy. "It's so nice to see you again—but what exactly is going on?"

Hearing Tandy's calliope-full-of-notes laughter, Fletcher's knees felt weak.

"I forget how you like to get to the heart of things, Wanda," said Tandy. "And I love that you're here." Her gummy smile stretched across her gaunt face. "I guess things aren't so urgent that we can't have a little party. What do you say, Charmat?"

The alien leader stood with his hands on his narrow hips, but the scowl on his bulbous forehead softened, and smiling, he held out a finger, directing its strong pulsing light at something on the other side of Tandy's lawn chair. "Fletcher, crack open the cooler, and let's get this party started."

The two humans exchanged a long look before Fletcher followed Charmat's order. He felt as if his emotions were on a chain, being yanked this way and that, but if the aliens thought it was now time for refreshment, he wasn't about to protest.

As the waves beat out their relentless rhythm and the moon shone yellow, the odd quartet sat quietly contemplating the bonfire, downing their beers in varying speeds. Charmat was a guzzler, opening a second bottle and pouring it into his glass before Wanda had taken two sips out of hers.

"Beer," said the alien leader, "you were so right, Tandala. It's got a bigger taste than a normal thirst quencher, almost like a liquid food." He took a long draw, smacking his lipless mouth. "And you're right that it's best drunk out of a glass so that one can enjoy the foam— foam is like a dessert—not sweet but a treat nevertheless. A texture that makes you feel good."

Fletcher and Wanda laughed; to hear an alien expound on the merits of beer while sitting by a bonfire on the coast of Mozambique was not how either one had anticipated spending their Thanksgiving.

"Oh, but piña coladas," said Tandy. "Piña coladas are like drinking a coconut that's been crossbred with sugar cane and whipped up by very happy Hawaiians."

"I was in Hawaii once," said Wanda. "On a college break. I thought I had landed in the place where perfume was invented."

Fletcher wanted to kiss her then, to taste the beer on her lips, to burrow his nose into her neck and smell traces of Molokai and Oahu.

"'Joshua trees whose branches are lifted in prayer!'" said Charmat, standing now. "'The brown velvet of a horse's nose! Singing 'Git Along, Little Doggies' with a bunch of weepy cowboys!'"

"He's quoting me," explained Tandy, and her smile was so big it erased all signs of sickness from her face.

"My interceptor could barely contain all the sense-o-grams and messages that were being transmitted," said Charmat. "I expected them to taper off, once she became more acclimated to earthly ways, but they never did. And the smells—'fresh cut hay, a rain-scrubbed morning, the sun on Grazi's flank'—I was nearly in overload with just samples of these, and here poor Tandy was immersed in them."

"Not *poor*," whispered Tandy. "Lucky."

"'The pleasure of a noisy fart and the laugh of cowboys afterward!'" said Charmat. "And of course, Tandy had to include the smell in that transmission!"

In the firelight, Fletcher saw Wanda's features tighten and a second later heard the unmistakable sound of a fart ripping through the air.

"I can't believe you just did that!" he said.

"I know," said Wanda, giggling. "I scold my kids for that kind of behavior, even while I'm thinking, 'Is that all you've got?'"

The aliens—and Fletcher—thought this was near the top on the humor pyramid.

"Oh," said Charmat finally, rubbing his backside. "Please."

Fletcher explained to Wanda that the aliens' bebobs hurt when they laughed too hard.

"*Bebobs?*" said Wanda, delight caressing both syllables. "My kids will love that word!"

Charmat, who was proving to be something of a party animal, regaled them with more stories of Tandy's transmissions—"'Ice cream cones, Charmat—ice cream cones! With a cold sweetness that leaves a softness in your mouth when it melts, and then you get the crispy hello of the cone!'"

"You know, you're right," said Wanda, nodding. "If ever there was a friendly food, it would be an ice cream cone."

Fletcher would have loved the laughs and conviviality of this beach party to go on and on, but he couldn't ignore the anxiousness that settled in his stomach like gas. He felt like the worrisome kid at the kegger who just knew the cops were about to close in.

"Tandy," he said, leaning toward her from his perch in the sand. "Why are you here? Here at the Indian Ocean?"

The alien-cum-Jamaican's dark brown eyes held Fletcher's before looking straight ahead, toward the sound of the waves.

"I love the ocean, Fletcher, and I wanted to see all seven before I die."

The air was punched out of Fletcher—he hadn't meant to ask a question that would return that kind of answer.

"What do you mean, *die?*"

Tandy waved a hand, the bracelets surrounding her thin wrist tinkling.

"Die. Expire. Cease existing. Sign off. Cash in the chips. Kick the bucket. Buy the farm—"

"Tandy, this isn't funny!" He looked to Charmat for some indication that yes, this was a joke, a *bad* joke but a joke nevertheless, but in the alien's face—not exactly built for expressiveness—Fletcher only saw sadness.

"But you're a superior being," said Fletcher, forcing lightness into his voice. "You guys live forever!"

"We didn't count on how much energy it takes to be human," said Charmat. He looked mournfully at his half-full glass before flinging the beer out into the sand. "It was a gross miscalculation on our part."

"Well, get off Earth, then!" shouted Fletcher. "Go back to your alien form and leave!"

On Tandy's face was a tender mix of apology and amusement.

"I can't, mon. It's too late."

"We had calibrated Tandala's energy reserve to handle all the travel in and out of parallel universes and fantasies," said Charmat. "We thought that's where the depletion would occur—your fantasy life is pretty dense, Fletcher, sort of like being in the thick of a jungle without a machete. But it wasn't the zamooshing in and out of time and space that proved destructive, but what she experienced in that time and space."

"It was all so . . . beautiful," said Tandy.

"Too beautiful," pronounced Charmat. "We had no idea of the depth and breadth of your fun."

Bowing his head, Fletcher squeezed his eyes shut, so that he missed the shooting star that fell from the sky like a dud firecracker.

"Charmat," said Tandala urgently, "it's time."

"Yes, I saw it," said the Lodge leader. Silhouetted in front of the fire, he held out his long spindly arm. "Fletcher, we must go. They're warning us to make haste."

Tandy's laugh was weak. "It's always rush-rush-rush with them."

"Okay," said Fletcher, rising. "Tandy, put your arms around me."

Surprise widened Tandy's eyes. "Fletcher, I'm not going anywhere. I can't."

Charmat shook his head. "She hasn't the strength to travel where we're going."

The panic that had been nibbling and grazing in Fletcher now burst inside him like a racehorse through an open gate.

"Well, then I'm not going! I'm not leaving her here to . . . to die by herself!"

"Fletcher, it's all right," said Tandy. "Please, go."

"No!"

Regarding the sky, Charmat said with urgency, "It's time now."

"I'm not going!" said Fletcher, grabbing on to the arm of Tandy's lawn chair, as if that were enough to tether him to Earth.

The alien leader moved closer. "Fletcher, we need you to make our case—"

"Take me," said Wanda, stepping forward to meet him. "Let Fletcher stay here. I'll go in his place!"

Fletcher felt physical pain, as if he were being ripped in two pieces. One of the pieces wanted to tackle Wanda and tell her there was no way he'd allow her to go with the alien and the other piece shouted, "Thank you!"

Light pulsed in Charmat's forehead and a weaker one in Tandy's answered, and the molecules in the African air throbbed and shimmered and cartwheeled and turned colors, and Fletcher cried out as he saw Wanda Plum bid him a dimpled smile before she disappeared in a swirl of pink and violet sparkles.

The wind blew at the fire again and the waves rolled into shore, their sound like ten thousand librarians, warning everyone nearby to "Shhhhhh."

"Oh, my God," said Fletcher, and to him the night suddenly seemed a deeper, denser black. "What have I done? What have I done?"

"You made a decision," said Tandy. "And Wanda made hers. Don't worry, Charmat won't let anything harm her."

"But where did he take her?" He began pacing by the fire. "Where are they going? Where does the Universal Head Council meet?"

"They'll find out when they get there," said Tandy, her voice gentle. "Just know that all will be well."

"How can you say that? You're dying!" Fletcher plopped down next to Tandy's lawn chair and took her hand. "Oh, Tandy, why is this happening to you?"

"You heard Charmat. It was too much. It was like an addiction . . . an addiction to pie and I couldn't stop at one piece—I had to have the whole pie." She chuckled. "The whole beautiful, fantastic, amazing, and immeasurably fun *love* pie."

"I'd like to kill that Clarence!"

Tandy's laugh was three low notes in her chest. "Don't blame Clarence—you were an even bigger piece of it."

Fletcher snorted, mucus burbling in his nostrils.

"Don't tease me now, Tandy."

"*Fletch-aire.*" Her voice was both a scolding and a caress. Pushing her elbows against the metal arms of the chair, she straightened up, but the effort tired her and she sunk back down.

"Would you . . . would you hold me, Fletcher?"

A sudden gust of wind ruffled through the air and the flames of the fire leaned sideways before rising up again.

"Of course, Tandy." Fletcher wrapped one arm around her back and the other under her knees and when he lifted her, he forced himself not to cry out. The Jamaican had lost most of her curves and felt as light as a gourd.

He stood by the fire, his body naturally falling into the rocking motion parents use when comforting a baby. A light in Tandy's forehead pulsed.

"Fletcher, I'm sorry you felt I deserted you sometimes—"

"Don't even—"

"It's just that I knew you didn't need constant supervision. And there was so much to explore!"

A sob rose out of Fletcher's throat and Tandy placed a hand on his cheek.

"Shhhh," she whispered and Fletcher smelled the beer on her breath, and underneath it, lemonade, strawberries, black licorice, and movie popcorn.

I bet I smell like all sorts of things.

"Umm-hmm," said Fletcher, inhaling. "Jordan almonds and jasmine and lake water and rodeo dust, and—"

I've been collecting favorite scents as souvenirs.

"Hey!" said Fletcher. "You talked but I didn't see your mouth move."

That's right, it'll conserve energy if I communicate telepathically now. It saves me the strain of translation. She leaned her head against Fletcher's shoulder. *Let's walk toward the ocean.*

"Aw, Tandy." He shifted her in his arms, and as he began walking, he thought that his sadness weighed him down far more than she did. "Can't you do something—can't I do something to make you better?"

Fletcher, you mustn't worry about me. I'm leaving here wanting nothing— except more! Just because it was all so wonderfully . . . earthful!

Away from the fire, the air was chilly, and as he walked Fletcher held Tandy tighter, wanting to keep her warm. When he heard a rasping breath deep in his ears, he was alarmed and tipped back his head to look at Tandy's face.

The alien tried to smile, but it was too big an effort, like setting a two-hundred-fifty-pound weight in front of an octogenarian and asking her to bench-press it.

Fletcher, let's go to the water now.

He didn't know why, but the request filled him with dread.

Don't be afraid, Fletcher, there isn't time. And the reason there's not time is entirely because of me—I should have prepared you better, but I can't seem to escape Lodge 1212's reputation for screwing things up. I'd love to have a long, heartfelt good-bye and tell you all sorts of things—but you already know them. So I'll tell you what you don't know: your fate's being decided right now by the Head Council.

"My fate!" Fletcher's feet, in Mr. Plum's patent leather loafers, slipped in the sand.

Don't drop me yet, Fletcher!

The faint bells of her laughter rang inside his head.

And let me just tell you, Fletcher . . . oh, look, we're here!

They were at the water's edge, and the tide curled up around Fletcher's feet.

"Tandy, I don't want you to go!"

Fletcher—mystery and magic. They're everywhere, in everyone. Notice them.

"Tandy, if I could just get you to a doctor—"

There was the faint sound of a calliope, Tandy's laughter.

I'd like to see the face of the doctor who'd examine me!

Fletcher heard the sound of labored breathing in his ear.

That saying, 'You'll always be in my heart'? It's true, Fletcher, I'll always be here.

He felt the warm imprint of a palm on his chest.

"I don't want you in my heart! I want you here in the world with me!"

Fletcher, I just want to say thank you . . . and congratulations.

"Congratulations? For what?"

Fletcher felt Tandy in his arms, saw Tandy in his arms, and a second later he didn't. It was as if the water took her as easily as it tucked a shell into the pocket of a wave and took it out to sea. Where there had been two figures on a remote beach in Mozambique, there was now one, and Fletcher stood looking out at a horizon he couldn't see, listening to the churns and sighs of the tide.

Finally, he kneeled and cupping his hands lifted a handful of water to his face. As the water dribbled out between his fingers, he remembered Tandy, on the boat at Lake WoogiWikki.

"It's true," he said. "The ocean tastes like tears."

20

There was no way Wanda Plum could take in all that she experienced, but hers was such a sensible nature that she offered herself the same counsel she gave her students: you can only do what you can do.

I'm not an astrophysicist, after all; I'm a second grade teacher and I will call on all my skills as such!

Don't make room for fear now—it is an unwelcome guest that demands attention you can't spare!

This is the opportunity of a lifetime!

These and dozens of affirmations rang through her head as Charmat whisked her into the vortex of outer space, to a place where the air was so dense she felt she might smother and yet so light she felt it was dancing through her.

And when the whole mind-bending/-blowing experience was over, Charmat had, like a professional ballroom dancer, zamooshed Wanda back so smoothly that when she landed on her dining room chair, it was as if she had been swept in on a breath rather than by a tornado. She had been more jarred making stops at red lights in her Volkswagen Beetle.

Charmat resisted her offer of coffee as they tiptoed into the kitchen but did agree to a loaf of banana bread to go. Bowing with the courtliness that is inherent in many leaders, human or alien, he told her he had to get back to his Lodge to apprise them of what had happened at the Head Council and on Mozambique.

"Tandy is . . . ," said Wanda and when Charmat nodded, her hand went to her chest, as if to stanch the hurt.

"But just because she's dead doesn't mean she's done for," said Charmat, his voice wavering. "For all the superiority of our cosmic Lodge brothers and sisters, no one has been able to answer the what-happens-next question."

"I like that mystery," said Wanda.

"And I like you. Fletcher did well to find you, for you are—even with your human handicap—a superior being."

"Thank you," said Wanda, and her smile was so pretty and her dimples so deep that Charmat's forehead pulsed, taking a picture he didn't want to forget. Taking one of her hands and pursing the slit that was his mouth, he kissed it.

"Until next time."

"I hope there is one," said Wanda, and after the alien leader whispered something in her ear, he—and the loaf of banana bread—swirled and sparkled into nothingness.

"I have got to write this down," she said aloud, but first she washed her hands, because after all, she had no idea what she had just been exposed to, and it was always better to be safe than sorry.

Satisfied all outer-space germs had been scrubbed away, she set up her portable typewriter on the kitchen table.

Dear Fletcher,

she typed, her flying fingers keeping pace with her thoughts.

I wish I had had a film crew with me to document all I saw and heard, but I will do my best to relay what happened at the Head Council meeting. Right now I feel like a giant dryer and everything is tumbling and spinning inside me, but as I tell my students (and told you once), "Begin at the beginning."

The zamoosh felt as if I were not just a rocket but a rocket whose propellant didn't come from the fossils of some slow, plodding dinosaur but from the sun. Really, I felt a yellow blast that turned blindingly white, and then I was off into a darkness I didn't know could exist. But that's what the entire experience was often like. I'd feel like I was upside down at the same time I felt right side up!

When I felt as if motion had stopped (and yet felt movement I couldn't see all around me), Charmat and I were in a room with no walls. He was no longer the alien who looked as if he'd stepped off a movie set; he was a ball of light. I was, too, and oh my, gosh, Fletcher, the sensation of my body being nothing but a glowing sphere! It was like being one enormous electric shock, only it didn't hurt. It was as if I had the power of a volcano while my entire body weight was less than a gnat's. There were twenty other balls (I counted) and they vibrated and hummed and dipped and darted in the room, and then I got a sense of weight, as if something very important—a cloud of knowledge—had descended on us. And then the room with no walls formed walls and the balls of light became shapes and we were all sitting at a conference table!

Looking into its reflective surface, I could see I was no longer a round glimmer of light but myself. And surprisingly, considering the speed in which I traveled, my hair looked none the worse for wear.

"All of this, of course, is a nod to you Earthlings," said the apparent leader, waving a one-fingered hand at the thermos pots of coffee and legal pads on the table, a flow chart positioned nearby. Like the aliens that sat on either side of her (I took her to be female on the basis of her high voice—you of course know that these aliens manifest themselves with no marked characteristics denoting gender), she was wearing a cap—which looked, by the way, like those worn by the Green Berets—with the letters UHC sewn on.

Across from me sat an Asian gentlemen, quite nervous, adjusting his glasses every which way, as if pushing them a centimeter to the left or right would make all that he was seeing make sense. Next to him was an alien (all of them, except for slight color variations, looked just like Charmat and wore their lodge numbers) and next to the alien was a silver-haired woman, wearing a ski sweater and a bemused look on her face. Another alien, then a dog! A well-behaved golden retriever, who sat on his chair with great nonchalance, as if dogs everywhere sat at conference tables in outer space (although, come to think of it, humans are probably aliens to them anyway).

All in all, there were, including me and the dog, seven Earthlings. A beautiful woman with a headscarf and kohl-rimmed eyes. A very large man who shifted in his chair as if it were impossible to get comfortable. Another man tapped his fingers on the table—he was as black as Tandy but as thin as she wasn't. And me. I think we would have been friendlier to one another if we weren't so discombobulated. In any case, we sat silently, with our particular fidgets, until the alien who sat at the head of the table spoke.

"Welcome," she said. "I am Borlot, Acting Chair of the Universal Head Council. And for those of you like me who appreciate knowing where you are, we are presently in between Saturn's Ring A and Ring B because we find the light so flattering—but we could easily move if anyone gets chilly.

"We are aware you have traveled far and thank you for your participation in what we hope will be the commencement of a new age in Universal understanding. You were screened carefully, and we look forward to hearing what you have to offer us.

"We will now go around the table and each Lodge member will introduce its candidate and illuminate us as to why he or she was chosen.

"Plek, from Lodge 527, please begin."

The alien, who was a murky sort of purple color, stood up like a good student.

"As you know, we are the scientists—"

Charmat snickered and Plek glared at him.

"—and to that end, we chose Bhakdi Shinewatri, the premiere chef in all of Thailand."

"You claim to be a Lodge of science and you choose a chef?" asked Charmat.

Borlot leveled a gaze at him that would have singed hair, if he had any.

"We realize it's a point of pride for Lodge 1212 to get thrown out of every Universal gathering, but do you really want to get thrown out of this one?"

Charmat's rubbery knee nudged mine under the table, but his apology to the Head Council leader sounded sincere.

"Our belief," continued Plek, "is that Thai food answers questions that haven't even been asked yet."

"And we shall explore those more deeply in Phase II," said Borlot, making a notation. "And now, Veztar, let's hear from you."

A khaki-colored alien stood.

"I represent Lodge 103—the healers—and to that end, I would like to introduce Guri Ramstad—

The silver-haired woman bobbed her head and smiled.

"—who at the age of sixty-five human years treats her body as if it's twenty and her body responds in kind."

"Ja, I tink—"

"We'll have time to hear what you think later," said Borlot, not unkindly, but not kindly either. "Merdor?"

"Greetings," said the gray alien. "As you know, I represent Lodge 720, whose motto is, Seek and you'll no doubt have to seek some more. We're the spiritualists, of course, which is why we've chosen Buster."

The golden retriever thumped its tail against the chair.

"Because we feel the true heart of a dog might possibly lead us to the great unknown."

"Thank you, Merdor," said Borlot, making another notation. (I tell you, Fletcher, she was all business.) "Shezbar?"

The blue alien introduced himself as coming from Lodge 623—"the Lodge that seeks beauty"—and said that Hammar was an Egyptian poet whose words created little rest stops for weary souls. (I'd like to read a poet like that!)

Next an alien named Rex (!?) from Lodge 204 (the landscapers) introduced Balan from Samoa, saying that his candidate understood both land and water in ancient ways that need to be reclaimed for all planetary success.

From Lodge 115, Zek introduced Mr. Kwaqui, a concert pianist from South Africa whose hands "speak the healing and mysterious language of music."

Finally, Borlot got to Charmat and after he stood and introduced himself, he said, "My candidate, unfortunately, couldn't be with me, but I have in his place—"

"What? This isn't—" The head council leader scrunched her bulbous forehead as she looked at the legal pad. "—Fletcher Weschel?"

Charmat issued a dry, dusty cough. "No, this is his proxy, Wanda Plum, a second grade—"

"Brother Charmat, this is unacceptable. As it was, you were almost late for the session—reason enough for disqualification—but this—"

Holding up a finger in a time-out gesture, Borlot conferred with her other council aliens.

Nodding her head, she looked up. "Yes, we are all in agreement. Lodge 1212, in its perpetual puerile quest for fun, has disqualified itself and its candidate."

"Madame Borlot, please," said Charmat, leaning over the table. "Fletcher's reasons for not being here are precisely why he is the ideal person for this job."

The golden retriever growled.

"Sorry," said Charmat. "The ideal Earthling. His escort, Sister Tandala, was in the final throes of expiration, and Fletcher didn't want to leave her."

"Sister Tandala has expired?" asked Borlot.

Charmat nodded and the aliens in the room sounded a one-note sound of distress, so high that the poor golden retriever yowled in protest.

"Our condolences," said the chair-alien, and suddenly they all stood at attention as the walls and ceiling of the room disappeared so that we could view what Charmat explained telepathically to me was the three-hundred-nebulae salute that is standard operating ritual when an alien passes.

Fletcher, there is no way I can explain the profound beauty of that sky show; it would be like asking me to build the Eiffel Tower with toothpicks. Suffice it to say that those burning, streaking colors were an appropriate display for Tandy.

We shared a long feeling of reverence until the ghostly tails of the lights disappeared and the walls and ceiling returned, and the aliens and Earthlings sat down and the foreheads of the other Head Council members scrunched down as they leaned into one another, conferring.

"While the sympathy card is a crafty play, our edict is still the same. Fletcher Weschel is not—"

Before I could hear anything else, I was sucked up in that vacuum of speed and color, and the next thing I knew, Charmat and I were in my dining room.

Wanda sat for a long time, staring at the words she had written before unrolling the paper and adding it to the small stack next to the typewriter.

After exhaling a long sigh of effort, she said out loud, "I guess I'd better put that lasagna in."

It was the smell of tomato sauce and garlic that woke Fletcher.

For a moment, he was allowed the sweet sleepy fuzz of knowing nothing more than he was awake. Consciousness of where he was came next—*Why, I'm at Wanda's. On her couch*—and it was a comforting and happy consciousness but short-lived, shoved aside by the memory of himself kneeling on the Mozambique shoreline.

"Tandy," he had cried, and as the waves lapped against him, he felt he was shrouded in a loneliness so black he didn't think it could ever be lifted.

But it was.

"Fletcher," said Revlor, his rubbery one-fingered hand on the human's shoulder. "Look."

He was surprised by how pleased he was to see the smart-aleck alien, and his eyes followed the direction where the alien's other finger was pointing.

The sky was filled with swirls of color—the northern lights, although it reminded Fletcher of the lights in which the aliens would appear and disappear.

"That's for Tandy's send-off," said Revlor, his voice clotted with emotion. "Anytime you see the aurora borealis, know that a Lodge member has passed into the great beyond."

He and Fletcher stood watching until it evaporated.

"Godspeed," said Revlor reverently, and then, remembering who he was and in what Lodge he was a member, he added, "Whatever that means."

—

Sighing, Fletcher got up and folded the afghan that had covered him in a precise rectangle. After using the bathroom he went into the kitchen, and when he saw Wanda, wearing a gingham apron with the silhouette of a turkey stitched onto the bodice, he felt a little wobbly in the knees.

"Fletcher," said Wanda, who had been greatly relieved to see him asleep on the couch when she had zamooshed into the living room with Charmat. "You're awake."

With outstretched arms, they stepped toward one another, and their hug was long and hard.

An oven timer went off.

"Time to put the garlic bread in," she said, gently pulling away from him.

"Wanda, what happened? Where did you go?"

"It's all there, Fletcher," said Wanda, nodding toward her typewriter on the table. "You can read it while I work on dinner."

And as Wanda dipped a brush into melted garlic butter and painted the French bread with it, as she mixed the salad and uncorked the wine, Fletcher did.

"Hoola, baby," said Fletcher after reading it for the second time.

"I know," said Wanda. "It's a lot to take in, isn't it?"

Fletcher, overcome, nodded and shook his head at the same time so that it looked like he was tracing out erratic figure eights.

As a teacher, Miss Plum knew when her children needed a break, which is why story time came after the rough-and-tumble of recess, and why sing-a-longs at the piano followed math drills. As a woman, Wanda knew that Fletcher was overloaded and needed, for just a little while, to decompress.

"Let's eat now," she suggested. "I'll bet you're starving. I know I am."

By the light of the candles that flickered like little buds of flame on the branch centerpiece, Fletcher ate three helpings of lasagna, three pieces of garlic bread, and two bowls full of salad.

While Wanda enjoyed her own smaller portions, she told him all about the school pageant that had taken place the day before and the strange pumpkin fudge Caroline Seeholt, the kindergarten teacher, had brought to the teacher's lounge.

"Jim Manning, the fifth grade teacher, had to spit his into a napkin."

She told him that Reed Quinn, a student of hers, was going to Mount Rushmore over the holiday weekend and that Reed's brother had told him that birds nested in all the presidents' noses so it looked like they all had boogers.

"You wouldn't believe all the things Reed's brother tells him."

Fletcher was grateful for and entertained by the one-sided conversation, but finally he dabbed his mouth with his napkin and pushed aside his plate.

"Thank you," he said.

"You're welcome," said Wanda. "I know it was sort of a strange dinner for—"

"Not just for the dinner. Which was wonderful, by the way. Thank you for everything."

"I say the same to you," said Wanda, and they looked into one another's eyes and into a deep place.

———

The afternoon darkness—but not the snow the weatherman had promised—began to fall and they moved from the dining room into the living room, taking Wanda's report and cups of spiced apple tea with them.

"All those people assembled!" said Fletcher. "And a dog! What were they thinking?"

"I'm sure I would have learned a lot more had I stayed," said Wanda. "Phase II was coming up after the introductions."

They sat next to each other on the floor, leaning against the ottoman and facing the fire that snapped in Wanda's feminist fireplace.

"Do you suppose they all had the same fantasy experiences I had?" asked Fletcher. "Did the dog get to see what it was like to be a cat? Did the guy from Samoa get to experience life as a stockbroker in New York or a male stripper in Milwaukee?"

"Charmat was of the mind that only you got that particular honor, because you needed to be reminded why you were recruited."

"I'm sort of following you, and sort of not."

Because they were sitting so close together, Fletcher felt the little shake of Wanda's shoulders as she laughed.

"Remember, all Lodges were ordered to recruit a candidate truest to their values. Lodge 1212 thought you best exemplified fun—but they had to make sure you believed it."

"Do you know that there isn't a single human being I've ever met who would accuse me of exemplifying fun?"

"Aliens are smarter than human beings. They saw the real Fletcher."

"So what was this contest for? I mean, all these Lodges swooping down to Earth and gathering their candidates—these people and a dog—but their candidates for what?"

Wanda took a sip of tea and held the taste of apples and cinnamon in her mouth for a long time. This was what she had been waiting to tell Fletcher, the last words that Charmat whispered in her ear.

"Well, believe it or not," she said, "they were looking to elect the Mayor of the Universe."

For a long time, they watched flames leap and the wood spit sparks, and then, in a very small voice, Fletcher asked, "I was Lodge 1212's candidate?"

Wanda nodded. "And Charmat said that disqualified or not, as far as he was concerned, you *are* the Mayor of the Universe."

Fletcher felt an odd charge of fear and glee. "But what does that mean?"

"I don't know. Maybe we'll find out. Maybe not." Holding up her teacup in a toast, she said, "Either way, Happy Thanksgiving."

"Happy Thanksgiving," answered Fletcher, and the sound of their clinked china was a soprano's high note that still sounded after their lips met.

21

The Tuesday after Thanksgiving they were married in the Aberdeen City Hall during Wanda's lunch break.

"So where should we go on our honeymoon?" asked Fletcher, driving his bride back to school in her VW.

"As if I need one after Mozambique and outer space."

They laughed, something they found they did a lot together.

When Miss Plum brought her new husband in for Show and Tell, Katie Charbonneau asked her what was so funny.

"What do you mean, Katie?" asked Miss Plum, who stood in front of the class holding Fletcher's hand.

"Well, you two keep laughing."

"We do?" said Miss Plum.

"It's because we're so happy," said Fletcher.

Katie Charbonneau, who was prepared to not like Miss Plum's new husband (who could be good enough for her?) lowered her head and smiled. She liked when adults gave sensible answers.

Matt Hefflinger raised his hand. "Are we supposed to call you Mrs. Wisher now?"

"Weschel. My husband's last name is Weschel. So now I'll be Mrs. Plum-Weschel."

"And I'll be Mr. Plum-Weschel," said Fletcher proudly, and the couple laughed.

"That's awfully long," said Reed Quinn. "My brother says teachers should just be called 'Teacher' because that's what they are."

"Does your brother's teacher call him 'Student'?" asked Mrs. Plum-Weschel.

"No, 'cause his name's Bruce."

Always encouraging her kids to figure things out for themselves, Mrs. Plum-Weschel said nothing further.

Now, on the first day of winter break, they were headed to Fletcher's home in Pierre to pick up his roomier car and begin a two-week road trip.

"You don't have to be nervous," said Wanda, who, Fletcher was finding, sensed what he was feeling almost as soon as he did. She took her hand off the gearshift to pat his knee.

"I know," said Fletcher, blinking back tears. That was another discovery he and Wanda had made; the fire had been turned up under all their emotions.

With a laugh, Fletcher might recall for Wanda the sight of Tandy doing a handstand on the hood of a Cadillac in her cowgirl outfit, or of Deke Drake and Millie outrunning their pickpocketed victims, or of Shark and Tandy waltzing on a glittering strip of moonlit water, and three seconds after the words were out of his mouth, he would be sobbing.

Even as Wanda comforted him, her own tears fell.

"How can we not cry, Fletcher?" she said, after they'd reminisced about the sensation of zamooshing. "We've seen so much . . . wonder."

"Yes, we have," he said, looking into the lovely face of his bride.

———————

The snow that had made the drive pretty but not dangerous picked up a couple of miles outside of Pierre, and by the time Wanda turned the Beetle into Fletcher's driveway it was coming down fast and furious.

"Weschel?" cried Dodd Beckerman, who liked to do what he called a pre-shovel even before all the snow had stopped falling. "Weschel, is that you?"

In his bulky army coat, he leapt over the narrow strip of whitened lawn that separated his driveway from Fletcher's.

"Hey, Dodd," said Fletcher, getting out the car.

"Hey?!" said Beckerman, yelling as the snow swirled. "You've been gone almost a month and you just say, *Hey*? Where the hell have you been?"

"I got married," said Fletcher, opening the driver's-side door. "This is my wife, Wanda."

For a moment, Beckerman was rendered speechless by the announcement and the small pretty woman who emerged from the car, but then the butcher bawled, "Married?!" and invited the newlyweds into his house for a drink.

"Now, come on!" he shouted. "I won't take no for an answer!"

———

When you've been a pulsing ball of light flitting through the rings of Saturn, an invitation into a home with its knick-knackery of beer bottles and paintings of topless women on different makes of motorcycles isn't all that daunting an experience. Or so Wanda tried to telegraph to Fletcher with her eyes as he telegraphed his apology with his.

"First snow of the year, and it's a doozie," said Beckerman, who after dumping their coats over the banister gestured toward the Naugahyde couches.

"Now you two make yourself at home whilst I retrieve our libations." Dodd made a move toward the kitchen but froze for a moment before making a slow pivot to face his guests with an apology.

"Oh man, I haven't made my beer run yet."

"We're fine," said Fletcher.

"I might have some schnapps."

"Really," said Fletcher. "I think we're fine."

"You let the old man speak for you?" asked Dodd, throwing a little wink Wanda's way.

She winked back at him. "Only when we're in agreement."

"Okay, then," said Dodd, gesturing that they all sit.

"So," said Beckerman as they all slid into position on the slippery Naugahyde. "You are the talk of the town, Fletcher! Quitting your job and running off with some black babe!" He shrugged at Wanda. "Sorry, but that's the scuttlebutt."

"The scuttlebutt is true," said Wanda.

"So you knew about her?"

"Oh, yes," said Wanda. "I met her several times. But she wasn't really black, Dodd. She was green—at least in her presentation to us Earthlings."

Fletcher had two simultaneous reactions, but the volt of shock zapped the laughter like a laser cauterizing an internal bleed. He sat frozen on the slick couch, his hands between his knees, waiting for whatever was going to happen next.

Dodd leaned forward and rifled the pages of the *TV Guide* that normally served as a coaster on his coffee table. He cocked his head and offered Fletcher and Wanda an uncertain smile.

"Whatever you meant by that, I didn't get it."

Wanda's smile was certain. "What I mean is that Tandy—that's the 'black babe'—was really an alien."

Dodd's eyes traveled the short distance from Wanda's face to Fletcher's and back again.

"I take it you're not talking about some wetback without a green card?"

Wincing at his remark, Wanda said, "I'm talking about an 'alien' alien—from outer space."

Beckerman winked at Fletcher, an insincere gesture that was enough to nudge Fletcher from his daze: if Wanda wanted to tell his neighbor about their experience, she must have a good reason and he would back her up one hundred percent.

"That's right, Dodd. I was visited by aliens. Right there in my very bedroom"—he pointed behind him, in the direction of his house—"and you know why? Because they were looking for the Mayor of the Universe."

Beckerman snorted. "Oh sure!" he said. "Of course! Out of all the billions of people in the world, aliens are going to decide *you're* the Mayor of the Universe." His smile and rolling eyes demonstrated that he got the joke, and he shook his head and chuckled as he traversed the matted path in the shag carpeting to the kitchen.

Fletcher and Wanda shared the kind of look two neophyte sky-divers do before jumping out of an airplane but remained silent until he returned, unscrewing a small bottle of whiskey he'd saved from his last plane ride.

"I forgot I had this," he said, twisting off the bottle cap and taking a swig. "So I get that the two of you are practical jokers—"

"Well, not exactly, but it is my sense of fun they were drawn to," said Fletcher.

Dodd rubbed his jaw and it was hard to tell if he was smiling or grimacing.

"Okay, because I'm your host and I'm glad to see you—by the way, I let myself into your house with the key your ma had given my ma, and I ran the water a couple times just to make sure the pipes wouldn't freeze and turned on the lights so it would look like someone was home, so don't ever say I wasn't a good neighbor." Beckerman took another swig from the bottle. "And I'm gonna play along with you because I can see somehow this game means something to you."

"You're right," said Wanda. "It does mean a lot to us, but it's not a game."

Fletcher couldn't help it. He let out a little cackle.

Beckerman was reminded why it was he had always picked on Fletcher: *because the jerk asked for it!* But intent as he was on making a good impression on his wife, he stifled his desire to flick Fletcher on the forehead (an old practice). "Okay, so why did they decide you were Mayor of the Universe?"

"They didn't decide I was the mayor," said Fletcher, "only that I was a candidate. I was in the running, but then I was disqualified."

Before he could censor himself, Beckerman asked, "What for? For being the world's biggest dork?"

Wanda's smile was the one she used on kids like Sean Douglas, the best-looking boy in her class but also the most cold-hearted.

"Dodd," she said, and although her voice was friendly, sharp ears would hear the distain in it, "they chose Fletcher because they realized the importance of a deep, loving fun and how much he exemplified it."

Beckerman coughed down his whiskey "Deep, loving fun? *Fletcher?* They must have misread their flight plan—their space ship must have zigged north when it was supposed to zag south—they must have confused Fletcher for someone like me!"

Hearing the desperation in his voice, Fletcher decided now wouldn't be the time to tell Beckerman that the aliens not only didn't choose someone like him but in fact short-sheeted his bed.

"Because," continued Beckerman, "what kind of aliens would take the trouble to come all the way to Earth and not want to meet me?"

Feeling like the guy brought in to dismantle the ticking bomb, Fletcher said, "For all I know, Dodd, it was totally random. The luck of the draw. Maybe next time, they'll pick you."

Outside, the snow was not so much falling to the ground as attacking it. Bent over against its assault, Fletcher led Wanda across Beckerman's snowy yard and to his own, up the back steps, and into the area Olive called the mud room. When he turned on the light in the kitchen, Wanda issued a small sigh.

"Oh, Fletcher," she said, "I can just see you sitting there as a little boy, eating your TV dinner alone."

"It wasn't so bad," said Fletcher, his arm encircling his bride's, "I love pot pies."

Later, as they lay so entwined in his old bed that he was hard pressed to identify which limb was his and which was Wanda's, they talked about what had happened at Dodd Beckerman's house.

"Why did you tell him, Wanda?"

He had left the rickrack-trimmed curtains open, and outside the snow twisted and swirled. It was in this room, the night the aliens came, that he had been the most terrified, but now he was certain that there was no place warmer, safer, than in the childhood bed he now shared with his wife.

"I hadn't planned to; the words just came out of my mouth." Wanda lay on her side facing him, her head resting on her hands. "But maybe that's how we should approach it, Fletcher. Maybe if we just tell people the truth, it'll help us sort out everything that happened."

"But they'll never believe us," said Fletcher.

"I don't think we should live our lives concerned about what *they* believe. I think we should live our lives concerned about what *we* believe."

"Will you marry me?" asked Fletcher, pressing his head into the blonde curly hair that smelled of apples.

"If I hadn't already," said Wanda, "I most certainly would."

In a diner in North Platte, Nebraska, they had gotten friendly with a jovial farmer and his wife while waiting out a snowstorm. As fellow travelers often do, they exchanged stories, the farm couple relaying their story of surviving the Good Friday earthquake while visiting relatives in Anchorage, Alaska, and Fletcher and Wanda sharing the tale of their alien encounter.

"Okay, are we on *Candid Camera* or something?" asked the farmer, no longer jovial.

"No," said his wife, gathering up her purse. "*Candid Camera*'s funny. These two weirdos aren't."

At another roadside diner in Colorado Springs, they shared counter space—and their story—with a trucker who sat nodding his head and stroking his long beard as Fletcher told him about waking up to a room full of aliens and Wanda imitated the robotic voice of the chairwoman of the Universal Head Council.

"That reminds me," said the trucker, dragging his fingers through his beard, "of the time I sold my soul to Satan while I was hauling chickens on Highway 61."

The poor waitress, who had overheard everything, wrote out their checks, her hands trembling.

"Please don't hurt me," she said softly to both the newlyweds and the bearded trucker.

They'd hustled out of the restaurant, leaving the waitress a forty percent tip by way of apology.

"I take full blame," said Wanda, once they were on the highway, both of them checking mirrors to make sure the bearded trucker with the sold soul wasn't following them. "Seeing as I was the one who thought we should be open and honest. But now . . . well, now I think we should be a little more circumspect in telling our story."

"I agree," said Fletcher. "But what about your parents?"

Wanda's lower lip trembled.

Fletcher rubbed his wife's arm.

"They're your parents, Wanda. I'll take my lead from you."

———

The newlyweds arrived in Silver City just after five, and even though the backyard thermometer read fifty-two degrees, Wanda's father, Clifford, insisted they eat their first meal together outside.

"Could we do this in Aberdeen three days before Christmas?"

As they enjoyed Irene's taco hot dish (she had combined her midwestern love of casseroles with her new appreciation for southwestern spices) and cornbread, the older couple regaled the younger one with their own courtship story.

"We were in the same freshman comp class in college," said Irene. "I was a Patterson and he was a Plum so I sat ahead of him, and the professor starts off the first day by reading Schiller's "Ode to Joy" and tells us one of our assignments will be to write our own ode to our own particular joy. After class, this impudent boy taps me on the shoulder and tells me, 'I've been staring at your hair the whole class, and I decided I'm going to write an ode to it.'"

"A certain cascade of honey-colored hair," Clifford recited. "Invites me to swim in its waves, heart opened in prayer."

Irene tucked her chin into her upturned jacket collar and smiled. "And you only got a B- on that?"

"What words could do hair like yours justice?" asked Clifford, whose own hair, a thick silver swoop, was odeworthy in its own right.

"But you've already heard this story," said Irene, looking across the table at her daughter, and even though she smiled, there was a tiny pucker of a frown on her forehead. Although some of her misgivings about her daughter's hasty marriage had been assuaged by meeting Fletcher and seeing the obvious love the two shared, she still felt there was something fishy going on. "Now we want to hear every single detail of your own. You haven't given us much in the way of details."

"That's right," said Clifford. "The last we've heard from you, you were planning a nice quiet Thanksgiving by yourself, and there's not one word of a special fellow, and then we get a call a couple days later telling us you're married!"

"I know," said Wanda. "It's just that everything happened so fast and—"

"Let me apologize, too," said Fletcher. "Not for marrying Wanda—of course it's the most wonderful thing I've ever done—but to deny you of your daughter's wedding, of walking her down the aisle—well, for that I'm truly sorry."

Wanda nodded and nervously gulped her ice tea, swallowing so much so fast that it hurt going down in her throat.

"It's just," continued Fletcher, "it's just that we'd been through so much together that we needed to—"

"Been through so much together, like what?" said Irene, folding her arms.

"All we know is you met in Wanda's classroom, as part of some sort of teacher rewards program," said Clifford, folding his arms, too.

"And I'm curious," said Irene, "what would an actuary have to do with that?" She was shivering, and even though it was not wholly due to the chill night air, she suggested that they all go inside. "And then," she said, with the same no-nonsense look Wanda used on unruly students, "you're going to tell us everything."

———

Irene decided Wanda's uncharacteristic coyness was because *everything* must mean a pregnancy, and she was flummoxed why her daughter didn't just come out and tell them the reason behind their sudden marriage. It wasn't as if she and Clifford hadn't been waiting and waiting for grandchildren—how could Wanda think they would be anything less than delighted?

The lights of the tree blinked in their cheerful, Christmasy way as they all sat down in the living room, and Irene wondered if she should feign surprise or not at the big announcement. She listened eagerly, but as Wanda spoke, and then Fletcher, and then Wanda again, she realized that their rushed marriage wasn't because they were expectant parents but because they loved each other deeply. *And oh yes, their intense experience with aliens from outer space had forged a profound bond that they felt a need to legalize.*

In telling their story, Wanda had only dared look at her hands, and it was only when she and Fletcher were finished that she raised her head. When she saw the look of fear on her parents' faces, she burst into tears.

"I'm so sorry to make you feel this way!" she wailed. "We debated not telling you—but we had to! It was so wonderfully, beautifully fantastic!"

"It was," said Fletcher, tightening the grip he had around his wife's shoulder. "But that's because it happened to us." He mashed his lips together, as if he were trying to evenly distribute lipstick. "If the situation was reversed, and you told Wanda and me the same story, I'm sure we'd be just as upset as you. I'd be so scared that the people I loved most had gone crazy. But Clifford, Irene: we haven't."

"It's late," said Clifford, standing up (and trying not to notice that his legs were shaking). "Let's all get a good night's sleep and we'll talk everything over in the morning."

Irene, as shaky as her husband, scavenged for some hopefulness.

"So you're not pregnant?"

"Not yet," said Wanda.

There was much whispering in the old-married-couple's bed as well as the newlywed's.

"Could she be . . . ," said Irene, facing her husband under the patchwork quilt she and her quilters' group had pieced together. "Could she be on drugs or something?"

"I wondered the same thing," said Clifford. "And then I thought, did he somehow brainwash her?"

"But she's always been so level-headed!"

"I'll bet Joan of Arc's parents said the same thing."

They allowed themselves a sad little laugh before Irene began to cry in the safe shelter of her husband's arms.

When Fletcher and Wanda woke up, they found on the kitchen table a note:

> We're running errands and then off to hike in the City of Rocks State Park. We packed enough lunch for four if you'd care to join us, say noon, here?*
>
> XXX, Mom and Dad *Directions on next page.

Wanda smiled. "This has to be Dad's doing. Whenever I had a problem or was stuck on something, he'd say"—here Wanda cycled her arms—"'Start some motion; that's the potion!'"

"But first the joe," said Fletcher, pouring himself a cup of coffee, "and then we'll go."

Threaded with thin wisps of clouds, the sky was a magnificent aqua, a different color from a South Dakota sky. The hiking path they were on was a fair grade, and Fletcher was surprised, and a little embarrassed, to find himself more winded than his in-laws.

"It's the altitude," said Clifford, hearing him pant. "Plus Mother and I get out for a good walk every morning."

"Well, why aren't you out of breath?" Fletcher asked Wanda.

"I guess I'm just more fit," she said, sashaying her hips.

"Could be that space travel," said Clifford.

"Yes," said Irene adjusting the small pack on her back. "Maybe it did something to your lung capacity."

Wanda stopped in her tracks, her shoes making a scudding noise on the hard dirt path.

"Are you kidding?" she asked cautiously.

"Kidding about what?" asked her mother.

"About space travel. Are you making fun of me, or are you trying to tell us you believe what we told you?"

Fletcher stepped closer to his wife and took her hand.

"Trying to tell you we believe what you told us," said Irene.

Wanda grabbed her mother into a hug that Fletcher, whose hand she still held, was automatically pulled into.

"All right, all right," said Clifford. "We had enough waterworks last night. Let's start some motion—that's the potion!"

They ate their lunch in the shadow of huge rock formations that jutted out of the earth in tall oblongs, in squat stacked circles, in irregular squares and triangles.

"They say that all of this was made from a volcanic eruption," said Clifford, sweeping the hand that held half a peanut butter sandwich. "And the rocks themselves were sculpted by erosion."

"It's beautiful," said Wanda.

"It is," said Irene. "It looks almost like a lunar landscape, don't you think?"

"Is that why you brought us here?" teased Wanda. "Do you think it makes us feel more at home?"

Chuckling, Irene elbowed her daughter's side. "Maybe."

A cloud covered the sun and made shadows on the strange rock formations.

"Irene and I stayed up a long time last night," said Clifford.

"So did we, Dad," said Wanda.

"We figured as much."

Clifford took a bite of his sandwich and as if they were playing Follow the Leader, everyone did the same.

"It's still pretty hard for us," he said.

Wanda nodded, swallowing a lump that wasn't peanut butter.

"But that's our problem," said Irene. "And I'm not saying it won't take some time to adjust to everything you told us."

"But," said Clifford, "we asked ourselves, 'Why would Wanda make up a story like that?' and we realized there was only one answer: she wouldn't. So we have to go from there, kitten."

"Thanks," said Wanda.

"It means a lot to her—and me—that you believe us," said Fletcher, undoing the top buttons of his shirt and pulling down his collar. "Now I know this doesn't look like much, but right there is the lodge medallion they burned into my skin."

Both Irene and Clifford leaned toward Fletcher to examine the tiny little scar hidden in his sparse chest hair.

"It sort of looks like a vaccination mark," said Irene.

"Look carefully. The Lodge numbers are etched into it."

Both Irene and Clifford stood hunched close to Fletcher's chest, lifting and lowering their glasses.

"I can't make them out," admitted Irene.

"Me neither," said Clifford.

"Well, they're there," said Wanda as Fletcher buttoned up his shirt, feeling like the dramatic display of proof was pretty anticlimactic.

A lizard skittered out from under a century plant and, seeing it wasn't alone, skittered back.

"We just don't want you to get hurt," said Irene. "We're afraid if you tell a lot of people—and you said you weren't going to hide what happened—you'll be treated differently."

"You mean like we're nuts?" asked Fletcher.

Clifford nodded. Tearing off a corner of his sandwich, he threw it at the cactus, hoping to lure the lizard.

"The trouble is, usually people who say they've had alien encounters *are*. Nuts, that is. I mean, have you ever been up to Roswell?"

"We've already decided we're going to be careful about who we tell," said Fletcher.

"That's right," said Wanda. "All tabloids, talk shows, and Star Trek conventions are absolutely off-limits."

Clifford's laugh was grudging. "Come on, honey, we worry about your job. We worry about your standing in your community. We worry—"

"I get it, Dad. Of course you worry. And since I hate to be a source of that, you can count on us to not announce to the world at large that I was in a conference room between the rings of Saturn with the Universal Head Council and that Fletcher was a candidate for Mayor of the Universe."

"But as far as I'm concerned," said Fletcher, wanting to be absolutely straight with his in-laws, "the campaign is still on."

"What does that mean?" asked Irene.

"We're still figuring it out, Mom," said Wanda, and just then a squirrel streaked past them, grabbing the square inch of peanut butter sandwich the lizard had no interest in or not enough bravery for.

That evening Arnie, who had the same luxuriant silver swoop of hair as his brother Clifford, came over for cocktails, bringing his wife, June.

"We were dying to come over right away," said June, "but we wanted to give you a chance to get to know Cliff and Irene first."

"And now that you have," said Arnie, clapping Fletcher on the back, "it's time to meet the fun relatives!"

Clifford suggested gin and tonics outside (reminding everyone that outdoor cocktail parties were impossible in Aberdeen in December), but he was outvoted and the fireplace was lit in the living room.

"I hear you're a South Dakotan like the rest of us," said Arnie, after an appreciative sip of his drink. "And you win points for that. What else can you tell us about yourself?"

Fletcher was aware that his wife and her parents seemed to be holding their breaths. "Well, I'm an actuary—or was. Right now I'm thinking about getting into some other line of work."

"Like what?" asked Arnie.

"I don't really know," said Fletcher, accepting a bowl of chips and a relieved smile from Irene. "I'm just looking for a change."

"I myself was in the same line of work for forty-three years. Never a dull day either, I'll tell you that."

"Arnie was a private detective," said Clifford. "Although he's lying about there never being a dull day. You used to tell me how deadly dull staking out a wandering husband or wife could be."

"Your memory's fading, brother," said Arnie. He offered a smile with teeth a bit too perfectly square. "Now, Cliffie here was a podiatrist. There's a thrills-a-minute job."

"Do you two know where you'll live?" asked June, whose little cactus earrings swung as she turned to the newlyweds.

"We're going to make that decision this summer," said Wanda. "I want to finish the school year in Aberdeen and then we'll see."

"It'd be a shame to give up that cute house of yours," said June. "Doesn't she have a talent for decorating, Fletcher?"

"I think she's the most talented person I've ever met."

Wanda's dimples flashed. "See, I learned from you, Mom: marry a man who appreciates you."

"What about your folks?" asked Arnie. "Are they still in Pierre?"

"My mother died several years ago, and I have no idea where my dad is," said Fletcher. "He ran off to California when I was nine. With a Brownie leader."

"Oh, my," said June sadly.

"Were you named after him?" asked Arnie. "Can't say as I've heard the name Fletcher much."

"No, my dad's name was Wendell," said Fletcher. "But everyone called him WW."

"And this WW didn't keep in touch with you?" asked Arnie, whose profession had taught him to ask questions others might have been too polite to pose.

"Did you know I'm from Mitchell?" asked June, who for years had been deflecting the awkwardness her husband's questions raised. "Ever been to the Corn Palace?"

"We went there once on a field trip," said Fletcher. Turning back to Arnie he said, "He sent my mother money for about three years and then we never heard anything else from him."

His in-laws had already heard this story, but still, hearing it again didn't make it any less painful and in a testament to the love Irene already felt for her son-in-law, she thought, *I'd rather believe that story wasn't true than the one about the aliens.*

———

"Should I open it now?" Fletcher asked on Christmas Eve when Arnie gave him an envelope.

"Well, I don't want you waiting around 'til Easter!" said Arnie.

Unused to so much attention at Christmas, Fletcher flushed. With mock outrage, Wanda had pointed out that her own parents had given him more presents than they gave her; now he had another gift to add to his pile.

"What's this?" he said, puzzled, as he pulled out a slip of paper.

Arnie didn't say anything, letting Fletcher read the words he'd written.

Grateful for the nearby chair, Fletcher sank into it.

"Fletcher?" said Wanda going to him, her words coated with worry.

He handed her the paper.

"Oh my, gosh," she said, sitting heavily on his lap. To her parents, she said, "It's Fletcher's dad's address."

"Sure wasn't the toughest job I ever had," said Arnie with a bluster in his voice. "Made a few phone calls is all."

"Are you sure this is him?" asked Wanda, knowing that's what her husband would ask, if he had the wherewithal to talk.

"Wendell Vernon Weschel—that's the only match I came up with."

"That's his middle name," whispered Fletcher.

"So, you think you'll see him?" asked Arnie, who in his detective work didn't always get the happy endings he would have liked.

"Honestly, Arnie, let him think about things for a while," said June, fingering one of her cactus earrings.

Arnie tapped his watch. "Well, like I always say, there's no time like the present."

22

Driving into Los Angeles on New Year's Eve was like being on a carnival ride for which you hadn't made the height requirement but had been strapped into anyway.

"Holy Mary mother of God," Fletcher muttered under his breath, feeling engulfed in the swarming traffic.

For their big road trip, they had consigned Wanda's VW Beetle to Fletcher's garage and taken his old Monte Carlo, for which Fletcher was glad. Surely, in the car crash that seemed inevitable, they had a better chance of surviving it.

"You're doing fine," said Wanda, whose right foot was pressing against an imaginary brake pedal on the passenger side. "Just pretend you're on a country road that happens to have six lanes in it."

They welcomed in the New Year in a motel that, according to the map, was only several blocks from the apartment complex where Fletcher's dad lived.

"Happy New Year, honey," said Wanda, after Guy Lombardo's TV band began to play "Auld Lang Syne."

Fletcher kissed her as hard as he ever had, with a prayer that, yes, it would be.

———

While Fletcher's intentions had been to start out the New Year with a bang, visiting his father immediately after breakfast, his courage had waned by his second cup of coffee, and both he and Wanda agreed there'd be nothing wrong with taking a side trip to Hollywood—"as long as we're so close." Their whirlwind tour included the Walk of Fame, lunch at Schwab's Pharmacy, and a drive through Beverly Hills, and it wasn't until late afternoon that they arrived in Van Nuys. As they walked into the shabby apartment complex, Fletcher realized the old man limping across the concrete courtyard was WW, and he called out to him.

His father's first words to the son he hadn't seen in twenty-eight years were, "Fletcher? Oh, shit."

Thinking he heard more sadness than rebuke in the words, Fletcher embraced the seventy-five-year-old man whose bathrobe was stained and covered a frayed pair of swim trunks.

"I . . . I," said WW. "How did you find me?"

"A private detective I know."

"I was just on my way to the Jacuzzi."

"Well, don't let me stop you, Dad," said Fletcher, surprised that it didn't take but a minute in his father's presence to feel the old familiar sting of rejection.

"My doctor says it's good for this damn phlebitis." He looked at Wanda. "You and your lady friend could join me, I guess."

"This is Wanda," said Fletcher, pulling her closer. "My wife."

"You've got yourself a pretty one. Like a little doll."

"I'm so glad to meet you, Mr. Weschel," said Wanda, forgoing his proffered hand and hugging him instead. "Fletcher has told me a lot about you."

"I'll bet he has," said WW.

Whereas in the past, both Fletcher and Wanda might have been unwilling to strip to their underwear to join an old man in a whirlpool, that particular self-conscious behavior had pretty well been zapped by recent experience. They were the only ones in the pool area anyway, and even if they hadn't been, it wasn't as if underwear didn't closely resemble swimsuits.

"Jesus Christ, this is just so hard to believe," said WW, after they all settled themselves in the Jacuzzi, each finding a strong jet to throttle their back muscles. "One minute I'm wondering if my towel from last night is still out here—it was my favorite towel and I think one of the young punks in the building stole it—and the next minute my son who I haven't seen for forty years shows up."

"Twenty-eight."

"Huh?"

"It's been twenty-eight years since I last saw you, Dad. Not forty."

WW waved his hand. "Twenty-eight. Forty. When you get to be my age, there's not much difference." He hung his thin flabby arms along the tile edge of the whirlpool. "So how's tricks, Fletcher?"

Tricks? How's tricks? Well, Dad, if you mean "How am I?"—fine, thanks. Except that for a long time I was sad and lonesome, missing you and trying to make Mom feel better; then for years—now that you're asking—I think I was in a low-grade depression, always sort of disengaged, I guess. But now, now I married the best woman in the world whom I met, funnily enough, through aliens!

Instead, Fletcher answered by asking, "How've you been, Dad? Tell me everything. Did you ever get that patent number? Did you remarry? Have more kids? Did you ever want to contact me? Wonder how I was doing?"

Wanda, hearing his words grow in speed and volume, waded through the pulsating water to sit next to her husband and finding one of his hands underwater squeezed it.

"Always full of questions," said WW. "That much I do remember." He flapped his fingers against his thumb in a "talk, talk, talk" gesture. "Always bugging me with question after question. So let's see . . . I did invent a couple of board games, but when I showed them to an investor, he stole my ideas. You can go in any store these days and find at least three of the games I thought of, but did I ever see any money for them? Not on your life."

"That's too bad," said Wanda.

"You're damn right it is! I should have been a millionaire, and instead I had to make do with managing a dinky little film processing lab."

He shoved the water with the heel of his hand.

"And no, I never had any more kids—that I know of!—and yes, I did remarry. Not Shirley, who I came out here with—oh my God, did that woman turn out to be *poison*—but a gal named Jan. A real beauty, Jan was—a showgirl in Reno! You can't say I didn't know how to pick 'em, although maybe you could, considering I picked Olive."

"Please don't say anything against my mother," said Fletcher, clenching his wife's hand. "You didn't make it easy for her."

WW shrugged and wiped sweat beading under his nose. "I probably didn't. Didn't make it easy for Jan either. She said words to that effect—and worse!—when she left me. Then there was"—his tongue poked out of his mouth and he shut one eye—"oh yeah, Rita . . . no, not Rita, what was her name? Oh yeah, Reva. Took her to see Frank Sinatra after our wedding. Christ, that guy can sing."

He tipped his head back and began to sing "High Hopes," and while Fletcher knew it was not a personal serenade, he pretended it was, for as far as he remembered, his father had not sung so much as "Rock-a-Bye, Baby" to him.

WW's voice was slightly flat, but what it lacked in tonal precision it more than made up for in salesmanship, and both Fletcher and Wanda felt compelled to join in on the refrain, and with the same vigor. The trio belted their "High Hopes" so loudly, in fact, that two different tenants were inspired to stick out their heads from their respective windows and offer their own requests.

"Shut up!" yelled the one from Apartment 103.

"Yeah!" shouted the one from Apartment 205. "High hopes, my ass!"

They stood in front of WW's linen closet, which was crowded with foot powders, bottles of liniments and antacids, a hot water bottle, and an enema kit.

"Here they are," said WW, finding two thin towels among the sundries of the aged. "I'd give you my favorite towel, but I think one of the young punks in the building stole it." Nodding to a door, he said, "You can dry off in there, and when you're ready I'll meet you at the bar."

The living room, decorated in what looked like 1970s hotel furniture, was separated from the kitchen by a counter, and it was behind this that WW stood, shaking a tomato juice can. Fletcher was touched to see some of the old WW flair now that the old man had cleaned up; he wore a silk dressing gown and pajama pants (smelling of moth balls and BENGAY, but elegant nonetheless) and the comb marks were visible in his dyed black hair.

"Hope you two like Bloody Marys," said the host. "I can't eat all the vegetables my doctor tells me to—so I drink 'em!"

His was a bar well-stocked enough to provide almond-stuffed olives as a garnish, and he handed Fletcher and Wanda their glasses with the pride of a man who knows how to mix a drink.

"Bottoms up," he said. Realizing the toast was too small for the occasion, he added, "To my son, Fletcher. And his lovely wife."

He toasted me! Fletcher thought, his heart swelling as they clinked glasses.

"I wasn't really sure I was glad to see you—"

Fletcher felt his effervescence flattening.

"—at first, but I am now. And I hope . . . I hope it won't be another forty years."

"Twenty-eight, Dad," said Fletcher.

The old mischief flashed in WW's magnified eyes. "Kidding, Fletch. I'm kidding."

He suggested they retire to the living room, and Fletcher and Wanda sat on an orange- striped couch and WW on its matching side chair.

"Now, Fletcher," said WW, yawning deeply, "it's time to tell me about yourself."

"Dad, it's late," said Fletcher, fairly certain (but not completely) that it was the time and not the subject that was responsible for his father's fatigue. "We'll come over tomorrow before we leave and catch up."

"You're leaving tomorrow? But you just got here!"

"I'm a teacher," said Wanda, "and I've got to be back when school starts."

"I thought . . . I thought we could spend at least the weekend together."

Pleasure filled Fletcher's chest.

"We'll stay as long as you like tonight," he said. "If you're sure we're not keeping you up."

WW stifled another yawn. "Don't worry about me, I stay up late all the time. It's just that that Jacuzzi sort of wears you out." He crossed his legs and Fletcher saw that the leather slippers he wore were cracked. "Now go on, I want to hear everything about you."

Fletcher had just finished talking about passing the first of his actuarial examinations when he could no longer ignore the fact that his father was sleeping.

"Gee, I really know how to tell a good story, don't I?" he whispered.

Wanda chuckled. "It's late, Fletcher. Most people his age would have been out hours ago."

"Still, I bet I could have kept him awake if I'd told him about the aliens."

Wanda squeezed his arm; they had decided to take a wait-and-see approach as far as telling WW about *everything.*

"Have you decided to?" she whispered after a moment.

"I don't think so. I don't want to scare him away, now that I've found him again."

Wanda nodded and then covered her own yawn. "Then let's get him to bed."

WW was snoring deeply and did not respond to the gentle shakes of his arm. Fletcher worked his arms under his father and lifted him up, feeling an immeasurable tenderness toward this old man whose bones he could feel under the silk fabric.

Wanda pulled down the covers—Fletcher was touched again, and heartened, that his father kept a neat room—and after he set WW down on the bed, he covered him with the sheet and comforter, tucking him in as carefully as a regular old son who loves his regular old father.

"See you in the morning?" asked WW.

"Dad!" said Fletcher. "I thought you were asleep. And yes," he said, kissing the old man's forehead. "We'll see you in the morning."

———

WW didn't answer his doorbell, or their repeated knocks.

"Do you suppose he went somewhere?" asked Fletcher, trying not to worry.

"Maybe he's a heavy sleeper," said Wanda. "Or maybe he didn't expect us so early and is out running errands."

Fletcher paced in front of the door, rang the bell, and knocked again.

"Maybe. But he said he'd see us in the morning, remember?"

"I remember," said Wanda, worry beginning to flutter in her own chest.

Fletcher was wondering if he should find the building manager to open up the door when he was startled by a sharp whistle.

It was a shockingly familiar whistle, one that he had forgotten all about until he heard it now, the whistle his father could make by placing a circle of fingers against his tongue. WW had used it constantly when he wanted Fletcher to do something for him.

"Dad?" he said, looking through the iron railing that surrounded the second-floor open hall.

"I was just getting my laundry," said WW, placing a filled plastic basket on a patio table. "Did you just get here?"

"Yes," said Wanda, and taking Fletcher's hand they made their way down the single flight of stairs and to the patio area.

"You've got to get up early to get a machine in this place," said WW, sitting at the table. "Can you believe a big place like this only has two washers and two dryers?"

"Dad, I hope you haven't eaten, said Fletcher. "We'd love to take you out for breakfast."

WW scratched his long old-man earlobe. "Uh . . ."

"What's the matter, WW?" asked Wanda, taking a seat next to him.

"No, I . . . well, the thing of it is, I've got an appointment. Absolutely forgot about it, and absolutely can't miss it."

"That's all right, Dad," said Fletcher, feeling concerned, as well as rejected. He dragged over a plastic chair from another table and sat down. "Is it a doctor's appointment? Is everything okay?"

WW waved a hand. "I'll be singing at my doctor's funeral is what I'll be doing. Nah, this is . . . well, it's a lady friend of mine. Jolene is her name. We go to the racetrack every Friday."

"Oh," said Fletcher, as the sting of rejection intensified. "Well, that's fine, Dad."

"Hey, you could go with us—we'll be back by supper!" said WW. "You ever been to a horse race? I'll spot your first bet!"

"We . . . we need to be on the road by noon," said Fletcher.

"I would have canceled, Fletcher, but it's sort of this ritual we look forward to. You know, when you're older, there aren't a lot of—"

"It's okay, Dad. Really."

The three of them sat in the early-morning California sun, smelling the chlorine a man in a brown uniform was dumping in the pool.

"Fletcher, will you come to see me again?" asked WW, his voice wavering with age and emotion.

"Of course, Dad," said Fletcher, covering his father's hand with his own and squeezing it. "And maybe you can come out to see Wanda and me."

"In Pierre? I don't know if I want to go back to Pierre. Too many bad memories." WW needed a new eyeglass prescription, but he was still able to notice the look on his son's face.

"Aw, Christ, Fletcher, I'm sorry. That was a stupid thing to say." His cheeks puffed and sagged as he blew out air. "Another in my long list of stupid things said, stupid things done."

"That's all right, Dad."

"You're a good man, Fletcher." WW turned to Wanda. "You got a good man, you know that?"

Wanda nodded. "Do I ever."

"Me . . . I guess I just wasted so much time being a big shot. A big shot at the wrong things." WW slapped his thighs. "Well, them's the breaks. I should really get this stuff upstairs and get ready. Jolene'll be here soon."

Still, he didn't move, nor did Fletcher.

"It's not what you can do," said WW suddenly, "it's what they *think* you can do!"

"I beg your pardon?" said Fletcher.

"That was one of the things I used to say to you when you were a little boy. You know, some words of wisdom. I was always trying to think up snappy slogans for you, to help you out in life."

"You were?" Fletcher's recollection was that the things his father shouted at him were more like recriminations than snappy slogans.

"Sure! Well . . . sometimes."

WW fiddled with the plastic woven strips of his laundry basket.

"You know, I read Napoleon Hill and Dale Carnegie and all those guys, and in the end all you really need to know is this: life is funny." Reaching into the plastic laundry basket, he took the hat perched on top of his folded T-shirts and put it on.

Fletcher's mouth dropped open. Wanda covered hers with her hands.

"What?" said WW. While he knew what he had said was true, he didn't think it merited their exaggerated reaction.

"That hat," whispered Fletcher, his hazel eyes wide. "Where did you get that hat?"

"In the laundry room wastebasket! " said WW, taking the cap off. "Can you believe someone threw this away?"

He fingered the lettering on it.

"It's an old Yankees cap, and see, it's got Whitey Ford's signature— it's probably worth a pretty penny."

He reached over and plopped it on Fletcher's head.

"From me to you, son."

He sat for a moment, wondering why Fletcher and Wanda were giggly as lunatics when just seconds before they had acted like they'd seen a ghost. Nothing against them, but in WW's opinion, his strange son and daughter-in-law were perfectly matched.

"You mind telling me what's so funny?"

"Well, it's like you said, Dad," said Fletcher, catching his breath. "Life."

23

Sometimes we turn the page faster than we should.

That was the thought that ran through Wanda Plum-Weschel's head as she sat in the teacher's lounge, casually leafing through a copy of *Minnesota Monthly* someone had contributed to the magazine pile. Uninterested in the ads for cosmetic dentistry and spa weekends available in her neighboring state, she was about to jettison the magazine in favor of *Redbook* when she flipped back two pages to more carefully study an image her conscious mind had barely registered. It was a photograph of a woman and an announcement under it that read: "Hear prize-winning Egyptian poet Hammar read from her new collection."

Wanda's heart hammered as she telephoned her husband.

"Fletcher," she said, "we're going to Minneapolis on Saturday."

"O-kay," he said.

In her eighth month of pregnancy, his wife had been making some strange requests, but they usually had to do with food. This appeal entailed a fourteen-hour roundtrip, but Fletcher was of the mind that whatever Wanda wanted, he would help Wanda get.

"I saw you right away," said Hammar.

"I know," said Wanda. She had been slightly uncomfortable when so many in the audience had turned around in their seats to see the person at whom the poet on stage had directed her forceful stare.

"You must be Fletcher," she said, offering her hand.

"Yes," he said, feeling as if he were in a trance.

"You remember his name!" said Wanda.

"I remember everything about that . . . incident."

"Me, too," said Wanda.

The poet had directed an usher to escort the Plum-Weschels backstage while she signed books for a long line of people.

"Boy, how do you rate?" said the chatty young woman. "Isn't Hammar great? I just discovered her poetry and I love it! She writes like the daughter of Emily Dickinson and Rumi!"

In the dressing room, Hammar had directed Fletcher to take the chairs that sat under the long vanity and assemble them into a ring at which they now all sat, knees touching.

"When is your child coming?" asked the woman, and with no self-consciousness she held out her hands, inviting Wanda and Fletcher to take them.

"Next month," said Wanda. "We're thrilled."

"As you should be," said Hammar.

Even in this exchange, there was an intensity that raised the hairs on the back of Fletcher's neck.

"Did you win?" asked Wanda. "Are you the Mayor of the Universe?"

Years dropped away from Hammar's face as she smiled. "I won merely by being considered. And you should feel the same," she said to Fletcher.

There was a knock on the door, the voice behind it reminding the poet that she must leave in five minutes to catch her flight.

"To further answer your question, Wanda, I did not officially win. No one did."

Both Fletcher and Wanda asked the same question.

"What?"

"The Universal Head Council deemed the whole contest, as you say, a bust. They felt none of the Lodge members made a solid enough case as to why their candidate should assume the mayoral mantle. Borlot—you remember, Wanda, she was the chair—said her only defense was that there must have been something in the subatomic atmosphere to make the UHC even consider for a light year that someone from the human race was the one who could save the universe."

"Oh my," said Fletcher, "is it that imperiled?"

"Her statement was that the universe is at a crossroads; traffic is heavy and there are no stoplights."

"That's exactly what Charmat told me," said Fletcher. "The night I met Lodge 1212."

"But we, the candidates, beg to differ. We all agreed that we would use the talents that drew the Lodges to us in the first place to better direct traffic and put up those stoplights!"

She leaned into them; the trio was now sitting so close their foreheads almost touched.

"For me that means I must figure out how to help the world with my words."

"Have you told many people about—"

"About transforming into a ball of fire? About the grace that allowed me to exist for that sublime moment between the rings of Saturn with alien Lodge members?" Shaking her head, Hammar flicked her swath of black hair behind her shoulders and shook her head. "No, no. All the important things I have to say would be dismissed by those afraid to imagine a world other than their own."

"We told a few people at first," said Wanda. "But we didn't exactly get a great reaction."

"And now," said Fletcher, nodding toward his wife's big stomach, "we've got the baby to protect."

Hammar nodded, her eyes on the bloom of Wanda's stomach.

"I do hope you realize, Fletcher," she said after a moment, "that considering the UHC called off the competition, your disqualification is invalid. Therefore, I urge you to continue with your mayoral duties. All of the other candidates—including myself—are."

"Hammar—please!" came the voice behind the door, with a forceful knock.

"And Wanda," said the poet, standing up. "You're a part of this, too. Figure out what you can do."

"I will," she promised, and after a long hug that thrummed with a warm energy, Hammar was off to a reading in Chicago and the Plum-Weschels on their way home, with a stop at the Happy Chef because Wanda was craving a hot fudge sundae with extra pecans.

———————

"Hello, kids," said Fletcher to a grade school assembly in Port Angeles, Washington, and after introducing himself he added, "and I'm Mayor of the Universe."

It was the 157th time he had introduced himself to a group of children in this way, the first being to the kids at his wife's school.

He had originally planned to address only second graders, reminding his wife that Tandy had once said their minds were the most exquisite open flowers in the garden of human thought.

"Oh, Fletcher," said Wanda, "I think every teacher feels that way about her students. At least every good teacher. Speak in front of the whole school."

She was on maternity leave but brought their daughter Tandala Olive (whose nickname would become Tandy-O) and sat in the back of the auditorium as Fletcher began his presentation by introducing himself as the Mayor of the Universe. She was proud that after the snickering and whispering died down, Katie Charbonneau, now a self-possessed third grader, asked the first question.

"What does that mean?"

"Excellent question, and one I asked myself many times," said Fletcher, coming around the podium to stand at the lip of the stage. "What our mayor does—what any mayor anywhere does—is to help his or her town or city run as well as it can. Our mayor wants to make sure that citizens have what they need, but his real goal is to make people think that Aberdeen is the best place in the world."

"It is!" yelled a few young boosters.

Fletcher smiled. "Then our mayor's doing his job. My job is to make you think that our universe—and all the towns, states, countries, continents, and worlds it contains—is the very best. When a person thinks he or she's part of the very best, they want to work hard to keep it that way."

"How do we do that?" asked Matt Hefflinger, also a former student of Wanda's.

"That's what *you* need to find out. For instance, I found out I was very good at having fun—"

The children giggled and whispered and little Raymond Erk (who would be in Wanda's class when she returned to teaching after the new year) said, "I like to have fun!"

"Excellent!" said Fletcher. "Who else does?"

Every hand belonging to every student and teacher went up, and Mr. Manning, the fifth grade teacher, continued to hold his up after everyone else's had gone down.

"Yes, Jim?" said Fletcher, calling on him.

"What does a person who's good at having fun do—I mean for a living?"

"Well, for example, in my wife's case, and your case—they teach. In your wife's case—kids, for those of you who don't know, Mrs. Manning owns the the Cupcake House—you bake. You do whatever makes you happy, because that makes other people happy, and so on and so on."

"What if doing bad things make you happy?" asked Luke Peterson, a boy who considered the principal's office his second home.

Fletcher pondered what he considered an excellent question.

"I don't think you can do bad things when you're happy. In fact, I think people have to be unhappy to do bad things. And those people need to figure out what makes them so unhappy, and then I'd hope they'd find people to help them not be so unhappy."

He looked at Wanda for reassurance—he didn't know if that answer had made much sense—and felt better when she nodded.

"How did you learn to be a Mayor of the Universe?" asked a fourth grader named Roberta who already knew she was going to grow up to be a microbiologist.

"Well, it never hurts to study hard," said Fletcher, playing to his audience, "but I had a lot of help."

"From whom?" asked Roberta, who excelled in English, along with every other subject.

"Oh," said Fletcher, "from a couple of aliens."

He got a big laugh, and he would soon discover that line always got a big laugh.

Fletcher ended the talk by telling everyone that they should act as if they themselves were Mayors of the Universe and do what they could to make sure the place where they were was the best place ever.

Soon he was receiving invitations to speak at schools throughout the state as well as in Minnesota, Iowa, Nebraska. His reputation spread and he had to hire an agent out of Minneapolis to keep up with his engagements.

He was the keynote speaker for fund-raisers and conventions across the country, and the press noticed.

"Are you the Mayor of the Universe?" asked a headline in *USA Today*.

"Fun: The Ultimate Answer?" was an anchor's lead-in on a nightly news show.

"Daddy, he's talking about you!" said Charles (a name his parents felt honored Charmat without burdening the boy with a name certain to cause undue teasing) pointing at the television set that displayed a picture of Fletcher to the left of the anchorman's molded hair.

"*Is* fun the ultimate answer?" asked Tandy-O. She was a child for whom, her parents were certain, little got past.

"We think so," said her mother. "Right, WW?"

They had convinced Fletcher's father, after suffering the blows of a minor stroke and the death of his lady friend Jolene, to come live with them. It was an arrangement that lasted a little over a year, until his death, and while Fletcher could never say his father completely changed his stripes, at least the stripes had faded.

WW could be a cranky grandfather who more than once provoked hurt feelings or tears in his grandkids, but he also participated in tea parties and games of Slap Jack and Mouse Trap and was easily cajoled into singing a goodnight song. It gave Fletcher immeasurable joy to see his children in their pajamas, jumping on the bed as WW crooned "High Hopes" or "In the Wee Small Hours" or "My Way."

———

Obeying his father's wishes to have his ashes thrown into the Pacific ("I might have been born a Dakotan," he wrote in his will, "but a bold guy like WW has got to wind up in California!"), Fletcher stood solemnly on a cliff in Big Sur, looking down at the rough slate-colored water.

"I keep thinking about where the waves will take him," he said. "Maybe toward Tandy."

"Definitely toward Tandy," said Wanda.

Taking a deep breath, Fletcher tipped the urn, and as his father's ashes blew into the ocean, he was moved to shout, "It's not what you can do, it's what they *think* you can do!"

"Nice eulogy," Wanda said dryly, as they watched the gritty cloud of fragments that were WW blow into the Pacific.

"It's what popped into my head," said Fletcher. After thinking for a moment, he cupped his hands to his mouth and shouted, "You weren't the greatest dad, but you were my dad! And you sure had a lot of pizzazz and flair!"

"Pizzazz and flair—he'd like that."

They stood on the cliff for a long time, the stiff ocean breeze flapping Fletcher's pant legs and flipping up Wanda's skirt. They watched a ship so far away that it seemed as if it were unmoving, pasted on the horizon. They watched as a teenaged couple set a blanket on the beach and then grab it when they realized they were not out of the range of the ocean's spray.

"It's too bad people don't get to hear their own eulogies," said Fletcher presently.

"Well, we could think that every time we hear someone say something nice about us, or do something nice for us, it's sort of a eulogy. A living eulogy."

"A living eulogy, I like that," said Fletcher, wrapping his arm tighter around his wife. "How would you eulogize me?"

Staring out at the horizon, Wanda said, "I would say, out of all the billions of people on the planet Earth, a group of astute aliens thought Fletcher Weschel was the most fun."

"It does top 'He had good hygiene,' or 'He never had an overdue library book,' doesn't it? You know what I'd say about you?"

His wife looked into his eyes, and returning her soulful gaze, he said, "I'd say, 'Wanda Plum has over a dozen handmade blouses made out of fabric printed with fruits and vegetables.'"

"Oh, thanks a lot!"

"And that at their request she painted Vikings on the walls of her daughter's room and dinosaurs on her son's and when he got scared because the T-Rex was so lifelike, she redid the eyes so they looked crossed and painted a beanie-copter hat on its head!"

Wanda laughed and Fletcher drew up his pretty blonde wife in his arms, and his lips lingered a long time on hers, tasting the salty tang of the ocean on them.

"Hey you!" he shouted to the teenaged couple when their kiss ended. "Never forget to eulogize one another!"

"What?" came their voices, made faint by the wind. "What?"

Fletcher and Wanda were holding each other, laughing hard as the young couple climbed the rocks, getting closer to them.

"Be the mayor of her universe!" said Fletcher.

"Be the mayor of his!" said Wanda.

"What *are* they talking about?" the girl asked the boy.

"Just ignore them," said the boy. "Coupla freaks."

But when Fletcher dipped Wanda backwards and planted a mighty kiss on her, the teenagers stopped their climb to watch, and if their adolescent selves didn't understand it, their primal ones did: something grand and glorious and very strange—awaited them.

Epilogue

Decades have passed since aliens dropped into Fletcher's bedroom on a cold and windy November night. The Lodges that make up the communities in outer space and beyond had great expectations for the inhabitants of the planet Earth, but unfortunately, they have come to realize that evolution does not always move in a forward motion.

There was much argument and no consensus as to who should assume the title of Mayor of the Universe. Many Lodge members wondered why it was that the UHC thought this officeholder would be found on Earth; oh sure, humans had managed to retain archaic notions like hope and love, but hadn't they been stymied by the very same things? There was such heated debate about the unworthiness of each Lodge's candidates that eventually the Universal Head Council disbanded, recognizing that it may, in fact, know nothing (giving those scientists who believe in the chaos theory of space much to support their arguments).

Lodges that had previously thought the members of 1212 trivial and their behavior childish now recognize the worthiness of their pursuits.

"Who knew," said a member of 720, the spiritualists, "that it wasn't cleanliness that was next to godliness but fun?"

There have been hard and wicked times on the blue and green planet, and while there are those arguing for a galactic intervention, Charmat chooses to believe its inhabitants are figuring out for themselves what needs to be done. If he were a cheerleader, he would shake his pompoms for the human race, for every day metaphysical touch-downs, goals, baskets, and holes-in-one are being made.

"Rah," Charmat shouts. "Gooooooo, Earth!"

He sees progress.

The complexities of Thai food are now appreciated all over the world. A farm boy visiting Des Moines and eating pad thai for the first time realizes that yes, his mother makes the best macaroni and cheese, but someone's mother from across many oceans does something completely different, and wonderful, with another kind of noodle.

People are taking better care of their bodies, realizing the holiness of dancing, of sex, of napping. The practice of yoga has skyrocketed, and Wall Street hustlers and radio talk show hosts are calming down in Downward Dog and Half Pigeon poses. Fake food and trans fats (which Lodge 527, the refrigerator scavengers, wouldn't even touch) are being phased out.

Music, which arguably has lit more fires than matches, is taking its rightful position next to spoken language. International choirs are being organized and people are finding that it's hard not to like some-one you jam with, or stand shoulder to shoulder with, singing.

One über-alpha golden retriever is behind the therapy dog move-ment, whose message is being spread by urine on fire hydrants, saliva on abandoned balls at dog parks, by howls in the night. For now the movement is content to aid and assist, to soothe and charm those whose minds or bodies are in disrepair, but it gives Charmat great pleasure to know its eventual goal is to infiltrate world governments. Presidents, prime ministers, and emirs, emerging after deadlocked meetings, will be in such good humor from dogs who greet them with wagging tails and sloppy kisses, from dogs who happily play the twen-tieth game of fetch as if it were their first, from all the raised endorphin levels that a good dog causes that peace will for once be considered something more than a slogan, and good men and women will get to work on ensuring it, while absently scratching behind the ears of their Lab, their corgi, their Portuguese water dog.

The poet Hammar, previously known only in Cairo's literary circles, is now published worldwide, and her poems about loneliness cured by curiosity, about love being the Sequoias and hate being the crab grass are recited by schoolchildren and studied by scholars everywhere.

In Samoa, there is an international oceanography group that has been building artificial reefs out of recycled Nerf balls and restoring life to dying oceans. On the island of Tonga, two brothers have figured out how to corral wind power with break dancing and use gum tree extract to patch the ozone layer.

A widow in Moldavia, whose husband beat her, is teaching inmates ballroom dancing as a form of anger management. A master gardener in Tokyo is trying to graft a walnut tree to a cocoa plant to sugarcane, his goal being an instant candy bar. A zoologist in New Orleans is training alligators to act like carrier pigeons and sends riddles and Sven-and-Ole jokes through the waterways. Thanks to Fletcher's co-option of Tandala's favorite phrase, "Hoola, baby" has entered the worldwide lexicon and is used to express any number of emotions.

Charmat looks at all of this with great pride, but it is the senior citizen in South Dakota who gives him the most hope.

Fletcher's seminars have become a global sensation; the title *Mayor* is a form of address that is now commonly used to replace *Mr.* or *Fru* or *Senora* or *Sahib*. Study groups gather to debate what exactly a mayor of the universe is and what the mayor's duties are. Charmat sees a day when there are billions of mayors of the universe, understanding, of course, that the universe needs every single one.

He still checks in on Fletcher and was pleased to see him the other day, standing in a shorn wheat field outside Pierre with his granddaughter, Alice.

"I used to come here and dance," said Fletcher, who has a slight stoop now and whose cowlick is about all that remains of his hair.

"Why?" asked Alice.

"Because the ladies begged me to," said Fletcher, with a swivel of his artificial hip.

"Gross," said Alice, using a word that like cockroaches will never die, and yet she did not pull away when her grandfather grabbed her hand.

"This is what they called the Twist, said Fletcher, demonstrating the dance move. "And this is the Bugaloo."

The old man and the girl danced, kicking up snow.

"This is the Snarl," said Alice, winding her arms around each other. "And this is the Owie-Wowie." She flailed her body as if she were holding on to the electric fence that surrounded the cow pasture down the road.

They hopped and gyrated together, their laughter making little visible puffs in the frigid air.

When it got so cold that even the wild moves of the Bugaloo or Owie-Wowie failed to keep them warm, Fletcher held the driver's side of the car door open for Alice.

"Can I really drive, Grandpa?" she asked.

"Sure," said Fletcher, handing her the keys.

She wouldn't get her permit until next year, but they were out in the country and the old insurance man had measured the risk (the likelihood of passing another car was low and nothing in the girl's personality suggested an untamed need for speed) and decided the fun and thrill factor outweighed it.

Charmat watched as grandfather talked granddaughter through the steps.

Alice buckled up, checked her mirrors, and started the engine, and even though the roads were empty in all directions, Fletcher advised her to turn on her blinker to indicate her merge into traffic.

The windows of the sedan were closed against the winter cold so the old man and the young girl didn't hear the low rumble of laughter, which is, really, when all is said and done, the universal way of saying *thank you.*

Acknowledgments

Thanks to Erik Anderson and everyone at the University of Minnesota Press for giving Fletcher Weschel a second chance. He and I are thrilled.

Mike Sobota, Patti Frazee, and Mark Thomson were all a big help at the beginning, and I'm grateful.

Special thanks to Sarah Stonich for her generosity and to Pat Rishavy, who kindly offered to help me clean up many typos those rascally aliens had put in.

Sometimes kind and encouraging words, a good laugh, or a big "Rah!" are delivered just when you need them, and for those I thank Renee Albert, Doug Anderson, Cindy Benton, Stephen Borer, Susan Davis, Anne Gandrud, Mary Gielow, Cynthia Glock, Judy Heneghan and Peter Staloch, Kimberly and Killian Hoffer, Lynn Ketleson, Ruth Krebs, Jennifer Lund, Janice McCormick, Joanne Messerly, Terri Mickelson, Brian Motiaytis, Nancy Olson, Vicci Pederson, Kirsten Ryden, Kimberly Sabow, Joel Sass, Karen Schwartz, Barb Shelton, Jim and Cindie Smart, Wendy Smith and Dave Drentlaw, Dawn Stattine, Kelly Steinwand, Karen Stuhlfeir and Walt Cygan, Sandy Thomas, Anne Ulseth, Kristin Van Loon, Bonnie West, and Brenda Young.

Tusen takk to the Norse women of Lakselaget, for the salmon lunches as well as the continued support and interest in my work. Merci beaucoup to the patient profs at Alliance Française who put up with me in their classrooms. A big thank you to all the book clubs who uncorked a bottle of wine or two and welcomed me into their homes. Namaste to my yoga teachers—sorry about all the sweat.

Thanks to Sue Krieg for generously sharing her lovely cabin.

To my friends and colleagues at the Loft Literary Center, thanks for doing the good work of supporting writers and readers.

WWW: I'm so glad to be one of ten in this most excellent literary sorority.

And to Charles, Harleigh, and Kinga: thanks for being the biggest stars in my celestial skies.

Questions for Book Clubs Reading
Mayor of the Universe

1. As the author was writing the book, she claims she was surprised when aliens suddenly showed up in Fletcher's bedroom. Were you surprised? Were you expecting a different kind of story?

2. How did Fletcher impress you at the beginning of the book? Did your feelings for him change as the story progressed?

3. Fletcher was bullied as a child, and we don't see a lot of adult intervention. How did your school/neighborhood/parents treat bullies?

4. Dodd Beckerman was Fletcher's childhood nemesis. Did you have one? If so, who was she or he and how did she or he treat you?

5. Fletcher escaped his loneliness by creating fantasies as well as dancing in farm fields. What unusual method have you used to make yourself feel better?

6. The author thought it was fun to imagine a universe populated by alien lodges. Lodge 1212 could turn themselves into any human form they wanted. If you had that talent, who would you turn into and why?

7. Fletcher and Wanda are reluctant to tell Wanda's parents about their alien experience. Have you ever protected your loved ones from information you didn't feel they could process?

8. What does it mean to you to be a mayor of the universe? How do you think our world would change if everyone took on this role?

9. Tandala is enamored by many Earthly delights. If you were trying to impress an alien about your world, what would you show her or him (or it)?

10. Wanda Plum feels privileged to be a second-grade teacher. Who was your favorite grade-school teacher, and why?

11. The author doesn't consider this book sci-fi despite its alien visitors. Do you?

12. If you were given the opportunity to go on a space mission, would you? What would you bring with?

Lorna Landvik is the author of ten novels, including the best-selling *Patty Jane's House of Curl, Angry Housewives Eating Bon Bons,* and *Oh My Stars.* She performs stand-up and improvisational comedy around the country and is a public speaker, playwright, and actor, most recently in her one-woman all-improvised show *Party in the Rec Room.* She lives in Minneapolis.